Morr
novel

mes
30 J.
ch.
rs.

D0342629

NAUVOO

NAUVOO

The saga of a city of exiles – the passions that built and destroyed it.

To Cliff –
with my best wishes –

Jim French

JAMES R. FRENCH

CONCORDIA UNIVERSITY LIBRARY
PORTLAND, OR 97211

Copyright © 1982 by James R. French

All rights reserved. This book or any part thereof may not be reproduced in any form whatsoever, whether by graphic, visual, electronic, filming, microfilming, tape recording, or any other means, without the prior written permission of Raymont Publishers, except in the case of brief passages embodied in critical reviews and articles.

ISBN No. 0-934126-27-5

First Printing, November 1982

Raymont Publishers
P.O. Box 780
Orem, Utah 84057

Printed in the United States of America
Publishers Press
Salt Lake City, Utah

For Pat

Foreword

As I was preparing this book, I mentioned the project to the eminent novelist, Ernest K. Gann, whom I had just interviewed on the occasion of the publishing of one of his best-selling novels. To my surprise, he seemed to know a great deal about the epoch of the Mormons at Nauvoo, Illinois, and he commented that this segment of American history was "the last, great, untold story of the developing West."

I agree. In fact, as I began researching the subject, I saw that the bitter defeats and the unyielding hopes of the Mormons, as they struggled from one precarious haven to another in their moves out of the East, were a living microcosm of the whole westward expansion of the nation, following what a future president would describe as their "manifest destiny." Except that the Mormons' goals were different from the "Gentiles'." Freedom, elbow room, money; those were major goals to most expansionists. The Mormons, most of whom had been converted to their faith only recently, followed what they believed was a divine injunction to establish a utopian way of life under the leadership of one man, the controversial dynamo, Joseph Smith. They, too, wanted freedom—from religious oppression; elbow room, in which to construct a perfect classless society; money? They were learning the law of sacrifice and had contributed far more of their own money than they were taking in. Still, they endured persecution and mobbings, brutalization and destruction, on their way to a refuge where they wouldn't be hounded again. They believed, most of them, anyway, that Joseph would lead them to it. And at last, he did. On the malaria-ridden banks of the Mississippi he purchased a tangled hillside of scrub trees and underbrush, named it with a Hebrew word no one had ever heard, and proceeded to direct the construction of the dominant city in the state of Illinois.

Now, in the face of such improbable courage and determination, a novelist need not add much of his own invention to make a dramatic saga. Accordingly, I have crafted only a few characters to the list of those who actually lived in the Nauvoo period. I have also taken a few liberties with the family trees of some of those real people; Thomas Sharp, the lawyer-turned-editor, had no brother Andrew, and kindly Willard Richards never adopted a Louisa Stephens. The McCann family is representative of many hardy immigrants who sailed to the United States to follow the prophet. And I have peopled my story with a handful of others who sprang from my imagination.

But the background events and the leaders of the Church and its opposition actually lived. The gathering perils which were finally to enfold Joseph and his councilors are a matter of well-documented history.

And, finally, the remains of Nauvoo, the Beautiful, are still there, hugging the banks of the Mississippi, to bear testimony to the fact that the faith and hopes of over ten thousand people did come together in one of the nation's first experiments with a totally pre-planned community, an oasis on the ragged edge of western society. Only a few buildings remain, but most of the roads are still maintained. The glorious temple, of course, is gone—blown down by the elements after it was defiled by mobbers taking over the city.

But that is getting ahead of my story. And I am anxious to be sharing it with you. The story of Nauvoo is an important, necessary part of the tough fabric of our nation's development. In fact, Ernest K. Gann confided that at one time, he had considered writing the story of Nauvoo himself! *"So do a good job,"* he admonished.

That objective has been echoing in my brain all through the months of work on this book.

Now that it is complete, I only hope it is worthy of the vivid personalities who lived the real life story of Nauvoo.

James R. French
September 1982
Bellevue, Washington

Author's Note

I would like it understood that I am a story-teller, not an historian; this work is fiction based on historical events. Some of the characters I have used in telling this story, however, actually lived. Into their mouths I have been obliged to put my own words, as a novelist and not in any attempt to represent actual relationships or conversations. Where this was done, however, I have tried to remain true to what is known today about their motives, movements and characters. But my objective has been to dramatize one of the most turbulent eras in U.S. history, by placing fictional characters among real ones. It is my hope that, in this blending of fiction and fact, no damage will be done to the memories of those figures out of the past, whose lives added such rich texture to that time and place called Nauvoo.

Andrew, Louisa, the Gaines and the McCann families, Mrs. Wilson, Mr. Ketchum, and assorted minor players—are all figments of my imagination; consequently, their relationships with Joseph Smith and his church, and with Dr. John C. Bennett, never took place.

This is not the story of Joseph, Hyrum, or anyone—it **is** a story of NAUVOO.

Acknowledgments

If many faithful historians had not written their books, I would have been unable to write mine.

In particular, my thanks go to Joseph Fielding Smith, Donna Hill, Keith and Anne Terry, Erwin E. Wirkus, Leland R. Nelson and Robert B. Day, for many references.

I am also indebted to Jim Kimball, David Kreuger, Doyle Mortimer, Weldon Sant, and Curtis Taylor.

To my dear friend and traveling companion to Nauvoo and many other destinations—Vic Schoen— a special debt of gratitude for inspiration.

And to my devoted wife, Pat Soule French, for encouragement and comfort, and for reminding me as to what I needed to do whenever I felt downhearted about the project, my eternal thanks. The help she guided me to seek never deserted me.

JRF

Prologue
October 27th, 1838

Lilburn W. Boggs was so nettled that he jabbed the wrong end of his dead cigar into his mouth, tasted the gritty ash and spat it out. "By damn," he roared, "then it's war all across the state of Missouri!"

Jim Tick, the young captain, had ridden through the night to reach the governor's mansion in Jefferson City with the news that the Mormons had launched an attack on Crooked River. He stood uneasily now, legs apart and hands clasped behind his back, watching the squat man in nightdress pacing around the heavily-furnished room.

"I'm afraid so, sir," Tick said.

"Five years," grunted the governor.

"Sir?"

"Five damned years I've been fighting the Mormons. I thought I had 'em when I was lieutenant governor and sent word our boys would throw down their arms if they would. Thought I had 'em when they promised to clear out of Jackson county. Hell, I own a deal of land around there, and those Mormon abolitionists would free the slaves and have darkies living everywhere! They're nothing but a plague," Boggs stormed, pointing a pudgy finger at the captain. "So damned many of 'em, they outnumber the Missourians at the polls, and they'll fight to vote!"

From a sideboy, the governor took a decanter and two cutglass goblets, and motioned for the captain to be seated on a settee by a low table. Boggs sat down heavily beside him and poured whiskey into the glasses. "Are you hungry? I can raise my wife, and she'll fix something. . ."

The weary rider shook his head. "No, thanks, Governor. This will be enough." He picked up the heavy glass, not knowing whether to drink from it until the governor had taken his drink first. The florid-faced politician studied the glass, took a deep gulp, swirled the dark amber liquid in the goblet, then drank the remainder.

"Unless we exterminate those wild men, they'll take over the whole state of Missouri!" Boggs made a bitter face.

"Governor, pardon me—but I was just called up recently and I don't understand what the fighting's all about."

"Well, I'll tell you what it's all about," Boggs snorted. "These fanatics outnumber us in any county where they settle. And they tell you right out, they intend to turn Missouri into 'Zion,' and drive the old settlers out."

"But why?"

"Because they think their leader, Joe Smith, is a prophet of God, that's why," Boggs roared. "And they do anything he tells 'em to do! He tells 'em to buy up land, they buy up land. He tells 'em to build a militia, they build a militia. Like as not, if he tells 'em to die for the cause, they'll die for the cause!"

The young soldier looked troubled. "Is that why the citizens have formed up against them?"

Boggs looked at the young officer with exasperation. "You own any property?" he asked.

"No, sir."

"Well, if you owned any property, you'd feel the same as the rest of Missouri feels. The Mormons are too thick here. They all vote the same way, so they can influence an election. They're against slavery, they brought a lot of peculiar ideas into the state . . . hell, son, they don't **belong** here!" He poured another drink for himself. "Besides," he added, "we got here first!"

The captain looked dubious. "Except for the Indians," he said.

"What?"

"The Indians got here first."

The governor glared at him over the edge of his glass and downed another gulp of whiskey. "Mormons and Indians," he muttered.

There was a rapid knocking on the front door. Boggs, surprised at another caller in the dead of night, went out to the hall and asked through the door who was knocking. Satisfied it was one of his own men, he unbolted the door. An exhausted rider in civilian dress stumbled in, removing his hat.

The governor gasped, "Henry, what's the matter?"

The rider, a man in his forties with wispy black hair streaked with sweat, took a deep breath and let it out in a huge sigh. "The Mormons have teamed up with the Indians across the Platte," he said, then took another gulp of air. "Fourteen thousand of 'em."

"But Bogard's militia. . . ?"

"Massacred! Not a man left standing!"

In the parlor, the young captain jumped to his feet. "Are you sure about that, man?"

Henry nodded, getting his breath back. "That's what I rode here to tell the governor. Folks are running from their homes. Governor, you got to do something!"

Boggs stood absolutely still. Then he said, almost to himself, "And by God, I will!" He stalked to his writing desk, snatched a piece of official stationary and a quill pen, and began writing furiously as the two men stood behind him.

"The Browning House"
Painting by Al Rounds
Courtesy of Lowell Benson

Part One:

The Journey

Chapter 1

"Torches, Pa!"

Louisa's eye had been caught by a yellow glimmer through the small cabin window just as she carried a bowl of cornbread to the table. Her father, Asael Stephens, sprang from the table and joined the slender 16 year old girl at the window. Sure enough, through the naked tree branches between their cabin and Haun's Mill, flashed several fiery daubs of light, bobbing up the hill toward the little Mormon settlement.

He studied the route of the marchers in silence for a moment, then turned to the small woman, her spoon poised in midair over the bubbling pot hanging over the hearth. "Put out the lamp, Mother," he said grimly, and took the bowl from his daughter's hands, placed it on the table and blew out the candle lantern. His wife snuffed the wick of the coal oil lamp hanging above the kitchen table. The one-room cabin was plunged into darkness, relieved only by the red tongues of flame licking in the fireplace. The feeble glow caused the single table with chair and benches, the total furnishings of the room, to cast dancing shadows against the log wall.

From the sleeping-loft came the feeble wail of Bobby, Louisa's four-year old brother, sick for the past three days with the fever. "Why did you make it so dark in here?" he demanded. His mother hurried to him, soothing him with soft whispers.

"Penelope, get a blanket to wrap him in," Asael directed his wife, not taking his eyes from the torches. Then, in a lower voice to the golden-haired girl beside him, he said, grimly, "Louisa, you know what to do."

Louisa swallowed the lump of fear that had been growing in her throat, and nodded. "Yes, Pa." Her father had rehearsed the family well in preparation for attack. Asael owned a squirrel gun, which he would use alternately with an old English pistol. Penelope had been trained in the fastest method of loading the single-shot weapons. If it came to a standoff, Asael planned to fire through spots where he had worked the chinking out by both the front and back doors, or through either the east or the west windows, while his wife reloaded. Louisa was to take Bobby and run to a pre-determined oak tree which would offer concealment for them during a skirmish. Louisa had thought it a great lark the first time Asael had put the family through the drill. She made a game out of it for Bobby, who had no memory of the mobbings the Mormons had suffered in times past. As she had grown into her teens, Louisa had made friends with some of the other girls in the settlement, and together they had decided that they would become nurses to the valiant Mormon defenders. Untouched by any of the violence which had flared wherever the Latter-day Saints ventured in their westward migration, Lousia had only heard stories the boys repeated—of how the prophet had been tarred and feathered, of how farms had been burned, and how some of the elders of the church had been tortured and imprisoned. She didn't understand how a peace-loving community of people, God-fearing and religious, could provoke such outrages from the settlers in the area. But the thought of warfare thrilled her and she and her friends had spent hours in daydreams of heroism, bandaging handsome young men and saving their lives to fight another day for the glory of the gospel.

She hauled the blanket off her parents' bed and held it in front of the fireplace to warm it. How childish those fantasies had been! How stupid of her to think that there was any glory in bloodshed—in murder. The knot of fear was now growing cold within her breast and she felt her mind whirling, scarcely knowing what to do. Suddenly she didn't want to leave her parents; she longed for them all to run, to hide, to be invisible when the maurading bands came looking for them! The familiar smells of the cabin, the smoke from the fire, the cooking aromas, her mother's faint rosewater cologne and the sweet smell of sweaty leather that was a part of her father, were the most precious things in the world to Louisa. She had to fight to suppress the strangling sobs welling up in her chest.

Asael looked at the cold October night and saw the branches shudder in gusts of Missouri wind—saw the baleful face of the moon rising through the clouds. It would be uncomfortable out there for his two children, but far safer than to be found in the cabin if the mobbers came this way and did what they had done to other Latter-day Saints.

"What's going to happen?" Bobby wailed as his mother helped him down to the floor.

"Nothing, Bobby," Louisa said, brushing away the tears that swam in her eyes. "We'll just go out and hide in our tree again. You liked that, remember?"

"But not when I'm sick."

His mother pulled the boy to her and put her cheek against his forehead. He was still feverish, the smooth skin still parched. She looked over at the spare man standing by the window. "We can't send him outside now, Asael," she said. "he'll take more cold."

"I'll keep him plenty warm, Ma," Louisa said, wrapping the warmed blanket around the little boy. Then she stooped and gathered him up, tucking the blanket around his bare legs. "Ma, please get me his boots."

"They're not dry yet," her mother replied. Bobby had explored the nearby creek in his boots three days ago and his mother assumed this was what had given the boy his fever. The boots were well soaked and were still damp, but Louisa had a sudden presentiment that he would need them. "Please get them, Mother," she said.

Penelope looked into her daughter's face. The two were the same height now, and it had seemed to Penelope Stephens that her daughter was becoming a woman overnight, complete with the intuitive instincts Penelope believed were the inheritance of all women. In Louisa's eyes she saw an intense, desperate **knowing**. It frightened her and she hesitated for a moment before going to the corner where Bobby's boots had been kept to dry out.

Asael went to the front door and peered out. "Yes, they're coming toward the mill. Give you time to get up the tree. Go on, now."

"Asael." Penelope looked up at her husband. "Give her a father's blessing."

It was a custom among the Mormons to invoke God's protection before embarking on any enterprise, and the Stephens family had been taught by the prophet's brother, Hyrum Smith, that holders of the Priesthood were authorized to pronounce a blessing on the heads of family members when the need was felt. Asael looked down at the pale face of his daughter and at the wan young boy she held in her arms. "We haven't got time, Mother," he said.

"Take the time."

His wife looked again into the eyes of her daughter. In the darkness they were devoid of all color, the cornflower blue now two pools of black.

A low rumble could be heard coming from the direction of the torches. Asael looked back through the doorway. "They have horses, too. A lot of them. Louisa, you'll have to hurry." But then he suddenly placed the palms of both hands on the head of his daughter, then, remembering Bobby, moved one hand to his son's head. With eyes tightly closed, he spoke in the personal, conversational way he always did when he prayed. "Dear Father in Heaven," he began. "I want you to watch over these precious children tonight. And watch over Mother and me too, if you please. And inspire me Father, as I pronounce a blessing on their heads." And then, as if speaking directly to the boy and girl before him, he said,"Louisa and Robert: I bless you that you will be safe from all harm, and that you will not cry out or let anyone know where you are, until your mother or I come for you. In the name of Jesus Christ, Amen." Louisa was suddenly aware that the fear she had felt was not for herself or Bobby, but for her parents. "I wish I could give a daughter's blessing, Pa," she said.

"Run to the tree now, Louisa," Asael said gruffly. "Your mother and I will be fine."

Louisa slipped out the door. The chill of the October night made her eyes, still damp from tears, water more as she edged around the side of the cabin and moved west into the stand of oaks. She stole a glance over her shoulder and saw the group of torch-bearers assembling near the small grist mill which supplied the little settlement with its meager output. She turned back to the woods and plunged ahead in the pale light of the rising moon. She hadn't been in the scrub oak after dark before, and she was intent on finding the tree her father had designated. He had blazed toe-holes in the trunk so she could scale the six feet up to where it divided into two main limbs and formed a natural couch, where she and Bobby could remain in relative comfort.

Within moments, she found it.

In the cabin hasty preparations were being made. Asael shoved the heavy planked table against the front door while Penelope dropped the bar across the back door. Theirs was one of the few cabins with two doors. Asael had felt it would give better ventilation in the hot months, and Penelope favored it because it was one of the few reminders of the fine Ohio home they had left in 1832 when the prophet Joseph Smith had come through Mansfield. He had come preaching of the miracles which had restored the true Gospel to the earth. They had been swept up in the excitement and, being young, with only one child, felt the call to join with the migrating Saints in their push westward. But mingled with the joy of finding answers to religious questions was the hardship of frontier life, the toughening of the trail, and the ever-present persecutions by the old settlers through whose countryside the Mormons trekked. It had never been worse than in Missouri.

Beneath the torches spitting with flaming pitch marched a company of soldiers. Arrayed in a variety of costumes designed to give a military flair, the men bore muskets and a few pistols. Riding in their head was Nehemia Comstock, who now approached the clearing in front of the gristmill and held up his hand for a halt.

The horses snorted and their flanks shivered in the chill of the night, and from their heaving bodies, clouds of steam rose into the flare from the torches. Comstock cupped his hands around his mouth. "Halloo, Haun's Mill! We've come in peace!"

For several seconds Comstock waited. A horse nickered and the rider leaned out of the saddle and spat on the ground. Then the leader hailed the quiet settlement again. "My name's Comstock. We don't mean you no harm. We want to parley!"

First one man, then a few more appeared around the back of the mill, shotguns and muskets in hand. Only a handful of Saints had the new expensive percussion lock rifles.

In the torchlight the men from Haun's Mill could see that the leader, Comstock, appeared to be the only unarmed man in the company. He now strode forward to within a few feet of the defenders, accompanied by a man with a torch. Sweeping off his plainsman's cap, he nodded at his small audience. "My name is Nehemia Comstock," he said. "I expect some of you know me and my men."

"We know you." It was Isaac Laney, standing with Joseph Young at the front of the Mormons.

"Well, we consider it only right and timely to tell you," Comstock said, "that we mean you no harm. Some of your folk have trespassed on our property, and some of your men are awful braggarts, but I intend that we keep the peace, where you're concerned, so long as we're not provoked."

He seemed to fall silent as if waiting for a reply. Laney and Young looked at each other and at the other men. Finally, Young spoke in reply. "We're obliged to hear that, Captain. Our people are peace-loving and we intend to push on west in the spring. We're grateful for your neighborliness." Young stepped forward toward the leather-clad Comstock, his right hand outstretched. Comstock hesitated for a moment, then shook his hand. "Well," he said, looking around at his men for a moment, "that's what I come up here to say. We'll be wishing you a good evening. Looks like it's turnin' cold." And with that Comstock and his torchbearer turned around to rejoin their troop. Without further word, the company retraced their steps through the brush and their torches disappeared from view.

The men at the mill turned to each other, smiling cautiously. "Praise God," one of them breathed. "Spared again."

From her vantage point in the tree, Louisa had watched the brief event. She hadn't heard anything after the leader of the marchers had called out the second time, but it appeared that the brethren at the mill were walking back to their tents and cabins with muskets held low. Soon Pa would come out of her cabin and tell her it was safe to come down.

None of the settlers at Haun's Mill could have known that night that their fate had already been sealed two days earlier at Jefferson City. Word had reached Governor Lilburn Boggs of a battle which had taken place on October 25th at a place called Crooked River, in which some seventy Mormon elders had staged a raid on the militia under the command of Samuel Bogard. This supposedly was in reprisal for being driven out of their homes in Far West. The elders confiscated goods the Missourians left behind in their retreat from Crooked River, including some weapons and ammunition. By the time the reports of the encounter had reached Governor Boggs, they had been embellished and exaggerated into alarming proportions. Without troubling to verify the accuracy of the reports, Boggs issued an order to General John B. Clark on October 27, 1838. A copy of the order arrived in the camp of Nehemia Comstock while he was engaged in his peace-making visit to Haun's Mill. When he got home on the evening of October 29th, his sentry handed him the sealed communique.

Comstock snatched the envelope from the sentry and tore it open under the lamplight. He read,

> . . . I have received . . . information of the most appalling character, which changes the whole face of things, and places the Mormons in the attitude of open and avowed defiance of the laws, and of having made open war upon the people of this state. Your orders are, therefore, to hasten your operations . . . the Mormons must be treated as enemies and must be exterminated or driven from the state, if necessary, for the public good.

Comstock folded the letter again and placed it back in the dispatch case, conscious even then of the historic significance of the order. But then he put his mind upon planning the attack on Haun's Mill the next day. He knew there was one thing in his favor: after his reassuring words that night, the

Mormons wouldn't be expecting anything to happen.

After lunch the next day, Bobby seemed to feel better and asked to go down to Shoal Creek with the rest of the children. Penelope asked Louisa to take him there and keep him out of the water.

The afternoon passed quickly and quietly, the woman working in the tents and cabins while the men chatted at their chores. Almost forgotten was the warning from the prophet Joseph Smith, that they were placing themselves in jeopardy by remaining in this tiny outpost in the midst of hostile Missourians. News had not yet reached Haun's Mill of the fighting in Far West the previous week. Nor could they have know that at that moment, as the men stood leaning on their hoes in the afternoon sunlight, a cohort of well over two hundred men representing two counties of Missourians were thundering toward the settlement, armed with guns and swords.

As the afternoon sun began to sink toward the tops of the scrub oak west of Haun's Mill, Shoal Creek was already dappled with shadow, being the lowest point in the settlement. The rising dampness went unnoticed by the younger children, racing wood-chip vessels in the bubbling torrent that wound out of the millrace and down through the brush to the flatland. Bobby had by now recovered his vigor, almost as rapidly as he had lost it the week before, and it was all Louisa could do to keep him on the creek bank. With the others, Bobby guided his little ship with a long peeled branch.

On the higher ground, the men sang hymns as they weeded and harvested the knobby potatoes sewn in the unyielding soil the previous spring. Louisa, down by the creek, was comforted to hear her father's strong, melodious tenor carrying the melody above the prattle of the children nearby. The faint breeze stirred and brought a savory bouquet of woodsmoke blended with steaming vegetables and the salty smell of pork. Louisa hugged herself under the homespun shawl. Autumn was her favorite season of the year, poignant with the remembered gentleness of summer, poised for the winter's onslaught that slowed all human movement and turned each snug cabin into a citadel of mending, knitting, baking and preserving. It seemed to her that Nature was a huge, slowly turning wheel, irresistable as it brought the seasons in procession. It was Mankind's challenge to live upon the spokes of the wheel, adapting to each change as the celestial Spinner wound His eternal skein.

All things in their time, Louisa said to herself almost aloud. Turn, and the snow would fly. Turn, and she would be seventeen. Turn, and she would find the man even now who was hurrying along his own path as the wheel turned their lives ever closer together.

A tidal wave of sound broke over the settlement of Haun's Mill, caused by the onrushing of 240 galloping horses and the roar of as many riders.

The children at the creek looked up the slope to see swords flashing, smoke from guns marking the route taken by the charging men. For a second, Louisa thought they were a party of Latter-day Saints in high spirits, perhaps the vanguard of the Ohioans called to join the Saints in Missouri.

But then she heard the gutteral screams and curses as the party broke and rode among the tents and cabins. Because of the terrain, she couldn't see her parents' cabin, but there was a group of marauders heading in that direction. Volleys of shots pummeled the air. Women screamed.

When the realization struck the children by the creek, some began to run uphill toward the melee, some fled downstream toward the thicket of brush and scrub oak, and others—like Louisa and Bobby—were so stunned that they stood motionless as the terrible scene unfolded above them. The earth reverberated to the hoofbeats as the swirling gang of riders drove over every inch of the village. The mill was one of the attacker's immediate objectives, for it was presumed to be fortified. Nine elders were killed immediately, defending it. The horrible carnage broke before the children's eyes in rapid succession: an old man knocked to the ground and three riders circling him with swords savagely sundering him; women dragged by their hair into cabins where their screams pierced even the thunder of hooves and the bestial roar of the attackers. Louisa saw two men in white shirts, wading among the riders, waving their hats as if to ward off the assaults, and recognized them as Isaac Laney and her own father.

Louisa sprang into action. She leapt the creek and ran furiously up the slope toward the massacre. In her mind was one overpowering urge: to be with her father. But before going fifty feet, a rider fired a rifle at point-blank range at Laney and a companion swung a rifle at Asael, knocking him down. As he struggled back on his feet, half a dozen riders bore down on him, firing, and Louisa saw her father spin around in the dirt, saw his body convulse as the shots found their marks, and then he fell beside the other elder.

The girl was nearly under the hooves of the horsemen now, when suddenly a force lifted her off her feet, and a sweating horse appeared beside her, charging up the hill. She found herself deposited on the animal's heaving neck and she was being held, stomach down, by a huge hand. Louisa twisted and kicked until her tormentor came into her line of vision. The face was that of a man no older than her father, but leathery and stubbled, with a broad, misshapen nose and several missing teeth.

Louise saw his rein hand inches from her face. Lunging at the filthy knuckles, she bit him with every ounce of strength in her jaws and clung to the salty flesh as blood spurted onto her face. The other hand released her now and grabbed her flying yellow hair, but still she hung onto the hand like a wild animal. She was only vaguely aware of her kidnapper's scream of pain, for now as he stretched her neck back she spotted the hilt of a knife strapped to the rider's waist. Without hesitation, just as it seemed that her neck muscles would snap, she released her bite on the bloody hand, and her own free arm shot toward the knife and whipped it from its sheath. In a mighty arc her arm swung out from the rider and then back again, plunging the knife to the hilt in his ribs, just beneath the arm that held her by the hair. The hand loosened, the rider seemed to relax and surrender, as his curses ended in a pink foam on his lips. He slid off the saddle, his right foot still caught in the stirrup, and was dragged by the maddened animal until it reared up, freeing Louisa who slid off onto the ground.

Bobby had been left alone by the creek. She had to find it and retrace it to where Bobby was! Weak and bruised, in the shuddering chill of shock, Louisa staggered down the slope toward the creek, and saw the continuing slaughter in the twilight.

She stumbled forward. Her long dress and petticoats were spattered with blood and the hems had been ripped. Her golden hair hung in strands over her face and her eyes stared ahead uncomprehendingly as she placed one foot in front of the other. Near the village, the frenzy was just beginning to slacken.

Ahead was the place where she had left Bobby. Across the little draw and up the gentle bank lay the village gardens. The neat furrows had been trampled by scores of horses. Bodies lay in the field. The last house visible in the gathering dusk was Louisa's. The door stood open.

With a final circling of the tiny cabins, the horsemen reassembled into a loose formation and rode past the deserted mill. Some of the riders were as close as fifty feet from Louisa, who shrank to the ground in terror when she saw them approaching. One of the riders had a horse in tether, the horse whose rider had kidnaped Louisa and whom Louisa had stabbed with his own knife. That man was now lashed across his saddle, legs jouncing like a rag doll as the horse cantered with its hastily-balanced burden. Grimly now, with their lusts satiated, the riders were silent. They rode away from Haun's Mill, not one of them turning to look back at their work.

From the ruins of the settlement came the faint keening of a woman. In a moment her voice was joined from another quarter by a second tormented cry. From doorways, from the nearby copse of brush and from behind the mill, men and children crept, many limping and staggering with their wounds. From somewhere near the Stephens' cabin a man cried aloud, "Oh dear God, dear God, no! No!" The sound of his sobbing brought the tears to Louisa's eyes and she began to run blindly down to the creek. She splashed across it, scarcely feeling the icy water which rose nearly to her thighs. She started up the other side toward her cabin when a man intercepted her. She knew everyone in the camp, but she stared at him blankly, not recognizing him. He grabbed her firmly by her arms and stopped her from going any nearer the cabin. She wrenched, trying to get free. The man said something—something she didn't hear or didn't understand. He was trying to prevent her from joining her family.

"Sister Stephens, you mustn't go up there!" The voice was vaguely familiar, but she didn't turn her head to look at his face. She had but one objective and that was to be with her family. She had been away, had had a terrible nightmare, but it was over now and she would be content again, once she was in the bosom of her own family, in the snug cabin with her gentle mother and dear little brother and her strong, loving father. "Sister, what's up there ain't for you to see! There ain't nothing can be done for your Pa and

Ma now! You got to think about your brother!"

Brother! Where was Bobby? *I'm going up to my cabin and you can't stop me!*

"Louisa, it's Joseph Young. Don't you know me? Listen, the little ones are in the woods. Your brother's bound to be with them. They'll be needing someone to watch over them. You may just be a little older'n them yourself, but they'll be needing you. Won't you just go fetch 'em and keep 'em with you 'til we can . . ." He stopped, looked up at the destruction which lay only a hundred feet away in the settlement. He felt the strength go out of Louisa's arms and he cautiously released her.

"Have you been in our cabin, Brother Young?"

"Y-yes'm."

"And?"

"Ma'm?"

"Did my Ma suffer much, do you think?"

The rawboned young man considered the question, wiped the mucous away from his nose and rubbed his streaming eyes with the back of his hand. "No'm, I . . . I don't believe she suffered much. And I'm sure she . . . she didn't . . ."

"Didn't what, Joseph?"

"I'm sure she . . . died a lady." And the man's lip trembled and his chest heaved as the anger and tragedy within him began to burst out. He stood behind her, ashamed that he was sobbing convulsively and unable to stop. But Louisa's square shoulders straightened, and slowly she turned away from the silent cabin, turned slowly and saw men approaching where her father still lay, and turned until she was looking directly at the bereaved young man. He hung his head and huge wracking sobs shook his wiry body.

Louisa felt like a middle-aged woman. She felt like all the pioneer women who had made the ultimate sacrifice for the sake of their beliefs. It seemed to her that she was no longer a 16-year-old girl, but suddenly a woman with a grave understanding. A luminous tenderness was in her eyes, the ravaged look of the hunted animal had fled. "You're right, Brother Young," she said softly. "The children will be needing someone." And she turned and walked back down the slope toward the dark stand of oak. As she neared the forest, first one child, then another, appeared from the branches of the trees and ran to her. She held out sheltering arms and the children came and ran against her skirts and clung to her, crying. Among them was Bobby. Louisa busied them finding kindling for a fire, while she sat holding Bobby and trying to find the best way to tell him that they were now orphans, on this chill October evening.

Chapter 2

August of 1840 was characteristically hot in the town of Warsaw, Illinois. In front of a small office on Main Street stood a young man in his shirtsleeves, collarless, frowning up at the sign he had only that hour hung over his door. It had read: "Thomas Coke Sharp, Attorney At Law"; now it was almost undecipherable. The paint, so painstakingly applied to the wooden shingle, had run in the heat after it had been lettered and mounted. And the first caller in the office after the sign had been hung was, to Thomas' disappointment, not a client, but a town idler, who had only stopped in to notify the new lawyer that his handiwork was dripping paint on the wooden stoop outside his door.

The small office was dominated by the desk which bore scars from earlier owners and which Sharp had tried to improve by applying boot blacking to its battered corners and edges. The narrow wall behind the desk held a framed parchment which proclaimed that Thomas Coke Sharp had obtained a degree of Doctor of Law from the Allegheny College in 1839. A small bookcase containing the law books collected during Sharp's feverish pursuit of the law was close by. On the bottom shelf were stacks of newspapers. The old desk was, for the most part, innocent of any work relating to the practice of the law, but held several books of foolscap on which their owner had penned anecdotes, editorial comments, political and social observations, with an eye one day to seeing them in print. For Thomas Coke Sharp, while professing a love for the Law, was more in love with the printed word, and felt he had a flair for producing it which would some day bring him fame and, if not fortune, at least a comfortable living.

For the time being, however, he had put aside any active pursuit of his avocation in favor of following the profession in which he had been trained and at which there was promise of much employment. The Law was a noble calling and a young man with a flair for words might gain political office rather easily in this raw part of Illinois, might catch the eye of wealthy landowners along the Mississippi who needed a clever attorney, and might—who knows?—find a suitable young woman who would be willing to overlook the limp that had accompanied him since infancy, and the deafness which he feared was overtaking him. Yes, all in all, the practice of Law was preferable to the risks of newspapering. But on this hot August afternoon of 1840, he had no clients and no way of obtaining any, and he longed for having a product to sell: his journalist's skill; his way with words.

At the moment that he seemed the most forlorn, he heard a step scuff on the planks of the stoop and he looked up to see a young man peering into the shadowy office from the blazing street. "In here, Andy!" he called, and jumped up from the desk.

The visitor wore the cap and jacket of a traveler, and his dusty Gladstone bulged with the burden of too much clothing jammed into it. He dropped the bag and strode forward to embrace Thomas Sharp. "I've been looking all over Warsaw for you," he cried. "Why don't you hang up a sign?"

Tom looked sour. "I just took it down. I was afraid you'd find me." They both laughed and the younger man pulled up a chair as Tom sat back at his desk. "What are you doing in Warsaw?" the attorney asked. "Aren't you going back to finish school in the fall?"

"No. Now, don't lecture me like a big brother. Remember, you're only 13 months older than I am. Besides, it's time I made my way in the world."

"With what, Andy?" Tom asked.

Andrew Sharp pointed at both of his eyes with his index fingers. "With these," he said. "and my brain. I'm going to be a reporter, and a good one. Just like we always talked about."

It was a fact that Andrew and Thomas had both contemplated the life of newspapermen and had even turned out their own handwritten version of a newspaper back home in Meadville, Pennsylvania, when they were both approaching their teens. It had delved into intimate details of certain families known to them in their neighborhood, producing a minor scandal. The irate father of one of the subjects of an article demanded that their father confiscate any remaining copies of the offending edition which announced that a boy, whom they named, had been leaving school early every afternoon so he could spy on his mother and see if she had been entertaining any male guests, as the father had been fearing. The fact that they never turned up anything sinister only added to the intrigue of the story. The revelations made juicy gossip that spread far beyond the tiny circulation of their little newspaper. Thomas' and Andrew's father took them both into the woodshed and lashed them with a sycamore sapling, while demanding that they abandon their hobby, to which the boys had tearfully agreed. But by nightfall they were again conspiring to one day re-enter the newspaper field. They were now more impressed than ever with the impact of the brazen truth—and the power of the printed word—but were more cautious than ever when they realized that the daring publisher might risk all kinds of punishment, even from his father, for merely exposing truth to the light of day.

Thomas had his parents' blessing (and financial support) for the study of law, and he proved to be a remarkable student. He completed the prescribed course as fast as it was possible to do, and—reeling from the infusion of rapidly-learned knowledge, could hardly wait to put it to the test on his own. It seemed only appropriate that he open his first practice somewhere away from Meadville, and he chose Warsaw, Illinois after reading that it was a center for commerce along the Mississippi, and that the town was growing fast under the development of new businesses and homes. Furthermore, the town marked a boundary between the settled East and the turbulent and tantalizing West, and any young man with ambition was eyeing the new lands beyond the sunset as the place to make his own mark in the world.

Thomas, however, did not share some of the advantages of his brother. For one thing, Andrew was a handsome child and Thomas had been plain to the point of being nearly invisible to his peers. Had it not been for his limp, suffered as a result of falling into the spokes of a wagon wheel when he was three, Thomas might not have attracted any attention at all. But the limp, together with the pasty round face and small eyes fixed slightly too close together over a jutting, bridgeless nose, gave the young boy no advantage in gaining friends. He was never chosen for games because it was assumed he couldn't run, and he never made any attempt to curry favor with girls because he believed he was doomed to failure there, too. By the time he was 16, Thomas Coke Sharp knew that his success in life would depend on his brains and not his beauty. And so he determined to put every effort on building superiority in mental, rather than social, affairs. In time he developed a beard and groomed it into a vivid black frame that helped shape his face and hide the triangle of nose which protruded from the otherwise flat face. He had plenty of thick, black hair, which he allowed to grow long and develop a wave which he combed down over both ears. And he compensated for his physical deficiencies by becoming a first-rate orator. His arguments in the courtroom exercises at college won him the admiration of the other young men, most of whom were older than he.

Andrew, on the other hand, was only a mediocre student in school. His mind didn't lock onto the subjects his instructors offered; instead, it wandered out the windows of the classroom and into the life of the town, where he pondered the comings and goings of tradespeople, the glamorous work of the town constable, and even went beyond the horizon to Philadelphia, New York, and those near-mythical lands Westward where deeds were done which would pave the way for an expanding America. Life, it had seemed to Andrew, was at a standstill amid the paper and paste smells of the classroom, and was roaring by at a furious pace just outside. He was keen to run after it and catch it.

Andrew had made his infatuation with newspapers known to the editor-publisher of the Meadville *Journal*, Austin Crikette, and the tiny man whose name perfectly suited his spry and brittle manner held up a bony finger and shook it in Andrew's face. "The first rule of a good reporter," he had said, "is to get all the details. Not just the cream, but the whey as well."

Andrew enfolded himself around these words as an oyster builds a pearl around a grain of sand. His frequent visits to the old editor elicited other priceless lore: *Don't trust anyone else's story; get it yourself. When you're writing a story, keep asking yourself, is this a fact or is this what I think is a fact? Every story has two sides, at least. Get them all.* By the time he was seventeen, Andrew was a cub reporter for the *Journal*. Before he graduated from school, he knew that reporting was his life's work, and he dropped all other interests, much to the regret of his mother who had hoped he would become a physician and to the disappointment of many young ladies who had dreamed of snaring him one day. But Andrew forsook medicine, romance and the promise of financial independence in favor of landing a full time job with a good newspaper. And since good newspapers were not to be found in the precincts of Meadville, Andrew, armed with clippings of *Journal* articles he had written, had set out to seek his fortune in the world of journalism.

He sat now, carelessly astride one of his brother's creaking office chairs, arms folded across the chairback, enjoying the concerned frown on Tom's face. "You don't think I can do it, do you?" Andrew challenged.

"Do what? Write? Oh, you can write, there's no doubt of that," his brother replied. "The question is, can you make a living doing it?"

Andrew's eyes roamed over the barren room in which they sat, over the empty desk whose pigeon holes were still unburdened with notes or correspondence; over the plain walls where not even a curtain relieved the Spartan plainness, and to the new diploma on the wall, on which the ink seemed barely dry. "And you," Andrew said with a trace of irony, "can you make a living doing what **you're** doing?"

Thomas frowned deeper. "That takes care of itself in a town growing as fast as Warsaw is. Don't worry about me; I'll get my share of business and then some. But mind you," he said, leaning forward to waggle a finger in his brother's face, "if you're thinking of moving in with me while you look for work, I'm afraid I can't afford it."

Andrew leaned back to avoid the aroma of old cigars on his brother's breath. "Oh, that won't be necessary, thanks all the same."

"Won't be necessary?" repeated Thomas.

"No. You see, I have a job. In fact, that's one reason I came to Warsaw . . .that and to see you, of course."

Thomas' eyes narrowed. "What kind of job?"

Andrew barely whispered it, eyes glittering: "Thomas Coke Sharp, attorney-at-law—you are looking at Andrew Sharp, **special correspondent** to the Quincy *Argus*!"

The words caused Tom's jaw to sag, his eyes to bulge. A position with the *Argus* had been the fond dream of both brothers during their adolescent fantasizing about a career in writing. "Since when?" Tom cried.

"Last month. I made Ma and Pa promise not to write you about it because I wanted to tell you myself!"

Thomas fell back in his chair and, for almost the first time since Andy had come in his door, let a smile spread across his face. Here was his younger brother—in so many ways still a boy, now looking like an eager pup telling of his first real job, and at one of the state's finest and most respected newspapers! He began to chuckle, reached into the top drawer of the rolltop desk and extracted a roll of oiled paper which he unwrapped to reveal one unsmoked cigar, and another which had been partly smoked and then snuffed out. He handed the fresh one to Andrew. "I've been saving this for a special occasion," Tom said. "I know you don't use tobacco, but now that you've officially taken up a life of sin and debauchery in the ink-stained world of the scrivener, you must be officially indoctrinated!" He took the long cigar and shoved it into the grinning mouth of his brother, whipped a match against his boot sole and watched as Andrew sucked in the stinging smoke and let it puff out of his mouth. Soon the office had a blue cloud rising to the ceiling in the hot, still afternoon air.

Their celebration feast, that evening, took place at the Warsaw Inn, which stood on the post road just south of town. It was not only an event of note for Andrew, but in the few weeks that Thomas had been in Warsaw arranging for an office and furniture, he had forbidden himself the luxury of taking any meals except at the table of the home in which he rented a room because of his lack of capital. But tonight he threw caution and his usual sense of thrift to the winds, and the two brothers dined as well as men in that rustic frontier town could eat—with huge slabs of pork, ears of corn dripping with pork grease, and tankards of a locally made beer which both young men downed, although Andrew made a face when the bitter brew first reached his tongue.

Finally, their bellies were full, and the snapping fireplace warmed the room. "How much will you be paid?" Thomas asked.

"Well, six dollars a week to start. But when they've read more of my writing, I'm to get an increase."

"Bravo! And what is your first assignment?"

Andrew looked around the dining hall with deliberate caution and leaned across the table. "The Mormons," he whispered. "But I tell you this in strictest confidence, Tom. If it should be learned that I'm spying on them, I'll lose my job!"

Thomas was unconcerned. "The Mormons? You'll have no trouble spying on them; why, they make themselves a nuisance everywhere they go. First they took them in down in Quincy and gave them homes and loaned them money, and then from what I hear, the next shot out of the gun, they're trying to colonize and take over the state! I shouldn't wonder they'd put a cub reporter onto the Mormons; everyone who can scribble a line in English is writing about them!"

"But what an opportunity for a reporter's first job on a good newspaper!"

Thomas leaned back in his chair and wiped his mouth. "I hate to disillusion you," he said with a wry chuckle, "but there are many more important stories in Illinois than chasing Mormons. What about that congressman, Abe Lincoln?"

"What about him?"

"You've heard of him, of course?"

Andrew hadn't. "Why is he so important?" he asked.

Thomas snorted. "You call yourself a reporter and you don't know about Abe Lincoln? Abraham Lincoln headed a delegation from Springfield in '37, stumping to get the state capital moved to Springfield. Well, as you know, there was a lot of competition. Some wanted it back in Chicago, some down in Quincy; but Abraham Lincoln voted to spread a lot of internal improvement money around in the cities that had applied to become the capital, if they'd vote for Springfield in return—and they did.''

"Who is he, anyway? Some hero in the Black Hawk War?"

Thomas shook his head. "You've got a lot to learn, little brother. Lincoln's a backwoods lawyer. He's a crack politician. Why, when you consider that they made Vandalia the state capital in 1820, and she's had these last twenty years to solidify her position, Lincoln's tactics were pure poetry. You need a little brushing up in your history.''

Andrew was stung by the rebuke. "Look," he said, "I admit I did a lot of daydreaming in school, but there's one thing I learned about Vandalia: the state was only two years old when they made Vandalia the capital back in 1820, and they wrote a provision into the law that stated Vandalia couldn't remain the capital of Illinois longer than twenty years. Whatever your Abe Lincoln did, Vandalia couldn't remain the state capital after this year. Even a poor student like me knows that!''

Thomas grumbled something that was drowned out by a sudden burst of laughter from some men at a nearby table. Tom jerked his head in the direction of the noise and leaned closer to his brother. "Those folk,' he said under his breath, "are part of the posse that straightens out some of our Mormon neighbors from time to time. You might pick up some information from them if you want to know more about the Mormons.''

Andrew looked over at the group. Five men were gathered around a table. They were massive, sweating from the fire and drink, most with jackets removed and bulging forearms bared. Their laughter was punctuated by playful shoves which nearly sent one of them toppling over backward from the backless bench on which he sat. Summoned by the noise, the woman who had been serving the innkeeper's dining customers came in with a tray bearing fresh tankards. As she set them down on the table and retrieved the empty vessels, one of the men grabbed her around the waist and pulled her down onto his lap. She gave a playful shriek and pushed herself away, accompanied by more guffaws from the table. "Nice crowd," Andrew said to his brother.

"I wouldn't want to be in a Mormon's house after a night like this," Thomas mused. "Like as not, when they're through here, they'll warm themselves against the chill of the evening by burning out a Mormon family or two.''

Andrew stared at the boisterous men and then turned across his own table to look at Thomas, whose impassive expression showed no compassion or concern for the actions he had predicted. "Are you serious?" Andrew asked.

"Serious enough that I don't want either of us to be in a position to be witnesses," Thomas said, getting to his feet. "Come on. We can talk better in my room.''

The August night had a bite in it when the wind swept over the Illinois plain and down the dusty street. Clouds paraded swiftly across the sky while half a moon looked down on Warsaw's clapboard and brick dwellings. One of the earliest private homes in the town now stood near its center, and having fulfilled its purpose as a dwelling for the family that built it, was now reduced to letting three of its four upstairs rooms to tenants like Thomas, who could not afford better lodging at one of the three public houses in Warsaw. As a boarder, Thomas had dining privileges in the spacious downstairs dining parlor, and was invited to spend evenings in the front room or, as weather permitted, on the verandah which circled two sides of the building. It was plain but comfortable living for the young attorney; it provided respectable quarters, and it was quiet enough for him to study his law books with an oil lamp on the English dresser by the bed.

In the few weeks he had been living there, Tom had made no close relationships and was only passingly acquainted with the other two boarders and the widow who rented the rooms. Her husband had built the abode while serving as a foreman on the Illinois Levee along the Mississippi. During a flood following a storm upriver, the bank crumbled and the man was swept away in the muddy torrent—an event his wife related word for word to each new tenant, by way of explanation as to how it was that a comely women not yet forty was living alone in Warsaw, renting rooms to strangers.

Thomas undressed and sat in his underdrawers with a blanket around his shoulders, his legs under the covers. Andrew hadn't yet removed his traveling suit but was standing at the window, looking out across the rooftops of the town. Tom's lone oil lamp glinted dim amber in the tiny bedroom.

"Do you want to go to sleep?" Andrew asked his brother, not turning away from the window.

"Not especially. Do you?"

Andrew shook his head and sat on one corner of the bed. "I want to know everything you can tell me about the Mormons," he said. "I never paid much attention to them, and I'm supposed to become an expert on them for the *Argus.* Mr. Ketchum, the editor, says a contingent of them are moving north along the river looking for some place to build a town of their own. Since I knew you were here in Warsaw now, I thought I'd base myself here until I got my bearings."

Thomas drew himself up against the headboard of the bed and pulled the blanket around him higher. He enjoyed the prospect of administering some knowledge to his brother, and it gave him satisfaction to think that he could tell this fledgling newspaperman many things that would undoubtedly be used in print. It seemed ironic to him now, that he would be providing material which would find its way to the public under the byline of his younger brother, and not himself. But he spoke willingly, eagerly.

"Surely you know," he began, "that Quincy—the very town your newspaper publishes in—was where the Mormons landed after being driven out of Missouri."

"I know there are a lot of them down there," Andrew agreed.

"Very well. Governor Boggs threatened them with extermination if they didn't clear out of his state, so thousands of them poured into Quincy. I assume you've read the editorials the *Argus* ran, taking old Boggs to task for the violence?"

"I'm afraid I haven't."

Thomas sighed and shook his head. "Well, I can see I'll have to bring you up to date. The Mormons first came into Missouri nine years ago, back in 1831. Some of them stayed in Ohio, but a large body of them followed Joe Smith, their leader, to Jackson County, Missouri because he told them that's where 'Zion' would be established."

"'Zion'?"

"The 'Promised Land'. Well, when a thousand or so of these fanatics settled in Jackson county, that changed the voting balance. Every man Jack of the Mormons could be counted on to vote alike, and it upset the politicians. Besides, it got around that Smith and his bunch were going to bring in enough more of their lot that they'd push the old settlers right out of the county—maybe right out of the state!"

"Why would they want to do that?" Andrew asked.

"To make it safe for more Mormons, I suppose. But, that wasn't the worst. The Mormons no sooner set foot in Missouri than they began to preach that the Indians were 'our brothers', and ought to be treated peacably. Now, after President Jackson's 'Indian Border', where frontiersmen couldn't move on west to establish new lands, that meant that one day the food and the game would be gone in Missouri. But here come about a thousand do-gooder Mormons, preaching 'love the Indian', and what's more, where did most of 'em come from?" Without waiting for Andy's reply, he said, "New England. Never owned a slave in their lives! And so in they came, preaching abolition—in a slave state! Little wonder there was trouble for the Mormons in Missouri."

Andrew let this sink in. He sat, chin cupped in his hand, staring at the steady flame of the lamp. Then his brother continued. "There was a Mormon newspaper run by someone named Phelps. He wrote an article that as much as invited free Blacks to come settle in Missouri and join their church!"

"Oh, that must have touched them off!"

Thomas snickered. "I'll say it did. Three hundred men from Jackson county, mad as hornets, demolished the Mormon newspaper and tore up some Mormon bibles they were printing. There was tar and feathering. Some say some women and children got hurt, I don't rightly know. But it set the whole neighborhood against the Mormons."

"What did they do?" Andrew asked.

"The Mormons? Most of them promised to pack up and leave the county. But not all of them. Some of them retained a law firm in Independence, and when the settlers found out the Mormons were going to stay and bring suit, a few of them took to raiding a nest of Mormons west of Big Blue

River.''

Andrew stirred uneasily. "But that wasn't right," he said.

"Wasn't right?" Thomas parodied his brother's tone. "When a mob gets its mind made up to do something, it doesn't matter any more who's right or wrong. The mob has its way. And that is what happened to the Mormons in Missouri. They demanded that the Mormons turn over their arms to a militia and the fools did it. That same night the mob sacked and burned over two hundred Mormon houses!''

Andrew looked at his brother with concern. He seemed to be enjoying this tale of prejudice and bloodshed. "It seems to me that a good lawyer would never approve of such a thing," Andrew said.

Thomas was stopped by the remark. "What? Me?" he asked, "not much one lawyer can do when a whole county is up in arms. If I'd been asked to represent the Mormons, I'd have laughed in their faces. Shortcut to the graveyard, that's what that would be!''

Uneasily, Andrew shifted position on the edge of the bed and pulled off his boots. But Thomas was still full of the momentum of his narrative, and he plunged on. "Well, while all this is going on in Missouri, old Joe Smith is back in Ohio, getting madder all the time. And he decides to organize an army and march on Missouri to get the Mormons' property back. Well, they trained some in Clay County and the greater part of them came down with cholera. Died like dogs, they did. In time, it all came to nothing. The Mormon army faded away.''

"Then what's the trouble about?"

"Well, the trouble was, the Mormons began passing bogus money! They opened a banking company of their own in Kirtland, Ohio and it went bust. There was worthless paper money floating all over Ohio and some of it came into Missouri. They wanted Joe Smith arrested but he kept getting away. There was a terrific fight at Far West, where the Mormons were headquartered, and they finally arrested Smith and some others and threw them into jail. General Lucas ordered them to be shot. But another general—Doniphan, his name was—refused to obey the order and let 'em escape.''

"What did they do?"

"Well, they finally straggled into Quincy. You must've seen them, Andy, or heard about them at least. Your own newspaper, as I said, took their side. Everybody felt sorry for the poor Mormons. And they must have been a sorry sight, at that. A lot of widows and orphans and most everybody sick and as poor as beggars. And all this time, of course, Smith is in Liberty Jail.''

Andrew now had both boots off and was pulling off his jacket. "Well, why didn't they all just give up? What's so important about their religion?"

Tom's face curled into a sneer. "Why, hadn't you heard? Joe Smith is a prophet sent straight from God Almighty, and he can do no wrong!''

"They all really believed that?"

"They appear to. But, after all," Thomas said, a sardonic grin on his lips, "that's something for you to find out; you're the inquiring reporter. How do you figure on getting your story?"

Andrew was silent. In his mind whirled images put there by the tempestuous history his brother had just related. He saw stern, dedicated men resisting mobs, starving or being shot, and threats from the governor. What manner of people were these Mormons? How could he get close enough to these strange, deluded people? And suddenly the confusion of pictures in his imagination was replaced by the visage of old Mr. Crickette, the editor of the Meadville *Journal*. Andrew thought he saw the old man shaking his bony finger and saying, "*Every story has two sides, at least. Get them all!*"

He felt himself being kicked under the covers by Thomas, and it jolted him into consciousness. "Hey, Andy, are you asleep? You're sitting there with your eyes shut! Come to bed!"

Tom moved over and allowed his brother to slide into the bed beside him. It had been years since the two had shared the same bed, back at home, and it was comforting to Andrew.

He thought of the torrent of words which Tom had poured out, of the grasp his brother had of the bewildering affairs of this strange group of religious zealots. Never a churchgoer himself, Andrew had amused tolerance for his relatives and friends who "went to meeting" regularly on the Sabbath. There had seemed nothing wrong in it, a harmless ritual that only took an hour once a week. How could so many people—these Mormons—risk everything, including their lives, for something they believed in? He took a deep breath and let it escape, slowly. He seemed to remember something someone had told him about some people in the Bible who did something like that. But it didn't really matter to him now; he was too sleepy to think about long-dead prophets. As his brother said, "Good night, Andy," and turned to extinguish the lamp, Andrew was already dreaming. And he thought he saw Mr. Crickette again, saw his lips forming the words, "*two sides . . .two sides . . .*"

Chapter 3

"There are two sides to every story," the birdlike man had said. "At least two sides, sometimes more. If you're going to report a news story, you have to report on it from all sides. You know the story of the blind men and the elephant?"

The Sharp brothers shook their heads in unison.

"Well, a blind man was introduced to an elephant one day," the old editor began. "He walked up to the beast, felt its legs, and then said, 'Oh, an elephant is like a tree.'"

The boys giggled.

"Then another blind man comes along, and he feels the elephant's trunk. 'Oh,' he says, 'an elephant is like a big snake.'"

The boys giggled again, anticipating the next part of the story.

"Then a third blind man comes along, and grabs the elephant's little scrawny tail. 'Oh,' says this third blind man, 'an elephant is like a rope!'"

The boys broke out into laughter.

"Now, all three of them knew something about the elephant. But because they couldn't see the whole animal, they missed the biggest part of the story. You get the point?"

The brothers nodded. "Well," Austin Crickette continued, "when you report on a news event, you have to walk around and look at all sides. Otherwise, you distort the article and you never tell the whole truth. Now, let's have a look at your paper."

Andrew and Thomas had brought samples of their now-outlawed neighborhood newspaper to the office of the Meadville *Journal* for critical evaluation. The top issue contained the scandalous story which had brought about their father's ban on further publication. Crickett read it and a guffaw escaped his lips, which he tried to conceal by turning it into a cough. The boys looked at each other, shamefacedly. "This, I take it," the editor said, "is what caused the shutdown of your enterprise?" They nodded again.

"Aside from the—ah, implications of the story, was this fact?"

Thomas spoke first. "Yes, sir. Danny Oglethorpe told it to us himself." Danny was the boy whose father was suspicious of his wife's afternoon activities, and it was Mr. Oglethorpe who had stormed into Mr. Sharp's office, brandishing the incendiary newspaper, demanding the Sharp brothers be brought to justice for their sensational revelations.

"I see," Crickette commented. "And Danny was your sole source for this story?"

"Sir?"

"I mean, you didn't verify his story with Mr. Oglethorpe?"

Andrew spoke up now, "Gosh, no! We were too scared to talk to him!" Thomas nudged his brother sharply with his elbow.

"There is a school of journalistic practice," the editor said, "which employs the half-truth, the innuendo. Do you know what I'm talking about? We call it 'yellow journalism' because it is a cowardly, indecent practice. It is designed to create a sensation in the reader, from merely a one-sided examination of the facts. What you have here," he said, snapping the paper with the rap of his hand, "is a classic case of yellow journalism. 'Meadville Boy Spies on Mother for his Father.' What a dastardly headline!"

The Sharp brothers squirmed uncomfortably, wishing they had never shown him their literary efforts.

"You have only one person's word for what happened. How do you know he didn't lie to you? How do you know anything at all unless you personally investigate it?" The boys glanced at each other, and Thomas reached for the papers they had brought. "We'll be going now," he said.

"You will not!" Crickette cried, standing up behind his desk. He was barely taller than they were and weighed less than either of them. But when he strode out from behind the piles of books and papers and stood at the brothers' side, he was a terrifying sight, hands on his hips and his tiny round glasses perched at the very tip of his narrow, beak-like nose. He seemed like a vulture ready to pounce.

"You came here to learn something about the newspaper business," he said. "All right, here is lesson number one: a **lead** is not a **story**. Do you know what I'm talking about?"

Thomas, the older and braver, ventured a reply. "A lead is an idea?"

Crickette seemed satisfied, and nodded. "A lead is a clue that there **may** be a story. But until you investigate it, you do not have a story. You cannot print it, because readers of a newspaper have the right to expect that the paper prints **facts**—unless it specifies otherwise. Now, you heard a tale from another boy—what was his name? Oglethorpe. What should a good reporter have done with that tale?"

It was Andrew who answered. "Make notes, and then go ask his father?"

"Certainly."

"Yes, but if we had done that, it would've gotten Danny in trouble with his dad," Thomas protested.

"Did Danny request anonymity?" The boys looked puzzled. "Did he tell you not to use his name?" Crickette asked.

"Uhh—no."

"Then your first responsibility would be to visit Mr. Oglethorpe and tell him you are reporters, that you have been informed that thus-and-so is going on involving him, and ask him for his reaction. Don't ever put words in a witness's mouth. Ask for his reaction, ask him to verify it, don't frame a response and get him to say 'yes or no'."

"He'd have gotten pretty mad," Thomas said.

"A chance a reporter has to take," the editor replied. "But just suppose there was more to the story than either of you boys, or your friend Danny, understood. Suppose what Mr. Oglethorpe really was asking Danny to do was to protect his mother from an intruder! Your article has cast suspicion on a woman's character—and if you boys were of legal age, you could be sued for libel! Do you know what libel means?"

Thomas scratched his head as if trying to recall learning it; Andrew merely looked innocently up at Mr. Crickette, waiting to be told.

"Then boys, I think you ought to consult a good dictionary. Do you have one?" Andrew shook his head.

"Every newspaperman needs a dictionary. There—" and he pointed to a huge volume on a bookstand beside his desk, "go look up the word 'libel'," and he spelled it. Thomas, nearest the dictionary, sprang to his feet and consulted the enormous book. He pawed the flimsy pages until at last he looked up at the editor.

"You've found it? Good. Read it out loud for your brother to hear."

Haltingly, Thomas read, "'Libel, deflamatory writing; bringing a person into public contempt through misrepresentation.'"

Crickette nodded. "Exactly. Now, gentlemen, there are laws against libel. When you libel someone, you take away his or her good name, you damage a reputation, you diminish someone's standing in their community. How many people do you suppose heard about poor Mrs. Oglethorpe from your article?"

Thomas, returning to his seat, said "Not very many. We only printed up about twenty copies.,"

Crickette raised a long, bony finger. "Ah! But what if those twenty copies were read by twenty more people? And they told twenty more? Scandal is the fastest thing in the world, and the hardest to put down. Once scandal is begun, nobody wants to hear a denial. The damage is done."

"But, we didn't mean anything by it," Andrew said. "We didn't mean to hurt anyone."

"Yeah, they were only words," Thomas added.

Crickette laughed at that. "Only words? The Sermon on the Mount was only words, the Magna Carta, the Declaration of Independence! Only words—but words can change the world!" The editor walked back behind his desk again, hands behind his back. "What are words?" he asked.

The boys were silent. "Words," Crickette said, "are the keys to our thoughts. They express, from one mind to another, the ideas and feelings of humanity. Language is what separates Man from the apes. Words are imperishable. Especially the printed word. Laid down on paper, a man's thoughts and dreams can outlive him, can live forever—influencing unborn generations! That's what words can do!"

The Sharp brothers looked sheepishly at each other. Then, as he sat again at his desk, Crickette asked, in a softer voice, "What happened to you two as a result of this thing you printed in your little paper?"

Thomas replied, "Our father got real mad at us and we took a licking."

"And we had to promise never to make another newspaper," Andrew said, his voice breaking slightly.

"Well, I'd say you got off pretty lightly," the editor commented. "If I had printed something that defamed a citizen, I'd be hauled into court and sued for everything I own. And deserve it."

The boys were silent. At last, the editor leaned forward across the littered desk, pushing a stack of papers aside. "Do you still want to be newspaper men?" he asked softly.

The boys looked at one another, then at the editor. "Yes, sir," they said earnestly, in unison.

"Well, I'll tell you: I don't know which of you wrote what, but you do show some talent. Now, I know our local school doesn't have a journalism class, but I would encourage you to prepare yourselves now so that you can go on to college and major in journalism. Your father is fairly well-fixed; I presume he hopes you'll go to college?"

"But not to learn journalism," Thomas said, gloomily. "He's an engineer and he says the future is in civil engineering."

Crickette nodded. "I see. Well, meantime, prepare yourselves. Do you like to read?" The boys nodded. "Excellent," the editor said. "No one can write if he doesn't read."

"Our dad wants me to be a lawyer," Thomas said.

"And me, an engineer," Andrew added.

"But you think you want to write?" the editor queried. The two brothers nodded.

"Why? Writers are seldom rich. Few attain any fame to speak of. Many have extremely bad habits and not a few of us die young. Why do you want to write?"

It was Andrew who spoke first, a faraway look in his eyes. "I like to think of people I've never even met, reading something I wrote," he said.

His brother said, matter-of-factly, "I like the feeling of power. Newspapers can change things—like you said."

"**As** I said," Crickette corrected. "You like the power and the influence of being writers. All well and good. But not good enough. Those are selfish reasons. Do you know why I like being a newspaperman—despite the fact that I am always not more than one jump ahead of the bill collectors and am headed no doubt for an early grave from too little sleep and too much dissipation?" The boys waited silently for him to continue.

"A good newspaper offers a valuable—no, a **noble** service to the community. It collects and condenses all the events and happenings of interest and service to its readers, and offers all this—one would hope, coherently—in a handy form. It examines all sides of an issue, not just the obvious ones. And a newspaper chronicles the human events which future generations will regard one day as history. It marshalls all the facts on an issue, so that the reader may make an informed decision. That," he said, taking a breath, "is why I like being a newspaper man."

It had all tumbled out of the little man so rapidly that the two brothers had to sit and digest the statement. Austin Crickette took the pause as an opportunity to roll himself a cigarette, which he did inexpertly, dropping tobacco on the paper-strewn desk. He leafed through one of the copies of the Sharps' newspapers and blew smoke at it. "Actually," he said, mellowing, "there is some literary promise in some of this. Which of you wrote about the closing of the Indian cemetery?"

"That was Andy," Thomas said. "He went over and watched from behind some trees while they did their crazy ceremony."

"It wasn't crazy to **them**," Andrew protested.

"Well, this is a nicely-done story," Crickette said approvingly. "Good observation. A touch of heart, but pretty objective. So you wrote this all by yourself, did you, young fellow?" he asked Andrew. Andrew nodded.

"Yes," the little man had said. "You could do it. If you wanted to apply yourself, you could write."

That had been the beginning, for Andrew. Mr. Crickette had trained him, after school hours, to do everything from running errands as a printer's devil, to composing, editing, writing and pressmanship. While Thomas had gone on to law school on a scholarship, Andrew, to his parents' disapproval, had come home late many nights each week, hands black with ink, but with a goal growing in his heart. He loved the tedium of type setting, the craft of word assembly, even the acidy smell of the ink. But most of all, he loved knowing that now and then, words of his were being read afar, by people he didn't even know.

Five years passed in the part-time tutelage of Andrew Sharp by Austin Crickette. In time, Andrew knew, he would have to prove what he had learned in a distant town, a larger town. In April of 1839 he arrived in Quincy, Illinois, having received favorable comment from the editor of the *Argus* in response to a letter of application. He was far from home, for the first time. But he was closer to the cutting edge of America's westward expansion. Here were frontier problems: Indians, Mormons. It was where an ambitious young reporter needed to be, in this medium-sized Illinois town in the spring of 1839.

Chapter 4

One month earlier, the bulk of the Mormon population had yet to cross the Mississippi into the sympathetic arms of the Quincy townspeople. Many, in fact, held no hope of a permanent refuge in Illinois; they only knew that Illinois could be no worse for them than Missouri had been. Hundreds shivered miserably on the banks of the frozen Mississippi in Marion County, Missouri, awaiting the thaw.

Louisa was among them. She gently removed Bobby's arm from around her neck, where he had thrown it during his fitful sleep. The gray dawn of March 8, 1839 diluted the eastern sky, and Louisa painfully elevated herself on one elbow to survey the scene outside the tent.

The frigid ground for a thousand yards around was littered with frost-covered mounds, some of which moved from time to time, giving evidence their inhabitants were still alive. Scores had died from exposure since the more than 130 families driven from Far West and Haun's Mill had taken refuge beside the river, awaiting the spring reopening of the ferry.

But how many would be left to make the crossing? Louisa shuddered as she looked at a vacant space near the shelter she shared with her brother and the Gaines family. Yesterday morning as she had tried to awaken a widow whose bedroll was near the Gaines' tent, Louisa had gotten no response. She pulled the frost-rimed blanket away from the woman's head and found herself staring into a blue-lipped face, mouth agape, eyes and nostrils silver with ice. The woman had died sometime during the night. The elders had carried her body to the makeshift morgue, a wagon whose burden increased daily—the ground being frozen too hard for grave-digging. There were no relatives to mourn the woman's passing, and Louisa tried—but found no tears left in her body.

A woman moved now among the few tents and the many bedrolls laid out without any shelter. She was tall and graceful and almost elegant in her movements. As she spoke to the awakening refugees, the camp seemed slowly to come alive again, and shortly over a hundred people were standing, stretching, beating their arms together in an attempt to restore circulation. A thin vapor was generated over the camp by the exertions of the waking sleepers. Mothers began leading their young children off toward the latrines, and in the still, frigid air the smoke from the cooking fires went straight up, faintly brown against the slate gray of the sky.

Louisa would have given anything for a bath. Like all the other refugees, she had been deprived of even the scantest elements of civilization on the march from Haun's Mill.

Louisa and Bobby had been taken in by the family of Brother and Sister Samuel Gaines. They had a daughter, Rebecca, who was only a year younger than Louisa, and a younger daughter, Elizabeth, only four years old. The family had arrived in the United States from their home in Plymouth, England four years earlier, at the time of Elizabeth's birth. But like the other Saints, the Gaines family was impoverished. Louisa had gathered what valuables she could from the wreckage of her family's cabin after the massacre, and had gladly contributed them to the Gaines' belongings. But generally, as outcasts in a forbidding land, the Saints were unable to care for much more than their most basic needs. Almost all of their money had gone to purchase food and medicine, and many fortunes had been lost through the razing of homes and farms and the wanton destruction of herds and flocks. If the Lord humbled those he loved, Louisa thought, he must love the Mormons a lot.

The tall woman waking the camp wore a faded blue cloth around her hair; her skirts and the shawl over her shoulders showed the wear of constant use. Still, there was a regal quality about her which seemed to make her a natural leader among the women of the camp, something quite apart from the fact that Emma Smith was also the wife of the prophet Joseph. Although she held no ecclesiastical authority in the Church, she was looked up to with respect by all. She now made her way toward Samuel Gaines who was folding his bedroll as his wife, Maude, prepared to lead Elizabeth to the distant latrine. There was a beauty in Emma unspoiled by the dangers, grief and privation she had suffered.

"Louisa, dear, good morning! Did you sleep well?" she asked.

Louisa tried lamely to return her smile. "Not badly, Sister Smith, and did you?"

"I dreamt last night of Joseph. I've had a letter from him in Liberty Jail, and he gave me such hope! I'll read some of it to the sisters today. I'm sure we only have to be patient a short while longer, and we'll be across the river and in safe hands once again."

They both turned then to look at the river. Slabs of ice had been cracking and sliding downstream, promising that the spring breakup would soon come, permitting the ferry to run across the huge torrent to the town of Quincy. Everyone in the camp seemed to believe that once Missouri was behind them, their troubles would be at an end. Louisa didn't understand their feelings, and tried to avoid looking forward to anything. That way, she had reasoned, she wouldn't be disappointed. She didn't want to have her hopes raised and then dashed, ever again. "I believe it's breaking up, don't you think so?" Emma asked.

"Maybe so. I don't know. It's such a big river."

"Well, I'll look for you at morning prayer, Sister," Emma said, and moved off.

The conversation had awakened Bobby, who now sat up, blinking, scratching his head under the wool cap he wore. "What are we going to do today?" he asked.

"Maybe we'll get to help make kindling for the fires," Louisa improvised, knowing that Bobby enjoyed being near the roaring blaze that was kept going all day for warmth and cooking. Samuel Gaines was on his feet now. In his rich English accent, he greeted Bobby and asked him delicately if he wanted to "take a trip." By now the lad understood what this meant and he nodded, giving his hand to the tall, thin man, who led him away to a distant wagon draped with canvas, at which a number of men stood.

Alone, Louisa snatched her own blanket and quilt from the ground and bundled herself in them. For the hundreth time, she asked herself how she had become this wretched, humbled girl in a wilderness populated, it seemed, with hostile people. She took a mental inventory of her recent past. One minute she had been comfortable in a loving family, and the next, a band of maniacs had killed her parents, and she had become an animal, she had taken a human life. She could still feel the knife in her hands, still feel it as it drove into her attacker's ribs, and she still saw his body slide off the horse, to be dragged along the ground. The scene repeated itself in her mind whenever she had nothing to do. She had killed. She had murdered. How could she get into heaven now, she wondered, having taken a human life? How long would it be before she lost her grip on sanity?

Louisa had fashioned one defense against the tide of panic when it rose in her and its name was revenge. She was able to put herself asleep every night by envisioning a scene in which she, the avenging daughter, slew the attackers at Haun's Mill. If she were bound for hell, she would take those others with her. She saw her bloody hand strike again and again, each time destroying one of the men she had seen that horrible October day—only five months earlier—until the entire mob lay at her feet. And then she would see the cabin she had lived in, and run to it. But then, all went black. She couldn't bring back her parents, no matter how often her hand fell with the dagger on a screaming enemy.

The more than three hundred refugees along the Mississippi had gathered there after being dispossessed of nearly everything they had owned. They had spent Christmas of 1838 in hiding, a few families here and a few there, as they sought to evacuate Caldwell, Daviess, Clinton, Carroll and Livingston Counties in Missouri. One of the final battles between the old settlers and the Mormons had come at DeWitt, which had become largely populated by Latter-day Saints. There had been burnings and lootings, which led to an attack in reprisal by some forty Mormon men on the town of Gallatin, where a store was burned and the stock carried back to the community called Adam-ondi-Ahman, which the Mormons had dedicated to the Lord. This touched off the eventual fall of Far West and Haun's Mill, on extermination orders from the Missouri governor, Lilburn W. Boggs. The survivors had been driven to the very banks of the Mississippi, and might have been slaughtered there but for the strident editorials in two Missouri newspapers, which seemed to have a temporary cooling effect upon the mobs. But Mormons were still unwelcome in most of Missouri and the Saints, for their part, could hardly wait to leave the state for refuge in Illinois, across the Mississippi.

Again this morning, as for the past week, an awkward young man, Tom Haggart, came to Louisa's tent. It was something in his manner—his stumbling, bashful words and his feeling of being somewhat lost amid the hardships, as she was—that caused Louisa's heart to soften for him. She knew he was trying to gain a closeness with her which she neither wanted to encourage, nor knew how to fend off. Her heart, she believed, had been clamped shut forever by her unspeakable experiences. There was nothing there for anyone anymore, except for the last of her own kin, Bobby. Certainly there was no tenderness left for an outsider. Gratitude—she felt that for the Gaines family. But she knew she was staying now with the Saints only because there was no other place to turn, and no other people with whom to live. She looked at the ragged figure of the tall young man as he picked his way toward her through the tents and bedrolls on the ground. "Mornin', Miss Louisa," he said, removing his cap as he spoke. How curious, she thought; until now he had always called her by the more formal term, "Sister Stephens."

"Good morning, Brother Haggart."

"They say the ice is breakin' up," he blurted, accompanied by a wholly inappropriate smile.

"I can see that."

"T'wont be long now afore we can take an' ride right acrost t' Illinois, I reckon."

Louisa kept her distant, civil attitude. "Well, I certainly hope so."

She turned her back on him and made herself busy shaking out and folding the quilt she was holding, but Haggart stepped around until he was facing her again. Twisting his cap in his hands, he mustered up another broad-toothed smile. "You be needin' someone to carry your things? I'll be glad t' do it."

Louisa didn't look up from her folding. "Thank you, but Brother and Sister Gaines and the girls and I can do it quite nicely." There was silence for a moment, and she looked up at the young man who was agonizing over a rebuttal which his shyness—or his lack of vocabulary—prevented him from voicing.

"Well," he said at last, "If'n ye need any he'p, just give me a holler." And at that, he began to retreat, smiling still, backing away from Louisa as if he were taking leave of a queen in her throne room, until at last he turned, planted his cap on his head, and fled from her presence, leaping over piles of belongings and dodging between tents.

Louisa frowned at the echo of her own voice in her mind. Surely she could have been more civil to him; hadn't her mother taught her respect and manners? But then she felt the icy memory of other men, saw the spectre of the massacre at Haun's Mill, saw again and again the bloody frenzy of men—what they could do! What devils they could be!—and she felt the ice of her grief begin to melt under the fire of hatred she nurtured, deep within herself, and brought out each night to curry and preen in her imagination, and then she felt perfect justification for treating young Haggart—and all strange men, for that matter—as potential enemies. She clamped her lips together and felt the skin tighten over her knuckles as she gripped the quilt as if it were something she were trying to choke. Nobody would ever be close to her again. Those devils had made her kill, had robbed her of the heaven her family believed in and had been working for. She was doomed now, and she would live as a doomed person—shutting out all others from her private prison.

Maude Gaines reappeared with the four-year-old Elizabeth in tow. The little girl dove for the small box in which her eating utensils were kept. Maude looked freshly scrubbed, her cheeks aflame with the cold water and lye soap which made up their morning toilet in the camp. She was small and round, with sparkling blue eyes and brown hair cut short. Her voice was a rich contralto, throbbing with the tones of her English homeland. "I see young Haggart stopped by to pay his respects again this morning."

Louisa sighed. "Yes, as usual."

"You know, my dear," Maude said, moving closer, "he may not be the pick o' the flock, but it's nice to know you've got your charms."

Louisa folded her arms over her bosom. "I really don't care."

"Oh, you say that now," Maude crooned, "but just you wait. One of these fine days, you'll be living in a proper house and life will seem much better to you than it does now. Then's the time when you'll appreciate the attentions of a fine gentleman or two. And from the looks of you, my girl, you'll have plenty of them!"

Louisa clapped both hands over her ears. "Hush!" she cried, and whirled away from the Englishwoman, shaking her head. "I don't want to hear anything about that!"

Mrs. Gaines rushed to her side and put a stocky arm around her waist, but Louisa wrenched herself away and turned to face her, her face contorted in rage. "I don't want any man near me, do you hear?" she shouted, so loudly that people nearby turned to look at her in astonishment. At just that moment, Samuel Gaines reappeared with Bobby. He looked on silently, then Bobby darted to his sister's side and Louisa held him protectively against her skirts. "Aye," Gaines said softly. "We'll be seeing you at prayer, Sister Stephens," then he led his family toward the group assembling by the largest of the fires, where morning prayers and the blessing on the food would be asked.

Bobby looked up questioningly at his sister, who stood trembling with her arms locked around him. "What's the matter, Louisa?" he said in a small voice. "Are you scared?"

Louisa fought for control, then she looked down at the little boy who so

31

poignantly reminded her of her parents. Remembering that it was now her responsibility to be both mother and father to her brother, she said, with resolve, "No, Bobby. I'm not scared. Not of anything—not any more."

The bitter March cold abated four days later, when the afternoon sunset promised warmer weather on the morrow, and in fact it began to rain—a warm, gentle rain—during the night. Louisa lay under the tent, listening to the familiar sound of Brother Gaines snoring, and the short, gentle breaths of her sleeping brother nestled beside her, and she heard the patter of the raindrops on the canvas and knew for a moment that feeling of calm, of oneness with the universe, which had been her way of expressing a unity with God's plan—the image of Nature's wheel, slowly turning from one season to the next. Let calamity fall, let men work their mightiest wonders, Nature still slowly turned her wheel from winter to spring. The pattering raindrops reassured her for a few minutes that somewhere in the universe, God was still in charge.

But He had forgotten some of his choice children.

She bit her lip to hold back the tears, yet they came and flooded her eyes as the rain began to flood Mormon Camp. Bobby stirred, rolled over, and went back to sleep. Louisa held him, firmly, close to her body. It was not yet time to be awake. She lay back and watched through closed eyes as the grim procession began again. She saw her father slain, saw men slaughtered like cattle, saw women ravished and children shot. And then she saw herself, knife in hand, executing the murderers, one at a time, saw them scream silently and fall under her thrusts, until at last she slept. She slept rigidly, and when she awakened an hour later, she had the taste of blood in her mouth where she had again bitten through her lip in her sleep.

Chapter 5

The morning was already hot when Andrew realized that he was awake and in a strange place, but had simply not opened his eyes yet. He lay silently, letting his mind assemble the realities. He was in his brother's room in the rooming-house in Warsaw, Illinois. They had eaten well, talked late, and now it must be well into the August morning. He opened his eyes and looked for Tom, but his side of the narrow bed was empty and there was a note on the pillow. Blinking the sleep out of his eyes, he rolled over and read it.

Have some breakfast and see me at my office.   T.

Andrew stretched and stood up beside the bed. Warsaw's main street sent the odor of horses and dust into his nostrils as he took a deep breath out the single window of the room. Mingled in the aroma he detected the smell of coffee and sausages, and hoped this was part of the service his brother's rent paid for, for despite his casual confidence to Tom about his earnings, his salary was far less than he needed to live in the manner his family had lived back home.

Hastily dressed, and running his fingers through his touscled hair, Andrew hurried down the narrow staircase in search of the food. He followed his nose and the sound of utensils banging, and found himself in a back kitchen, catching sight of a mantle clock which surprised him by registering ten-fifteen. There was a pot on the huge black iron range that dominated the kitchen, and a woman stood with her back to him, beside the sink, black hair done up in a bun, sleeves rolled above her elbows, energetically scrubbing dishes. An iron pot of scalding water steamed on the sideboard between sink and range, and as the woman scrubbed food from the plates, she dipped them in the scalding pot and then stacked them on a butcherblock table in the center of the kitchen. As she swiveled with a steaming plate dripping from her hand, she suddenly saw Andrew, and the plate fell out of her hand smashing to pieces on the brick floor.

"Oh, good grief!" she exclaimed, keeping her eyes on Andrew as she bent down to pick up the crockery. Andrew sprang to her side to help gather the debris. "I'm sorry if I startled you," he said.

"I didn't hear you ring the bell," she said, accusingly.

"I didn't," Andrew explained. "I just came downstairs. I've spent the night here."

The woman scowled as she looked at him closely. Their heads were only inches apart. "You're not one of my people, are you?"

'I'm Tom Sharp's brother."

The woman continued to look perplexed for a moment, then her heavy dark eyebrows shot up and the wrinkles left her brow. "Oh, Mister Sharp, the lawyer," she exclaimed, and smiled. Andrew marveled at how important professional labels were to older people.

"That's right. I just got in town last night." They had by now collected the last of the broken plate, and he deposited the shards in her hands. He noticed how pink and plump they were, puckered from the hot water. "I'm sorry about the plate."

"Pshaw, it was my own fault," the woman said, opening a wooden hamper and depositing the pieces inside. "I'm Mrs. Wilson and this is my house. What was your name?"

"Andrew. Andrew Sharp. I'm a reporter for the Quincy *Argus*."

Mrs. Wilson looked at him appraisingly; "A reporter? My, you hardly look to be old enough. Your first job?"

Andrew's cheeks glowed, and he checked the impulse to tell her he had been writing newspaper stories all his life. "No ma'am, not exactly. I've had other jobs. None as good as this one, though." He glanced at the earthenware coffee pot on the range.

"Have some coffee," Mrs. Wilson said, reaching for the pot with one hand as she selected a large cup from an open cabinet nearby.

"I'd like some, thanks."

The woman pulled out a chair at the table, and he sat down as she set the steaming cup before him. "I guess I slept too long," Andrew put in, hoping it would be obvious to his hostess that he hadn't had breakfast.

"Well," she said, turning back to the dishes in the sink, "it's halfway to dinnertime. If you want to eat dinner here, better tell me now so I can plan on it. Otherwise, might not be enough to go around."

"Oh, no—that's all right. I have to meet my brother and we'll probably want to go out to eat."

There was silence while the scrubbing continued, then Mrs. Wilson paused and turned around, pushing a wisp of black hair off her damp forehead. "What kind of things do you report?"

It was the first time he had been asked that question. Andrew framed a reply that he thought would impress her. "I'm actually here on a special assignment."

"Oh? That sounds important."

"Well, I think it is." He longed to tell her about the assignment; she would be impressed. But he forced himself to say no more, and she turned back to the dishes. "I can't say what the assignment is. You understand."

The woman nodded. "Running a boardinghouse," she said, not pausing in her scrubbing, "you learn not to poke your nose into other people's business." She sniffed and wiped her nose with one sweaty forearm.

"I guess so," Andrew answered. "Come to think of it, I guess that's just exactly the opposite of what a reporter does."

She turned toward him, a half smile on her face. "And you feel good about that?"

"Well," he said, feeling the color rise again in his cheeks, "the people have a right to know.''

"To know what?''

"To know . . . the truth.''

The woman nodded agreeably. "Oh. And so you just have to find the truth, and print it?''

"That's right.'' Suddenly he saw he was being baited.

Mrs. Wilson planted both fists on her aproned hips. "And what gives you the ability to see the truth?''

Andrew was momentarily confused. An able and spirited debater, he and Tom often engaged in this very kind of verbal sparring as an exercise, but this woman was older—a stranger—and he had misjudged her as being **only** a housekeeper. "What gives me the ability to see the truth?'' he repeated. "I'm trained to get the facts. Like a lawyer.''

"Or a judge?''

"That's right.''

"Ah, then, you judge your fellow man? I thought only God did that.''

Andrew thought, *why is she trying to make me so uncomfortable? Is she laughing at me, ridiculing me for having a responsible job at my age*? He protested, "You don't understand. People don't have time to collect all the facts on a news story; that's why there are journalists. We put all the facts together and let the reader decide.''

The woman surveyed Andrew silently for a moment, hands still on her hips, her lips slightly parted, and then she nodded again. "I see,'' she said. "I understand. Just so long as your stories—your **facts** aren't just your opinions.

Andrew spied a clean dish towel and picked it up. Mrs. Wilson dipped a dish in the scalding pot and handed it to him, and he began to dry it. "Well, newspapers do print editorials,'' he said. "Those are one man's opinions, but you don't have to agree with them''

"But a lot of folks believe anything that's printed on paper.''

"That's not the newspaper's fault. It seems to me that a story in a newspaper shouldn't close people's minds on a subject; it ought to open them.''

Mrs. Wilson seemed to be considering Andrew's words for a moment. Then, removing the dried dish from his grasp, she said, "I think I'd like to read your reporting, Mr. Sharp.''

Andrew glowed. He had held his own with this very alert lady and had won! "I would be honored to have you read my articles,'' he said, but then he remembered his assignment. "However . . .''

"Yes?''

"However, I'll be writing under a "nom de plume,'' an assumed name.''

Mrs. Wilson dipped another dish and handed it to him. "Oh? Why's that?''

"It's because I'm on a . . . a confidential assignment. If I used my own name in the newspaper I couldn't report on the story any more.''

35

"As if you were a spy?"

It was strange how the woman could cut through the details and get to the heart of things. He saw now that he had been too frank with her and had confided too much. It was time for him to withdraw, before he had told her too much. "Oh no," he said lightly, "nothing like that."

Hens scattered across the dusty road at the eleven o'clock hour and the sun bore down mercilessly on Warsaw's main street, as Andrew stepped into the shade of Tom's office. He found his brother busy writing something at his roll-top desk. He looked up when Andrew walked in, nodded at a chair, and continued scratching the pen on the paper for several seconds before setting it down by the ink bottle. "Sleep well?" he asked, arching an eyebrow.

"Too well. Then I met your landlady."

"Ah, Mrs. Wilson. Did she feed you?"

"Only coffee. But she's some talker."

"And they claim Morse invented the telegraph," Thomas chuckled, "but my dear landlady is the original telegraph. I hope you didn't tell her anything you don't want spread all over town."

Andrew sat down, unbuttoning his jacket in the stifling office. "No, nothing much," he replied. "Do you like her?"

Tom shrugged. "Well enough. She's a fair cook and the rent's cheap, but she'll talk a man's ears off. Have you gotten the sad tale of how her poor husband drowned when he fell into the river? Every boarder gets that lecture."

Andrew smiled and changed the subject. "What's that you were writing?"

"A dunning letter for my rich landlord."

"You're the landlord's lawyer?"

"When he needs me to help him collect money. I take my fee in reduced rent. But so far, that's the only work I've been able to do for him."

"Do lawyers have to write dunning letters?"

"It's part of the profession. See," Thomas said with irony, "my writing talent is paying off after all."

Andrew was troubled. "You sound bitter, Tom. In fact, you've sounded bitter ever since I came in here yesterday. Do you really like what you're doing?"

There was silence in the office. A team drove by on the street and dust drifted in the open doorway. Tom leaned back in his chair and studied the ceiling, then he swung around to face Andrew. "Do you know what it was that attracted us to the idea of reporting, back when we were kids?" he asked. "It was the **power** of it! Oh, there's power in being a lawyer. The title, 'Attorney At Law' on my letterhead may scare the poor sod behind in his rent because he's afraid the big, important lawyer may take him to court. Yes,

36

people respond to power, Andy, they gladly pay for it. But the power of the printed word is often greater than the most powerful court in the land. Why we saw the power of even our childish newspaper back in Meadville!"

"And got a licking for it."

"My point exactly," Tom exclaimed. "We tapped a source of power with that make-believe newspaper of ours, and when that power—the force of public opinion—got too hostile, we were punished. Same thing happens in real life: when you write a sensational story, you draw fire from the people it hurts."

"But suppose the story has to be told?"

"Ah! That's why people sometimes die with pens in their hands." With that, Thomas picked up his pen and dipped it in ink, then, in a bold swirl, addressed the envelope on his desk, blotted it and folded the letter into it, sealing the envelope with wax over the candle burning atop the desk. Andrew watched his brother's movements with fascination. "It makes me sorry to see your writing going to a readership of only one," he said.

Thomas tucked the envelope into a pocket of his coat hanging over the back of his chair, then leaned back against it, lacing his fingers behind his head. An expansive smile lit his face. "What would you say if I told you I just might be running a newspaper one of these days?" he asked.

"I'd say hurrah, if that ever happened."

"Well, I'm telling you this in strictest confidence. The gentleman to whom this letter is addressed happens to be the owner of the Warsaw *Signal*. He is rather seriously in arrears on his rent. And by the time he receives this little missive here, he will be very vulnerable to an offer of a purchase."

Andrew's brows knitted. "Where would you get the money to buy him out? You said yourself you're nearly broke."

"I wouldn't need my own money," Thomas replied, enjoying his brother's puzzlement. "Because, you see, the landlord doesn't care who runs the *Signal*, so long as it makes money. The landlord knows something of my ambitions as an editor. If I were in charge of the paper, and it were successful, he would get his rent plus a share of the profits. You see how simple it is?"

"Why do you think you can make a go of the newspaper when the present owner failed?"

"Because I know what sells papers," Thomas said, swiveling in the chair and pointing to the groaning lower shelf of the cabinet behind him, jammed with folded newspapers. "Those are the best newspapers from all over: Springfield, St. Louis—yes, even the Quincy *Argus*. They know how it's done. I've studied them. The secret's there if you know what to look for."

Andrew turned to look at the stacks of papers, as if their hidden success would leap out at him.

"Some newspapers just print the daily happenings in their town," Thomas went on. "Not these. And, under me, not the **new** Warsaw *Signal*. The successful newspaper reports on issues!

"Issues? Such as what?"

"Such as slavery, such as the Indian lands, the dangers and the threats of living on the frontier of the West."

"And what will your issue be?" Andrew asked.

Thomas smiled. "Why don't you wait a couple of weeks and then come to work with me on the *Signal*?"

Andrew drew back in surprise. "Are you serious, Tom? I'm already working for the *Argus*."

"Is blood thicker than water?"

"But I've accepted an assignment. Besides, the *Argus* is already a successful newspaper. You'll pardon me, but you haven't got hold of the *Signal* yet."

"Give me two weeks."

"Tom, I can't. You know I can't."

"Suppose I tell you what the issue will be when I take over the paper."

Andrew scratched the back of his head vigorously. "I don't know, Tom," he said uneasily. "I've promised Mr. Ketchum . . ."

"Suppose I tell you that the issue I'm going to write about is the Mormons!"

Andrew felt as if the breath had been sucked out of him. He gripped his knees, and found himself standing up, trembling. "Tom, I should never have told you my assignment," he said accusingly. "I trusted you!"

His brother's eyes narrowed to two slits. "Let me remind you that the Mormons are nobody's exclusive story," he said, measuring his words. "And, in view of your ignorance of them, which one of us has the better right to report on them—you, or me?"

"Right? Neither one of us has any more right than the other . . ."

Thomas held up both hands, stopping Andrew's objection. "No. You're quite right. As I said, nobody has an exclusive on them. But can't you see what a team we'd make, just as we did when we were youngsters? With my knowledge and your flair . . ."

Now it was Andrew's turn to interrupt. "Tom, don't torture me with this. I'm not going to betray the *Argus*."

"But you can change your mind."

"No! It's too late. Besides, I've got to see this through on my own!"

There was a pause, and then Thomas seemed to relax in his chair. His hand went to his wounded leg and began rubbing the spot where he had been injured as a child. "Of course you have to," he said softly. "I shouldn't have asked you to change your plans on account of me. I just thought," he said, looking away wistfully, "it would be the fulfillment of our childhood dreams, in a way . . ." his voice trailed off, then turned back to Andrew, a reassuring expression on his face. "Just a momentary thought," he said. "And you're right, I haven't got control of the *Signal* yet. Maybe I never shall. And it would be a crime to delay your career, when you have a good job in the making." He braced his arm on his leg and straightened into a standing position, revealing a little pain. "No hard feelings?" he asked, extending his hand.

Andrew clasped his brother around the shoulders. "Of course not, Tom," he said. But why, Andrew wondered to himself, did he feel so strange now? And why had the elation over his new adventure turned suddenly to a vague feeling of guilt?

Tom evidently had gotten over the sudden animosity that had flared between them. Stepping back toward his desk, he pulled open a drawer and brought out a sheet of paper. "Now you'll be wanting to locate the place up river where the Mormons are building their town," he said, wetting his pen and nodding for Andrew to sit beside him at the desk. Andrew drew his chair up as his brother began describing a careful series of lines in ink on the paper.

"Here's Warsaw," Thomas said as he drew, "and here's the Mississippi. Now, there is a trail of sorts heading north of Warsaw, but the most comfortable way to go is by steamboat."

"I haven't got the price, I'm afraid."

"But I notice you also haven't got a horse. Of the two, I'd say the price of a steamboat ticket beats the price of a nag."

Andrew nodded and watched as Thomas continued making his map. "The place the Mormons are," he said, sketching in a bend in the line representing the river, "is here—at a spot called Commerce City. Only the Mormons call it something else. 'Nauvoo,' I think it is."

"What kind of a name is that?"

"Mormon word, I guess," Thomas shrugged. "The place is swampy and the air is foul. I understand there've been a lot of 'em dying of swamp fever up there, probably because the Mormons won't touch whiskey. So I prescribe you take along a supply if you want to keep healthy."

Andrew nodded. "How far is it from here?"

"About fifteen miles. And there'll be a boat tomorrow about ten o'clock in the morning. Can you be ready by then?"

"I'll be ready."

"What are you going to tell them when you get there?"

Andrew was thoughtful. "Tell them? The Mormons? Do I have to tell them anything?"

Thomas looked at him and shook his head. "You still don't seem to understand that the Mormon is a different breed, like an Indian. You can't treat them like you'd treat ordinary folks. They're going to want to know your business when you land at their town dock."

"Then I'll tell them."

Thomas groaned. "You're going to tell them you're a reporter come to spy on them?"

"Of course not! And I don't intend to spy on them, exactly. I'm just going to live among them and report exactly what I see."

Tom turned and placed his hands on his brother's shoulders, a look of compassion on his face. Smiling and speaking as he would in trying to teach a child, he formed each word distinctly. "Do you think they'll take you in and let you watch their inner workings, Andy? Do you really believe that?"

Andrew said nothing, but his heart began to sink.

"These people," Tom continued, "have been robbed, mobbed, beaten, chased out of their homes, they're the most unwanted people in the country except possibly the Indians. They keep to themselves and they have secret ways. You let them know you're watching them and every door in Nauvoo will slam in your face. You'll be lucky to get a meal. And you'll be back down here in Warsaw, asking me for a job."

Andrew's head was down. His brother's reasonable, plaintive tone pierced through his conscience and somehow he felt as he had as a child when their father or mother had tried to explain how he had done something wrong. "So how," Thomas said quietly, his hands still gripping Andrew's shoulders gently, "are you going to do it?"

Silently, Andrew shook his head, without lifting his eyes.

"Well, I know what I might do if I were in your place."

Slowly, Andrew looked up. "What would you do, Tom?"

He pulled his hands back and folded his arms over his chest, smiling a tolerant smile. "What would I do? Why—I'd become a Mormon!"

Chapter 6

Mrs. Wilson had packed a box filled with enough food to see Andrew through the day, including fried chicken, hardboiled eggs, cheese and a warm loaf of bread baked early that morning. She had refused payment for the food and had even found a small wicker box into which she tucked it all, wrapped in a freshly laundered dishtowel. As they left the boarding house, Thomas extracted a small flask of whiskey from his briefcase and found room for it in the lunchbox. "And I have something else for you," he said, but wouldn't elaborate as the brothers walked down to the Warsaw dock.

Four people were already there. A tall man with a curly black beard and a cap covering part of his overly long curly hair; two smaller men who were younger and dressed nearly alike in shabby tweed trousers and homespun shirts, and a woman—evidently expecting a baby—who sat beside the tall man on a pile of luggage.

"Mormons," whispered Tom out of the corner of his mouth as they approached the dock.

"How can you tell?"

"I never saw them before, but there's a look about them," Thomas replied, guiding Andrew to a spot along the north side of the dock. Here the two brothers leaned on the railing and looked down at the brown Mississippi as it glided beneath their feet, gurgling around rocks and pilings.

Andrew, standing close by his brother, turned to steal a glance at the others, when he felt a nudge from Thomas and looked down to see something in his hand, glittering in the morning sun. It was a pistol, a Hall flintlock with a small deerskin bag containing powder and balls wrapped around the barrel. "What's this?" Andrew asked.

"Just take it," Thomas muttered. Andrew felt the heavy iron in his hand. He had never held a pistol before, although every young boy in Pennsylvania learned how to hunt with a long-gun of some kind. Pistols were rare because they were used only in closer quarters. There was something about them Andrew had never liked, possibly the fact that they were designed for human targets, not for game.

Andrew did as he was told, and Thomas then slipped the deerskin bag into his brother's pocket. As Andrew began to protest that he didn't want to accept such a costly item from his brother, a shrill steam whistle split the heavy morning air. They both turned and saw a puff of white vapor drifting up in the sky, and edging into view from around a stand of willows came the steamboat, paddles kicking spray into rainbows in the bright sunshine.

The vessel, the *George Washington*, was tall and resplendent in its white paint. Lining the promenade on the upper decks were scores of travelers, while deckhands on the broad lower foredeck stood with hawsers in their hands, swinging them in preparation to make the craft fast to the shore. Roustabouts had appeared on the dock to receive the lines; and stevedores, black and emaciated, shambled up to unload any dunnage coming ashore at Warsaw. Another shriek from the whistle, caused the woman to clutch her hands over her ears. The four strangers now clustered together and moved aside to give the dock hands room to work. From the pair of tall funnels surmounting the ship, thick brown woodsmoke drifted on the breeze. From somewhere within the ship a bell clanged, and the steam and smoke poured more heavily from the stacks and the huge paddlewheel dashed faster against the muddy current which constantly tried to sweep the big vessel back to St. Louis. Only by keeping the paddlewheel churning could the ship move slowly up to the dock. Tiny whitecaps dashed against the prow of the ship, only inches below the decking where the men stood now, hurling the lines out and up. The men on the dock caught the lines and bent them expertly around stout stanchions as the ship continued to move closer to the pilings.

Negroes aboard the *George Washington* were tossing firewood for the boiler from a rack on the lower deck into an open hole, where the engineers and firemen had to keep the hungry flames fed. At last the ship was secured to the dock and a gangway was carried into position and dropped. More sweating black men carried freight off the ship, as apparently nobody aboard was scheduled to disembark at Warsaw. This wasn't surprising, as Warsaw was not a large town and the ship stopped only once a week. Mail and packages were placed in a wagon drawn up at dockside. A passenger agent, spry and businesslike on the one day a week that the boat came, crisply tore Andrew's ticket and then hurried off on other duties, leaving the brothers at the foot of the gangway. The four Mormons passed them by, heads down, watching their footing. Thomas waited until the four were aboard and then turned to Andrew and gave a playful tug to the brim of his hat. "Now take care of yourself," he said, "and save some ink for a letter to me now and then."

"Aw, Tom, I'll only be fifteen miles away. It's not as if I were going to another country."

Tom's expression changed. "In a way, you will be," he said seriously. He cast a glance in the direction the Mormon quartet had gone. "You're going into a different world. Watch yourself."

Andrew drew back his jacket and looked at the butt of the pistol hooked in his belt. "You really think I'll need that?" he asked, nodding at the gun.

"Better to have it and not need it than to need it and not have it," Thomas said.

Andrew had run out of words to say, and stood awkwardly silent, pretending great interest in the handle of his traveling bag. "Well, good luck, Andy," Thomas said, finally. "And if things don't work out for you on the *Argus*, you'll have a job waiting on the *Signal* right here in Warsaw."

"**If** you get it."

"Sure. **If** I get it."

The *George Washington's* whistle shrilled a long, piercing note, and Thomas stepped back as the stevedores shoved the gangway up onto the deck. Lines were loosed, and a gap widened between the deck and the Warsaw dock. The rhythm of the plunging paddlewheel increased and the ship creaked as the rudder bent the vessel out into the current. Andrew gave one final wave to Thomas and then turned to duck inside the salon, which was filled with travelers who had already returned to their cards and drinks. The men were at circular tables. The women lined the chairs and benches near the windows. There didn't appear to be any place for Andrew to sit without either interrupting a game or joining the ladies, so he turned and stepped back onto the deck, and decided to walk around the superstructure. The ship was picking up speed now, forging into the wind. The bright morning sun warmed the air and the breeze was bracing. He walked around the front of the main salon and found a handful of passengers seated on the left side of the ship, enjoying the sun. Among them were the four travelers Thomas had labeled as Mormons. The motion of the ship propelled Andrew toward them a little faster than he had intended. *Well, this was as good a time as any to start making friends with the Mormons*, he thought.

He approached the foursome, who were just getting settled in their chairs, and nodded to an empty fifth chair. "Care if I join you?" he asked, and the older man turned the empty chair around for Andrew to sit in, saying not a word.

They seemed to be preoccupied with the far shoreline. Across the river lay Missouri's northeastern boundary, a low profile of trees and shrubbery nearly a mile away. The four had been looking at it on the dock, and they continued to stare that way aboard the ship. Andrew decided to try again to engage them in conversation. "See any landmarks you recognize?" he asked brightly.

It was the woman who replied. "Do you know if that's Missouri over there still?" she asked. Her voice had a foreign lilt to it.

Andrew knew that Warsaw was almost directly opposite the boundary between Missouri and the Iowa Territory, and he told her he thought Missouri was falling astern rather quickly now.

Without looking his way, one of the two smaller men said, "That's good."

Andrew recalled what Tom had told him about the Mormons' persecutions in Missouri. Maybe that was what they were thinking about. To the older man he asked, "You folks from Missouri?"

"Aye, we just came from there," the tall man replied in his deep voice, "and we're not anxious to go back."

The woman touched the man's sleeve, darting a fearful glance in Andrew's direction.

So Tom had been right! They **were** Mormons. Suffering from the mobbings, on the run to greener pastures. How he handled himself in the next few moments might spell the difference between acceptance in Nauvoo, and the cold shunning Thomas had warned him about. But what to say now? If he remained neutral he would appear indifferent to their feelings and they probably wouldn't open up within earshot from now on. But if he appeared sympathetic, they might accept him as a traveler who had read about the Mormons' difficulties and would tell him things he could incorporate in his dispatches. Yes, that would be the right course to take. He would choose his words carefully and see if he could encourage them to talk.

"So, you're going to Nauvoo, too?" Andrew asked them.

The black-bearded man seemed interested. "We are. Do you know the place?"

"No. This is my first trip."

"Ah, then you're only visiting?"

"No, no. I'm hoping to settle down there."

"And may I ask, why?" The dark brows lowered over blue piercing eyes.

Have I given him some reason to be suspicious of me already? Andrew wondered. Better be very careful; this fellow is trying to figure me out. Suddenly the words formed in his mind and without a moment's hesitation he heard himself utter them: "Because that's where the prophet is."

Four pairs of eyes turned to look at him. The two other men, who had been listening but had not participated so far in the conversation, exchanged glances and then turned back to Andrew. The woman was the first to reply. "Then, are you . . .?"

The older man held up his hand and cut her off. "Perhaps," he rumbled, rolling his r's ponderously, "the man is referring to another kind of profit, the profit a businessman nets after expenses. Would that be your meaning?"

Andrew tingled with a heightened sense of alertness. What had just happened here, he realized, was his opportunity to do exactly what Tom had said **he** would do if he wanted to ingratiate himself with the Mormons: join up with them! Andrew weighed the alternatives; he could tell them the truth, that he was merely interested in Nauvoo as a visitor, or let them think he was a Mormon himself. The latter course was the most dangerous one, he knew, but the only one that would propel him into the inner circle (whatever that might turn out to be) from which he could write unique dispatches no other reporter had ever filed—from the inside of Mormondom! He decided his conscience could tolerate a little deception if he chose his words carefully and permitted the Mormons to believe, if they wanted to, that he was one of them. His deliberations, however, were misinterpreted by the woman, for she suddenly broke the silence.

"Sir, you needn't be afraid to be frank with us. I believe you are going to Nauvoo for the same reason that we are! You **are** a Latter-day Saint, then?"

How easy this was going to be, Andrew thought. "I must look it," he said, noncommitally.

"Ye do well not to advertise your faith," the older man said gruffly, "as we found out in the state of Missouri."

Now one of the two younger men joined in. "You'll have to forgive us, brother for being careful. We're the McCann family—what's left of it—and we came from Far West."

Andrew nodded, as recollection flooded into his mind from the details Thomas had given him about the fighting in that Mormon town. "Of course, Far West," he repeated. "You must have had a terrible time of it."

"Our parents were murdered," the young woman said, "and Jock, here, was wounded. Oh, but we haven't introduced ourselves properly. This is Jock McCann and these are his brothers, Angus and William."

"And this is my wife, Anne," the man called Jock said, his voice softening as he spoke her name. They shook hands with Andrew.

"And I'm Andrew Sharp," he said. "I'm please to meet you . . . Brethren. And you, Sister McCann."

"And where do ye come from?" asked Jock.

Andrew decided then and there to conceal any connection with the town of Quincy, in which his newspaper contact was located, and so he truthfully replied, "Pennsylvania, originally. A place called Meadsville." He hoped they wouldn't ask him for details about where he had joined the church, for he knew nothing about whatever ceremonies might attend such an event, except that he had heard that Mormons believed in full immersion, rather than sprinkling.

"We're from Edinburgh, Scotland," the woman declared. "Baptized in England, and we got on the boat for America straight away. But I must say, it's not like they told us it would be."

"Not that we expected the streets to be paved with gold, like some addled persons have said," Jock put in, "but this is a harsh and unfriendly place. We're hoping to see better."

Andrew enjoyed the soft sound of their accents, their humble and earnest way of talking. At all costs, he wanted to avoid as much deceit with these folk as possible, so he tried to let them dominate the conversation by asking them as many questions as he could, without arousing their suspicions. "Are there any more Mormons on the boat?" he asked.

Jock scowled. "I dinnae like us calling ourselves 'Mormons'," he said sternly. "That's what our enemies call us. Heaven help us if we begin to talk as they do!"

Andrew paled slightly. His first mistake, and an obvious one. They called themselves Latter-day Saints, or just Saints! He should have been listening more carefully to their conversation, and he resolved to tune his ears more sharply to the terms they used that were different from his own. "You're right, of course, Brother McCann. It's a habit I got into because so many of my friends talk about . . . us that way."

"It's probably nothing harmful," Anne added. "The Saviour's church became known as the 'Christian' church that same way. It was what His enemies called it.''

That struck Andrew as odd, hearing her refer to the Savior just as Christians did. He made a mental note to do some research on Mormon beliefs as soon as he got settled in Nauvoo.

"What will ye be doing in Nauvoo?'' Jock inquired.

What do I tell them? Andrew wondered. "Well, I do a little of everything," he said, smiling to cover his uncertainty. "I ought to find something they need me to do.''

"I thought," Jock said slowly, "ye might be a detective. I see that ye wear a gun.''

Andrew suddenly remembered the flintlock tucked under his belt. Looking down now, he saw that he had unconsciously unbuttoned his jacket as he had sat down, and the butt of the firearm was in plain view outside his shirt. "Oh, this?'' he said, forcing a laugh. "I've never shot one of these things in my life. My brother gave this to me just as we said goodbye back there in Warsaw. You saw him, I suppose. He was worried about me. You know how older brothers can be!''

"Aye, we know," said Angus, and William joined him in laughter, provoking somber-faced Jock into a hesitant smile. "And your brother, is he a member as well?'' Jock asked.

"Uh, no. In fact, he—doesn't quite approve of me.''

"Well, we know how that is, don't we?'' William said, looking meaningfully at Angus.

"Our rector back in Edinburgh read our whole family out of the church records one Sunday," Angus said, a mischevious smile on his face, "and nobody in the whole town would speak to us after that, except of course for the other Saints. It was as if we'd taken the plague!''

Anne shifted in her chair, elevating herself slightly and then lowering herself in a different position. Andrew knew that no man of good breeding permitted himself to seem to notice if a woman was **in confinement**, and in fact few expectant mothers appeared in public after they had begun to show visible signs of their condition. He averted his eyes and looked out across the rolling Mississippi. The water and the banks on either side were featureless, and he wondered why the Mormon prophet had chosen to lead his people so far away from civilization to found their city. "Tell me how you came to join the church, Brother McCann," Andrew said.

Jock hitched his chair closer to Andrew's. "Well," he said, appearing to relish the opportunity to respond, "we are ship-builders, and my father and I had business in Liverpool. I did his accounts for him, and we had gone to England to purchase supplies for our works up in Edinburgh. While we were staying in Liverpool, we learned of a meeting at which an American minister was speaking, and since we knew not a single American at that time, we decided to attend. Mind you," he said, holding up a long finger, "we were Presbyterians, of course, and not at all dissatisfied with our church.

However, we looked up the meeting hall and took seats near the rear. The gentleman preaching was Willard Richards.'' Here, he paused, evidently expecting some reaction from Andrew, who only nodded and smiled—knowingly, he hoped—and remained silent.

"Well, Elder Richards was, as I say, a total stranger to us, but as soon as he began to speak, our hearts went out to him."

"Is that so? Why was that?"

"Why, the room was filled with hostile parties," Jock said, "hardly giving the poor man a civil chance to state his position. We had never heard such discourtesy. I will say I became somewhat agitated, as did my father."

"What they did was stand up and silence the lot of those English rabble," chortled younger brother William. "They marched right down to the front, they did!"

Jock nodded. "The man couldn't make himself heard over the catcalls and shouting," he continued, "and someone had to bring order to the meeting. So we did." Andrew had a vision of two stern, six-foot Scotsmen confronting a room full of unruly protestors. If the elder McCann bore any resemblance to Jock, Andrew could see how they could command respect from any group. "Go on, I'm fascinated," Andrew urged.

"Well, Elder Richards must have spoken for more than an hour, and he touched on how the Gospel of Jesus Christ had been brought to the earth, just as we have it in the New Testament, but then how it was misinterpreted—how the Church fell into error. He saluted John Wesley and Martin Luther and of course our own John Calvin, the founder of Presbyterianism, for their attempts at reform. But he said that what was needed wasn't reformation, but **restoration**—a restoring of the original powers and offices of the primitive Church as founded on earth by the Saviour, himself. And that was when he told about Joseph Smith and his vision of the Father and the Son, and about the visitation of Moroni, the discovery of the plates and the publication of the Book of Mormon.''

Plates? Moroni? What was the man talking about? Why didn't I take the time to study what these people believe before plunging in among them?

"Naturally," Jock was saying, "there were hundreds of questions put to the Elders, but they answered each and every one of them to our perfect satisfaction. Well, by the end of the meeting, I knew that what we had heard was true—so did my father."

"But they still had to come back to Edinburgh and convince us," Angus put in. "They bought two copies of the Book of Mormon and when they returned, it was 'here, read this and shut up until you've finished!' Well, William and I, we didn't much care for that!''

"I'm afraid that's how it happened," Jock smiled ruefully. "You see, we had felt the Spirit there in that meeting in Liverpool and we wouldn't rest until the rest of the family felt it, too."

"And did they?" Andrew asked.

"Not at first, and not all at the same time," Jock continued. "Anne here," he said, placing his hand on hers, "was the dutiful wife. She said she would be glad to join me in any religion I had reason to believe in, but I'm happy to say that I had learned from my studies that each of us must come to an understanding of the Gospel for himself—and herself. We read the Book of Mormon together, and gradually we all came to know the truthfulness of it."

Anne, now over her earlier discomfort, leaned as far forward as her stomach permitted. "It was really so simple, you know," she said earnestly "to find out the truth. After you study the Book, you pray about it, and then you obtain a sure and certain testimony. Isn't that right, Brother Sharp?"

Nothing to do but agree with them, he thought, and nodded enthusiastically. "That's right."

"And so we were all baptized," Jock concluded, "we sold our business in Scotland and took passage to America."

And got your parents killed in the bargain, Andrew thought. "Tell me something," he said. "After your mother and father died at Far West, why are you continuing on? Why not go back to Scotland?"

Jock looked insulted. Andrew knew by the dumbfounded expression on their faces that he had said something no real Mormon would say. "Why because, mon," Jock replied reprovingly, "we're following a prophet of God! Look what he's been through for the Gospel: he's been beaten, tarred and feathered, driven from his home any number of times, robbed of his rights as a free citizen, thrown in jail for nothing, his family and friends insulted . . ." his voice had risen in pitch and again his wife touched his arm. He broke off, shaking his head. "No indeed, Brother Sharp," he said, his voice low and trembling. "The McCanns are made of better stuff than to turn our backs on a prophet of God!"

I have got to get off this subject, Andrew thought. It was clear that he was out of his depth now and risking detection. Now they might just think he was a weak member of their faith, but if he persisted in his awkwardness and demonstrated more of his lack of knowledge about things a Mormon ought to know, there was no telling what these three sturdy Scotsmen might do. Still, he knew he had obtained some vivid and colorful information from them, material he would weave into his dispatches back to the *Argus*. He was anxious to set pen to paper, before the impassioned words faded from his memory. "I wish I had your testimony," Andrew said, using a word he had heard devout Baptists use. "Would you take offense if I were to jot down what you've told me in my journal? I like to keep a diary of important events that happen to me."

Jock seemed impressed. "Why, not at all, Brother," he said kindly.

"Thank you," Andrew replied, and brought out paper and a stub of a pencil which he always carried with him. *Here I am, writing my first actual dispatch on the Mormons, right under their noses!*

"Let's see, the date is August 17th, 1840 . . . aboard the *George Washington* bound up the Mississippi to Nauvoo . . ." Andrew purposely kept up a narrative as he wrote, using a shorthand he had developed which included key phrases and abbreviated words that permitted him to take notations that nearly kept up with a normal conversation pace. As he spoke, seemingly to himself but more for the benefit of the McCanns, he occasionally looked up to comment, "I don't want to forget your beautiful words," or "one day perhaps I'll put this all in a book." His small audience seemed to approve.

Andrew had nearly finished making his notes, when Anne McCann, speaking sweetly, destroyed his composure. "Now, Brother Sharp," she said in the most innocent manner, "we'd love to hear about your own conversion."

Andrew pretended to study his notes for an instant longer, fighting for time. Then he closed his journal and said, "Why, I'd enjoy that a great deal, Sister McCann, but shouldn't we have some lunch first? Frankly, I'm starved."

The two younger McCann brothers agreed on the instant, and chairs were shifted and preparations made to open food boxes on the windy deck. The five formed a circle, and then there was a pause. *They're going to say a table grace! What if they ask me to do it?* Andrew's conscience burned within him again and he summoned a silent prayer, *Not me, not me, please!* But Jock was standing now, his hands clasped before him. All heads were bowed, and Andrew was glad they could not see him shaking, nor hear the thunder of his hammering heart.

"O Lord, who hast been our guide and comfort on our long journeys, bless us now we pray with safety on this voyage, bless our family and our newfound friend, Brother Sharp, and bless this food, we pray, that we may benefit from it, and gain strength for today. In the name of Jesus Christ, Amen."

A chorus of "amens" replied, and Andrew placed his lunch hamper on his lap and prepared to untie the cord around it. Then he suddenly remembered what was nestled atop the morsels provided by Mrs. Wilson, and what would instantly command the attention of the McCanns as soon as the noontime sunlight illuminated the contents of his box. Like the unwanted firearm digging now into his belly, the brown flask of whiskey was going to be as out of place among Mormons as a fox in a henhouse, and—taken on top of the other suspicions his performance this morning might have aroused—could be almost as deadly. Yet, he had to open his lunch box and there would be no way he could conceal the whiskey. Fighting down panic, Andrew slipped the twine off the box. "My brother packed this for me at his boarding house," he said. "I'm afraid he's still trying to be a mother and a father to me."

With that, he opened the hamper. There glistened the unwelcome liquor jug, just as it had been packed. A glance around the circle told him, however, that nobody else was looking at his lunch. Still, he would have to go through with it.

"Wait a minute!" he cried. "What in the world is this?" All eyes looked up at him, then down into his lunch box. Taking the neck of the jug by thumb and forefinger, Andrew raised the flask into the air as if he were holding a dead rat by the tail.

"Where did that come from?" he asked himself. "If this is what it looks like . . ." and with that, he uncorked the flask and took a suspicious sniff. He made a disgusted face. "Whiskey!" he snorted. "My brother's idea. He was telling me about the swamp fever up at Nauvoo, and how I ought to be sure to keep whiskey on hand to prevent it—but I never thought he'd provide it!"

Andrew wondered if his performance had been a shade overdone. The others were silent. Finally, Jock said, simply, "Well, I'm sure he meant well. Ye can just heave it overside." Which is exactly what Andrew now did, wondering as he watched the flask arc out and splash among the brown waves of the river, whether he should try to obtain another bottle secretly as a prevention of sickness in the new country they were approaching.

Chapter 7

Something sparkling in the air caught the corner of Louisa's eye as she sat at a window chair on the second deck. She turned quickly to look out on the monotonous river, but whatever it had been was lost now in the brown silt that slid past below. Then she noticed a young man standing near the rail, brushing his hands together as if he had just tossed something unwanted into the water. The four others seated nearby turned their attention back to their lunches which they were eating, and the young man joined them.

What she needed, Louisa knew, was a real diversion. All morning since getting on board at Quincy just past dawn, she had been trying to keep Bobby amused and out of mischief—what a lot there was to intrigue a six year old boy on a steamboat!—and she had tried to show interest in the whispered declarations of passion shared about every eligible boy on board, from Rebecca Gaines, who had discovered the fascination of the opposite sex rather recently in Quincy.

But Louisa, robbed of her adolescence by the Haun's Mill massacre two years earlier, shunned men of any age and could barely tolerate the stream of young men who presented themselves to her on the boat. Most were rich tourists up from St. Louis, headed to Nauvoo for a holiday among the fabled Mormons. Dandies, pampered and innocent, dressed like Easter paraders, made their way past the chairs where Louisa, Rebecca and the Gaines family sat. The boys were silly, grinning, childish monkeys, posturing and posing and hoping to catch a nod of approval from the girls. Rebecca gave them every encouragement; Louisa kept her eyes on her crocheting, watching her fingers fly as she constructed a lace doily to add to Maude Gaines' growing collection. At her age, other girls blossomed into young womanhood and had beaux. But now, Louisa had charge of her brother Bobby, did at least if not more than her share of the chores for the Gaines family, and tried to be a companion to the bright but light-minded Rebecca.

Yet, she was aware of the changes taking place in her body. The clothing suitable for her just a year ago no longer fit; she realized that her pale brown hair was glinting now with golden highlights, that somehow her eyes were changing—the blue becoming deeper and the lashes growing longer. Her voice, too, was maturing. Nature's wheel was turning, but it brought her no joy. She seldom wore the flattering new dress with the pinched-in bodice sewn for her by Sister Gaines, nor the saucy lace-trimmed cap given her the previous Christmas by Rebecca.

How comforting it would be, she thought, if she could be like Maude Gaines, who was intent on preserving her English heritage here on the raw edge of civilization, who believed that one day she would again have a polished dining room table to hold her lace doilies. How could people who had been through such brutal times have faith in the future? What made them believe there was a city, **anywhere**, where they would be safe from the ravaging of men who hated enough to rape, burn and kill their fellow human beings?

Louisa turned and looked at the lower deck again. The five people eating their lunch there were obviously not tourists. The tourists were loud, anxious to explore the steamboat, wearing bright, modern clothes and new, expensive shoes. The shoes were the invariable guide: Mormon refugees wore boots or worn-out and resoled shoes that testified to hundreds of miles of rough wear. Their clothes were homemade, patched, cut-down, threadbare. And their clothing tended to be dyed dark colors, because these would mask the stains of dirt—maybe even blood—which never washed out.

But one of the five didn't belong. It was the man who had tossed something into the river. His clothes, while not expensive, were lighter in color and more fashionable. And the cap he wore was more scholastic than practical, made of a tweedy material that matched his traveling jacket. Whereas the woman and other men in the group all tended to look like drab ravens, their companion seemed more like a robin, somewhat out of place in their company. But Louisa wasn't interested. If they were going to Nauvoo, no doubt she would encounter them there sometime. But it really didn't matter to her. Whatever the reasons they were bound for Nauvoo, Louisa knew why she was going there; she simply had no other place in the world to go.

Six-year old Bobby appeared at Louisa's side, demanding to be fed. Maude Gaines put down her crochet hooks and suggested to the girls that they prepare the cold lunch they had packed before leaving Quincy. Seeing the travelers on the lower deck eating had not stirred any hunger pangs in Louisa, but she began now, opening the food packages and hoping her appetite—whetted by the river journey—might return. Sister Gaines was forever urging Louisa to "eat while food is plentiful," and indeed she took her own advice devotedly; but Louisa's desire for food, as for most other pleasant things in life, had deserted her. She knew she was steadily losing weight, as her clothes seemed to hang more loosely on her each week. She glanced down at the group lunching on the lower deck. The young man in tweed certainly seemed to have a healthy enough appetite, she noticed; his cheeks were packed full of food.

They can't ask me to talk while I'm still stuffing my face, Andrew reasoned, and practiced for the first time in his life the thorough mastication that his mother had unceasingly advocated. It was her conviction that digestion would be better served if one took small mouthfuls and chewed every morsel until it was reduced to a liquid. She had gone so far as to require Tom and Andrew to count in their heads until they had chewed fifty times

53

before swallowing—a practice which caused them both to gag one day. After that, family meals were conducted without their mother's admonition to "chew fifty times," but they both felt her disapproving looks when they shoveled in their food and only half chewed it.

Now, it was more a matter of survival than his mother ever knew, Andrew thought. *These Scotsmen have good manners and they won't be expecting me to start telling them how I got "converted" until I am conveniently through eating.* He broke another piece of bread from the loaf and, although he was in danger of bursting, shoved it in his mouth before he had finished the cheese and egg he had been munching.

The conversation around the circle had ceased except for a few diffident remarks among Angus and William, and concern from Jock for his wife's comfort. Their attention to their own interests at least gave Andrew a few minutes in which to ransack his memory for any bits of information he might use to stitch together a plausible story about his introduction to the Mormon church. It wasn't easy, planning his deception under the very gaze of the people he meant to deceive. How could he write honest articles if he obtained them dishonestly? He was tormented by the ethics of the case, but with a sigh—which nearly caused him to blow fragments of food out of his nose—he realized that he now had no choice but to pursue the role he had accepted for himself: a newly-converted Mormon with only a fractional knowledge of the ways of the church. It was in that part of the pose, however, that he recognized his best chance to successfully pull off his deception. *If I act confused about the church, they're the kind of people who will want to set me straight.*

Having settled that strategy in his mind, Andrew decided to broach the subject of his "conversion" himself. "Well," he said, wiping the last of the jam from his lips, "you asked how I came into the church."

"Yes, Brother Sharp," Anne replied, "we'd all love to know."

He cleared his throat and swallowed. *You don't know a word of scripture and you haven't anything but sheer nerve,* he told himself. But he plunged on. *God help me now and I'll repent as quick as I can,* he thought. *Repent!* That was a good place to start!

"I was a terrible sinner," he began, lowering his head. No reply. He looked up to see the four McCanns waiting expectantly for his next revelation. "And I thought I was lost forever, until I heard the Gospel."

"Then ye had nae church before?" Jock asked gently.

"No. Oh, my poor mother had tried, God rest her soul . . ."

"Ah, she's passed on, has she?"

"Yes. My father, too." *Criminy, where did that come from? I must be insane! First I make myself a Mormon, now I'm an orphan!*

Whatever the source of his inspiration, Andrew could see that he had touched Anne deeply. Her eyes suddenly rimmed with tears and she said, "Just like us, poor man. Do go on!"

He hated playing so falsely upon her sympathy and decided to try to conclude his recital as quickly as possible and hope for a different subject.

Jock spoke again. "Who taught ye the gospel? We might know him."

Andrew was trapped now. "Oh, I don't think you would," he improvised. "The chap was brand-new to the church himself, and right after he baptized me he . . ." *He what? What have I got myself into now? What can I do with him?* "He was killed."

"No!" It was Anne again. "Where?"

"Well, I heard he was killed. He may have just died. He was sort of—sickly anyway."

Jock wore a troubled expression on his face. "And how long ago was this?" he asked.

"Oh, just a short time back. Just a few months. Uh, January. But I never got to go to meetings much, so I'm afraid I don't know a great deal about the church and how things are done. Maybe you could . . . help me?" He made such a plaintive appeal he almost believed himself.

"We would be happy to," Jock said. "Have ye a Book of Mormon?"

"No. I . . . this will shock you, Brother McCann, but I've still not read one."

Oh, oh. Blunder. Look at their faces.

"That's most unusual," Jock said. "Imagine being converted without a knowledge of the Book of Mormon."

"It's the Spirit," Anne put in. "You just knew it was the truth, didn't you Brother?"

Andrew nodded, hoping to produce a facsimile of her own tear-filled eyes. He kept nodding, hoping he looked too emotional to speak.

Jock laid a large hand on Andrew's shoulder. "As soon as we get to Nauvoo, I'll see if we can't obtain a copy for ye," he said.

"Thank you, Brother McCann," Andrew croaked. *Please, please let these kind people leave me alone now,* Andrew thought; *I've sported with them too much.*

As if in answer to his supplication, Jock stood up, ending the conversation as decisively as he had begun it. "A mon's faith is his own business," he said. "We appreciate your sharing it wi' us." The others murmured agreement. Andrew let his breath out slowly. *Did I pass muster?* He couldn't be entirely sure of Jock. A shrewd customer, this canny Scot. Had he deceived him, or was this formidable black-bearded man just letting him off the hook for now, to snare him later? Andrew's knees had grown stiff, sitting in one place and holding the hamper of lunch on his lap. He needed to limber up, and he excused himself to take a stroll around the deck.

Away from the McCanns for the first time in well over an hour, Andrew now felt the sweat trickle down his spine to flood the small of his back. He had been under such tension as he tried out his Mormon role on this little group—how could he survive living in a whole city of them? One little slip here, another one there—and someone would finally add up the evidence and there would be an ugly confrontation. At such a time, he had better be prepared to prove the basic honesty of his intentions, he decided. *I'll just write the truth. They shouldn't be afraid of that.*

He walked toward the stern, the most interesting part of a steamboat, where the huge paddlewheel, driven by a pair of thrusting, clanking beams emerged from the hidden machinery below decks. Spray fanned out into a continuous rainbow behind the vessel, and the feel of the steady, irresistible power of the steam engine thrilled him.

He stood now, holding on to the rail, feeling the trembling work its way from the paddlewheel, through the soles of his feet, and into his entire frame. *One slip and I'd be in the maelstrom*, he thought, recalling the terror of a childhood experience at Niagara when he envisioned being swept over the falls, unable to do anything but let Nature pulverize him.

Nature. Is Nature that *God* we pray to, fear, struggle to understand? Do the Mormons know so very much more than other people about Nature, about God? Is that why they can face danger and death rather than give up their beliefs? Do they know something I don't know?

Andrew shook himself out of his reverie. *Watch out, young fellow. From now on, you must learn to act and think like a Mormon. No—like a Latter-day Saint.* He turned away from the noise and walked back up the deck, close to the rail, studying the featureless brown river as it slipped past, inches below his boots. He longed to set pen to paper and begin drafting his first dispatch from Nauvoo.

Farther up the river, the Des Moines River emptied into the Mississippi, adding its bulk to the brown flood which coursed beneath the rolling wheel of the *George Washington*. As the ship plowed northward through this merging of a mighty tributary, the ship slewed like a man trying to stand on melting ice, giving uncertain footing to anyone walking aboard the vessel. It was an unnerving sensation and Andrew sought a solid foundation from which to view the scenery as it inched past. He saw a stairway leading up toward a small room surmounting the upper passenger cabin, and—assuming the view from there would be superior to that at deck level—climbed to the roof of the cabin. Just behind the little deck house sprouted the twin smokestacks which belched forth the brown sooty woodsmoke from the boilers below decks. Nobody else was on this upper deck, and then he saw the probable reason: in the small deckhouse stood a man with a blue cap with a short bill, whirling a huge brass wheel, his eyes riveted out the windows in front. From his position there was a commanding view of the river, and of stumps and branches which dotted the course as the flood swept them toward the ship. Now, seeing the whirling wheel spun back and forth in answer to the ship's movement against the currents, Andrew realized that the man at the helm had all matters under perfect control, and that whatever sensations were generated by the slewing of the big ship were natural. Andrew edged closer to the open window of the wheelhouse, and there he saw a second man—older, full of paunch and shorter by a head than the man at the wheel. At the moment Andrew saw him, he too was seen, and the older officer strode quickly to the door of the enclosure and stepped onto the open deck to confront Andrew. He wore an impatient scowl and his eyes were embedded in layers of wrinkles from squinting into the shining river.

"No passengers allowed up here," he barked.

Normally, Andrew would have meekly followed orders, but there was something in the brusqueness of the man's manner that challenged him. Andrew reached into a pocket and handed the man a folded packet of paper, much creased and soiled. In a low voice he hoped sounded mature and confidential, he said, "I think this will explain what I'm doing." Somewhat irritated, the man took the paper and unfolded it, scanned it to the bottom and handed it back.

"Reporter, eh? Doesn't cut any ice, young feller. No visitors allowed up here."

Andrew refolded the letter, which was a routine credential signed by the editor of the *Argus* intended to display only to the police or other authorities in an emergency. "And what is your name please, sir?" Andrew asked, drawing out a pencil stub.

"Captain Evan MacKenna, that's M-a-c," he spelled proudly. "Be sure you get it right, and then you can go below."

"Yes, you're the man I'm told is something of an expert on the Mormons up at Nauvoo," Andrew said as he wrote.

There was a slight hesitation before the captain answered. "Well, I don't know as I'm an expert, exactly. I sure have carried a bunch of 'em up there, though, and talked with some."

"You see, captain, I need background for my assignment. It is a **confidential** assignment. The *Argus* has sent me here to report on them. Absolutely confidential, you understand."

The captain's eyes flicked to Andrew's waist and then up again. "That why you're packing a pistol?" he asked. "I could relieve you of that while you're on my vessel."

That cursed pistol again! Andrew pulled the flintlock out of his belt and handed it to the captain. "Certainly, sir," he said.

The captain waved his hand. "Oh, keep it, keep it," he protested. "But if you want to talk, you'll have to come inside the wheelhouse. And mind you don't stand in front of the helmsman!" With that, he jerked his head toward the open door and Andrew ducked inside.

The wheelhouse afforded a splendid view of the river stretching out in front, and on both sides. From this height, thirty feet or more above the water, the man who steered the boat could see flotsam and avoid it, to say nothing of another ship up to a mile away. The Mississippi seemed to be bending steadily to the east now, a fact Andrew had been unaware of when he viewed the river from the lower deck.

As they stepped into the shady enclosure of the wheelhouse, Captain MacKenna peered over the shoulder of the man at the helm, judged the position of the *George Washington* in relation to the channel, and said quietly, "two points port now, Mister Stenson," to which the helmsman replied, "two points port, aye aye," and swung the brass wheel easily to the left and neutralized it. A compass mounted on a binnacle in front of the wheel swung lazily, and the captain eyed its motion and said nothing more until he was satisfied with the maneuver. To Andrew, the big ship's direction hadn't changed at all, so minute was the correction in its course.

"Now, what do you want to know about the Mormonites?" the older man asked, perching on a tall padded chair.

"What do you think of them?"

The captain shrugged. "They're just people."

"Dangerous, would you say?"

The older man snorted. "Dangerous? To who? To preachers from other churches, maybe; they like to rob congregations, I'm told. Dangerous to the lazy, for certain. You catch a Mormon lying down, he's probably dead. Never saw such working fools! That what you mean by 'dangerous', young feller?"

Andrew didn't know what he meant; the question was merely a way to open a discussion, but he nodded and changed the subject. "Maybe you can tell me a little about their beliefs."

The captain reached into a pocket and drew out a pinch of tobacco, which he tucked into his jaw. Andrew then noticed the well-used brass spitoon on the floor near the captain's chair, and the brown stains on the floor and the wall nearby. The old man shifted the cud around and worked the juice through it then turned his head and spat into the spitoon. "What they believe," he said, wiping his white moustache with a large pocket handkerchief, "is all wrapped up in Joe Smith. You heard of Joe Smith, the Mormon prophet?"

"Yes, of course."

"Well, then likely you know that he wrote a new bible, and if you're a Mormoner you got to believe in it."

"Have you read the Mormon bible?"

"Well, no, 'course not. But those as have read it will tell you it's full of the most bloodthirsty stories you ever read. That's what stirred up the Mormon scare in Missouri, you know."

"Is that so? What about the people who mobbed the Mormons in Missouri?"

"Why, hell fire, son; all they was doing was taking back what the Mormoners stole from 'em. They're awful thieves, you know."

"They are?"

The captain spat again, wiped his face, and looked impatient. "I told you they stole congregations. They walk right in and convert people right out of their pews in other churches. And there's a few of them Mormoners who robbed stores in Missouri and took the loot with them down to the river, here. Claim they had a right to it because they'd been robbed by Missourians.

Trouble wherever they go."

Andrew tried a new tack. "Why do you suppose people would join the Mormon church, then?"

The captain paused and considered. Then his face lit up. "Why, it's because of Zion," he said.

"What about it?"

"Joe Smith, he promised the lot of 'em that they could have the whole state of Missouri for Zion. That's what attracted 'em from all over up east, and even from England, they tell me."

Andrew smiled at the irony of the statement, remembering the impoverished Scottish family only one deck below. Hardly enjoying the riches of Zion, he thought.

"They threw Smith in jail, you know," the captain continued. "Charged him with arson, murder, treason—you name it, they charged him with it. But he got loose somehow. Some say it was magic, some say it was God's will. But I say it was just good old bribery; plain and simple bribery. Anyway, he's free as a bird now and building a city out of the wilderness, in one of the most Godforsaken spots along this cussed river."

At this, Andrew looked out of the forward windows again in hopes of seeing some sign of their destination, but the huge stream continued to meander northeastward under a sky that seemed to be turning as brown as the water. As Andrew gazed at it, the captain commented on the scene. "Be having a thunder storm in an hour," he said in confident tones. "Just about the time we get to Nauvoo."

Andrew wondered fleetingly where he would be laying his head tonight; there was no way to send ahead for reservations and no way of knowing what kind of accommodation might be available. But then he turned his attention once more to the talkative old steamboater, who had just delivered another burden to the cuspidor on the floor.

"What does a person have to do to join up with their church?"

"Well, you gotta be baptized, I know that for sure."

"Anything else? How do you get to be an elder?"

The captain shrugged again. "I'm cussed if I know," he said. "Gotta swear loyalty to Joe Smith, I suppose, and other things. I really don't know."

"Suppose you were already baptized in some other church?"

"Don't make no difference to the Mormons; they got to do it their way."

"Why is that?"

"I told you, I don't know!" Then, to the helmsman, "Pull a little farther out around that bar up there, Mister Stenson."

The helmsman nodded, his back to the captain, and swung the wheel hard to the left. Andrew saw the horizon slowly answer by swinging to the right.

"'Course, you know all about their crops and such?"

Andrew shook his head.

"Well, where an ordinary farmer raises one crop, the Mormon raises two. Never saw such harvests. Prob'ly they put a hex on the seed or something. And their menfolk aren't only farmers, some of 'em are clever: mechanics; understand how to make most of what they need, so they don't trade with townsfolk much. Peculiar people."

Andrew groaned inwardly. If what Captain MacKenna was saying was accurate, there was so much lore in the intricate Mormon way of life that he would surely never be able to absorb enough of their ways to fool anyone. Yes, the best course is the one he had set already: pose as a hastily-converted newcomer to the faith. At least, he thought, he might survive a little longer without detection in that way.

His thoughts were interrupted by a knocking on the wooden side of the wheelhouse, and Andrew turned to see a black porter, a starched white mess jacket buttoned to his chin, bearing a tray with two cups and two pitchers on it. "Come in, John," the Captain said, and the porter walked in, casting a surprised look in Andrew's direction.

"Coffee, Captain," John said, placing the tray on a ledge under the side windows. "You want me to bring another cup?"

Andrew, feeling he was excess baggage, made for the door. "Oh, no thank you," he said. "I was just leaving. Thank you for the interview, Captain MacKenna."

"That's 'M-a-c,' mind," the old man said, his eyes on the river.

The Captain had been right about the storm. The northern and eastern horizons now were curtained in lowering billows of cloud, brown and purple and black which erupted into flickering bursts of lightning, illuminating the black hearts of the clouds.

The air on the river took on a heavy and pungent character, as if the very atmosphere was begging for the purging of a rainstorm. People on the decks fanned themselves and watched the display as the clouds closed dark above them. Trees on both banks reached imploringly for rain. Yet it was withheld. Suddenly above the tall smokestacks on the steamboat, a terrible green-yellow luminescence flickered from the bowels of the boiling cloudmass, and a thick ribbon of lightning stabbed the Illinois shore, accompanied by a piercing shattering cannonade of thunder that echoed back and forth across the river.

And the wind sprang at the river, gouging waves, blowing spray, tormenting the placid vessel into a heaving, prancing animal that seemed tethered to the bottom, unable to move forward but only up and down, burying her prow in the angry water and then lifting it like a stricken whale, only to bury more deeply with the next thrust. In the wheelhouse, the Captain rang for half speed, reluctant to risk losing way but more reluctant to risk breaking the wheel or any of the machinery as the sudden gale lifted the stern out of the water. Belowdecks, men swore and watched the towering steam boiler sway against its restraining rods and braces. The temperature gauge and pressure gauge registered danger to the engineer, knowing he must keep steam up but afraid to stand near the machinery for fear a fitting might burst. The works stank with a mixture of lubricating oil, river water and sweat.

And then the first raindrops came, each drop drowning-size, until the patter became a tattoo and then a torrent, and then a blinding, impenetrable sheet which bore down upon the river. The roar it made as it struck the *George Washington* drove a stake of fear into every heart aboard.

Water was everywhere, and only the dim outlines of the whitewashed ship divided the sky from the river. All passengers cowered under cover, and the sound of women and children sobbing was orchestrated with the groan of the ship's seams straining under blows it had not been built to bear. Glass shattered as wind-hurled waves jumped the ship and smashed through the panes. The ship rolled, pitched and suddenly lurched sideways. Few people attempted to stand without a firm hold on some part of the ship. Andrew was pressed into a corner between the main salon and the door to the deck, which had been strapped open to permit ventilation during the hot trip up the river, and which now permitted volumes of rain and river to pour in. The salon floor was awash, and Andrew found himself wondering why the captain hadn't sent a sailor to lash the door shut—until he realized that the ship's crew was busy just trying to keep the ship from foundering.

He saw a strap or a belt which kept the door open. Surely he could release it and shut it. He stepped across the open doorway, receiving the full slap of a drenching gust of wind and water, but he lowered his head and stepped onto the deck, taking care not to release both hands from secure holds at once. The door had a brass handle, and through the handle was laced a strap the thickness of a man's galluses. He tugged on the strap but it might have been of iron rather than leather. And then he realized that it was leather indeed, and in water leather **shrinks**! He feverishly tore at the knot which had made the thong into a loop, but the shrinking had already started and the leather resisted his frantic efforts. What was needed was a knife, and he didn't have one. This meant hurrying back into the salon and finding someone with a sharp blade. He turned and lowered his head again to dive through the doorway, when the ship suddenly lurched and, from above, something white and sodden plummeted into him, knocking him sprawling. The deck was streaming with running water the consistancy of liquid soap, and as he tried to scramble to his feet, a piercing pain shot through his side, shortening the gasping breath he sorely needed. He rolled onto his belly as the pitching deck delivered him the flailing white bundle full in the face. It was a man! It was John, the porter! In an instant Andrew realized what must have happened. The porter had fallen from the deck above and was unconscious, now being swept ever closer to the edge of the deck. The black man's arms were stretched over his head and a steady stain of rich red blood poured from the man's temple and made rushing veins on the flooded deck. Andrew reached for the man just as the ship rolled sickeningly again, and felt the inert body sliding away from him, toward the rising brown river at the very edge of the deck. In pain, he lunged after the porter and managed to seize both of his legs, but the man's torso and both arms were overboard. If he still lived, Andrew thought, the water will drown him, but he was too winded and in too much pain to shout for help.

Inch by tortured inch, he snaked his own body backwards toward the doorway. The unconscious porter was caught somewhere and he couldn't make his weight budge the burden. Then, at the last moment of consciousness, he felt hands, strong hands, on his own body. Hands went beneath his arms and as they yanked him into a standing position, the pain in his side crashed into his brain and he felt nothing but dark, warm peace, and cared nothing more for the world and all its storms.

As quickly as it had arrived, the storm swept past and the skies cleared, with the immediate effect upon the river being so dramatic as to cause many of the more devout on board the *George Washington* to pronounce it a miracle. As it happened, there were only two persons injured—Andrew Sharp and John Parker, the porter—and both now were being cleaned up and attended to in separate quarters. Parker was belowdecks being treated with a bandage and a drink of rum. For Andrew, there was more attention, concern, and—to his consternation—a degree of celebrity.

"You risked your life out there, young man," a bewhiskered gentleman said, his entire face shaking. Andrew was not sure of anything; what had he done, why this old man was bending over him, and why it hurt him so sharply whenever he drew anything but the shallowest of breaths. "I saw the entire thing," the pink-faced gentleman went on, "you should be awarded a medal!" There was a murmur of agreement among the several other passengers who stood around the improvised couch on which Andrew had been placed, in the main salon. His throat burned, flooded with the rancid taste of his own bile, and he licked his lips, looking around the room.

"He wants a drink, who's got a drink?" cried someone. Within an instant a bottle was uncorked and thrust under his nose. Andrew's lips formed a grateful cup as the bottle was tilted, but before a drop could find its way into the eager mouth, a large hand closed over the flask and snatched it away. "He won't be wanting that," said a deeply resonant voice with a Scottish burr.

Jock McCann towered above the couch, a commanding figure even in clothes drenched with water. His mass of black hair clung to the sides of his head like plaster to a wall, and his beard curled into ringlets. Then Andrew realized he was lying under a coat that was black and coarse enough to be Jock's. "Where does it hurt ye, Brother Andrew?" he asked.

Andrew tentatively inhaled to confirm the location of his pain, causing a spasm which jerked him half into a sitting position. "Here," he said, pointing to the right side of his rib cage.

Jock gently placed his hand on the spot, then he opened Andrew's shirt, removed the pistol still hooked to his belt, and with fingers remarkably gentle for their bulk, palpated first one rib and the another, until Andrew suddenly gasped and cried out in agony. "Ah," Jock said, smiling with satisfaction.

62

"It's as I thought. A broken rib."

"Are you a doctor, sir?" asked one man, offended by Jock's dismissal of his liquor flask.

"No, are you?" rumbled the Scotsman, closing Andrew's shirt. "Now, Brother Andrew, there's naught to be done about a broken rib. Have ye had one before?"

Andrew shook his head.

"They mend themselves in time. But I'm sure ye'd feel better if ye had a blessing. Would ye like one?"

Andrew nodded expectantly. The crowd in the salon looked at one another, some nodding knowingly. "William," Jock called without turning around. The younger McCann appeared beside his brother. "I'll be needing ye to join me in administering to Brother Sharp."

William removed his hat, and both men knelt beside the couch. Andrew closed his eyes. A voice in the crowd—the same man as before—now demanded, "Oh, then it's a preacher you are?"

It was William who responded. "That's correct, friend. And we'll thank all here to be silent and respectful." There was no other sound in the cabin, as Andrew felt a rough hand on the crown of his head, gently, and then the pressure of another pair of hands.

"Your full name," Jock whispered. Andrew didn't know what was expected of him. "Your full name, Brother Andrew," he repeated.

"Oh. Andrew James Sharp."

There was a pause. Andrew could feel warmth flowing from the huge hands on his head.

"Andrew James Sharp," Jock said in a quiet voice, "in the name of Jesus Christ and by the authority of the holy Melchizedek Priesthood which we hold, we lay our hands upon your head and pronounce a healing blessing upon you. We promise you that your wounds will heal, and that you will be blessed for the unselfish act you have performed in service to your fellow human being. We bless you with a speedy recovery, as you continue to live according to righteous principles. In Jesus' name, Amen."

The warm hands were removed. Andrew lay with his eyes closed, enjoying the delicious dizzyness that had started with the first words of Jock's blessing. At last he opened his eyes and the cabin jerked into focus. The two McCanns were looking down on him, looks of satisfaction on their faces. Others in the circle were more concerned and curious. "Thank you," Andrew said, raising up on one elbow and testing the pain in his ribs, "Thank you." He was surprised and a little embarrassed at the emotional sound of his own voice.

Suddenly from out on the deck, a boy rushed into the crowded cabin.

"Nauvoo!" he shouted. "It's coming 'round the bend! And wait 'til you see it!"

"Smith-Noble Home"
Painting by Al Rounds

Part Two:

The Arrival

Chapter 8

It might have been a scene out of an Italian landscape. The storm clouds, having moved from the northeast to the southwest, were now profiled against the sun just past its zenith, making an aperture through which a fan of golden rays slanted across the river. The rain had cleared the air of all dust; rooftops ashore glinted; red brick dwellings looked as if they had just been painted; the town looked almost unreal—a mirage of order and refinement emerging from wild and uninhabited land.

There had been small huts along the river, mostly unpainted and tumbledown, and even the sight of an occasional dun-colored boatman or fisherman. Then the storm had broken and now, almost as if the ship had sailed into another realm, the sky was clearing above a gently sloping tract which bore several imposing buildings, spacious homes, wide avenues and a number of white-fenced lawns. An American flag flew proudly from a two-storied building near the dock. A traveler at the ship's rail could take in a panorama of urban planning and architectural integrity not found west of Philadelphia. The city of Nauvoo sat on a half circle of the Mississippi, offering three fronts to the river, just at the head of the Des Moines Rapids. A gifted city planner had organized the plats so that the rich lower land, which had benefitted from centuries of waterborne topsoil, were dedicated to farms; and the farmers plowed with oxen in the field as the steamer arrived.

Up from the farms a riverfront avenue connected with north-south arteries which rose at easy gradients to residential districts in which not more than four lots formed each block.

Adjacent to the residential area stood a mercantile center, offering what appeared from the water to be shops of all kinds, a town square, and on the outskirts, a mill and a few factories whose smoke drifted away from the town as if by some previous design.

Samuel Gaines stood at the rail with five-year old Elizabeth in his arms and his wife and daughter at his side, admiring the city. Louisa and Bobby Stephens were beside them; Bobby insisting on standing on the lower rail.

"Now that's a fair-looking city to be sure," Gaines marveled. "Imagine—only a year old!"

It was the biggest city Louisa had ever seen. Bigger than the Ohio village where she had been born, bigger than Haun's Mill, certainly—even bigger than Quincy. Something about the brisk breeze that stirred the flag, the crisp white paint on the houses, the absence of dirt and mould, lifted her spirits slightly. After hand-me-downs, hunger, hiding from enemies, and being outnumbered by suspicious neighbors, here at last was **something** the Saints could say was theirs and theirs alone! She felt excitement kindled in her chest. She recognized a feeling that had returned after a long absence: she wanted to get off the boat and onto shore in this city of Nauvoo. She was actually looking forward to something!

Beside her, Rebecca Gaines peered intently at the few citizens moving in the street. "Not very many people there," she said in a petulant voice.

"The young men would be in school or in the fields," her mother explained, a trace of amusement in her voice.

"I didn't mean young **men**," Rebecca protested, turning toward impassive Louisa, who was silently enjoying her own growing interest in whatever lay before them in the new city.

The *George Washington* nudged the pilings near the landing dock, and crewmen hurled lines ashore where dock hands waited to make them fast. With a final burst from its whistle, the ship gentled against the dock, hay bales thrown into the gap to cushion the impact, and the gangway was hauled into place and lowered.

Andrew had found that he could stand upright without pain, but he could not carry his baggage without wincing and catching his breath. Angus and William divided their own loads with Jock, who was carefully guiding Anna onto the gangway. Andrew—keenly embarrassed by his unaccustomed frailty—shuffled down to the dock as part of the McCann party. He felt depressed. What he had envisioned as a heady adventure was beginning badly, what with being dependent upon strangers and suffering pain at every step. Besides, his conscience still bothered him, because he was accepting help and kindness from the McCanns under false pretenses. Would they have gone out of their way to help him if they had known he was a reporter bent on penetrating the inner sanctum of Mormonism? Andrew wanted to be independent of anyone here in this strange new town, and to commence his writing—bring his journal up to date, frame his first dispatches for the *Argus*—and begin to function in his profession. Without his profession he felt no status, and without status he felt invisible.

Several wagons were drawn up at the dock to receive incoming passengers and freight. Also on hand were groups of Nauvoo residents there to meet relatives, and touching reunions were being held all around as more arriving Saints hurried down the gangway and into the arms of loved ones. Jock McCann led his party straight for one of the wagons, where a rawboned young man was placing a step box for passengers to use in boarding. "Where does the mail come in?" Jock inquired. "I'm told it's handled by President Rigdon."

"The general store," said the driver. "Brother Rigdon's too sick."

"Will ye take us there first," Jock asked, "And then on to our home?"

"Whatever you say."

Jock began to assist Anne into the wagon, as porters arrived with boxes and trunks tagged "McCann—Nauvoo." Andrew, unable to lend a hand, protested. "You don't need to put me up, Brother McCann. I was going to take a room just anywhere, to begin with. I didn't know you already had a house here.''

"Well, we shall see whether we do or whether we don't," William said with a smile. "We contracted to have a house built for us, but we've never set foot here before this minute."

"What's the name?" asked the driver.

"McCann."

The driver paused, scratching his chin and then he ran a finger under his collar. At last he said, "Oh! McCann! Yes indeed, brethren, you have a house in Nauvoo! A very fine one! I'll take you right to it."

Andrew quickly revised his estimation of the "impoverished" McCanns. "Do you mean to say," he asked, "that you ordered a house built, sight unseen?"

Jock nodded. "Aye, we did. Well, a mon has to have a place to live, and what with Anne the way she is . . ."

"Well, you're very kind indeed, but I can't impose on you this way. I'll just find myself a room somewhere," Andrew said. To the driver he asked, "There are rooms for rent in Nauvoo, I expect?"

The driver nodded dubiously. "Some," he said. "But not many."

"Ye'll stay with us at least until you're well," Jock said, finality in his voice. Andrew could see it was impossible to argue with the Scot, once his mind was made up. "Well, I certainly thank you," he said meekly. "If you have the room . . ."

"Och, we'll have the room if the builder followed the plans I sent him," Jock said heartily.

By this time the brothers had counted and helped load the baggage and had swung Andrew's luggage aboard the wagon. Now, on Jock's strong arm, Andrew climbed painfully into a seat between Angus and William, and the party started off into the city of Nauvoo.

The storm had freshened every growing thing. Flowers of every color festooned window boxes provided even on some of the store fronts, and the town had an orderly look to it, as if it had been thoroughly planned before the first shovelful of earth had been turned. Rather than the spontaneous development to be found in most communities, Nauvoo gave the first-time visitor a cohesive organized look. The street along which they were traveling led gradually uphill to a block containing merchants and craftsmen's buildings. They passed neat, pale-gray painted clapboard shops with signs such as "Wm. Onyx, Tailor For Gentlemen," "M. Deveraux, Milliner," and "Heath's Booksellers."

There was a leather shop turning out harness, tackle, and fashionable belts for men, next to a bootery which was, in turn, adjacent to a large open structure which needed no sign to advertise its function as a tannery, as hides were stretched on frames and hung on the outside walls. Down by the waterfront, rows of fine new barrels graced the shop of a cooper, not far from the ringing hammer of a blacksmith, whose output included the shiny hoops used in the cooperage. The McCann men took all this in with evident interest, and there was talk in the wagon about the most likely spot along the river at which to establish a shipbuilding yard. Andrew made mental notes, later to be transcribed in his journal, about the energetic ambition of his host family. He speculated that the sale of their family business in Scotland must have netted them a sizable profit. An indication of their affluence was immediately ahead for Andrew, as the driver pulled up before a building marked "Jensen's General Merchandise." A smaller sign read "U.S. Post Office, Nauvoo."

Leaving Angus with Anne in the wagon, Jock and William helped Andrew down and went into the store. Barrels and sacks of various commodities were arrayed beneath a spring scale near a counter. There were tins of olive oil and kerosene, jars of salve and pickalilly, rolls of fabric and racks of farm tools. A series of hand-lettered signs festooned the back wall. Among them was a freshly-painted one which read, "We Do Not Sell Tobacco Or Spirits." Behind the counter was a balding man with a flowing beard the color of corn-silk, making change for a woman who had just bought a bag of horehound candy. She turned, popping one into her mouth, and looked up in surprise as the three newcomers darkened the small room. Stepping aside for her, Jock tipped his hat as she scurried out. "We'd be after our mail," Jock said to the counterman. "The name is McCann."

The storekeeper looked puzzled for an instant and then smiled, holding up a finger. "Ah, you're the McCann's from Edinburgh," he said, and bustled around the corner of the counter and into an enclosure in the back of the store. Out of sight, he continued talking. "Packages and letters have been piling up for you," he shouted. "I began wondering if something had happened to you."

"Something did," Jock replied, too quietly for the man to hear. "It was called Far West."

As Andrew took this all in, he suddenly realized that there might be mail waiting here for him, as well. He was on the verge of calling out his own name for the shopkeeper to hear, when it occurred to him that anything marked with the return address of the Quincy *Argus* might arouse suspicion. He decided to wait and call for his mail when he was alone.

The shopkeeper returned from the back room with his arms piled with packages and bundles of letters tied together with twine. As he unloaded his arms, he said, "Yes, indeed; all Nauvoo has been waiting for you McCanns to arrive. Of course, we've all admired that fine big house you had built. And then we're told that you're going to put in a shipyard right here in Nauvoo! My, won't that be a blessing!" William raised an eyebrow at Jock at the mention of a shipyard, but Jock betrayed no emotion as he examined the packages. At last he selected one, a sturdy box some 24 inches by 8 inches deep, which he handed to William—who took it and hefted it with a satisfied expression. Andrew burned with curiosity about its contents.

"And what do we owe ye now?" Jock asked.

"Oh, nothing at all," the shopkeeper replied. "It was all prepaid."

"And how often does the post come?"

"Every Monday from Carthage, the county seat."

The McCann brothers loaded their arms with the mail and packages. Andrew offered to help but they insisted they could do it themselves.

"Well, again, welcome to Nauvoo," the shopkeeper said. "If you'll be needing anything, remember our store has the best prices. I'm Linus Jensen and I'm at your service."

They returned to the wagon. Anne and Angus looked inquiringly at Jock, who nodded silently at William. William reached up and placed the long box between Angus and Anne. The driver shook the reins and clucked to the horse, and the wagon lurched on up the road.

There was the sweet scent of newly-cut wood in the air from a number of buildings being raised in the neighborhood. Jock asked the driver about them and the young man named all the families who were building them. "Where does the prophet live?" Anne asked.

The driver turned around to look over his shoulder. Nodding and pointing back toward the Mississippi, he said, "There's an old homestead down by the river—the White farm. He and Sister Smith live there."

Andrew, who had remained silent through most of the journey, felt an urge to begin getting a perspective on the site of his new assignment. "How big a homestead is it?" he asked.

"About 135 acres. They hold meetings down there. You'll be seein' the place." He, too, had assumed Andrew was a Latter-day Saint; this masquerade was going to be simple to sustain.

"Then it's a big spread?" Andrew asked.

The driver laughed. "Afraid not. Just a simple log house with a little addition to it. It was here back afore the prophet ever come to Commerce City and named it Nauvoo. Then Brother Turley, he put up another log house about thirty rods from the prophet's. And then they just commenced buildin' all over the town."

It was true; wherever the checkerboard of streets had been put through, trees had been felled and homes were either under construction or freshly completed. Nobody had ever seen anything like it. Concentrated development along strictly-planned lines, most of the buildings far more substantial than any frontier town could boast; the design of the homes was strictly Colonial and eastern in inspiration, with the emphasis on the practical rather than the ornamental.

Ahead on the same road was a wagon which had overtaken theirs when they had stopped at the post office. The family in it was sightseeing as the horse plodded along, and two small children—a boy and a girl—danced with excitement as they pointed to the new buildings, looked at the dogs which paced the wagons for a few yards, and their squeals of glee could be heard as the McCann's wagon approached. Obviously, these were newcomers too, just off the boat.

"How many Mor-" Andrew corrected himself, "How many Saints are

71

there in Nauvoo now?'' he asked.

The driver ran his finger inside his collar again. "Don't know exactly," he said. "More comin' every day. Quite a bit from England, like you folks, I reckon." Anne smiled quietly at Jock. It was not the first time that Americans had mistaken their accent for British, although to the Scots, a Briton's pronunciation sounded alien, easily identified as coming from the Southern Isles.

The wagon ahead now pulled over to the edge of the road, and the driver and the male passenger jumped down and went up to the door of a fair-sized house, leaving three women and the little children in the wagon. As they passed by, Andrew recognized the family as one he had noticed on the steamboat. The two younger women had impressed him as being attractive, although decidedly different in attitude—one withdrawn and the other almost flirtatious. If they were both Mormons, Andrew mused, there was more latitude for individuality than he had supposed was allowed in this authoritarian church.

Turning at a corner, the driver pointed at a handsome two-story brick home which stood alone in the next block. A whitewashed fence surrounded it on all sides, enclosing rich brown earth still soaked from the recent rain. An outbuilding was in back, beside a shed which fronted on an alleyway. All the buildings were painted white, with dark green shutters and fine millwork on the facia boards and eaves. Directly in the center of the front elevation was a six-paneled door with an arched and leaded window light above it, and two narrow leaded lights flanking the door. The work was of such excellence that Anne spoke first before anyone else. "What gorgeous windowlights," she exclaimed. "Were they done here or imported?"

The driver, delighted to brag, turned and said, "Right here in Nauvoo, and by none other than by Apostle Brigham Young himself!"

The name meant nothing to Andrew. He caught himself before he opened his mouth to ask who was Young and what was an Apostle. "He's a glazer, is he?" Andrew queried.

"One of the best," the driver said, pulling up in front of the new house. "Well, folks . . . you're home!"

The McCanns stared in silence at the house. At last, Jock nodded slightly and said, "Aye. 'Tis as I drew it, is it not, Annie?"

"Exactly," she whispered, and hugged her husband's arm with both of her own.

"Well then, let's go in and look around," cried William, leaping to the street. When all had assembled, the driver began unloading the wagon. Suddenly, Jock stopped and snapped his fingers in dismay. "Do ye know what I've clean forgot?" he asked. "The key! Surely in this stack of mail, the builder, Mr. Law, has sent me the key!"

"The key to what?" the driver asked.

"Why, to my house, man!"

"There's no need for a key, brother," the driver said. "Ain't no lock on the door." And as they all looked, they saw that that was true.

"No lock? Preposterous!" Jock stormed. "I never expected a man would build me a house and then go away leavin' it unlocked!" And he stalked to the gate, threw it open and marched up the brick walk to the front door. Opening it, he stepped inside. He was gone for several seconds, and then reappeared, scratching his beard. "I can't understand it," he said.

"Is everything all right inside?" Anne asked.

"Seems to be perfectly in order. Come on in, let's look around," Jock said, and the group followed him through the door into the hall, its varnished floors still slightly tacky and the smell of fresh paint heavy throughout the hot quiet air inside.

Opening off the hallway was a parlor, wainscoting finely made and plaster finished nicely. A fireplace held brass firedogs and a load of wood ready to burn. The lead-paneled windows fore and aft were shiny and bright. Up the steep staircase ran a bannister made of spindles turned identically by a lathe. On the other, right hand side of the entrance hall, double doors opened onto a dining room with a sideboard. At the end of the hallway was the kitchen, and it was there that Anne now ventured. The kitchen faced east and was bathed in shadow. An oil lamp stood on the drainboard. Beside it was a box of matches. Someone had been thoughtful enough to prepare their new house to make it livable from the very first.

Striking a match, Anne lit the lamp and the glow diffused through the quiet room. "Oh, this will be lovely," she whispered, holding the lamp high and inspecting the cabinets, the lead sink, and the huge stove which smelled of oiled metal. "Jock, I've never cooked on such a fine stove before," she said. "And look! Someone has already filled the wood box!" Sure enough, beside the stove were neatly cut stacks of wood just the size needed to charge the stove.

The younger brothers had gone upstairs and she could hear them walking and talking above her. Andrew and Jock stood with Anne in the kitchen. "Then ye like it?" Jock asked.

Anne turned, holding the lamp in front of her. Her eyes swam and she looked up adoringly at the tall bearded man before her. "Oh, Jock," she said, oblivious of Andrew standing behind her husband, "Now we can start our married life in peace!" And she reached for Jock's neck, pulled him down and kissed him. Andrew turned to the hallway but Anne's voice stopped him. "And Brother Sharp, you must feel as home here as if you were one of the family! We're only too grateful to have a place to share with you!"

"Aye, and thinking of that," Jock said, "let's go upstairs and see the rooms."

There were four bedrooms, opening off a hall that ran lengthwise at the upper landing of the staircase. Jock designated the north front room as his and Anne's, and left the selection of the other three to the brothers and Andrew. In short order each had chosen his preferred room, Andrew gladly receiving the back southern room which would give him a southeast light. He had preferred that exposure because he expected to do his writing early, with the first light of day, before he left for work. *Work? What work?* He was an invalid without a trade other than writing! How would he live if he didn't take some kind of job? The pittance from the *Argus*—although he expected a raise as soon as his articles began to be published—wouldn't suffice. It worried him and he dwelt on this problem as he watched William and Angus bringing up his traveling bag and then lugging the trunks and cases in from the wagon.

Among the cargo was the two-foot long box which had interested him at the post office. He noted that Jock seemed to keep it near him at all times, and he also noted that it was not half a minute before Jock had once again separated the box from the rest of the family goods, and had it now held beneath his arm as he directed the disposal of the final load from the wagon. Standing at the head of the stairs, Andrew saw that the driver was waiting payment at the front door. The other brothers were busy placing boxes in various rooms, a chore Andrew was excused from because of his broken rib. Whatever discussion had been made between the driver and Jock had taken place just before Andrew stepped out on the upstairs landing, but he stood there silently and watched as Jock put the box on the floor, pulled out a knife and carefully removed four nails which had kept the top on, then pried up the fitted cover. Inside was a layer of oiled paper of a heavy grade, which had been folded over and crimped. Carefully, Jock unfolded the paper and spread it back. Standing almost directly above in the dimly lit hallway, Andrew could see right down into the box. It was filled with gold coins, stacks of them! Jock carefully lifted out a small stack of them, selected one, put the rest into his pocket, fitted the cover back on the box and rose to pay the driver. Whatever the denomination of the coin, the driver was impressed and protested that it was too much to be paid for his services, but Jock, patting him on the shoulder, turned him around and headed him out the door.

Andrew hurried back into his own room, panting from the pain of bending his torso over the bannister railing to observe the scene in the hall. So Jock McCann brought the family fortune with him and had it sent to him! A clever man. He had outsmarted the mobs; and here he was dressed like a penniless immigrant carrying a fortune in gold under his mighty arm like a musician might carry a concertina! He was more intrigued than ever to be in the household of this stern and taciturn man, and he felt that his fortune might well lie right here, working for McCann—if he were extremely watchful.

Chapter 9

Samuel Gaines felt humiliated. At a time when he had expected his weary little family to be embraced by welcoming Latter-day Saints, he now found himself, hat in hand, begging at the door of a householder whom, he had been assured by the wagon driver, had plenty of room to rent. But he felt again as he had in Missouri, where Mormons were regarded as a pestilence. "I'm a journeyman bookbinder," he protested, "and I have skills that will earn me a fine living. We've just come from weeks along the river, for we lost all we had in Far West. Surely, brother, you'll trust me for rent until I can begin work here?"

The small man in the doorway seemed resolute. Arms folded over his elegant vest, small dark eyes darting beneath thin brows, John C. Bennett looked beyond the humble man at his doorstep to the dismal group in the wagon in front of his new house. He had only moved in four weeks before and had been so occupied with affairs vital to the embryonic city that he was not ready to let rooms to strangers. Besides, he was annoyed at the invasion of his privacy. He liked reading and research, and there were other, personal aspects of his life that he certainly didn't want hindered or observed by anyone. Then there was another thing. He, Bennett, was a doctor, having served as a surgeon in the Black Hawk Indian war; he was a Brigadier General of the Illinois Invincible Dragoons, and he had just been appointed Quartermaster General of the state of Illinois by Governor Carlin. Naturally, he chose his associates from among men like himself—men like Joseph Smith, for example—and the company of a poor bookbinder from England and his destitute family was out of keeping with the social orbit in which he gravitated. However, as he looked again at the hopeful faces in the street, he had another thought. The man would be out of his house, working most of the day. The women might be useful in attending to menial household chores for which he had no taste; as a bachelor he needed someone to do them. And besides, he thought—noticing that the two daughters seemed rather charming despite their soiled and wrinkled clothes—scrubbed up, these girls might be rather entertaining company. Intellectual company, of course, he reminded himself; they would interest him only if they were **intelligent**. Nothing improper about that. And as a newly-pledged member of the Latter-day Saints and the titular political head of Nauvoo City, one must be extremely careful.

Bennett deliberated no longer. Bathing the Englishman in a beatific smile, he said, "It may be unsound business practice to permit this, but never let it be said that John C. Bennett turned away a worthy family in their time of need."

Gaines was overjoyed. Grabbing his hand, he said, "Oh, Brother Bennett, you won't be sorry, I assure you! And, as you live alone, you'll find my wife is an excellent cook and the girls will attend to your every need. You'll come to love them very much, sir, as I do!"

Bennett stole a look at the two girls. He assumed them to be sisters, not certain which might be the oldest. But then, his eyesight was faulty at distances and since he chose not to diminish his looks by wearing spectacles, he would have to wait for them to come closer before he could really tell. Gaines hurried out into the street, crying, "Brother Bennett has agreed to rent us rooms! What a generous, trusting man!" He was careful to speak loudly enough for Bennett to hear.

As Maude led the procession, Rebecca, with young Elizabeth in tow, and Louisa, with her brother Bobby by the hand, eagerly filed into the house. Bennett stood by the door, every inch the baron of the estate, welcoming each one with a handshake. He was a compact, trimly built man, with black hair attractively flecked with gray, and flashing deep-set dark eyes which never seemed to be at rest. His attire was expensive and fashionable, and his voice seemed deeper than would be expected for a man of such slight stature.

At close range, the girls took on more individual character, he noticed, and he was particularly interested when Samuel Gaines introduced Louisa as their **foster** daughter. Although it was hard to tell because she scarcely lifted her head to meet his gaze as they were introduced, Bennett felt there was a maturity and depth to this Stephens girl which was rare in anyone so young. In contrast, the Gainses' Rebecca was open and coquettish, blushing as she curtsied, and he squeezed slightly as he took her hand. The flames in her cheeks deepened to his inner satisfaction.

Bennett proudly showed the newcomers through his home, pointing out prized furnishings, grandly displaying an array of framed diplomas and certificates on the wall of his study, and concluding with a tour to the two rooms he had designated for the family. The larger bedroom, at the rear of the house, would be for Samuel, Maude, and the two youngest children. The other room would be shared by Rebecca and Louisa. Rebecca was enthralled by the dainty bed, the dormer window and the comfortable rug on the floor. Louisa accepted it dully, fatigue coming over her.

Shortly, although they were all weary, the womenfolk set to work preparing a light supper to be taken in the elaborate dining room which was furnished with woodwork so finely made and highly polished that it was all Maude could do to tear her eyes away from her own reflection in the tabletop. In the pantry she had found sufficient food for a small army, much of it wilting in the humid weather. It had been some time since any of them had seen so much to eat, and when she remarked about it to Samuel, he said he supposed from what Bennett had indicated, that he was accustomed to holding large gatherings. But whom he had engaged to do the cooking wasn't clear, until, as they sat down for dinner, he remarked that the supper looked better than the most formal dinners prepared for him by his previous cook, whom he said he had discharged only that morning. "But I am often away," he said airily, "and so I take most of my meals out of the house."

Over the ham, peas and new potatoes, Bennett launched into a description of his medical practice. He was a gynecologist, he had said, and when all the faces at the table looked blank, he delicately explained that he was a specialist in "women's complaints," at which Rebecca turned to her mother and then sputtered into her napkin. Ignoring her, Bennett told how he had organized a medical school, had been a practicing preacher in Ohio, a teacher in West Virginia and Indiana, and in Illinois, Quartermaster General and a leader of the Illinois militia, the Dragoons. Louisa thought that if only half of the man were genuine, he was still too good to be true. Rebecca was suddenly clumsy, and could scarcely hold her tools without dropping food into her lap; and she was sure that all eyes—especially her fascinating host's—were upon her.

In fact, John C. Bennett's eyes roamed the table continually. Louisa looked at him only occasionally, but whenever she did lift her eyes to his, she found to her consternation that he had been looking at **her**, but would then shift his gaze almost furtively, as if he felt guilt at being caught looking her way. A nonsensical thought, she told herself. And she kept her eyes averted thereafter.

Bennett intended to establish to his new tenants precisely who and what he was. He delicately sprinkled his conversation with tidbits of gossip about the prophet, Joseph Smith; how he had assisted Joseph in laying out the city of Nauvoo, and now that all seemed to be progressing as planned, his next major move on behalf of his newly adopted church would be to secure a favorable charter—not only for the city, but for a greater and finer militia than Illinois had ever seen.

"But my first concern," he said, wiping his lips daintily, "is for the health of the city, and I am very much concerned about the swamp fever which is abroad here."

Now all eyes were upon him. "You may have noticed that nearly all the new construction is of two stories," he began. "This was upon my recommendation to the brethren. You see, the fever is brought on by exposure to night fogs which are generated by decomposing vegetable matter down in the swamps, and when night comes, this evil fog drifts low along the ground. If it is drawn into the lungs, as in sleep, it poisons the system. Nauvoo sleeps upstairs!"

Samuel Gaines looked worried. "Can nothing be done once you get it?"

"There is a substance—quinine—which seems to help. I have laid in a substantial supply."

"Has it taken many lives here, doctor?" Maude asked.

"Sadly, yes," the doctor replied. "Even the prophet's first counselor, Sidney Rigdon, is very ill with it; I have had to assume most of his responsibilities, in addition to my other ones," he said with a sigh of resignation.

A small insect, attracted by the candelabra burning in the center of the table, landed on the doctor's wrist as he blotted his mouth again, and he swatted at it with his napkin. "Mosquitoes," he said, testily. "Harmless, but a confounded nuisance."

Maude saw that all appetites seemed to have been satisfied, so she rose and began clearing the table. Louisa and Rebecca took their cue and helped carry out the rest of the dishes, while the two younger children were sent up to bed. Long shadows stretched across the raw brown landscape outside and the sun through clearing skies lay low across the Mississippi. As Samuel sat at the table, letting the peace of the early evening sink into his weary bones, he was moved again with gratitude. "You can't know how it feels to be safe in Nauvoo at last," he said, "and in this lovely home. After so many miles and so much heartbreak . . ."

Bennett shook his head in sympathy. "It must have been dreadful. When I read of the atrocities committed against the Saints, that was what compelled me to write to Joseph Smith, offering all possible aid. And, in his gratitude, Joseph has given me much responsibility here—fully as much as vouchsafed to me by Governor Carlin—and I only hope to be worthy of the great trust placed in me by so many fine people."

It was a habit of Bennett's—the process of turning every conversation to the subject of his own accomplishments and influence, perhaps because no subject interested him as much as himself. But in his mellow mood, Samuel Gaines was only too happy to hear this eloquent and accomplished man dominate the conversation. Something about him was reassuring to Samuel. For one thing, he represented a cultured class he had not known on either side of the Atlantic, having risen from the ranks of workers, sharing privations with other Mormons who, like himself, had little education and few tangible assets. To think that an autocratic gentleman like Dr. Bennett would also join the young church movement seemed to validate Samuel's own testimony. For another thing, he seemed so self-assured in matters pertaining to power and influence, that surely the church would be stronger for having his counsel. Perhaps the worst days for the Latter-day Saints were over.

Their first nightfall in Nauvoo was, for the refugees off the steamboat, a discovery of the delights of peace and order among friends. Volumes of hot water were brought in, and the children bathed in delicately-scented soap imported by their host from France, then each bed was turned down and six grateful heads bowed individually for prayers before Maude and Samuel in their back bedroom, and Louisa and Rebecca in the adjoining front bedroom, snuffed their candles and slept.

Several rods away in the new McCann household, all lights were extinguished except for the one in the east upstairs room. Andrew had arranged a comfortable place for writing, and although he was nearly dead from the rigors of the storm on the river, he disciplined himself to begin his first article. He penned his first impressions of Nauvoo, the storekeeper, the wagon driver, the minute details which, if left until later for recording, might escape his memory. He wrote until he realized he was asleep with pen in hand, and at last turned out his lamp and climbed into bed. He tried to organize his thoughts as to what he must do in the morning. Beyond visiting the Post Office for any mail that might have been sent him from the *Argus*, he couldn't force his weary mind to concentrate, and in moments he was sleeping deeply.

The men, women, children and beasts of the recently-reclaimed land fell silent, and as a gentle night breeze high above the earth propelled drifting clouds across the eastern horizon, a moon rose above the prairie of Illinois and replaced twilight's dusky rose with a paler blue. From the river's backwash came the throaty rasp of thousands of frogs, while crickets joined in upland. Vapors formed on the river, as moisture and warm loam blended with cooling air to soak the tilled acres near the water in a thickening blanket of fog. It was this fog, mysteriously forming nearly every night, which was accepted as the cause of "swamp fever," and the accompanying swarms of mosquitoes were thought of as nothing but an inconvenience—their delivery of virulent malaria not suspected, nor the disease identified. All those who could, avoided the low-lying fog and slept upstairs.

But not all Nauvoo slept. Down near the river landing, far below the new construction of the city, stood a lone old homestead of logs and rough board siding. It was built long before a quarry or brick kiln existed in the region, so it rested upon a foundation of boulders. Growing thickly on its east side were tangled willow trees, and a tidy home garden occupied the rich soil just south of the building. The fireplace wall was moss covered, and lichen crept up the west front, facing the rolling Mississippi, only a hundred feet away. From a window in the west wall shone a single twinkle of yellow light, barely enough to illuminate the face of the man seated at the table by that window, who leaned his head heavily upon his left hand as he worked.

The tips of his fingers were in the thick auburn hair which crowned a high forehead. Fatigue drew his brows down, and his large and luminous eyes were heavy-lidded. His cheekbones were accentuated by the dim candlelight. As he pondered, he tapped the tip of his pen against closed lips which concealed a chipped tooth, suffered when a vial of poison was forced against his clenched jaw in one of the attempts that had been made upon his life.

He sat astride a kitchen stool, coatless, the sleeves of his shirt unfastened and rolled up below the elbow, exposing muscular forearms tanned and scarred by a youth spent at hard physical work. The shirt was of fine linen. The collar was undone, but hanging loosely around a neck corded with muscles which had been developed as much through frequent wrestling games, as by the tons of earth the man had shoveled in his teen years while working as a digger.

Joseph Smith opened his journal to a blank page and had written **Monday, August 17, 1840,** and then the following entry:

> Met with the High Council of Nauvoo at my office,
> also the High Council of Iowa. John Batten preferred

many charges against Elijah Fordham.

He rubbed his eyes. Into his mind came the image of Elijah Fordham as he had seen him just over a year earlier, on July 22, 1839. He had recorded in his diary then how the elderly Fordham, believed to be dying of the fever, had appeared lifeless when Joseph had at last broken away from his other pressing duties to rush to his bedside; of how he had taken Fordham's hand and held it for a minute, until he had detected a slight change in the sightless stare of his glazed eyes. Joseph remembered that when he had asked the man if he had the faith to be healed, Fordham had rebuked him by saying, "I fear it is too late; if you had come sooner I think I would have been healed." But nevertheless, Joseph had asked him if he had faith in Jesus Christ, and when the old man had answered "I do," Joseph had stood, still holding his hand, and in a loud voice said, "Brother Fordham, I command you, in the name of Jesus Christ, to arise from this bed and be made whole!" Joseph smiled now at the memory of how the old man fairly sprang from his bed, kicking off the poultices in which his feet had been wrapped, and pulled on his clothes, ate a bowl of bread and milk, and followed Joseph into the street.

Yes, Elijah Fordham had been spared death that night across the river in Montrose, and tonight he had been spared disfellowship in his new Nauvoo home, again by the intervention of his friend and prophet. Joseph dipped the pen in the inkwell and wrote:

> After the testimony and the councilors had spoken, I addressed the Council at some length, showing the situation of the contending parties, that there was in reality no cause of difference; that they had better be reconciled without an action, or vote of the Council, and henceforth live as brethren, and never more mention their former difficulties.

As he wrote, he heard the floor squeak upstairs and he knew Emma was up. He dipped the pen a final time and concluded the entry:

They settled accordingly.

Better, he thought, not to elaborate.

Emma descended the stairs with a candle. "I thought I heard something," she said. "How did your meeting go?"

Joseph leaned back as his wife stepped behind him, cradling his head against her. She smoothed the lines out of his temples, rubbing just at the hairline, where he loved the feel of her slender fingers. "It will be all right," he said, closing his eyes.

Emma looked down at what her husband had written. "What was the trouble with Brother Fordham?"

Joseph opened his eyes and swung the large journal closed. "Nothing very serious," he said, looking up with a smile. He knew Emma was a woman of strong opinions, active intelligence, and curiosity. It would not do for her to be burdened with information that could kindle her suspicions against any of the Saints. Gossip was inevitable—he knew that—but he realized that Emma was looked on as something as an authority among the other women of Nauvoo, because she was the wife of the prophet, seer and revelator of the Church, and would be thought to be privy to many confidences. It had been that way from the very beginning of their marriage. He took pains to keep personal matters very private, and instructed his councilors and bishops to do likewise. Yet, he shared all other interesting information with her because he believed that wives needed to support their husbands in the Priesthood, and it was a tenet of the religion restored through his writings that the glory of God was intelligence. And intelligence couldn't flower without information. He told her everything he felt that he could. "Nineteen more Saints arrived on the boat today," he said.

Emma nodded knowingly. "Including the McCann family. They say there are only four of them; the parents were killed in Far West."

Pain creased Joseph's face. Far West. More Saints' blood spilled. As much as he loved the United States of America, he was disillusioned about its lawlessness—even at the highest level. Constituional law was ignored or enforced only at the whim of local lawmen. Only the past spring he had returned from Washington D.C. where he had appealed to President Martin Van Buren for relief in the mobbings the Saints had suffered in Missouri. His case had been plain: the Church members had been denied their Constitutional rights, had been hounded, pillaged, ravaged and murdered—and when they had tried to resist, they were accused of the very crimes their attackers had committed. Van Buren had said, "What can I do? I can do nothing for you!" It was an election year. The President was more concerned with votes than with a few "Mormons." And the McCanns—whom Joseph had not even known—had suffered simply because they were "Mormon." He winced at the thought, and Emma tried to smooth out the wrinkles.

"I can never get used to people suffering on account of the religion I brought forth," he said.

"What about your own suffering?" She was thinking of the tar and feathers, the threats and beatings, the months he had suffered in prison under sentence of death.

"I endure it," he said, "because I know more than the others. I can't deny the truth, no matter what is done to me. After all, I know what God has commanded me to do, and God knows."

Emma froze on hearing those words, and her hands slipped from his brow as she moved imperceptibly back from him. For the thousandth time, she wondered what God **had** commanded of her husband—what dark doctrine had been revealed, that Joseph knew but couldn't tell her about? There was something, something he had taught to a few of the elders—or so the rumors had it. Something that had to do with relations between husbands and wives. But that is all she knew, and she feared the fact of a secret being kept from her, as much as she feared the secret—whatever it was—itself.

"How is baby Don Carlos?" Joseph asked, rising from the table.

Emma pushed a wisp of rich brown hair back under her nightcap. "Sleeping," she said, and turned away. Silently, so as not to awaken the infant and their three other children, Emma climbed back upstairs, and presently Joseph followed her.

They lay in bed in the darkness while the sounds of frogs, crickets and the eternal murmur of the Mississippi drifted in on the fog. Emma knew Joseph was not yet asleep by his breathing. Questions hung like storm clouds in the heavy air above them, ready to break. Should she tell him of the tales she had heard? The questions women were asking her?

She listened to the measured, gentle intake and exhale of breath beside her. How many nights she had longed to feel him there, when he had been away, preaching, on business, or imprisoned. How gentle he was with her, always. How reassuring he was, because he seemed so assured of himself—who and what he was, what he had to do. He knew God, and he knew Satan—he had said so. Was it Satan who stirred questions in her mind? Was it Satan who now was stirring these fears and doubts in her?

Joseph lay with his eyes wide open in the dark, tired but not yet capable of sleep. He had sensed her sudden drawing away downstairs at his mention of God's commandments to him. He longed to practice with Emma the candor he had so often preached on, counseling husbands and wives to share their innermost thoughts. He had learned that wives were to share in the powers of the Priesthood, and that meant total honesty between both parties to a marriage. And yet—there was one awful matter he had not yet shared with Emma because the very hint of it—which she had heard from others—had sent her into a rage. *If only* . . . it was the same thought he began shaping now which he had tried so many times before to dismiss. *If only the Lord would lift this from me!* He thought back to that unforgettable night in 1823, when he was only eighteen, when his bedroom had grown brilliantly white with the presence of the angel who had given him such unmistakable directions that were to change his entire life from that moment forward. How he longed to have such a new revelation now—tonight—rescinding what he had been commanded to do. But the night remained dark and his mind remained troubled. He knew his wife so well, that he knew exactly what was burdening her at that moment. She might well burst forth with all her anxiety and pent-up suspicion at any second.

He rolled onto his side, away from her, squeezing his eyes shut, forcing himself to relax and at least feign sleep. *"Help me, Father,"* he breathed, almost audibly, into his pillow. And then mentally he prayed that Emma had not heard.

Chapter 10

Andrew was awakened by a slim shaft of sunlight which angled through his bedroom window. The bed in which he had slept had its headboard against the west wall, close to the southern corner. The rising August sun cast its first rays into that corner of the McCann house, and served as an effective—if accidental—awakening arrangement.

Andrew let himself respond to the room, and then he became aware of pleasant sounds. Chuckling hens. A bird, somewhere far off. And below him in the house, conversation. He had slept deeply and had dreamt of being in a cradle with warm hands on his head. Details of the dream began now to slip away as he opened his eyes against the brilliant silver of sunlight which moved almost visibly across his bedcovers. He raised his arms to stretch, and was seized with a viselike stab of pain on his right side. He let out a shrill gasp of pain as the broken rib forced air from his lungs. He had forgotten all about it. What if he couldn't move around? What if he couldn't get out of bed? Panic rose in him, and he steeled himself for the pain as he gingerly slid his elbows back alongside his torso to elevate himself into a sitting position. So far, so good! He found that, by moving cautiously, he could get into a sitting position. Then, arms straight down, he swung himself slowly out of the bedclothes until his legs dangled over the edge of the bed. Still no pain. He tried standing up, and again was struck with the lash of agony. He fell back, panting, and tried again, this time moving deliberately away from the source of the pain, and he was at last on his feet. Perspiration stood out on his forehead.

A tap at the door, and it swung open. Jock McCann stood filling the doorway, a breakfast tray in his hands. "Ah, ye're awake at last," he said with a grin. "And likely t'be hungry." He hooked a chair with the toe of one boot and hauled it around in front of him, then set the tray on it. He cast a critical eye on his guest. "And how are ye feeling this morning?"

"It hurts in certain positions."

"Aye, and it will until it begins to set. We'll be havin' a doctor for ye, as soon as we find the best one."

Andrew shook his head emphatically. "You mustn't do that, Mr. McCann; I'm sure I'll be fine . . . " He saw the Scotsman's face change, the heavy black eyebrows rise.

"But I want to do it, **Brother** Sharp."

Andrew realized he had omitted the Mormon way of addressing a fellow church member, and now something was troubling Jock McCann, and his face closed like a shutter against a storm. He stopped over and took a towel off the tray, disclosing a bowl of fried mush in thick cream, a plate of eggs, and sliced fruit. "There's nae bread in the house yet," he said. "Anne's baking this morning. She said if ye want more, there's plenty." He stood up and turned to go.

"Brother McCann!"

The Scotsman turned back to Andrew. "Aye?"

"I . . . I just want to thank you, you and your family," Andrew stammered. "And I want you to teach me the things I should have learned . . . about the Church, I mean."

Jock's face softened slightly. "Ye'll learn as fast as ye want to," he said. "It takes time to change the old ways. I know." He turned and closed the bedroom door behind him, softly.

Andrew slumped, was hit with another spasm and straightened up again. He looked down at the food Anne had prepared. What kind, generous people, he thought. Whoever said Scottish folk were stingy? He pulled on his trousers and a shirt, and attacked the breakfast with a will.

In John C. Bennett's house, unpacking had begun. Clothes and linens salvaged from the years of trekking were once again shaken out, the iron was heated and the wrinkles pressed out. A wash boiler was heated downstairs and Maude bustled about, already taking over the kitchen and washing room, humming softly as she arranged things to suit her convenience. Breakfast has been as successful as supper. Dr. Bennett had complimented Maude and her daughters on the quality of the food, and then he retired to the room in which he did his studying. The young children were attended to by Louisa, while Rebecca did up the breakfast dishes, chattering happily to whoever passed near enough to hear. Samuel Gaines was anxious to obtain employment, and Bennett had suggested that he talk with Don Carlos Smith, younger brother of the Prophet, about work in a publishing venture which was beginning in Nauvoo. On that errand, Samuel left the house and walked toward the cluster of shops downhill from the Bennett house.

As Louisa turned Elizabeth and Bobby loose after cleaning jam from faces and hands, she became aware of a rapping noise from the front of the house. Realizing that perhaps nobody else was going to answer, she dried her hands on her apron and hurried to the front door. Standing at the door was a young man she had seen the day before on the boat.

"Would this be Doctor Bennett's house?" he asked, with a thick Scottish burr to his voice.

"It is."

"Well, my name's Angus McCann," he said, thrusting his hand out to be shaken, and grinning widely. "And who might you be?"

Taken aback by his boldness, Louisa almost physically shrank back into the doorway. "I—we live here with Dr. Bennett," she said. "Step in, I'll get him."

The Scot swept his cap off his head and took a long pace inside the doorway, looking around at the crystal ornaments on the wall sconces. Louisa hurried to the doctor's study and tapped on the door. "Yes?" The voice was tinged with annoyance.

"There's a person to see you, Doctor," Louisa said. "Angus McCann."

Presently, Bennett opened the study door and came out. "Yes," he said, examining the young man in his hall. "I'm Doctor Bennett."

"Ah, good morning, sir," Angus said, pumping the doctor's hand. "I'm told ye're a medical doctor, and we have a man hurt at our house."

"I am a **gynecologist**," Bennett said primly. "Is the man hurt badly?"

"Och, he's got a broken rib, Jock says."

"And who is 'Jock'?"

"Why, he's our older brother."

"And he has diagnosed the case, you say?"

Angus scratched his head uncertainly. "Well, that's what he says Brother Andrew has, a broken rib. He'd like you to come see what's to be done."

Bennett looked around at Louisa with an exasperated frown, then back to Angus. "If you wish me to look at the patient, kindly have him come here," he said. "I assume he can walk?"

"Aye. Jock whittled him a cane this morning."

Bennett sighed. "I shall be here for another hour. Bring him over within that time and I'll have a look at him. What did you say his name is—the patient?"

"Andrew Sharp."

Bennett shook his head. "Never heard of him."

"Nae, nor would ye have," Angus said cheerily; "he landed only yesterday from the boat, same as we did. He was hurt in that great storm we had on the river." Louisa, still in earshot, recalled seeing a crowd around someone who had been knocked to the deck in the storm.

Bennett conducted Angus to the door. "We live close by," Angus said, pointing to the McCann house, plainly visible around the corner on the next street. "Oh, so that's your place?" Bennett asked.

"Aye. Well, we'll be bringing Andrew right over, Doctor, and thank ye." With that, Angus slapped his cap on his head and skipped the front steps, dashed out to the gate and was gone, trotting up the street.

"It's always like this," Bennett said with a wry smile to Louisa. "Nothing but interruptions when I'm trying to work."

"I'm sorry, Doctor; I didn't know you weren't to be bothered."

"Oh, no, no," Bennett explained. "You were right to call me. A doctor is sworn to help the sick, never mind when or where. When they come back, you may show them in to my study." He walked back in and closed the door.

Louisa stepped to the dining room window and watched Angus McCann make his way to the house around the corner. She felt the muscles at the pit of her stomach begin to relax now, as the tension receeded. She would force herself, she thought, to associate with strangers here in Nauvoo. It would either be that, or live as a prisoner of her own fears.

Across the hall in his study, John C. Bennett also looked out of the window at the McCann house. Gossip in town had already given him some information about the newcomers. William Law, the builder, had let it be known that he had received fully one half of the price of the new house by mail from Scotland, and had been told to select a good lot on high ground, and to follow the plan enclosed with the retainer as closely as possible. Law had been promised the balance of the price when the new owner arrived and had inspected it and found it to be built to his satisfaction. And McCann had sent William Law a bond underwritten by Spiers & Sons, Ltd., of Edinburgh, a prominent insurance firm. This had been an impressive introduction to a family of substance which obviously knew what it wanted and how to go about getting it.

Anyone of substance interested John C. Bennett. He had spent his life cultivating important people, and repeatedly had been rewarded for the effort. Both his medical degree and his position as a minister had elevated him above reproach, and in this position of trust he had met many who respected him. Men admired him for his scholarship and credentials—although some were amused by the delicacy of his manners. His political connections were genuine and his command of English was persuasive. Women, on the other hand, were fascinated by his elegance, and many a trusting patient or parishoner became his admirer, and some admirers became his secret lovers.

Bennett had always been able to balance these associations without harming his reputation; such was his stature in whatever community he lived, and even after he had abandoned illicit liasons, the women in question remained his admirers and not one of them ever betrayed their clandestine romance with the glamourous doctor. This helped him to feel that he was somehow exonerated from responsibility for his behavior. And what little he knew of the new city of Nauvoo, which in fact he had helped Joseph Smith establish, made Bennett feel that he was making a fresh start in a new place. Only his excellent accomplishments were known to the locals here, he was looked up to by all as an authority on Illinois politics, an officer in state government, and a medical doctor. He had only to quell his other passions, and he sensed that he might use the burgeoning city of Nauvoo as a springboard to prominence and political advantage.

But now, the McCanns had moved in. What was the base of their fortune, and what power would they represent once they became established here? Word had it that the McCanns would build a shipyard in Nauvoo and would need to hire scores of craftsmen. This would give them a prominence overnight, an importance to the economic and social life of the young city that might shade that of his own. Bennett stroked his chin as he contemplated the best way to probe their situation. Then, as he watched, he saw the front door of the McCann house open and Angus help another young man over the threshhold and down to the walk. That would be his patient. He tore himself away from the window and opened a cabinet, taking out a container of plaster of Paris, rolls of bandage and adhesive, and other necessities which he placed on his desk.

He let the girl, Louisa, answer his door for him again, feeling it a nice touch—one he certainly hadn't enjoyed with the frumpy woman recently discharged. She had been no credit to his household and he hadn't been any fonder of her independent attitude than he had been of her cooking. But this Louisa—she might be a different story. If only he could break through that deferential shyness of hers. Ah well, he thought, time enough for that. For now, it was pleasant that she had fallen into the duties of a maid; it fitted his sense of his own importance. Louisa now tapped at his study door to announce that his patient, Mr. Andrew Sharp, had arrived. Bennett sat behind his desk, straightened his vest and aligned his sleeve cuffs, and said, "Yes, send them in, please."

Louisa opened the study door for them. Yes, she had seen both men on the steamer, and in fact was sure that the man called Andrew Sharp was the same man she had noticed throwing something into the river. He was physically more attractive to her than McCann, who was a swarthy, stocky type. But of the two, McCann had a nicer smile, while Sharp seemed to be preoccupied with managing his cane. She closed the door behind them and then realized she was standing still in the hallway, thinking about them. She brushed down her apron with both hands, as if brushing her thoughts away, and hurried into the back of the house to see if Sister Gaines needed help.

"Yes, Brother McCann was quite correct in his diagnosis," Bennett said pleasantly, as he smoothed the last of the bandage around Andrew's chest. "No heavy lifting, no bending for four weeks, and don't be afraid to walk with that cane." He handed Andrew his undershirt.

"How much do I owe you, doctor?" Andrew asked, knowing that his purse was almost empty.

The doctor waved his arm and turned away. "This didn't require much doctoring." He returned to his chair behind the desk. "But mind that you don't expose yourself to the swamp fever. Until we can drain the rest of the lowlands, we may have more trouble with it. Sleep upstairs if you can. Don't inhale the fog."

Andrew nodded, buttoning his shirt. "I'm very grateful to you, sir," he said.

"Andrew's new to the Church, newer than we are, even," Angus put in.

Bennett looked up at him. "But I fancy I'm newer baptized than either of you. Only last month!"

Angus reached over and pumped the doctor's small hand in delight. "Congratulations, Brother," he cried. "We weren't sure as you were a Saint or not."

"Well, I may have been only recently baptized," he replied, "but my loyalties have been with the Prophet and his people for a long time. I wrote to

Brother Joseph several months ago, offering my help in obtaining this very property we're standing on. You see, I happen to hold some rather high offices with the State of Illinois.''

Angus and Andrew looked properly impressed. "Why did you want to help the Latter-day Saints?'' Andrew asked, proud that he had avoided the less-favored term of "Mormon.''

"At first, simply that their plight appealed to my sense of fair play. Then, as I grew to know and respect President Smith, I realized that here truly was the religion I had been searching for. You see, I am also a licensed preacher in the state of Ohio.''

Andrew was impressed with the doctor. "So you moved here.''

"Yes, to be of more benefit to the Saints. Now, from this point, we can consolidate our strengths and build Zion—a city that will be the shining symbol of our faith from sea to sea and from Canada to the southern borders! Why, do you know we already have over 250 homes in Nauvoo? One day this city will be the largest in Illinois, and then it will rival Boston and Philadelphia, perhaps even New York, as people realize the perfection of our system!''

Andrew had never heard anyone speak so easily, so eloquently. He was a gifted spellbinder, a man anyone could listen to in rapt attention for hours. "Do you think the persecution is over, then?'' Andrew asked.

Bennett smiled. "The city of Nauvoo is prepared to mount a militia that will be second to none in the States,'' he said in a confident tone. "We shall train them, equip them and mount them to be the envy of military commanders the world over!''

This was news to Andrew. "To defend the city?''

"To make sure we are never again at the mercy of mobocrats,'' the doctor replied. "Now we need not ask a perfidious President to defend our rights; we'll defend them ourselves! And he smacked his fist on the desk for emphasis. Then he consulted his pocket watch, snapped the case closed and stood. "I am sorry, gentlemen,'' he said, gliding out from behind his desk, "but I have an important appointment in a few moments. Mr. Sharp, take care of yourself and do not strain your body. Your youth and good health will provide you with a sound body again—with God's help—in about a month. Good day.''

The men stepped out into the hallway. The plaster seized Andrew's chest like a fist, and he couldn't inflate his lungs fully, but he did feel more comfortable in a standing position. "Now, ye said ye want to go to the Post Office,'' Angus said. "Can ye find it or shall I go with ye?''

"Oh, no, Angus, don't bother. I may just wander around the town for a little bit of sightseeing.''

"All right. Mind ye don't run any footraces, now.'' And he was out of the door and gone.

Andrew prepared himself for a walk, hefting the cane and hitching up his trousers. He left the Bennett house a few moments later and turned to his left to walk down the slight hill toward the cluster of shops.

A few moments later, John C. Bennett hurried out of his study, locking the door to the hall. He was wearing a dove-gray morning coat, neatly tailored in a manner seldom seen on the western frontier, and a matching tall-crowned hat. His boots were polished, but not so much as to distract the eye, so that the fact that the heels were over an inch higher than the custom for men to wear was scarcely noticeable. The net effect was to make Bennett appear taller than he actually was. He walked into the street and stood impatiently in front of his house. A few moments later, a carriage drew up to the edge of the road and the driver helped the doctor in and drove smartly away.

Louisa observed all this from her position of concealment behind the dining room curtain. Now she hurried to the back of the house and informed Maude Gaines that she was going out for some air. Maude, caught with a mouth full of pie dough, seemed about to protest but the much quicker girl had waved and gone, hurrying upstairs to remove her apron and find a suitable bonnet. Half a minute later she was down the stairs and out the front door. She looked down the long street and found that Andrew Sharp was walking haltingly with his cane, taking in everything around him with interest. Louisa waited until he seemed far enough away that she could walk in the same direction, unobserved. The last thing that she wanted was to meet him alone. Not yet, at any rate. She turned in the direction of the center of Nauvoo, took a deep breath, and stepped into the sunshine.

Linus Jensen, the shopkeeper, handed Andrew two letters. "Been here a week," he said. Sunshine filtered in the window of the store, bathing the floorboards in a golden pool. Appearing from somewhere, a yellow cat selected the center of the sunbeam, circled it once, stretched, and curled up in its warmth. "Stay awhile if you've a mind to," the bald proprietor said, resuming the sweeping Andrew had interrupted. The broom drove cyclones of dust motes into the sunlight.

Andrew leaned against the door and examined his mail. One of the letters, as he had hoped, came from Mr. Ketchum, the editor of the Quincy *Argus*. The other envelope bore the familiar, strong hand of Andrew's father. He ripped open the *Argus* letter first, and out of it floated a check. The cat, alerted, pawed at it as it sailed to the floor, and Andrew rescued it. To his dismay, it was for only twenty-four dollars—a month's pay. Andrew had been sure Mr. Ketchum would have advanced him more than that, to see him settled with a few necessities. He folded the check into his pocket and read the single sheet of notepaper included in the envelope.

Andrew:
Find out about the "Danites," the "Mormon Army"
and how many wives Jos. Smith has. Expecting your
first article Aug. 21.

Ketchum

The twenty-first? Three days away! He turned to the shopkeeper. "Can I send a letter to Quincy and have it get there by the twenty-first?"

Jensen paused in his sweeping. "The twenty-first? That'd be Friday. Hmm . . ." and he scratched his bald head. "Not by the U.S. Mail, of course. They only pick up on Mondays. Best way would be to give it to a rider who's going down that way—or put it aboard a boat."

"What would that cost?"

"By boat? Twenty-five cents ought to do it."

"When would I have to have it ready to go?"

Jensen walked back to the Post Office area of his shop. "Be a packet boat putting in this afternoon sometime, going down river," he said. "Best I have it in hand no later than one o'clock, in case he's early. Or, you could hand it off yourself, down at the dock."

Andrew nodded and said, "I'm grateful for the information." He hurried to the door, stepped out into the bright sunshine, and collided with Louisa Stephens, who was just walking past. Thrown off balance by his injured ribs and the cane he wasn't used to relying on, he dropped the cane and had to hang onto the surprised young woman with both hands. At the same moment, she reflexively clutched at his arms. They stood staring at each other for a moment in the street, then each backed away, embarrassed.

Each stammered apologies, and then Andrew said, "I just saw you up at the doctor's house, didn't I?" Louisa nodded, adjusting her bonnet. "My name's Andrew Sharp."

"And I'm Louisa Stephens," she replied, managing a faint smile. At close range and in the bright light, she had an impression of an angular face, pale blond hair, blue eyes and cheeks covered in a faint golden fuzz. Then she looked away.

"I didn't hurt you, did I?" asked Andrew.

"No. Are you all right?"

"Just clumsy. I'm not used to wearing a plaster on my chest, and I guess it threw me off." He knelt to retrieve the cane, which lay in the dust. "Oh, let me get that for you," Louisa said, and their hands touched as they both reached for the cane.

This brought their faces close together and Andrew turned to look once more at the girl. She was so close that he could smell her skin and hair and see the dark lashes that framed her large blue eyes. He noted that the two of them shared much the same coloring. He wondered how old she was. Flustered, Louisa stood up quickly and brushed her skirts.

"Thank you," he said, bracing himself on the cane and standing up again.

"Well . . ." Louisa began, wanting to go, wanting to stay.

Andrew couldn't seem to look away from her. He knew he was staring and that it was making her uncomfortable, but he couldn't seem to help it. "Are you going to one of the shops?" he finally asked.

"No. I mean, I don't know anything about Nauvoo and I was just . . ."

she hesitated, wondering just what she **was** doing here in fact.

"Sightseeing?" Andrew asked. "Same here. I just got here last night."

"I know." Louisa realized how that might sound—as if she had some interest in the young man and had been watching him. Her face flamed anew and she looked away again. "I mean, I heard it mentioned."

"Are you in Dr. Bennett's family?" Andrew asked.

"No. My brother and I are living with Brother and Sister Gaines, and Dr. Bennett is our landlord."

"Then we're neighbors! I'm staying with the McCanns, you know."

"Yes." The conversation seemed to be stuck, and Louisa felt she had already been too bold in speaking at all to a man to whom she had not been properly introduced. Abruptly, Louisa turned away and said, "Good day, sir."

Andrew watched as she walked down the street. Then he turned and limped hurriedly after her. "Perhaps we could explore Nauvoo together," he panted, catching up with her.

"Please, not today."

Andrew paused and she walked daintily on. "Sister Stephens." She paused and turned. "Perhaps I could call on you?"

Louisa felt a curious reaction. There hadn't been that taut feeling; she hadn't felt as guarded as she had around young men. Was this a sign? She looked at Andrew, the sun framing his tall, thin body and forming a halo of his mop of straw-colored hair. As he leaned hopefully on his cane, waiting for her answer, something relaxed inside her. She smiled at him, a hesitant, tolerant smile. "Perhaps," she said, and turned away. Louisa was suddenly conscious of her every movement, of the length of each step, the way she held herself, for she could almost feel his eyes watching her.

As she walked away from him, Andrew felt that a thin strand still connected them, a sense of closeness that had transformed strangers into something else—something promising—and all of a sudden he felt an elation he had never known before. He watched as Louisa stopped in front of the milliner's shop and looked in the window. And then, as he had hoped, she looked back at him, and smiled! He waved at her, eagerly, foolishly, for only a hundred feet separated them. And she turned away, still smiling. Andrew wheeled around on his cane and headed up the street towards home. He seemed to hear Louisa's voice in his ears, the half whispered reply, "Perhaps." It repeated over and over, until he found that he had returned to the door of the McCann's house. And he couldn't recall a thing about the walk back from the store.

The seductive smell of bread baking wafted out of the McCann's kitchen, but Andrew hurried upstairs. William and Angus were working in the back, Anne was in her kitchen, and Jock was nowhere to be seen. All the better, Andrew thought. Ketchum had expected him to have arrived in Nauvoo a week earlier, and now he was in danger of missing his first deadline on the *Argus*. He needed to marshall his thoughts and write something presentable for an introductory article. **And** rush it down to the dock.

Andrew slipped quietly into his bedroom and eased the door shut. He was chagrined to see that Anne had made his bed—something he had neglected to do when he had left the house to be examined by Dr. Bennett that morning. He drew the chair over by a desk and took a pencil and writing paper, smoothed out the creases it had developed from weeks in the bottom of his traveling bag, and sat down to think.

He pulled out Mr. Ketchum's note and read it again. Who, or what, were the "Danites"? Andrew hadn't heard the word before. The "Mormon Army" could refer to the militia Dr. Bennett had mentioned—he would try to find out more from him on that. But then there was that curious reference to "how many wives Jos. Smith has." Was there rumor that the prophet was a bigamist? Andrew realized how much he had to learn, and how much was expected from him. He tapped the pencil impatiently on the desk and waited for inspiration to arrive. From some distant lesson, he remembered being taught that you can't pour cream out of an empty pitcher, and he sadly realized that his pitcher of experience—as far as Nauvoo and its people were concerned—was almost empty. All he could do was write what he had seen—what he **knew**.

A DISPATCH FROM A TRAVELER IN NAUVOO:
August 18, 1840

The Latter-Day Saints are building a new city where had been nothing but swamp and forested tracts a few months before. Imbued with much optimism and energy, the followers of the man they revere as a prophet have divided the old city once known as Commerce into building and commercial lots, dedicated wide streets, with considerable forethought as to future growth—and have already erected some 250 buildings.

Prominent among the citizens here is one John C. Bennett, a physician and preacher, living in one of the finer of the new residences now gracing the spacious hillside city. Like the other homes, Dr. Bennett's is large and much reminiscent of the Eastern school of architecture.

Nauvoo shows signs of civic planning. If it survives to grow as it is now intended, none of the haphazard development common to most cities will be seen here; to this extent, it may indeed qualify as a "model city" for any metropolitan planners to study.

A steam vessel serves Nauvoo from St. Louis & points north on a weekly basis.

Chapter 11

The carriage brought John C. Bennett to the small wooden house by the river landing. As he alighted, Bennett saw the prophet in conversation with three other men, standing in the tiny garden where Joseph had been hoeing. Bennett recognized the visitors as Howard Coray, Joseph's clerk; young Edwin Bottomly, a convert from Europe, and the prophet's younger brother, Don Carlos Smith, a tall and handsome young man who had been Bennett's patient and was often in precarious health. In addition, several children lingered, some clinging to the prophet's trouser legs, and two or three neighborhood dogs ambled through the garden patch. As he approached, Bennett mused at how Emma would scold over the trampling of her vegetables. It seemed that her husband attracted a crowd wherever he went—even if he had merely stepped outside to hoe a few weeds.

Seeing him approach, the other men bade farewell to the prophet, and walked out of the garden, saluting John C. Bennett as he walked up. Don Carlos was coughing again, Bennett noted; not a good sign. Joseph looked well, and Bennett told him so as the two met and shook hands.

"I am well, Brother Bennett, thanks be to God. And how are you?"

"Busy, as always," Bennett replied. "I was interrupted in my planning for our meeting. We have some new neighbors and one of them was hurt in the storm on the river yesterday, so I treated him."

The two men now walked toward the house. "Who was that?"

Bennett had to stop and recall the name. "Sharp," he said at last. "Andrew Sharp. A young fellow, broken rib or two."

Joseph shook his head, marveling. "Nauvoo is growing so fast I can't keep up with it," he said.

"Precisely why we must have a city charter," Bennett said as they reached the door and went in. The children followed, and Emma, young Don Carlos on her shoulder, greeted them as she worked in the kitchen. "We're going to have a short meeting," the prophet told his wife. "Perhaps Dr. Bennett will join us for dinner?"

Bennett held up his hand. "No, no, I thank you all the same; I'm to meet with some of the brethren concerned with drafting our plans for a university, and we'll be having something to eat then."

Emma was glad to have a man of the standing of John C. Bennett in their home, and proud that he and her husband had become such close associates. Almost the same age, Bennett was well educated while Joseph had little formal education; yet the two men seemed to complement each other, and she felt that her husband was rapidly absorbing some of Bennett's knowledge as well as his graceful use of the language. She smiled and continued her work, as the two men sat at the small table.

"We were well advised to wait upon the results of the election, Brother Bennett, before submitting our petition to Springfield. Now, as you said, they'll see the strength of the Saints' voting power."

Bennett pulled his chair up to the small table and from his letter case, unfolded a series of note papers. "Yes, Nauvoo seems to have voted very much along the lines you favored. All the Whigs were elected, except, of course, for Lincoln. Your good friend James Ralston is about the only Democrat who has shown any support for our cause."

"And we have put him in the legislature," Joseph added. "That will show Mr. Lincoln a thing or two."

Bennett arranged the notes before him. "Well, we'll probably hear no more from Lincoln since Ralston's defeated him. Now, shall we consider the city charter?"

Joseph agreed and pulled his chair beside Bennett's to look over the notes. "I have assembled the elements you called for," Bennett said, "and encompassed them into these petitions to the governor. The chapter should provide for a mayor, four aldermen and nine city councilmen. This body would have authority to formulate all city laws and ordinances."

"Excellent."

"And the council would have authority to sit as a municipal court."

"Excellent indeed."

"And, as you requested, we petitioned the state for a franchise to organize a militia."

"The Legion. Yes, absolutely vital."

"You do realize, President, that the mayor would have considerable power in Nauvoo? He would regulate all affairs of the city; he would be in charge of the Nauvoo Legion, and the Legion would enforce the city's laws. In effect, the mayor would have his own police force."

Joseph considered this for a moment. "Yes. It must be that way," he said, nodding in agreement.

"Then there is the matter of jurisdiction. The court of Nauvoo would be empowered to hear any case which took place within its city limits involving any of its citizens."

"And no extraditing," Joseph emphasized.

"None. In short, should any of us again be subpoenaed to appear in any other court in the land, we could refuse on the grounds that our own municipal court can hear the case."

Joseph beamed his satisfaction. "And an end at last to the influence of mobocrats from anywhere else." Then he became serious again. "Tell me, Brother Bennett, what are our chances for this petition being accepted at Springfield?"

"Well, inasmuch as you agreed that we shouldn't submit our petitions until the Legislature felt the weight of the Mormon vote, I should say we shall be taken much more seriously than ever before."

"Good!"

"And, President, it will be my pleasure to accompany the petitions to Springfield, I'll address the Legislature, and I'll speak personally with Tom Carlin."

"Excellent, Doctor. With your influence, we shall not fail."

Bennett returned to the carriage and Joseph watched him depart up Water Street. *At last we're making some real political progress,* he thought. As he walked back to the house, he remembered the two letters Bennett had sent him, offering to come to the aid of the Saints. At that time, he had disregarded the offer because he still expected his mission to Washington, D.C. to bear fruit. But when it became evident that the Congress wouldn't vote to censure Missouri over their mistreatment of the Latter-day Saints, and that Martin Van Buren was a weakling President concerned only over his popularity, Joseph had seen that he would have to continue as he always had: on his own initiative, breaking his own trail, trusting his own judgment. And as he had grown to know John C. Bennett, he had become greatly impressed that the man's credentials were just as genuine as he had claimed they were.

The only thing was, Port Rockwell had brought him disquieting information that suggested Bennett might have been promiscuous in the past. Sexual instability was not tolerated in the Church. But Bennett had sought baptism, and was intelligent enough to know what repentance was all about. For now, Joseph decided, he would take John C. Bennett at face value.

"I do believe ye've gone sweet on her!"

The taunting voice of William McCann floated up on the balmy afternoon air from the backyard, where he and Angus were working, into the open bedroom window where Andrew was trying to marshall his thoughts. In fact, he had been trying to get his mind off the chance encounter he had had with Louisa, and back onto the immediate challenges of investigating Nauvoo and the rumors about its leader. Because the words he had just heard from William matched his own thoughts about his reaction to Louisa Stephens, he moved close to the window, remaining hidden from the ground by the curtains, and listened.

"I have not," Angus replied indignantly. "I've only met the girl. Hardly that, in fact."

"Aye, but ye can't stop talking about her."

"And what of it?"

"Well, what are ye going t'do about it?"

"Nothing; that's my business and none of yours!"

"Will ye be mentioning her to Jock?" There was an unmistakable meaning in William's tone but Andrew couldn't imagine what it was. Its effect upon Angus, however, was interesting. What had been good-natured banter between the two brothers now changed completely. Angus didn't reply immediately, but when he did, his voice was low and threatening. "No, I will not," he said, "and neither will you, if you know what's good for you!"

There the conversation ceased, and as Andrew peeked cautiously out of his window to the ground below, he saw the two young men vigorously hoeing weeds. They had both stripped off their shirts and the sweat highlighted the rippling muscles on their backs as they worked. They hacked at the hard ground with short, angry thrusts, turned away from each other.

Andrew edged back into his bedroom, a troubled uneasiness in his mind. There was no doubt that William and Angus had been talking about Louisa Stephens.

Why should he care whether Angus was interested in her or not? Didn't he have enough on his mind without romantic notions? He sat on the edge of his bed, trying to marshall his thoughts into an orderly rank of priorities. There was so much to learn and so little time to learn it before another dispatch was due to be sent to Quincy! He felt he was wasting precious time. He got up, made a stab at smoothing out the wrinkled bedspread, and quickly went downstairs and out of the house.

The west breeze was cooling the dusk, and he turned into it, toward the Mississippi. He walked briskly, every step bringing a sharp nip of pain, but he believed that if he kept active he could minimize it.

His route took him downhill, down Sydney Street, past Carlin, Main and Granger, to a well-traveled thoroughfare named Bain. There he turned to the left and continued toward Water Street at the river's edge. The town's few original structures were on this route, and some were little more than moldering log cabins now.

As he explored, his nostrils received a familiar scent that cut through the fetid marshy smell of Mississippi backwater. Following his nose, he came to a small structure with a freshly-lettered sign over the door which confirmed what his nose had told him. Coming from inside the shack was the rich, acidic aroma of machine oil and printer's ink! The sign read PRINT SHOP, and below it, *Times & Seasons*.

He hurried to the door, which was standing open, and walked through it to the dark interior. The setting sun had thrown the shop into shadow and lanterns burned beyond a primitive counter where two men labored in a dark basement down steep stairs.

It appeared that the two men were brushing and chipping on a large object, but from the distance, Andrew couldn't tell what it was. His presence in the doorway was still unnoticed and the two men worked on. Evidently the print shop was not yet open for business. Boxes of paper stood unopened on the floor, and there was no evidence of a printing press to be seen. Unless . . .

One of the grimy men looked up. "Hello," he called.

"How do you do?"

"Looking for printing?"

Andrew stepped closer. "I'm a newspaperman looking for work—I just got into town yesterday."

The two men stopped and looked at each other. Andrew saw that the man who had spoken was tall and well-built, perhaps six and a half feet high. "You're looking for work, are you?" he asked. "What kind of work?" He climbed up, followed by his partner.

"Writing, reporting; I've set type and run a press. I've deviled, done just about everything in a newspaper shop."

The two men broke out into simultaneous smiles. "You don't say," remarked the shorter man, "where do you come from?"

"Heaven, probably," the tall man said. He wiped his hands on his apron. "I'm Don Carlos Smith and this is Robert Thompson. We're the *Times & Seasons*. And who might you be?"

"Andrew Sharp from Meadsville, Pennsylvania. I apprenticed to the Meadsville *Journal* for five years, and I'd really like to get back into the business."

Don Carlos turned and made a sweeping gesture toward the grimy pile of dried mud on the basement's damp floor. "So would we," he laughed, "and we shall, just as soon as we remove a few more pounds of Missouri from our old friend here. Oh, by the way, this **is** a printing press despite appearances to the contrary."

Andrew climbed down the ladder. "What happened to it?" he asked.

"We buried it in someone's back yard," Thompson replied.

Andrew looked bewildered. "You buried a printing press? Why?"

"To keep the mobbers from smashing it," Don Carlos answered. "That was in Far West. We just got it back here last week."

"Oh." Far West—the scene of the Mormon massacre he had heard about. He walked around the dirt-encrusted machine. It was a Stanhope model, made of iron, entirely hand-operated, capable of turning out only one sheet at a time—a tiresome process for production of a newspaper. "You surely aren't going to try to print a periodical on this antique?"

"We have a new Konig press ordered," Thompson said. "But it will be months before it gets here. Meantime, we will publish once a month, with a circulation of about one thousand."

"I hear Konig's new press is steam-driven," Andrew said.

"The one we've ordered is run by a crank," Don Carlos said ruefully. "But if we do well enough, maybe we can hook it up to a steam engine."

Andrew looked around the shop. Hooks on the walls held back numbers of the *Times & Seasons*. Shelves held boxes of type.

"We buried all the type, as well," Thompson said. "We could use some help cleaning it."

"Where is it?"

"Over here." He walked over to several trays which were sitting in oily-looking water. "We have to brush each piece, dry it, and oil it to keep it from rusting."

"I'd like to help," Andrew said. Excitement was running through him like a current.

"Well, I guess you can consider yourself hired," Don Carlos said. Thompson nodded approvingly. "What was your name again, Brother?"

"Andrew Sharp."

The two printers shook his hand again, and before he could say anything else, they draped a spare apron around him and gave him their only pair of gloves.

It was dirty work, extracting stubborn Missouri mud from each piece of type, but it was **work**.

"So you got here yesterday?" Don Carlos said. "Where did you leave from?"

"Oh, Warsaw."

"You have a family with you?"

Andrew was on guard now. "No," he said without elaboration. The men were silent for a few minutes.

Don Carlos spoke again. "I'm curious. What brought you to Nauvoo? You had no family, no job . . . Why?"

Andrew remembered the answer he had given the McCanns when they had asked him the same question the day before. "There's a prophet here," he said. Let them think what they liked, that was as honest an answer as he could give. Andrew looked over at Don Carlos.

Don Carlos nodded, saying nothing. Robert Thompson asked, "Do you know the prophet?"

"No. I suppose you do, though."

"We know him," Don Carlos said. "I'm his younger brother."

Andrew paused, controlling his elation. It was the end of his first full day in Nauvoo, and he had landed a job in a newspaper office, working for the brother of the very man on whom he had come to report!

"Well," he said finally, "I feel very lucky that I met you."

"That's how we feel too, Andrew," Don Carlos said. "Very lucky."

"Brigham Young Home"
Painting by Al Rounds
Courtesy of Nancy Rounds

Part Three:

The Powers

Chapter 12

It was a Saturday with the promise of autumn in the air. Laborers worked half a day, then lit fires to burn the dried grass and weeds and the snags and scraps that were the debris of construction. The tang of smoke blended with the freshening afternoon breeze to put new vigor in every breath drawn in optimistic, burgeoning Nauvoo.

At the end of his third week in the city, Andrew's body once more was responding without pain, and the savory meals prepared by Anne McCann were putting flesh on him.

He had filed two tightly-written dispatches to the *Argus* which contained the unmistakable authority of a correspondent who lived in, and understood, his field. He had written of the surprisingly high sickness and death rate from swamp fever, or "ague," as the locals called it. And he was able to report that the prophet, himself, had been desperately ill but had risen from his sickbed after two weeks of confinement and had sailed across the Mississippi, to Montrose, to lay hands on similarly stricken church members, most of whom were reportedly recovering.

He had written authoritatively about the self-sufficiency of the Latter-day Saints, and of their plans to set up a charter that would give them legal protection from outside forces, plus a militia which would function as a personal police force under the command of the mayor. But as yet, he pointed out, Nauvoo had neither the right to call itself an incorporated city under Illinois law, nor a mayor to govern it. Ketchum's terse note accompanying the weekly pay was as complimentary as the man could be. But he reminded Andrew that he still wanted the facts about the "Danites" and Joseph Smith's marital status.

It troubled Andrew that he still had not found a way to meet Joseph Smith. He had attended meeting with the McCanns on each of the two Sundays since arriving, but Joseph had been away, and the preaching had been done by Sidney Rigdon, who was recuperating from a serious bout with the fever, and on the following Sunday by the prophet's older brother, Hyrum. In neither sermon could Andrew find any hint of the aberrant doctrines whispered about outside of Nauvoo.

Don Carlos had introduced him to Emma Smith, the wife of the prophet, whom he found to be handsome and gracious, if somewhat distracted by the fact that a number of women were seeking to talk to her all at once—hoping, it seemed to Andrew, to gain stature by being recognized by the prophet's wife.

With this acquaintance with a part of Joseph's family, Andrew began to feel familiar around the center of authority in the city and the church. Don Carlos had a delightful sense of humor and was well-liked by everyone who knew him. Hyrum, the oldest of the brothers, was large and handsome also, but had a sublime peacefulness about him that made it a pleasure to associate with him and hear him speak. Andrew had also seen the prophet's mother at Sunday meeting, but she had hurried home to nurse her husband, Joseph Smith, Sr., who was still recuperating from exposure he had suffered in Missouri. And Emma was an enigma; pulled in every direction by her children, the other ladies of the church, as well as by her responsibilities to Joseph, Andrew felt he knew her least well of all.

He cut across fields to reach the McCann house, and as he did so, he saw a wrestling match nearby on a grassy plot. Two bodies were flailing on the ground, while a group of boys and men stood around, cheering. Andrew walked over for a closer look.

The contest was between a boy about eighteen, and a man in his mid-thirties—and the boy was having the worst of it. Stocky and powerful as he was, the younger contender at last gasped, "Quarter! I give up!"

His opponent instantly sprang off him, gave him his hand and pulled him to his feet, hugging him fiercely and pounding him on the back. "You were brave and strong," he announced, throwing his mane of light auburn hair back on his head and running his hand through it. "We'll be sending you to Springfield as our champion wrestler one of these days!"

The younger man grinned and shook hands with him, thanking him for the contest. Andrew hadn't seen either contender before, but from the respectful attitude of the onlookers, the victor seemed to be someone of importance. Andrew asked one of the spectators, in a low voice, for the name of the older man. The onlooker was startled by the question. "That's the prophet Joseph Smith!"

Andrew was dumbfounded. He looked at the panting gladiator, and took in the sight of the tall, lumbering, well-muscled 200-pounder whose white shirt now bore the stains of wet grass and mud, whose neck, above a wrinkled collar, was sunburned and thick. A man who now wiped a wet nose with the back of a hairy hand, and who seemed to enjoy throwing his arm around people—he was walking ahead of Andrew, embracing every man who came up to him to congratulate him—this was a prophet of God?

When he recovered from his surprise, Andrew hurried beside him. "President Smith," he said. "I'd like to meet you."

The keen blue eyes, mirthful and large, looked down on Andrew. The prominent nose, the arrowhead-shaped point of it still wet from the exertions of the wrestling match, the deep lines from nostrils to lips, the wide, generous mouth and the firm chin—all combined to create a face of strength, yet intelligence and sensitivity. A **sensuous** face, Andrew would later write to himself in his shorthand notes. "And I'd like to meet you," Joseph said.

"My name is Andrew Sharp. I work with your brother at the *Times & Seasons*."

"Of course," the prophet said, pausing to grab Andrew's hand in both of his. "Don Carlos has told me all about you! Welcome," he said, and enveloped Andrew's shoulders in a hug he would feel for hours.

He touched, he charmed, he bewitched. The man was every bit as dynamic as Andrew had been told he was—you could feel it from your first meeting with him. He liked to be close to people, to touch them and create emotions within them, that was evident. A bit of a show-off, Andrew thought, wrestling out in the open with a much younger athlete. "I've been looking forward to meeting you ever since I got here," he said, "but the last thing I expected to find a prophet doing was wrestling!"

Joseph laughed and nodded his head. "Yes," he said, "you thought I'd be wearing a long white beard and carrying stone tablets!" The onlookers roared with him.

"Well, Brother Sharp, look me over," he said, pausing as he tramped through the field to hold out his arms from his sides. "I am a man; nothing more."

"Well, you're a better wrestler than I am, Brother Joseph!" his opponent said, and the crowd laughed again.

Andrew felt a rush of questions about to tumble out of his mouth. "When might I have a few minutes of your time to interview you, Sir?" he asked, as the party began to move toward the road.

"On what subject?" the prophet asked.

"On doctrine, on your plans for Nauvoo . . ." Andrew wanted to enumerate the areas, but feared he would give away his non-Mormon status if he went further.

"I am expecting my carriage," he said as they walked, "but I may have a few minutes now before returning home." The knot of spectators had not disbanded, but were surrounding them now in a devoted crescent, every ear straining to hear whatever Joseph might say. "What points of doctrine are unclear to you?" he asked Andrew.

Andrew adroitly shifted to a safer field. "Your vision of Nauvoo?" he asked.

"My vision of Nauvoo," mused Joseph. "I founded this city in a dismal swamp, when it was unwanted by anyone else. I saw then exactly how it could be. What you see here," he said, stopping to sweep his arm in a circle taking in the entire community, "is only the beginning of the largest and finest city in the state of Illinois. We drained the swamp. We cut the underbrush. We established farms on the rich soil down by the river front, and cut roads so that farms could be worked by day and the farmers return to their pleasant homes in the city at night—free from unpleasant odors and noisome sounds." Then he pointed in another direction. "No resident of Nauvoo lives more than a short walk from all needed amenities—stores and shops—and the industries that support us are grouped down there," pointing to the southern section," where sound and smoke blow in the other direction. It was all worked out, given to me—perfected." He smiled with the sublime self-confidence of a man who knows he is indisputably correct, and walked on.

Andrew hurried to stay abreast of him. The man had long legs and took large, exuberant strides, his head held high. "Tell him about the temple, Brother Joseph," one of the younger lads said.

Joseph stopped again and pointed east, to the brow of a hill which surmounted Nauvoo, over which white clouds now boiled. "On that site, we shall build the House of the Lord," he said, a reverent note in his sonorous baritone. "It will surpass the Kirtland temple not only in glory, but in purpose. The Lord will send down more endowments than have been on the earth since the Savior came!"

A thrill ran through Andrew. The words were meaningless to him, but he had the sense that they were significant, and should be remembered. He had left his notepad and pencil at the printing office, but he made a determined mental note to remember what he was hearing. He was quite sure it had never been quoted in the outside press.

At that moment, a carriage approached on the road nearby, being driven at a speed out of all reason for the kind of rig it was. All eyes turned as the driver pulled up and jumped down. A small man in buckskins ran up to the prophet, a long horsetail of hair flailing behind him. He stood barely to Joseph Smith's shoulder as the crowd parted to let him through. Andrew noted with surprise that the small man wore a bandolero across his shoulders, and sported a holstered weapon, one of the new revolvers called a Pepperbox.

"Joseph, bad news," the man said tersely. "Your father is dying."

The spectators gasped. "I'll go there at once," Joseph said. He started away, then turned to Andrew. "My brother tells me you have a way of transcribing the spoken word very rapidly. Is that correct?"

"Yes, sir, I---"

"Then I need you to come with me now!"

Andrew had never ridden in a carriage at the speed the driver now demanded from the lathering horse. It was hot, and flecks of foam flew back from the panting animal. Holding on for dear life, Andrew turned to Joseph and said, "I didn't bring anything to write with!"

"Never mind," Joseph said, "Mother has writing materials."

The carriage made a final turn and hauled up before a house where a small group of people waited. They made way for Joseph as he jumped down from the carriage, their faces filled with sympathy. Andrew hurried in behind him and the driver followed on his heels.

Inside the small house Andrew recognized Hyrum and Lucy Mack Smith, who came downstairs as she heard the three men enter. The tiny, frail mother of the prophet looked petrified. Joseph met her at the foot of the stairs and enfolded her in his arms. Behind her on the stairs, Hyrum told his brother, "He's going fast, Joseph."

"Let me see him," Joseph said, taking the stairs two at a time.

Andrew felt out of place. He was reasonably sure that the Smiths, under such intense concern, didn't remember who he was; he'd met them only once at a Sunday meeting in the bower above the town, and under the circumstances he wished he could wait with the others, outside. But just then, Hyrum said to him, "Brother Sharp, it is good of you to be here."

"President Smith asked me to ride here with him, and he thought I might be needed to take dictation."

Lucy Mack Smith looked up at Hyrum. "Oh, then, oughtn't he to be up with Father?"

Hyrum made a sign for Andrew to wait, and he hurried up the stairs.

Mrs. Smith turned and noticed the buckskin-clad man for the first time, and the small man took her hands fondly, saying nothing. He was weeping.

Hyrum reappeared at the top of the stairs and came down quietly. "Joseph is giving Father a blessing. He seems quite a bit calmer."

Lucy Mack Smith seemed relieved with this news. "We can all wait in the parlor," she said, and graciously showed the three men to chairs; but the small man elected to lean in the doorway where he could keep an eye on the stairs.

"He began to vomit blood, you know," the tiny woman said. Andrew turned away from the doorway to find she was talking to him.

"We had Orrin send for Joseph because he always knows exactly where he is," she said. "Don't you, Port?"

The small man nodded slowly, not taking his eyes off the top of the stairs.

Andrew didn't know what to say. "Do they know the nature of his illness?" he asked.

Hyrum answered for his mother. "It began in Quincy after the family escaped from the attackers in Missouri. Father was hurt and he never really got his strength back. Then this swamp fever hit him, and he's never rallied."

"Does he have a doctor up there with him?" Andrew asked.

The small man in buckskins spoke at last. "He has the best doctor on earth with him this very minute." His high voice was filled with emotion.

Hyrum smiled sadly. "You're right, Port; he's in God's hands now. If anybody can save him, it's Joseph."

The small man stiffened as steps were heard on the stair, and Joseph Smith came down. "He is better," he said, and Lucy and Hyrum both sighed with relief.

"You all have met Brother Sharp," Joseph continued. "He will act as scribe. If the—if anything happens to the Patriarch, we shall want his final words."

"Of course," Andrew said.

"Would you find it convenient to remain here?"

"Of course, President."

The shadows lengthened. Upstairs, Joseph Smith, Sr. slept and his wife faithfully sat with him, as other women shuttled between their homes and the

Smith's with food and freshly laundered linens. There was quiet compassion and organization in everything being done for the Smith family, and Andrew, seated still in the parlor, remarked on it to Hyrum.

"It is the work of Emma, the prophet's wife," he said. "In time of need, she is always there, a ministering angel. This spring, when so many were sick with the fever, she turned her home into a hospital and tended everyone who lay ill. She was the same in Missouri before coming across to Quincy."

A steady procession of townspeople made their way to the door, where they were greeted by Hyrum or Don Carlos, taking turns, thanking them for their prayers and concern. Night fell and the elder Smith still slept. Andrew had been fed by the neighbor women as if he were a member of the Smith household, although few if any of them knew his name. There were still many questions to ask, and since Hyrum seemed agreeable, Andrew ventured to seek some more information. "Just who is the small man in buckskins?"

Hyrum smiled. "Orrin Porter Rockwell. Joseph's oldest friend, and bodyguard. We grew up together back east in New York state."

"Your father is the 'Patriarch' of the Church? Excuse me, Brother Smith, but nobody ever explained that term to me."

"The prophet ordained Father to the office of Patriarch in '33," Hyrum said. "He also serves as Assistant Counselor in the First Presidency."

"This office of Patriarch—what does it mean?"

"He holds the Patriarchal priesthood, and all the keys of that ministry."

Andrew nodded, understanding nothing, but assuming that the title gave its holder a fatherly dominion over the membership of the church. He dared not to ask any more just now.

Fitfully, Andrew dozed through the night. He was dimly aware of whispered conversations near the couch on which Lucy Mack Smith had insisted he sleep, but he slipped in and out of consciousness until some time after dawn. He was awakened by Orrin Porter Rockwell and a sheaf of papers and pencil were handed to him.

"Upstairs," the small man whispered. "They want you in the Patriarch's room."

Shaking the sleep from his head, Andrew made his way up the stairs. He found the small bedroom already crowded with Lucy, the old man's wife; Hyrum, Don Carlos and Joseph, and Dr. John C. Bennett. The doctor edged his way through the relatives, eyeing Andrew with surprise, and stood at the door. The room was almost airless, the single window being closed. On the bed lay Joseph Smith, Sr., gaunt and parchment-white, but he was looking around the room, taking in all who were there. Standing by the head of his bed, Lucy stroked his hair. Then, in a voice made hoarse by age and weakness, he spoke to her, and Joseph moved aside, beckoning Andrew to stand on the other side of the bed so that he could hear and take down the words.

After carefully expanding his shorthand notes into readable English, and making an unspotted copy for the family, Andrew sat in his room at the Mc-Cann residence and re-read the dying words of a man he had never known—but felt curiously close to.

"The world loves its own," he had said, "but it does not love us. It hates us because we are not of the world; therefore, all their malice is poured out upon us, and they seek to take away our lives. When I look upon my children, and realize, that although they were raised up to do the Lord's work, yet they must pass through scenes of trouble and affliction as long as they live upon the earth; and I dread to leave them surrounded by enemies . . ."

A DISPATCH FROM A TRAVELER IN NAUVOO
September 15th, 1840

This writer attended his first Mormon funeral today, and found it altogether different from those grief-filled gatherings dreaded by all in the ordinary world.

It is fair to say that not a tool was put in hand nor a coin exchanged in Commerce on this day, Monday, September 15th, in which the father of the prophet Joseph Smith was laid to rest. Well over a thousand persons attended the services, which were conducted by the prophet himself.

Noteworthy in the eulogies for this elderly victim of violence against the church his son had founded, was the absence of malice toward the mobbers who had wounded him, and the circumstances which forced him and his family to flee to the unhealthy climate only now being improved to a livable degree in Nauvoo. Instead were proclamations of the hope this people has in a life eternal, and the certainty that there is much work for the deceased to do on the "other side." It was as much a celebration of life, as it was a recognition of death.

The Latter-day Saints are single-minded and unswerving in their devotion to their prophet, and this feeling seems to embrace his entire family, as well. All kinds of Christian services and assistance were provided to the Smiths during the final illness of the man they recognized as a patriarch, which would do justice to the best-organized Methodist or Presbyterian congregations in our larger cities. . . .

Lilburn W. Boggs' rage had been gestating for months, ever since he was first alerted to the fact that a delegation of Mormons headed by Joseph Smith himself had gone to Washington to petition for redress of grievances against Missouri. Grievances against Missouri! Boggs smashed his ham-sized fist on the desk in his Jefferson City office and cursed.

"Thieving, murdering, traitors!" he roared. "Jail-breaking, sanctimonious hypocrites!" The object of his anger was an edition of the St.

Louis *Bulletin* devoted almost entirely to a recitation of the Mormon charges against Missouri mobbers, and it specifically charged Governor Lilburn W. Boggs with dereliction of his duty to control the lawless element in his state. He gripped the offending newspaper with both fists and tore it apart, threw it on the floor of his office and stamped his boots on it.

Witnessing this outburst was an aide, Arnold Best, who was as mousy as the governor was leonine. Boggs now turned his rage upon the small, narrow-shouldered man, who had retreated from the governor's desk as the volume of Boggs' anger increased.

"I read it from those damned Illinois milk-sops, but I never thought I'd read it from St. Louis," he shouted. Then, he hurled himself into the tall-backed chair at his desk. "All right," he said, nodding to himself for emphasis. "All right, this has gone far enough!" He scrabbled his spatulated fingers through piles of papers, flipped open a large law book and slammed it again, and then waved a mighty paw at Arnold. The aide crept closer.

"What do they call it when you demand prisoners from another state?"

Arnold's brain raced, driven by nervousness. "Ah . . . requisition?"

"Requisition, that's it! No," the governor said, shaking his huge head. "You requisition furniture and stuff such as that! I want Tom Carlin to go arrest Joseph Smith and his lot and send them to me! Now, what's that called?"

"Extradition," the small man cried victoriously.

"Extradition! Right! Now, here's what you do: you draw up the papers and have them sent to Governor Thomas Carlin in Springfield, requiring him to extradite . . . where is that list?" he muttered to himself, "I ought to know their names by now!" Finding the list on his desk, Governor Boggs enumerated the names: "Joseph Smith, Sidney Rigdon, Parley Pratt, Lyman Wright, Caleb Baldwin and Alanson Brown. I want 'em all here, right here!" He threw another smashing blow to his desk.

"On what charge, sir?"

"**On what charge?**" The aide retreated another step. "On the charges of treason, arson and attempted murder," Boggs roared. "Oh, and add to that—flight from the law! They're fugitives from justice!"

Arnold Best was making notes on a pad of paper, backing toward the door. "I'll see to it right away, your Excellency," he said, slipping quickly out the door and easing it shut behind him. Best was the only member of Boggs' retinue who ever called him "excellency," and Boggs, as bluff and square-cut a son of the southern soil as ever to hold high office, enjoyed the title, even if it did come from a man he considered a pipsqueak. Boggs leaned back in the executive chair, enjoying the spectre of a line of Mormon antagonists, chained, appearing before him on the very carpet of this office, trembling as they awaited their fate. He folded his thick fingers over his paunch, flicking the watch chain spanning his pockets with both stubby thumbs, and finally translated his anger into a rolling, phlegm-laden chuckle, and he rewarded himself with a new cigar.

One week later, the extradition request was delivered to Governor Thomas Carlin in Springfield, Illinois. Carlin knew the perils of politics included supporting an unpopular cause, even if the cause was just. The issue of the Mormons had already caused his neighbor state, Missouri, great troubles and had generated so much bloodshed that he feared the same could happen in Illinois. "After all," he told his wife—in whom he confided all of his concerns, "Joseph Smith betrayed me only two months ago, when he claimed Boggs' men were trying to entrap those four Mormon thieves."

What he alluded to had happened in July. A party of Mormons, including Alanson Brown, were kidnaped and beaten until they confessed to stealing a large quantity of goods from an area around Tully, Missouri. There were rumors that Joseph Smith himself had authorized the Mormons to compensate for their losses at the hands of the mobs by stealing from Missourians, until they had recovered three million dollars' worth of goods—representing the value of property taken from them by the mobbers. Hyrum Smith was later to repudiate these rumors, but they were being widely accepted as fact in Missouri.

Joseph had been enraged when he learned of the kidnappings and beatings, and he wrote to Governor Carlin of Illinois, requesting that he protest the action by the Tulley Missourians, claiming they had planted the contraband near Nauvoo themselves, in order to justify their attack on the Mormon men. But investigation later indicated that the huge amount of stolen property found in Hancock county, and well within "Mormon territory," made it seem unlikely that it all could have been carried across the Mississippi in secret by plotters from Missouri. Furthermore, Alanson Brown had confessed taking part in an organized burglary ring—and this without the beatings his brother Mormons had suffered.

When these particulars were reported to Governor Carlin, it had the effect of turning him from a friend of the Saints to a badly disillusioned, suspicious man, and he readily signed the extradition order requested by Boggs.

The ride up from Springfield to Hancock county took the Illinois officers over some of the worst roads in the state, so that by the evening they had reached the county seat, Carthage, they were ready for some relaxation before riding the final few miles into Nauvoo the next day. One of the party mentioned their mission to a local in Carthage, and that news was relayed into Nauvoo the same night. By morning, when the Springfield deputation rode into Nauvoo, Joseph Smith and the others named in the writ had disappeared, nobody seemed to know where they could be found, and the lawmen had no choice but to ride back to Springfield emptyhanded.

Louisa Stephens' elation at her chance meeting with Andrew Sharp was fading, as the memories of the Haun's Mill massacre returned to haunt her. *What did she know of this Andrew Sharp anyway?* she asked herself. She knew nothing about him, except that he was as new to Nauvoo as she was.

From her window she had watched him set off somewhere every morning, for he walked past her house, and she had seen him return in the evening, often at late twilight, leaning less and less upon his cane. Then she was told he was working at the *Times & Seasons*. But he hadn't come to call on her, and when she had seen him at Sabbath meetings in the grove where the services were held, he stood with the McCanns and although she could tell he was glancing at her from time to time, he never spoke, except for a brief greeting.

The only other young man she had met was Angus McCann, and she never saw him at all except in the company of two other men whom she assumed were family members, but except for courtesy greetings at church meetings, they never spoke, either.

Louisa was achingly lonely, but wasn't aware that it was her expression of unutterable sadness that kept others away. It masked her natural beauty and dragged her features into a perpetual pout.

And so she passed her days in gloomy isolation, certain in her heart that she was paying now, in mortality, a down payment on the eternal debt she would have to pay as punishment for killing a man at Haun's Mill. She was so ashamed of her deed that she had never confessed it to a church authority, who might have speedily set her mind at rest; she lived with the certainty of eternal damnation, and it grew within her like a malignancy.

Chapter 13

Springfield became the capital of Illinois only the year before, in 1839, and still lacked the imposing government buildings needed to house the legislature. The taxpayers had been busily financing railroads, canals and turnpikes, and so the Senate and the House met in makeshift quarters.

On Wednesday, December 16th, 1840, as one of their final acts before quitting for the Christmas holidays, the lawmakers enacted into law eight city charters which were before them, uncontested and unhindered. Nauvoo's was among them.

On that morning, John C. Bennett had spoken before both houses, outlining the persecutions the Mormons had endured in Missouri and emphasizing the need to redress the injustices they had suffered. The legislature did not feel it necessary even to hear all of the provisions of the Nauvoo charter; it was enacted into law with dispatch. Even Secretary of State, Stephen A. Douglas, supported it. There was popular sentiment in Illinois to show up their Missouri neighbors as ruffians for their treatment of the Mormons, but there was also the fact that the Mormons, voting *en bloc* as they had done in August, would be a formidable ally for any politician to have on his side. The Whigs had learned this to their pleasure, as all but one of them were voted into office at Mormon polling places. That single exception, a tall and bushy-haired individual, now made his way through the cluster of men standing around the door to Governor Carlin's office. John C. Bennett had just stepped out of the office and was replacing the signed papers of incorporation in his portfolio.

"The gentleman from Nauvoo, I believe," the tall man said, ambling in his awkward way toward Bennett. The doctor looked up into the sad but kind eyes of Abraham Lincoln. At thirty-one, beardless, his square jaw blue from the ever-present stubble he had to shave twice daily to remove, the rawboned back country attorney had a diffident manner that betrayed the keen mind and orator's skill behind it. Bennett was annoyed to see him, expecting him to complain about how he was the only Whig the Mormons voted against in the recent election. He rubbed the mole on his nose.

"I just want to congratulate you on receiving your city charter," Lincoln said. "I want you to know I supported it."

"Well, thank you," Bennett almost snapped. He was anxious to get away; he had other business on his mind.

"And I wanted you to tell your friends out in Nauvoo," the attorney drawled, "that I understand the reason they voted for my worthy opponent, James Ralston. I can appreciate that he and your prophet are good friends, and that Ralston can do a lot of good for your cause."

Bennett was well aware that Ralston was the only Democrat Joseph had favored and he had let the Saints know his sentiments before the August elections. It was perfectly plain to most of them that the Democratic party, of which the hated Missouri governor Boggs and the do-nothing President Van Buren were members, had let the Mormons down in their hour of need. Only one of the Illinois Democrats had gone out of his way to befriend the prophet, and that had been James H. Ralston. The Mormons rewarded him and punished his Whig opponent, Lincoln, at the polls.

"But my philosophy and the Mormons' are just the same," the lawyer droned, "when it comes to human rights. We're probably both unpopular enough over our stand on slavery, for example," he said with a rueful smile. "So, when the time comes sometime in the future, that the Mormons need another honest man in the legislature, just remember A. Lincoln. Will you tell them that?" His eyes were twinkling in recognition of how irritated Bennett was becoming.

"Yes, thank you," Bennett said, pushing away now. "I'll tell them that." He left Lincoln standing in the throng, hand extended, and threaded his way out of the cigar smoke and rumbling cacaphony of voices, into the cold Springfield twilight.

When Dr. Bennett returned to Nauvoo, he saw that major changes had occurred in his two-month absence. Dozens of new homes and commercial buildings were started, lots were cleared and brush disposed of. The river bank down near Joseph and Emma's house had been shored up with rock, a second sawmill was nearly completed, as was a steam flour mill and numbers of other industrial plants. The streets seemed busier than they had been in October when he left for Springfield, and more of these broad thoroughfares were paved. The industriousness of the Latter-day Saints never failed to thrill him.

His very own house, as he alighted from the carriage he had hired to carry him and his luggage up from the landing, looked festive and cordial. Boughs of holly were festooned around the doorway and a Christmas tree stood in the window of the dining room.

Inside, all was bustle and polish. Maude Gaines had been baking pies and cookies for days in anticipation of the doctor's return. Rebecca and Louisa had been kept busy polishing brass utensils and ornaments, and the two younger children had been kept out from under-foot by Maude's encouragement to them to make tree ornaments from bits of yarn and dried fruit. The results were less than decorative, but they were hung on the tree anyway.

When Bennett walked into the entry hall he was greeted as a hero. The *Times & Seasons* had printed the announcement of his successful trip to Springfield, and the popular doctor was now spoken of in town as the logical choice to become Nauvoo's first mayor. This, after it was ascertained that the prophet had no designs upon that office himself. And so it was in the highest of spirits that John C. Bennett once more set foot in his house, and it never smelled nor looked more inviting.

Christmas was only five days off, and although this was Monday the 21st, and normally a working day, Samuel had left the bindery a bit early that afternoon so he could help his wife prepare the first real English Christmas they had enjoyed since emigrating in 1835. As the master of the household entered, the Gaines family formed a greeting line in the hallway, Samuel first, then his wife, rosy-faced and beaming, the girls—Louisa smiling shyly and Rebecca fidgiting beside her—and the two youngest, Bobby and Elizabeth. Bennett warmly shook hands with Samuel and Maude, then kissed the cheeks of the two girls, causing Rebecca to glow. He greeted the young children, then gifts were handed out from the large briefcase the doctor carried—apples and rare oranges, and sweets purchased at a post house in Carthage, the county seat.

They all tried to talk at once. The children demanded he come and inspect the tree. Maude asked him if he weren't hungry after the long journey. Samuel was anxious to show off the root cellar he had dug beneath the back of the house, an amenity the doctor, not being much for housekeeping, had ignored in the months he had lived there. But over the tumult, effervescent Rebecca cried, "And there's to be a Christmas dance, Doctor!"

He looked at her. It seemed to him that this adolescent, this child, had grown more of the allure of a woman in these two months, than he had remembered. In fact he hadn't thought about her at all on this trip. The women in his thoughts had been of a far different kind than this little English sparrow, trying to burst into maturity. But he had tired of the other kind. How delightful she was, eyes sparkling like fireworks, a provocative smile on lips so red he thought she must have gotten into her mother's rouge—if she had any. "A dance, eh?" he threw back at her. "Well, that's jolly! And will you be my partner?"

Louisa and Rebecca's parents turned to look at the girl. Two months ago she would have buried her blushing face in her apron and run giggling from his presence. Now, she parted her lips slightly, curtsied, never taking her eyes off him, and said, "Why, I would be honored!"

That night, after dinner, Louisa and Rebecca sat on the floor of the bedroom sewing flounces on the skirts they intended to wear to the Christmas dance. Their moods could hardly have been more opposite. Whereas Louisa continued her introspection, Rebecca wanted to gossip. Louisa saw no joy in the Yuletide season, Rebecca was a veritable Kris Kringle of good will. And with Louisa becoming pathologically afraid of romance, Rebecca glowed with the promise, however casually made, that she would be escorted to the Christmas dance by Dr. Bennett.

Rebecca chattered away happily buried beneath taffeta and crinoline, until she suddenly became aware that the only response coming from Louisa was an occasional sigh or a noncommittal remark. Rebecca threw down her needle and thread and said, with fists on hips, "Look here, Louisa, nobody likes to be around a pickle, and that's what you are tonight, a sour pickle! What in the world went wrong with you tonight?''

Louisa honestly couldn't have explained what had gone wrong. Unless it was the dramatic contrast between her own withdrawn manner and Rebecca's newfound sophistication; or the approach of a season, her second as an orphan, which she used to love to share with her mother and father; or the evidence that her one tentative foray into friendship with an eligible and attractive man in Nauvoo had come to absolutely nothing—Andrew had never called on her. But since she could not honestly reply to Rebecca's question, she chose to bite her lip and say nothing.

"You're always saying **I'm** acting childish; well, who's being the child now?'' Rebecca demanded.

That brought the tears. Huskily, Louisa said, "I could hardly expect **you** to understand!''

"You know what you look like?'' Rebecca asked. "You look like a jealous child!''

"Jealous?'' Louisa shot back, "Of whom? Of you? If I had to throw myself at a man old enough to be my father---''

"I knew it!'' cried Rebecca. "You can't stand it that Dr. Bennett thinks I'm attractive!''

Outside their bedroom door, John Bennett heard his name spoken as he reached the top of the stairs, and he paused to listen.

Louisa threw down her sewing and struggled to her feet. "Oh, Rebecca Gaines,'' she said, beginning to sob, "you are a fool! If you want to think that, then think it! I don't care what you think! I don't care about anybody or any thing in the world any more!''

With that, she threw open the door and ran blindly into Dr. Bennett, who caught her in his arms. She opened her eyes, horrified to see him an eyelash from her face, knowing he had heard everything.

"Louisa, my dear,'' he said soothingly, trying to calm her.

The jolt of surprise, the arms slipping around her, and suddenly the dam inside her burst. The grief and heartbreak that had been welling up inside her for two years exploded. Then, there had been no one to turn to, so she had buried her grief just as Haun's Mill's widows had buried their husbands and sons: hastily, immediately. But the pressure had become too great.

Louisa's body was wracked with uncontrollable sobs which burst out of her in great explosive spasms which made every muscle jolt and recoil. She slipped into hysteria in which she saw, heard and remembered nothing but the cathartic of lament, and her moaning and gasping brought the household up the stairs on a dead run.

She had sagged in John C. Bennett's arms and her jerking spasms—over which she had no knowledge or control—caused her to slip out of his grasp onto the floor, where she lay as if in a **grand mal** seizure.

Rebecca was standing, mouth agape, in the doorway. "Don't stand there like an idiot, girl,'' Bennett shouted. "Help me get her on the bed!''

114

Dumbly she picked up Louisa's heels, and they managed to get her into the bedroom.

Rebecca stood at the foot of the bed, tears starting to trickle down her face. Bennett bent over Louisa.

"What did you say to her?" the doctor demanded, as he untied the ribbon that secured the top of her dress to her neck.

"I didn't say anything," Rebecca replied in a defensive, little-girl voice.

"Of course you did, you must have," he said grimly, loosening Louisa's blouse.

"I didn't!" Rebecca whined. "She started it. She's jealous because you're taking me to the dance!"

"Taking you to the dance? You silly girl, I'm not taking you or anyone else to the dance!"

Rebecca began a shrill whisper of a wail, and ran out of the bedroom, across the hall and into her parents' room, slamming the door. Her bawling was heard, joined by her sister Elizabeth and Bobby, who cried in sympathy.

Maude Gaines appeared in the doorway. "Here's some cold water and a rag."

"Good, give it here," Bennett said, holding out his hand. He bathed Louisa's forehead with the cold rag, then placed his hand on her bosom, a bosom filling, he noticed, even more since he had last occupied the house. He felt expertly for the cartoid artery and did not like the faint pulse. He knelt and put his ear to her chest. The pulse was too fast and thready, not as strong as he liked to find it. "She is suffering shock," he said. "Delayed, I think, from the very day she saw her parents killed. Has she cried like this before? Grieved for her parents?"

Maude shook her head firmly. "Never once."

He rose and rolled one of her eyelids up. "Oh, mercy, doctor," Maude said fearfully, "will she be all right?"

He really didn't know. He had seen men suffer these same symptoms during major surgery—amputations, the like—never certain that they would recover. Some didn't. The girl was young; she had that in her favor. But she had suffered something in her brain; her system had rejected it, and now she was going through the agony she should have felt when the massacre happened.

Samuel Gaines hurried up the stairs with the doctor's bag. Bennett took it and extracted a small vial which he opened and waved under Louisa's nose. She began to shake her head, still unconscious, trying to avoid the acrid fumes. "Louisa, wake up," Dr. Bennett demanded. "You must wake up. You're all right now."

Her eyelids flickered, eyes unfocused, and then she looked startled to see where she was. Her mind fought to remember what had transpired, and then the memory lodged in place and she clamped her eyes shut again. "I want to die," she said, lucidly.

"Don't be silly," the doctor said, taking her hand. She pulled it away.

115

"I want to die."

"You don't want to die, you are a young and beautiful woman with everything in the world to live for." It was his most pursuasive voice, one which had seldom failed to accomplish his objectives.

"Yes, don't be talking like that, dear," Maude put in, moving beside the bed and taking her other hand. "We all love you and want you to be happy."

Dr. Bennett consulted his black leather case again and brought up another vial, a bottle containing laudanum. "Will you please bring me a spoon, Sister Gaines?" he asked. The plump woman hurried back downstairs. Samuel stood in the room, feeling helpless. Bennett looked up at him. "I think your own daughter needs your comforting right now, more than Louisa does. I spoke rather harshly to her, and she ran to your bedroom. Tell her I'm sorry and ask her to understand."

Gaines nodded and walked across the hall.

Louisa lay silently, staring at the ceiling. John C. Bennett sat on the side of her bed and leaned across her on one arm, looking at her face. It was ideally formed, a heart-shaped oval ringed by pale hair. Soft cheeks, tiny nose, wide-set eyes. But the eyes had seen things never meant for a child to see, the brain had rejected these things—filed them away for a time when events might trigger their explosion into the conscious mind. What had done this tonight? Something that foolish Rebecca had said? Or was it—could it be **himself**? Something about jealousy. Was this sweet-sad girl, Louisa, carrying a hidden longing—for him? And as he had comforted her in his arms—*that's all I was doing, God knows, merely trying to comfort her*—had he awakened some smouldering ember in her? Or was he reminiscent of her own father? Had her father held her and stroked her that way? He wished he could see inside her mind. But Louisa lay motionless, staring at the ceiling.

Maude Gaines returned, puffing, a spoon and a linen napkin in one hand, a water tumbler in the other. "Thank you," he said. "I am going to give her something that will cause her to sleep. I think it best that she sleep alone tonight. Can Rebecca sleep somewhere else?"

"Oh, of course; we'll fix a place in the parlor."

"That will be best. Thank you, Sister Gaines." He wanted her out of the room, and she did leave, a look of motherly concern on her face. She closed the bedroom door.

"Louisa." He spoke softly to her, his deep voice a caress.

She was silent, staring.

"Louisa," he said, taking her hand in both of his, with great gentleness.

"I hear you," she said, emotionless.

"What you have felt tonight is perfectly natural," he said. "I know what happened and why it happened. Tomorrow I'll explain it to you. But tonight, I want you to sleep. I'm going to give you something to make you sleep."

He poured a small amount of laudanum into the spoon. Then he reached around the back of her head, cradling her hair in the crook of his arm. He offered her the spoon. She hesitated, then opened her lips, only slightly. The silver spoon touched her lips, her lower teeth. He tipped it and the amber fluid drained into her mouth. Reflexively, she lapped at it like a nursing infant, then shuddered and turned her head away.

"Now, drink some water," he said, offering her the tumbler. She drained most of it. With her head still on his arm, Bennett thought she was a remarkably beautiful young woman. So much to live for—so much to give. She would make some man very happy. But only if she could overcome the blight of her memories.

"Are you feeling drowsy?" he asked.

She shut her eyes and nodded.

He put his head closer to hers. "All that happened to you is in the past now," he said. "It is all over."

"I know," she said. "But it keeps coming back. It will always keep coming back. I see it as if it's happening all over again."

"That's only your imagination," Bennett crooned. "Things like that may stay in your imagination for a while, but then they grow fainter and go away."

She shook her head and opened her eyes, looking at him with a defiant expression. "Oh?" she asked. "You mean God can forget?"

What was she talking about? It must be the opium taking effect. "God?" he asked with a smile. "What are you saying?"

"God never forgets," she said, closing her eyes again. "And when I die . . ." She turned her head away from him.

"And when you die . . . what?"

She said nothing for several seconds. Then she turned her head back again, eyes tightly shut. "Then he'll get me," she said. "That's why I want to get it over with now. I might as well get it over with, don't you think?" Her speech was slurred now, the drug taking over.

Bennett was alarmed. He shook her by the shoulder, gently. "Wait, Louisa," he said, forgetting to modulate his voice in its lowest range. "Why would God want to 'get' you?"

"Not God. Satan."

Bennett chuckled. "Now, why would Satan be interested in a lovely girl like you?"

She closed her eyes tighter, as if to force the words out. "Because I killed someone on purpose," she said.

"You killed someone? You?"

"Yes. A man. He put me on his horse and was taking me away, and I bit him to make him let me go, but he wouldn't. So I saw his knife and I took it and I stabbed him. And he fell, and his horse dragged him . . . and he was dead!" She uttered the last words in a wail, and turned her face into her pillow.

So that was it! The reason for her moods, her strange sadness. He had known of her parents' death in the Haun's Mill massacre, but had never known Louisa carried **this** burden. "Who else have you told about this?" he asked.

"Nobody. I was so ashamed. . . ."

"Louisa," he said, "listen to me! You think you're damned, but you're not!"

"Oh yes I am! It says so in the Bible!"

Bennett took her hand again. "You were innocent. I'll bring the prophet here to this very room and he'll tell you . . ."

"No!" Louisa opened her eyes and struggled to sit up. "I won't tell anyone! Oh," she cried, falling again into her pillow and burying her face in it, "I wish I could die!"

Dr. Bennett sat on her bed, holding her hand. He was becoming more concerned. The laudanum should be taking its effect any minute now, but laudanum was unpredictable; too much opium and a patient could lapse into a tormented nightmare. Or, the wine in which the opium was mixed could merely create drowsiness but not sleep. The trick was to compound exactly the correct balance.

At this moment there was a tap on the bedroom door. The doctor leaned over and pulled it open slightly. Maude Gaines stood in the door, puffing slightly from her recent trips up and down the stairs.

"It's Brother Andrew from across the street, Doctor," she said, apologetically.

Bennett was annoyed. "What does he want, did he say?"

"It's about your plans for an election."

Bennett hesitated. It was past the time for a social call, he was thoroughly worn out from the long trip out from Springfield, and he was concerned about Louisa. Still he had the future to consider, the city's—and his own. He was aware that the *Times & Seasons* had printed a flattering editorial calling attention to his mission to the state capitol in Nauvoo's behalf, and that only three days earlier they had printed his letter announcing the signing of the city charter and the permission to form a militia. On the ride from Carthage the driver had shown him unusual respect, commenting that he must be "the man of the hour" in Nauvoo. Yes, he decided, it might be important for him to make himself available to young Sharp, now that he was working at the *Times & Seasons*. "Tell him to make himself comfortable in the parlor," he said, "and I'll be down in a moment."

Maude Gaines departed silently and the doctor looked down at his patient. "Louisa," he said softly. Her eyelids worked, and she appeared to mumble something, but he could see that she was in normal slumber. His eyes feasted on her again for a long moment. He felt the old turmoil. The struggle was beginning again within himself, the aroused male fighting to defeat the professional physician. He had never been strong enough. But that had been before, never under his own roof, and never in Nauvoo. And not since he had taken the vows of the Latter-day Saint Church. Perhaps it was conquerable, he thought. He tenderly drew the covers up to Louisa's chin, blew out the candle by her bedside, and tiptoed out of the room.

As he walked down the stairs, Dr. Bennett switched his mind from the concerns of a physician to those of a consummate politican. Now that Nauvoo would become a city on the first Monday in February, 1841, an election must be held. Many municipal positions needed to be filled, but he was certain of the outcome of only one of them—the mayoralty; he would be chosen. Not only that, but since he had been the chief architect of the plans for the Nauvoo Legion and the University he felt he might well wind up leading the political, military and educational forces of the city—and justifiably, for it had been he, John C. Bennett, who had made it all possible. With great confidence, he strode into the parlor and greeted Andrew Sharp.

"Welcome back, Doctor," Andrew said, pumping his hand warmly.

"Ah, and how good it is to be back. I have lived in many places, but none attracts me as poignantly as Nauvoo. Perhaps that is because I feel that I, in some small way, have had a stake in building this place." He motioned for Andrew to sit down, and then he chose a wing chair by the fireplace and turned it so that the two men faced each other. "How can I help you?"

"Is the charter truly all you hoped for?"

"In every particular. It is one of the most liberal city charters ever designed. But let me emphasize," he said, holding up a cautionary hand, "it is the work of the prophet. His will is behind every part of it."

"Might I see it?"

Bennett hesitated. "I have but one copy of it."

"I can make a perfect copy of its language," Andrew offered eagerly. "And have the original back to you first thing tomorrow morning."

"Oh? And how will you manage that?"

"I developed a sort of writing shortcut," Andrew said. "It's been useful in taking down conversation. It works the same, copying a document or a letter. I'd be very careful, sir."

Bennett thought for a moment and then agreed. "Very well. You shall have the charter before you leave tonight. But now, you indicated you wanted to talk about the election of city officers."

"Yes, sir. How will that be done?"

Bennett was careful to defer to Joseph Smith. "Well, inasmuch as President Smith wants to administer the affairs of the city in a strictly democratic way, I am sure there will be nominations tendered, a public announcement made as to those who are candidates, and then all eligible citizens will vote as they feel to do."

"And will you be a candidate for mayor?"

"If there are sufficient citizens who wish me to serve, yes."

"But what if President Smith were nominated as a candidate also?"

John C. Bennett's eyes darted about the room, finally fixing again on the reporter. "Naturally I would defer to the prophet."

"In affairs of state as well as affairs of the Church?"

"They are one and the same, in Nauvoo."

119

"But that's against the Constitution, isn't it?"

The doctor uncrossed and crossed his legs. "I am sure neither President Smith nor I would do anything which is against the U.S. Constitution."

"But that would be a concern, wouldn't it, Doctor, if Joseph Smith were the mayor as well as the leader of the Church?"

Bennett was now annoyed. "I fail to see where this need concern us at this time. I have no concerns about the President's loyalty to the Constitution. Apparently you have."

"Oh, no, Sir; I'm just trying to understand the situation."

"The situation is very simple: whoever is elected mayor will serve in that capacity. If it should be the prophet, he will continue to be the prophet. If it should be me, I shall continue to be a physician—in addition to being the mayor. Where is the conflict?"

Andrew cleared his throat. "I see. Thanks for explaining it to me."

The doctor smiled and relaxed again. "The confusion you have is natural in a city in which the great preponderance of population is all of one religious persuasion."

"Like Vatican City?"

"No, no; Vatican City is governed exclusive of Italy. Nauvoo is responsible to the laws of the state of Illinois and of the United States of America. It is merely another city, like St. Louis or Springfield. All that is unique here is the composition of its citizens, being nearly all Latter-day Saints."

Andrew admired the clarity of the doctor's thinking. "Now I have it."

"We are both newcomers to the Church, Andrew," Bennett said. "There is much that must be understood."

Suddenly, Andrew recognized an opportunity to take advantage of the doctor's willingness to talk. "There's something else that I don't understand, Doctor, about the Church."

"Oh? And what is that?"

"Well, I've been hearing some things that worry me, and I don't know who to ask."

"What sort of things?"

"About . . . immoral behavior."

Bennett slowly uncrossed his legs again and sat upright in his chair. His eyes made another round trip about the room and returned to Andrew's earnest expression. "Can you be more specific? What kind of immoral behavior?"

Now it was Andrew's turn to be uneasy. "Having . . ."he began, and then swallowed. "Having . . . more than one wife."

"And who, in particular, are you asking about?"

"Uh. . . the prophet."

Bennett's birdlike eyes bored into Andrew's. "Where did you hear this?"

Andrew looked away. "Oh, in Quincy, in Warsaw."

"What are you hearing?"

Andrew squirmed into a more comfortable position. "That, uh . . . Joseph Smith has more than one wife."

The doctor, satisfied that the rumors had nothing to do with his own personal life, leaned back in his chair and tapped his fingertips together. "Well, can you tell me who is making these accusations?"

"No, I can't, Doctor."

"And do you believe them?"

"No, not necessarily; they're only rumors. That's why I'm asking you."

"And being a young man of high moral character, you were concerned lest these rumors be true?" A smile played on his lips.

"That's it, yes sir."

"Very commendable indeed, Brother. Sharp," the doctor said. "You wouldn't want anything to do with a man who would cohabit with more than one woman at a time, would you?" Andrew felt the sting of sarcasm. "Nothing of that sort would ever occur to **you**, for example?" Bennett asked. "You wouldn't be tempted to live that way?"

"I wouldn't know, sir. I was just trying to find out if you knew if Joseph Smith was . . ."

"A bigamist?" The doctor smiled. "I have no doubt his enemies call him that, and worse. Be very careful as to whom you listen to, my friend, and if you wish intelligence of that sort, you should ask President Smith."

Andrew nodded. "I meant no disloyalty, of course."

"Of course. Is there anything else?"

Andrew decided to pursue the opportunity to its fullest. "There happens to be one other thing I've been told about," he said. "Have you ever heard of the 'Danites'?"

Without hesitation, Bennett answered, "Yes, certainly, but not for some time now. What would you like to know about them?"

"Well, what are they?"

"I was given to understand that they were a group of men in the Church who had been given a special calling, as defenders of the faith. I must confess I know almost nothing more about them, except that they were formed in Missouri—I suppose, to help against the mobbers." His eyes narrowed. "Just what are you getting at?"

"I'm a reporter, and I'm new to the Church, Doctor," Andrew explained. "A reporter hears things."

The doctor rose. "In view of the depth of your interest, you should consult someone more expert on these subjects." Bennett was anxious to bring the conversation to a close, now that the subject of his candidacy seemed to be past.

"And I shall," Andrew said. "Now, Doctor, if I might have that city charter, so I can make a copy?"

Bennett had almost forgotten. He considered changing his mind, telling the persistent visitor that he couldn't part with such a vital document, even overnight; but then he thought better of it and shrugged. "I'll get it for you," he said, left the room and crossed the hall to his study, where he removed the heavy brown envelope from his bag and carried it back into the parlor. Handing it to Andrew, he said, "I must have this back first thing in the morning."

The man who had been outside, crouching in the newly-planted shrubbery just under one of the parlor windows, now shrank onto his haunches in the shadows. He was so compact and still that he might have been unseen, even if someone looked directly at him. He waited until Andrew left the street and re-entered the McCann house, and Dr. Bennett extinguished the lamps downstairs. Only then did he slip silently away, to disappear in the chill of the December night.

Chapter 14

Nauvoo was alive with festivities for its first Christmas celebration. The winter had been too fierce and the pioneer residents too busy to plan a city-wide event in 1839, but the phenomenal growth, coupled with the assurance that the city was about to be recognized by the state of Illinois, had lent an optimistic overtone to Christmas, 1840.

Joseph Smith was the chief promoter of the Christmas party. He had decreed that there be a dance, special parties and favors for all the city's children, gifts for every adult, and food enough to fill every stomach. The residents had turned to their larders and juice presses, had shared recipes and organized baking and cooking bees, while cargoes of merchandise from as far away as St. Louis were bought and festively wrapped. Considerable musical talent was recruited from the residents, and impromptu rehearsals were apt to spring up in the harness shop, the mercantile store or in numerous homes.

December 23rd, a Wednesday, was designated Nauvoo Christmas Party night, and by decree from the President of the Church, all work ceased in the city at noon, not to be resumed until Monday, the 28th. It was the longest holiday the Mormons had ever known, and their first of any consequence since arriving in Illinois.

It was a time of reunion. Latter-day Saints living across the Mississippi in Montrose were invited to attend the festivities, as were other members still living in surrounding Illinois communities. Even Gentile participants were selectively invited, including political and journalistic persons considered sympathetic to the Mormons.

The basement office of the *Times & Seasons* was closed at the stroke of noon, and Robert Thompson, Don Carlos Smith and Andrew Sharp stepped out into the thin sunlight, satisfied that the latest edition of the newspaper had caught the optimistic spirit that was in the Nauvoo air. It carried an editorial written by the prophet, announcing the signing of the city charter and the forthcoming election of city officers, now only ten days away. It congratulated the Nauvoo residents on their industry, welcomed newcomers, and prophecied that the city would become the finest in Illinois.

Certainly the signs of progress were everywhere. As the three journalists made for home, they walked through endless scenes of construction, and even on this holiday eve, oxen hauling brick and lumber stood shoulder to shoulder in the streets, their drivers anxious to complete one more load before the Christmas holidays.

At the Law Brothers' store—the polling place in the upcoming election—lively discussions over the candidates for the nine city council positions and four aldermen continued unabated, until boys—dispatched by anxious mothers—ran to the store to call their fathers home to change for the party.

As Andrew broke away from his companions to head up to the McCann house, his pace slackened somewhat. He reflected that this Christmas would be the loneliest one he had ever spent—away from his family, an imposter in a strange town—with no prospect of sharing the company of Louisa Stephens.

He found himself hearing voices from his memory. His mother's: *Friendships are like gardens—they need tending or they wither.* He had let the budding friendship with Louisa starve and die. And then other remembered voices—Angus and William McCann:

I do believe ye've gone sweet on her! Ye can't stop talking about her! And what of it?
Will ye be mentioning her to Jock?
No, I will not, and neither will you if you know what's good for you!

Andrew had puzzled over that overheard remark for these past four months. The three McCann men worked together all day. Had Angus never mentioned Louisa to Jock? Andrew knew her name had never come up at the dinner table. He found himself wondering about that now.

Up from the riverbank property they had bought, Jock, Angus and William walked. The family's wealth never showed on these rugged men, for they were singlehandedly digging a channel with picks and shovels, on property Jock had purchased their second week in Nauvoo. They had obtained land adjacent to the south boundary of the riverboat landing and were laying out the foundation of a shipyard with their own muscle and sweat.

They were similarly attired, in hip-high waders with broad suspenders hung over brawny shoulders. Their coarse shirts were wet with sweat and the lower parts of their bodies were caked in the stinking mud of the riverbed. Every day they arose at dawn and returned at dark, so exhausted they scarcely spoke to one another or to Anne, except in short, labored grunts around the table.

Anne spent her days caring for her nursing baby boy, robust little James, born two months earlier, and when he was not in need of her, she preserved fruit, cooked three huge meals each day, cleaned the dishes and the kitchen three times each day, did a mountain of filthy laundry each evening and hung the clothes out in the back yard to dry. She baked pies and cakes once each week, and ended each day under an oil lamp, sewing clothing for the baby, her brothers and for gifts. She was wispy but not frail. Jock had purchased a set of tiny gold spectacles for her when she had mentioned that she was having a hard time seeing the stitches. These she perched at the end of her petite nose as she sat in a rocker with her sewing basket at her side. That is what Andrew saw every night of the week as he bade the family goodnight before climbing the stairs to his room. Their industriousness made him feel exhausted.

But tonight was different. The McCanns slogged homeward earlier than usual to bathe and prepare for the party. Instead of the silent trek, the Mc-Canns were now talking and laughing as they approached the house, on a tangent from Andrew's own route there. When Angus saw Andrew, he hailed him with a wave and a shout, "Merry Christmas, Andrew!"

Their paths converged a few steps before they passed the home of Dr. Bennett. Andrew glanced at the stately home, decorated for the season with holly and green boughs, and longed to have a little time again with Louisa. Then he studied Angus for any sign that he was sharing these same thoughts, but there was no indication of it. Together, they walked on past the house, and up to their own home, where the McCanns, as usual, went into the back yard where pails of well water awaited them. Here, in a small enclosure made of strips of lath, the men removed their grimy outer garments and scrubbed with the heated water Anne had provided, removing the worst of the soil. They would conclude their bathing indoors.

Andrew went directly to his room where he wrote a few more lines on the dispatch he was preparing to send to Quincy. The experience of his first Mormon party lay ahead of him and he expected this to provide him with the grist he needed to fill out the article.

As he finished his notes and placed them in the drawer, he heard Angus enter the adjacent bedroom. A plan began to form in Andrew's mind. The two had never spoken of Louisa. Tonight might be a good time to establish just where things stood. Andrew wanted to see Louisa, but he had no wish to offend Angus. One man had as much right to her attentions as another, he thought, but there was the question of priority. Who had spoken to her first? To whom had she given encouragement? These seemed important questions to settle before the evening's entertainment began. Andrew knocked on Angus' door. "It's me," he said.

"Come on in," Angus called. Andrew found him pulling his undershirt off over his head. His body was shining wet.

Andrew began with small talk; how had work been, how was the shipyard progressing? Angus, perfectly unabashed, had stripped naked and towelled himself off. Andrew, unaccustomed to nakedness, stood with his back to the room, looking out a window to the house where Louisa lived. At last he came to the point. "I was wondering," he began, "if you're taking Louisa to the dance."

Angus chuckled. "Well, not likely. Seeing that I never learned how."

"But you'll be seeing her at the party?"

A slight hesitation. "I suppose so. Why?"

Andrew turned around now. "Do you like her?"

"Yes, I like her." Angus was pulling on his underwear.

"I mean . . . do you see her a lot?"

Angus laughed again. "See her? And when would I have the time to see anyone, the way Jock's working us? It's up before light and home to supper and bed six days a week and church on Sundays." Andrew thought he heard an edge of bitterness in his voice.

"I've noticed that you have time for little else than work," Andrew commented.

"Aye. Work comes first, everything else comes later, if there's time," Angus said, busily lacing the front of his undershirt. "Why are ye asking? "

"Well, it's because I . . ."

"You've been admiring her your own self?"

Andrew smiled. "That's it. Admiring her. But that's all I've done."

"Aye." The stocky Scot was hauling on fresh trousers, and seemed preoccupied with the project.

"I wanted to ask you about her because I didn't want to interfere." Andrew explained.

"And I appreciate it," Angus said. There was a tension in his silences now, and Andrew had the feeling he was holding himself back from saying more. "Well," Angus said at last, "you're not interfering. I'm afraid there's naught to interfere **with**."

There seemed nothing more to say. "Just thought I'd ask," Andrew said as he moved to the door. "I was thinking of seeing if I could get to know her better at the party, if she's there."

"Aye."

He saw Angus' expression as he left the room. It was a mixture of envy and forced amiability, and it left Andrew unsettled. Living here, among the McCanns, Andrew only wanted to maintain the most cordial relationships. Now he was afraid he had opened a forbidden door. Well, it was every man for himself and the devil take the hindmost, Andrew thought, as he latched his bedroom door and began to change from his work clothes.

The pungent aroma of roasting game filled the Bennett house. Hampers filled with bowls of sweet potatoes, the vanilla and almond scent of rich puddings and the spice of mincemeat pies blended into a symphony that promised lavish dining, and Maude had done it all. Louisa had wandered into the kitchen offering to help, but Maude saw that the girl was still so distracted that she might forget and try to lift hot things without pot holders, so she waved her out of her domain to supervise the children. Rebecca, sad eyes, remained in her room where she continued sewing.

John C. Bennett had been away since mid-morning, attending to matters concerning the well-being of the city, his household had assumed. He would depart with a loaded briefcase crammed with notes on which he had worked until all hours in his study, and the Gaines family and Louisa by unspoken agreement remained quiet and unseen as much as possible, to give the great man as much freedom as possible to pursue the weighty matters which concerned him. On occasion he would share at the dinner table some of the accomplishments he was proudest of that day. But most often, John C. Bennett remained an enigma to his own household, coming and going at all hours, often picked up at his door by a black carriage.

Louisa had delayed preparing her party costume until Maude insisted that she get it ready herself, or she would do it. Still in a languor since her collapse at Dr. Bennett's feet only two days earlier, and not yet fully recovered from the laudanum he had given her, she walked through the house as if in a daze. There was a chill between Louisa and Rebecca now, perpetuated by Rebecca's resentment of the doctor's rebuff and his attentiveness to Louisa. She was jealous, but too well-bred to say anything about it.

Samuel Gaines pulled up in front of the Bennett house in a small horse cart obtained to carry the provender from the kitchen to the party. Elizabeth and Bobby raced out to the cart for a ride, for the games were already underway on a grassy knoll visible in the far distance, and the squeals of the children were audible even down on Sydney street.

Soon the food was loaded and Samuel drove off, promising to return to escort the females to the bower. He traveled up Partridge Street to Knight and turned east, passing wagons being loaded with other party-goers.

The arbor-like clearing among the trees in a grove on the upper edge of town was where the Saints in the Nauvoo stake held their Sunday meetings, but today it was decorated with lanterns, festive bows made of imitation silk, and paper streamers.

There was music in the air, provided by the first of a small group of rustic musicians who had been practicing for the occasion. As the sound of the fiddle, the cornet and the dulcimer drifted across the city below, it acted like a magnet to pull the rest of the population out of doors and into the crisp, sunny December day.

Andrew's room lay downwind of the music and he tucked his *Argus* notes into a hiding place he had fashioned at the back of the desk, then hurried downstairs to join the McCann family.

The younger brothers, Angus and William, were wearing what they wore to church—dark colored tweeds. But Jock had transformed himself into a sight Andrew had never seen before—a Scottish highlander in full dress regalia—his jacket, a tamochanter on his head, and kilts! His great, hairy knees smiled beneath the clan tartan and a plaid was caught at the jacket's epaulettes and was thrown across one broad shoulder. Jock McCann was a striking sight.

The family waited in the parlor for Anne and the baby, and outside stood a hired horse and wagon to transport them.

At last, Anne came down the staircase with baby James in her arms. She was swathed in a deep blue satin gown with lace at the hem, a black velvet waistcoat with a fur-trimmed collar, and a stylish black hat. "Ah, how fine ye look," Jock said, rising. He held the door for her, while William ran out to help the party into the wagon.

They came on foot, they came in carriages and wagons, and most had their arms filled with gaily-wrapped packages. The grove was filling with chattering, laughing people, and Andrew now perceived Mormons from a new perspective. These people knew how to have a good time! Additional musicians joined the ones already playing, and on a bare wood floor assembled for the occasion, a reel was formed. Young and old alike pranced to and fro, bowing and smiling, while the savory smells of food wafted through the crowd. Aproned ladies rushed with plates filled with meats and vegetables, baked goods and jugs of cider and berry juice, pitchers of creamy milk and mountains of biscuits, ladles of gravy, tureens of soup, and locally gathered fruit. Colored lanterns were strung on clothesline rope through the tree branches and a lad with a taper was hoisted to the shoulder of a tall man who stood beneath each lamp as the boy carefully lit them.

The centerpiece of the celebration was a large Christmas tree which sparkled with dozens of tiny candles. Beneath the tree grew a burgeoning jumble of packages, and a pair of young men were assigned the job of seeing to it that none were placed too close to candles on the lower boughs.

Andrew took it all in. He recognized many of the people here as tradespeople he had seen every day in Nauvoo, but he had never seen them under such felicitous circumstances. Their faces were wreathed in smiles. The efforts of daily labor were erased, replaced by laughter and the promise of good food and fellowship. Andrew longed to set it down on paper, and searched through his pockets to find a stub of a pencil. He brought out his ever-present journal and made swift shorthand notes describing the scene.

This done, he set out to find someone to talk to, and discovered Robert Thompson of the *Times & Seasons* talking with Hyrum and his wife and another woman Andrew assumed to be Sister Thompson. He was introduced to the laides as **Brother** Andrew of the *Times & Seasons*. He glided from that group to another where his editor, Don Carlos Smith and his attractive wife, Agnes, were talking in a group around the prophet. Andrew attached himself to this gathering briefly. He enjoyed hearing any of the Smith brothers talk. They each had distinctive voices, but used language so effectively that it fell pleasantly on the ear, and their slight New England accent sounded more intellectual than the flat tones developing in the western lands of Ohio, Indiana and Illinois.

When Joseph Smith's eye fell on Andrew at the outside of the group around him, he smiled and stretched out his arm over the heads of the others. "Brother Sharp, Merry Christmas! Come join us." The others turned to him and smiled. Andrew edged his way into the circle of ten or twelve others. "We were just talking about the big election," Joseph said. "This marks an historic moment for the Church!"

"I'm sure it does," Andrew replied, noncommittally.

"A fully-chartered city with a recognized right to exist, and soon we shall have a militia second to none in the country! Isn't it a fine thing to be among the Saints at a time like this?"

Everyone agreed, but one man spoke up loudly. "There are many of us, President, who think you ought to be mayor, but you're not even running. Why?"

"My preference is for the experience of John C. Bennett. He has a knowledge of politics, and an acceptance in Springfield, which I have not."

"But he isn't one of us, truly," the man replied.

Joseph looked at the man thoughtfully. "Because he hasn't lived on the run or been hunted like an animal, you mean, Brother? These are not necessarily qualifications for high political office. It is time we turned over the affairs of this city to a seasoned politician. I am quite content if the people choose Dr. Bennett to be our mayor."

That seemed to end the discussion. Emma Smith, on the arm of her husband, suggested that the group find partners for a reel, and Andrew turned away. He felt a heavy hand on his shoulder and turned back to find Joseph towering over him, a smile on his face.

"Don Carlos tells me you are doing fine work at the newspaper. I'm delighted you have come to take up residence with us, Brother."

"Thank you," Andrew stammered. The big man squeezed his shoulder slightly and walked away with his wife toward the dance.

Andrew stood for a moment, still feeling the warm spot where the man's grip had touched him. Then, shrugging the feeling off, he began to wander in search of Louisa.

Louisa had tried to beg off, feigning weakness, and had asked to stay at home rather than come to the Christmas party, but Maude Gaines would have none of it. "You're a lass of eighteen and fully a woman now. You're not going to get well by staying at home and feeling sorry for yourself. Now, up!" And she had taken Louisa by the crook of her elbow and half pulled her out of her chair and onto her feet. As Louisa stood facing her, Maude took her face in both of her hands. "I love you like my own," she said, smiling. "And I do know what's best. Come on, now, love."

With forlorn feelings and no hope of a pleasant experience, Louisa dressed in the clothes she had sewn on for so many evenings, now far more festive-looking than her spirits felt. She pulled her long hair into a knot at the back of her head, found a complimentary ribbon and tied it, put on the bonnet Rebecca had given her, and joined the Gaines family in the little horse cart for the ride to the grove.

Rebecca still felt distant toward Louisa and neither girl was inclined to confront the other with an apology or a desire to regain the amiability they had felt before. Maude had seen this and had talked it over with her husband, and both decided that the girls would have to rebuild their earlier relationship at their own speed, so neither one mentioned it to either of the girls.

When they arrived at the party, Rebecca immediately attached herself to a group of other young ladies, and Louisa found an empty spot on a bench, where she sat watching the activity.

The bench she had chosen was the wallflower's row. Here sat the unattached extras to be found at any large social gathering. Some were too fat, some too skinny, some merely plain. By contrast to their pensive appearance,

Louisa was a picture of feminine beauty, but she was so consumed with her thoughts that most of the eligible men who glanced her way looked past her, for all that could be seen of her was an attractive dress and a bonnet which concealed most of her face.

Louisa had been a prisoner of her dispirited mood for so long that it was starting to become her habitual manner. Those who knew her sad history understood; those who knew nothing of it avoided her. Either way, she was lonely but unable to reach out from her shell of despondency, to cry for help. Her breakdown two evenings earlier had only vented a part of her storehouse of unexpressed grief. She still had to deal with the livid scar of stabbing her abductor, and the eternal consequences she feared. With that hopeless dread as background to everything, the antics of the Christmas celebrants and their joyous laughter fell bittersweet on her senses. *They may have something to look forward to,* she thought, *but I have not.*

Trays of food were being circulated, sweetcakes and freshly squeezed cider on trays decorated with holly. As Andrew took one of the small cakes, he suddenly saw Louisa. He had to look twice to be sure it was her. Among all the revelers she had a faraway, wistful look that he recalled she wore the last time he had seen her. On impulse, he seized a second sweetcake and two mugs of cider before the tray passed on, and he walked over to where Louisa was sitting.

She was lost in thought, barely aware that he was standing beside her. "Excuse me," he said. He cleared his throat and said it again. "Excuse me, it is Louisa Stephens, isn't it?"

She looked up into the quizzical eyes of the man who had been on her mind more than she had cared to admit. The straw colored hair, the pleasant, half-shy smile were as she remembered.

"I've brought you something to eat, if it's all right," he said, and she noticed now that both of his hands were full.

"I---I'm really not hungry right now," she said faintly. She saw the disappointment in his face.

"Oh, well, I---" he stammered. "I just thought we could---talk."

There was a space beside her on the bench. "May I sit with you?" he asked.

As if in a trance, Louisa extended her right hand to her side and gathered the taffeta of her spreading skirts closer to her, slowly making room for him. Just as slowly, it seemed to her, he sat down. Apologetically, he said with a laugh, "I can't eat unless you take one of these cider mugs out of my hand."

She saw that this was true, and turned half toward him, reaching for a mug with her left hand. He held it out for her and their hands touched, as they had at the moment of their first meeting, and again she felt the strange thrill she could not name.

"Thank you," she said, and sipped the cool cider.

"Have a frycake," he said. "Back home in Pennsylvania the Dutch make these all the time. Let's see if they're as good as I remember them."

And he took a generous bite from his. "Umm, they are," he said, smiling through a mouthful. He stuck the second cake in front of Louisa. "Try one."

She took it and bit a small piece off. She found nothing exceptional in the flavor of the cake, but she was beginning to be dazzled by the sheer enthusiasm of her companion. He seemed content to concentrate on her, as if he couldn't read her depression. *Could it be*, she wondered, *that I don't look as terrible as I've been feeling?*

"I've been meaning to call on you, but I was able to get a job at the *Times & Seasons* and I've been putting in some long hours."

"Of course."

"I really wanted to come over and introduce myself properly to your folks."

Louisa felt propelled back two years to Haun's Mill. "My parents are dead."

"Oh . . . I---I'm awfully sorry." The pall descended again, and neither Andrew nor Louisa knew how to break through to a more pleasant subject. *Does she just want to be left alone?*

An unattached man was walking past the row of seated damsels. Seeing that Louisa seemed to be sitting lost in her thoughts, and apparently not communicating with Andrew, he sidled up to her. "Care for a dance, Sister?" he asked, with a hopeful grin.

"No, thank you," Louisa sniffed. The grin faded, the man shot a glance at Andrew, and walked away.

"The last time we met," Andrew said to her, "I almost knocked you down. I hope you weren't hurt."

"Oh, no. And I see you have recovered from your injury. What was it . . .?"

"A broken rib, maybe two. Anyway, it's not bothering me now, at all."

"Doctor Bennett will be happy to hear that."

Andrew was stuck again. Maybe she just didn't like him. Maybe his memory of her inviting "perhaps" when he had asked if he might call on her had changed into disinterest because he had failed to follow it up. Yes, that seemed logical. He would try to explain.

"I've been thinking of you a great deal," he began. "I've seen you at Sunday meeting here; I've wanted to talk to you, but I didn't know if I ought to."

Have I been that repelling? she asked herself.

"I mean, a man certainly doesn't want to be too forward, or make a nuisance of himself. I hope I'm not making a nuisance of myself right now," he said with a nervous laugh.

She turned to him and said, "Oh, no—it's not that at all. It's just me."

"I mean, I would understand completely if you didn't want me to call on you, or even sit here and talk with you."

Louisa felt the urgent need to let him know that she was starting to want him to sit and talk with her, but she couldn't find the words.

"You see," Andrew babbled on, "I was a total stranger to everyone in town when I got here, and---"

"So was I."

Andrew paused. "You were? Well," and he laughed again, "that's a coincidence, isn't it?"

"Y-yes," she nodded, trying to smile.

"It can get pretty lonely, can't it?"

"Oh, yes," she said, her heart in her voice for the first time.

"Well, but the thing is," he pursued, "we don't have to be lonely. Not if we don't want to be."

She thought about that. Did she really want the loneliness she felt? Or was it something that was imposed upon her by the knowledge of her eventual doom? Was she punishing herself by not allowing anyone else into her life?

"We only live once," Andrew said, in the mellow wisdom of a twenty-one year old.

"That is true."

"And I think a person should try to get as much out of life as he can. Don't you?"

She consulted her conscience on that one. "Yes," she said, hesitantly.

"Now, take for instance, this broken rib I had," Andrew said, warming to his theory. "I could have just sat around and nursed it for four or five weeks like some people would do, but I said to myself, 'No sir! Get out and get moving! Get working!'"

"And did that help, do you think?"

"Well, I'm completely healed," he said. "But I haven't tested myself on the dancing floor."

She turned to him again. "Oh, I'm afraid I . . ." she began, but then she stopped to realize that he hadn't actually invited her to dance; it was only her heart that had formed the idea of dancing with him. Her color deepened.

"I really must try it to see if I've been made whole again," he said. "Would you help me?" Andrew was surprised at his glibness with this girl. He wondered if she would think him too forward.

"Why, I haven't danced . . ." she tried to think if she had ever danced, although the steps were certainly easy and the movements looked to be child's play.

"Then, will you?" he asked, and boldly took one of her hands, which had been folded in her lap. The touch of her skin, the warmth and softness of her hand, made his heart leap. To Louisa, it was an electric shock, like lightning, which seemed to stun her senses. She felt herself rising, felt herself smiling, felt herself being guided toward the dance with an arm at her back, as Andrew joined the circling, bowing group.

Louisa hadn't made her feet move this fast in months, and the stiffness she felt leaving her seemed to be departing, not from her joints, but from her

132

heart, for it began beating faster and faster and she began to **feel** again, feel a part of life. She found it possible to look on the ruddy face of this young man now, and she found it surprisingly pleasant. He was looking at her, smiling too, as she felt herself smile, and their eyes lingered on each other a moment longer than was necessary. "I can do it!" he cried. "I'm well again," and he laughed at his own joke.

On and on the music played, on and on the dancers danced, with Louisa feeling as if somehow she had graduated from an exhaustingly long term in some kind of prison, and was rejoining life as it was meant to be lived. She was thinking all kinds of thoughts now, thoughts apart from the past. How warm she felt, how the layers of clothing felt on her suddenly active body, how handsome her partner was, how joyous everyone was around her—why, if this is what life can be, this music-filled, laughter-filled celebration with pleasant people on every side—was the dark past only a bad dream? This was reality, and she suddenly knew how she had hungered for it. She threw back her head and laughed, laughed loudly enough that the woman next to her turned and smiled back.

"What is it?" Andrew asked, excitement in his eyes.

"We're both well, I think" she said. "I think we're both well again!"

If all her prayers, pleadings and exhortations, whispered, muttered and tearfully supplicated beneath the covers of her bed or under the angry skies of Mormon Camp, were to have been answered in the affirmative all at once, Louisa could not have felt more joy than she was feeling now. Her radiance had returned, multiplied tenfold—so much so that Maude Gaines, passing by with a load of food for the communal table, nearly dropped an armload of fresh-baked bread at the sight of the flushed and smiling face of Louisa Stephens, on the arm of Andrew Sharp, her head slightly inclined toward his, walking briskly toward the end of the feeding line. Maude stopped in her tracks to watch the couple, then lifted her eyes to the heavens still faintly visible through the treetops, and said aloud, "Saints be praised!" And then, realizing that was an expression from her Catholic past, smiled up again and shook her head.

It simply wasn't done, not unless a couple were married or at least betrothed, but they were doing it: arm-in-arm, in public! And yet there were no stern, reproving looks. Or if there were, neither Andrew nor Louisa were aware of them. They had been chattering to each other, anxious to hear what the other was saying but unable to keep their own voices stilled, in the way that lovers do when they realize that somehow they have at last found each other and there is so much lost time to be regained.

Andrew felt every inch a Mormon, if that's what it took to be a part of this community, a part of Louisa's life. Living a chaste adolescence among well-brought-up boys, his experience with girls had been scant, limited to cotillions rigidly supervised by school authorities. And he was never inclined to the freedoms other men away from home indulged themselves in, once he was on his own and far away from family and friends. No, Andrew was going through the thrill of discovery with every moment he and Louisa spent together, and he found that as they stood in the line where the food was being dished out, neither one wanted to move, if moving meant they might be separated by as much as an inch from the nearness of each other.

Louisa was suddenly aware that someone was saying her name, and she saw as she looked across the serving table that it was Rebecca. Rebecca, a symphony in pale blue and white, was standing right beside Dr. John Cook Bennett, and although he was chatting with some other man as they edged their way sideways through the serving line, Rebecca managed to stand close enough to him to make it appear they were together. "Louisa," she said again, "how are you, dear?"

"Oh, I'm fine, just fine," Louisa replied, and with such enthusiasm that Rebecca looked astonished.

Louisa was suddenly hungry. The food before her looked better than anything she had ever seen in her life, and she piled her plate high with everything she could reach. It was as if all her systems were reborn, for colors now looked more vivid, aromas were spicier, sounds were clearer, and she felt a new awareness of herself.

I'm looking for a place for us to sit," Andrew was saying.

"Oh, what? What did you say?"

"Well, where would you like to eat dinner?"

Tables had been arranged, some improvised from fresh lumber and others had been carried from homes, but it was evident there would never be enough space for the entire population to be seated at once. Someone banging on a pan for quiet had said something, several minutes ago, about those eating first and those eating second, but neither Andrew nor Louisa had heard or understood it. Now they could see there was virtually no seating left for them.

"I have an idea," Andrew said as they reached the end of the feeding line. "Look out there," and he pointed with his free hand to the lines of wagons and carriages which had brought celebrants to the party. "We could sit in one of those," he suggested.

It was a daring thought. An unmarried couple, unchaperoned, in a wagon or buggy was an open invitation to sin and, everybody would think there had been sinful activity, whether there had been or not. "We really oughtn't," Louisa said, with less than full conviction.

"Better than standing up to eat," he said. "I'll bet there are others doing it." He edged toward the line of vehicles, and Louisa walked slightly behind him, reluctant to go, more reluctant to let him leave her side.

Under the darkening sky, a dozen or more horses waited in their traces, tethered to posts. "There's a nice little buggy," Andrew said, pointing with his elbow. Louisa took his arm and they walked to a shiny black carriage. He helped her in under the folding top and then he walked around and climbed in beside her.

The noise seemed far away. From the nearby woods, crickets and frogs provided a backdrop. It was chilly, but the exiles sensed a warmth from each other, and were glad to be together, alone.

Louisa had never tasted food with the subtleties of flavor she enjoyed now. The pinpoints of stars were sharper, the tree branches etched against the twilight sky were more clearly defined than she had ever seen them. All her senses were heightened, and she felt in complete control of them all. She loved the feeling of the springs under the buggy, for when either she or Andrew shifted weight in any way, the entire vehicle trembled slightly, and the patient horse, standing so quietly, would sometimes quiver with the movement. It was as if she and Andrew were suspended in some sanctuary apart from the solid earth, a lily pad in a vast lake, where forces rippled through their bodies and made them one with the movement, not anchored to the ground. It was thrilling to explore the delicacy of her feelings, and she knew the reason she felt them was the presence of Andrew beside her. They were both conventionally and modestly clothed, but Louisa imagined she could feel the heat of his body beside her, through all her layers of cotton and crinoline. And the thought of it made her blush in astonishment at herself, and in shame. What if he read her thoughts? Still, there was magic in the moment, and she savored each passing second as a gourmet savors the most delicate foods, and all her senses relished the experience.

They ate in silence, finally. They ate slowly, occasionally stealing glances at each other and smiling. Andrew felt as he had never felt before, and his heart was racing, thudding against his chest. As eloquent as his thoughts could be, as fluent as his pen had been, now the young journalist could not think of one coherent thing to say, except banal comments on how bright the stars seemed, how pleasant it was for December, or how nice it would be to own a buggy like this. And her responses were just as trivial to her, just as precious to him. Andrew became aware that he was unable to eat any more. Swallowing with great difficulty, he announced that he couldn't finish his plate. "Neither can I," Louisa said gratefully, handing her plate to him. He took their plates and silverware and, hanging on to the seat, leaned far out and set them on the ground beside the buggy.

"Careful, you'll fall," Louisa cried.

"Hang on to me then," Andrew said, feeling himself slipping. She clung to his right arm, her hand locked in his, and helped pull him back into the seat. The momentum carried him into her waiting arms. Their faces brushed, as he turned toward her in the darkness.

"Are you all right?" she whispered.

"Oh, yes," he said, barely breathing. Her eyes, inches from his, glanced at his lips and then back to his own stare. Their lips grazed, then sealed in a moment of sweetness beyond dreams for Louisa, beyond hope for Andrew. There was gentle softness in the kiss, thrilling—promising—and he opened his eyes to her, to find that her eyes were already open, drinking him in with a questioning gaze. Suddenly, the spell was shattered by a lurching of the buggy at the same instant a voice, inches from their ears, called out.

"What are you doing here?"

It was impossible to see who it was in the darkness, but the voice was a treble screech, and the breath exhaled by the intruder was pungently sour with the smell of liquor. Whoever it was, was clinging to Andrew's side of the buggy, and something was prodding Andrew in the shoulder, something very much like the muzzle of a gun. Andrew struck it away, and the intruder was dislodged, falling to the ground on the china plates Andrew had placed there, and their snapping was clearly audible.

He jumped down as the stranger, on his back, was struggling to get up. Andrew called, "Run, Louisa, run to the grove!" And then the intruder was on his feet. "I've been watching you," he said drunkenly, steadying himself on the side of the carriage, "and you're trespassing on the property of Joseph Smith, did you know that?" Andrew could see that he still had the gun and was waving it under his nose.

Louisa started for the grove but only got as far as the horse, when she turned and ran back to stand behind Andrew. "He's got a gun," she gasped. "Andrew, he has a gun!" She shrank behind him, quivering from a terror that was welling up from deep within her. She felt her knees begin to give way and she held her arms out toward Andrew, but she did not reach him. She slumped to the ground. Andrew whirled and saw her lying just behind him, on her back. Then he turned to confront the gunman, but as he did so, the man wheeled and darted away through the other carriages into the blackness of the night. He made no sound as he left, and drunk as he was, his agility was that of a wild animal.

Andrew knelt beside Louisa, terrified that she had fainted, and cradled his arm beneath her head. She regained consciousness almost immediately, and as her eyes flickered open, Andrew fell to his knees on the ground beside her. "Oh, my darling, my darling," he heard himself say, and he covered her face with his kisses. She slipped her arm over his neck, and he gently brought her to her feet, and she clung to him until her head stopped spinning.

"Are you all right now?" he asked.

"I think so," she said. "Are you? Where did he go?"

"He ran when you fainted. Louisa, are you all right?"

She gulped air, felt better, and nodded. "I think so," she repeated.

"Scared?"

"I was. Not any more."

"You scared me. Frightened me to death. I forgot all about his gun. What made you faint? The gun?"

She took several more deep breaths, then thought of her appearance. She brushed the back of her dress several times with her hand, and pulled down her bodice, readjusted her bonnet, then looked at Andrew. "I think," she said, "I had better tell you about me."

Chapter 15

She had told him everything. They walked alone through the empty Nauvoo streets, far from the celebration, Andrew keeping an eye out for the will-o-the-wisp who had surprised them in the buggy, as she recounted how her parents had joined the Mormon Church in Ohio, of how they traveled with groups of other converts until they had found a tiny settlement at Haun's Mill, Missouri, where they hoped to stay long enough to plant and harvest a few crops. Of how, one October afternoon two years earlier, the settlement had been wiped out by a bloodthirsty pack of marauders on horseback. And she determinedly related her kidnaping, the knife, and the grisly outcome. When she had finished, her breath was ragged and her voice had taken on a harried, hopeless demeanor.

"Now what do you think of me?" she asked, not looking at him.

Bolder now, he gently took her by both shoulders and turned her to face him. He had been sickened by her story, told in her determined monotone and half under her breath, as if the telling itself were a catharsis. He visualized every moment she had lived through, and his heart was in his throat as he looked at her fixedly in the pale starlight. She was looking down. He willed her to look up at him, and at last, she did. The question hung in the air, and her eyes held a hopelessness that all but broke his heart.

"What do I think of you?" he asked. "I love you, Louisa."

She continued to look at him. "But you can't."

"Why can't I?"

"Because . . . I'm not fit for you. I'm not fit for any man to love!"

"How can you **say** that?"

"Because of what I did," she said, dropping her voice to a whisper as if the thought itself were too repugnant to give voice to. "I have taken a human life. **On purpose.** Don't you understand that?"

"Then I suppose every soldier in every war is damned, as well?"

Louisa stopped and thought. "But that's different," she said at last. "They are ordered to kill the enemy."

"Is this what the Mormons teach?" he asked, angrily. "That you can't defend yourself if you're about to be raped?"

She looked shocked, and put her hand to his lips. He grabbed it and kissed it. "Louisa, in God's name, don't carry this burden of guilt anymore! No court in the land would convict you for doing what you did!" His voice echoed in the silent street.

She looked at him strangely. "Andrew," she said, "aren't you a Mormon?"

His throat went dry. "What do you mean?"

She stared at him. "The way you said, 'is this what the Mormons teach?' . . . you sounded . . . like one of the . . ."

"Missourians?"

". . . Yes."

Hastily, he recovered his equilibrium. "As I told the McCanns, I guess I never did get very thoroughly trained in Mormonism. There's so much I still don't know. Why, would you believe it, I never even owned a *Book of Mormon*?"

He knew the reply didn't satisfy her, but she seemed willing to drop the subject. She turned away from him and, linking her fingers through his, started walking along the street again. "We'd best be getting back to the party, don't you think?" she said.

"If you like." They turned around and retraced their steps across the empty city. There was a heavy silence between them. Andrew could bear it no longer. "I meant what I said, Louisa," he said. "I knew it as we were dancing. I love you."

She shook her head slowly, as if replying to a thought in her own mind. "I'm sorry," she said at last. "Because right now, I don't know how I feel. Tonight I was happy for the first time in more than two years. I laughed, we danced; I never felt better in my life. But that was because I had forgotten . . ." she paused.

"And you should forget it, forever. Put it out of your mind!"

Her laugh was harsh, cynical. "Of course," she said.

They walked briskly back to the grove, meeting several families who were returning to their homes on the way. There would be talk, Louisa knew, if they were recognized as an unmarried couple, out alone on the dark streets. She slowed her pace and thrust her arm through his, as she had seen married couples do, promenading on Sundays in their finery. She tilted her head up, looked sideways at Andrew, and together they masqueraded into the bower, joining the hundreds of people still there, and there they separated, mingling with others. Andrew was momentarily taken by surprise as she slipped away from him and blended into the crowd. He turned and found her drifting between groups of celebrants, her head held high.

The musicians returned to the stand and presently an old English tune began. A few untiring couples pranced around the floor, but most of the crowd was satisfied to talk and sample the last of the food and drink. Andrew felt lost. Suddenly, a voice nearby called his name. "Mister Sharp? Why, where did you disappear to?" It was an English accent that caught his ear, and he turned to see the Gaines girl, Rebecca, carrying a large earthenware pitcher toward the waiting wagons. "Oh," she said, as if it were an afterthought, "you may carry this out to the cart if you'd be so kind."

He took it, expecting it to be heavy, but it was not. "Thank you," she said. "Ours is the little horse cart, right out there. Well, perhaps I'd better show you. Follow me." And she walked ahead of him. In the dim lantern light he was able to detect a determined sway to her movements which boys had always thought was deliberate. She kept it up until she reached the cart. "Right in here," she said, lifting the lid to a basket. He reached up and placed it inside.

"And have you had a good time, Mister Sharp?" Rebecca asked brightly.

"Yes," Andrew replied. "An exceptionally good time. Have you?"

"Divine," she said. They started back to the party, walking slowly. "You're a writer, I understand," she said, stating it as more of a fact than a question.

"That's right, I am."

"For the *Times & Seasons*?"

"Yes."

"Then no doubt you know we have a correspondent for the Quincy paper living among us."

Startled, Andrew nearly stumbled. "No, I didn't know that."

"Oh, well," Rebecca replied, "I would have thought you would have read all the other papers. It seems there is someone writing for the *Argus* who calls himself 'A Traveler In Nauvoo'."

Andrew felt his mouth go dry. "And you think he lives here?"

"Oh, I don't know anything about it," she said with a toss of her head. "But there was talk tonight—quite a bit of it, in fact—about who it might be." She turned toward him and smiled. "They think it's a newcomer to Nauvoo."

"I see," he said. They had reached the edge of the festivities again.

"Thank you for your help, Brother Sharp," Rebecca said, and hurried into the crowd. Andrew was left with a feeling of alarm. Of course he might have expected that word of his articles in the *Argus* would come to the attention of Nauvoo eventually, but so far he had been far from critical of the Mormons and always accurate in what he had written. How could anyone take offense? The evening was turning out badly and he began to look for Louisa. He had found love, been threatened by a mysterious man with a gun, discovered Louisa's burden of fear—and now Louisa's roommate was all but accusing him of writing secretly for the *Argus*. His mind was filled with concern and the only person he could talk to was someone he dared not confide in—because he feared destroying the fragile relationship begun this night.

He walked through the thinning crowd. Many women were packing leftover food and piling up serving dishes to be taken back to their homes. Louisa didn't seem to be in sight, but the fact that Rebecca was still at the party told him that the Gaines family hadn't started to leave.

The music had stopped, the musicians had departed, and now a group of men with their coats off were dismantling the platform on which the musicians had played, while other men took up the boards that had formed the dance floor. Andrew drifted over to help, and as he approached, he saw Joseph Smith among the workers, gathering planks with the rest. It seemed to

Andrew an opportune time to report the gunman episode, confess that he and Louisa had sat in his carriage to eat, and at the same time, confront Joseph with Louisa's fears and get his response. "President Smith," Andrew said, "may I talk with you for a moment?"

Joseph turned to Andrew as he straightened up with a great armload of planking. "Of course," he said smilingly, "and perhaps you'll walk with me to the lumber wagon with some of these boards." Andrew gathered as many as he could carry, and proceeded beside the prophet toward the wagon, which awaited with a lantern on its tailgate.

Andrew cleared his throat nervously. "I wanted to confess," he began, "that I—that a friend and I sat in your buggy to eat our supper this evening."

Joseph chuckled. "You are perfectly welcome to it, Brother Sharp."

"But a strange thing happened," Andrew continued, and told him of the brief encounter with the drunken man with the gun. Joseph obviously was troubled by the report. "Did you get a look at him?" he asked.

"No, it was too dark to see. He ran off like a deer."

"A large man?"

"Oh, no; I would say, rather small. Quite a bit shorter than I am."

The prophet said nothing, but rubbed his chin. "Well," he said finally, "alcohol does terrible things. I am distressed to hear of this, Brother Sharp, but thank God the ruffian didn't harm you or your friend." They had deposited the planks in the lumber wagon and were starting back for another load. Andrew cleared his throat again. "There was one other thing, President," he said.

Joseph paused. "Yes?"

"My friend is concerned about a point of doctrine: will a member of the Church be damned for killing someone in self-defense?"

The prophet studied Andrew, a serious look on his face. "I would have to know more," he said.

"Well, there is a young woman who was kidnaped by one of the Missourians who raided Haun's Mill. He hauled her up onto his horse and was riding off with her. She grabbed the man's knife and stabbed him with it. He fell off his horse and was killed."

Joseph considered this information, and then placed a hand on Andrew's shoulder. "Please have the young women come and see me about this," he said. "It is a serious matter, and I should rather interview her directly."

Alarmed, Andrew said, "But what else could she do? All around her there was murder and rape going on . . ."

"Just have her come to see me, Brother Sharp," the prophet said, "and the matter will be put right. I cannot interpret through a second party, nor should you."

"I'll tell her," he said. "Thank you, President Smith."

"You are welcome," he said, and strode away. Andrew was not much relieved. He needed to find Louisa and see that she got her explanation from the prophet as soon as possible. But the problem now was finding her. He hurried back to search for her, and met Samuel and Maude Gaines coming out of the grove, each with a sleeping child in their arms. He stopped them and asked if they knew where Louisa was. They looked surprised. "We thought she was still with you," Maude said.

"Would she be with your daughter, Rebecca?" Andrew asked.

"No, I think not," Maude replied. "Doctor Bennett has asked her to ride home with him." There was a hint of pride in her voice.

"Perhaps I should help look for her," Samuel offered. Andrew thanked him but declined. "I'm sure I can find her," he said.

"Well, Merry Christmas, Brother Sharp," Maude said as he hurried away. "And do come visit us during the holidays."

They must not know how she feels, Andrew thought to himself, *or they wouldn't be so unconcerned.* He hurried through the rapidly emptying clearing, looking for any sign of her. Only the black forest of trees and undergrowth remained to be searched, and there was little chance of finding anyone in there if they wanted to go unseen. The candles on the Christmas tree were being snuffed out, diminishing what little light was left to see by in the bower. He was becoming frantic. He wanted to shout her name, to organize a posse, to do **something** to find her, but he didn't dare, for the embarrassment it would cause them both—and in her precarious emotional state, who knew what she might do?

Terrifying thoughts ran through his mind as he strode among the last of the party goers. What if she encountered a wild animal? What if that drunk with the pistol saw her? What if she had fainted again and was lying somewhere now, as the night grew colder? And it **was** getting colder. He could see his breath and he shivered, thinking of Louisa in her light pink dress.

She had carried her head high as she parted from Andrew in the bower; it was easier to keep the tears from flowing when she did. In one evening her life had reopened as a perishing flower opens when at last it receives moisture, and she had known for a few minutes the feeling of sensual pleasure a woman in love was entitled to. But then the old spectre had come back to remind her of her bondage to Haun's Mill, where she had left her innocent soul. If only she could escape, start life over again without the stain of the blood on her hands, but still find Andrew and be worthy of him! But she knew, as she found herself walking north, away from the festivities in the clearing, that the only escape would be death. And then her eternal punishment would begin.

She walked along Wells Street buried in her desperate gloom until she ran out of street and had to turn west. The road was nothing more than a track, but it led downhill and there seemed to be no turning back for her now, as she stumbled through the darkness. Barely aware of the chilling night, she hugged her arms together and went blindly on, toward the Mississippi.

Over and over, her mind brought her memories of the time spent with

Andrew. She saw his face, felt his lips, heard his voice confessing his love for her, and then she felt her heart, locked with remorse, shut itself away from him—the one man she wanted to share it with.

She was unaware of the passage of time. She had no idea of where she had walked. Suddenly she realized the track had become only a path and the path was now surrounded by the spikes of tall, dead cattails and the smell of swamp was everywhere. Furthermore, she had been bitten repeatedly by tiny insects which rose in clouds as she passed. Then she heard the river.

It was just ahead of her, but she hadn't seen it because of the miasmal cloud of mist which was rising as the warmer temperature of the water struck the cold air. But now she heard the whispering, sighing torrent as it slid eternally past the shore—rustling higher on its banks because of fall rains which had swollen its tributaries to the north. The ground beneath Louisa's slippers felt marshy, but the relentless tempo of her downhill march carried her several steps closer before she came to realize that there was danger underfoot. The fog was rising all around her, and she was completely and frighteningly lost. She turned, wide-eyed with fright, looking for a tree, a house—any landmark she might recognize. But only the branches of dead trees appeared through the swirling mist, arms held mockingly to the heavens. She turned around and tried to find the trail that had brought her here, walked a few yards, then saw there was no trail left. She turned back, hoping to find where she had lost the track, and found to her horror that she was virtually at the water's edge again. She leaped back and fell over something unseen behind her, landing on her side in the dank brush. Inches from her face, a snake, disturbed in its den, slithered past her eyes and she screamed. The screaming and sharp intake of breath brought a cloud of tiny insects into her mouth, and she screamed again, getting to her feet, and ran blindly through the swaying skeletons of cattails and brush, heading she knew not where.

"I owe you my profoundest apologies," Dr. John C. Bennett said, as he sat beside Rebecca Gaines in the carriage taking them home. "At the moment I was concerned only for the welfare of our friend, Louisa, and I was unforgivably rude. Please say you'll somehow overlook it."

Rebecca nearly swooned at the pleasure of his rich voice, spoken now in a near whisper at her ear, realizing her most cherished imaginings. He had spoken to **her**, asked **her** to ride home with him, now was begging **her** to forgive him! She had nursed her wounded pride in ill humor ever since Wednesday night when Louisa had fainted and she and the doctor had carried her to the bed. It had seemed to Rebecca then that the doctor had more than a professional interest in Louisa, and had been so curt in dismissing Rebecca when all she had wanted was to help—that she had gone into her parents' bedroom and given vent to wails of anger, hurt and embarrassment, mixed with the frustration that came from realizing that this worldly man thought nothing of her, had even called her a "silly girl," hadn't even noticed that she was in fact a woman, with a woman's desires and a woman's allure.

142

Now, though, she was able to enjoy that sublimest of sensations, a man's tender petition for forgiveness. "Why, of course, doctor," she said, demurely.

"Thank you, Rebecca," he said, and he placed his gloved hand over hers. A tingle ran up her spine. "One of the penalties of leadership is a lack of time for the pleasant associations one might otherwise seek," he said. She thrilled at his choice of words.

"But I must say that these few months with you and your family sharing my home have given me much pleasure. **Much** pleasure!" With the last words, he gave her hand an additional squeeze, an intimacy that set Rebecca's blood racing to her face.

"Thank you," she whispered. "For us too, I'm sure."

He gave a great sigh and turned toward her, matter-of-factly. "Look here," he asked, "are you terribly worn out or might we take a few minutes to talk? I have some important things on my mind."

Important things? Talk? Rebecca would have postponed heaven and the celestial kingdom to hear John Cook Bennett talk to her! "No, not tired at all," she said, trying to sound bright.

"Good," he said, clucked to the horse, and turned right at Hotchkiss, and proceeded slowly west. "What I wanted to say would best be said in private, and our household," he chuckled benignly, "is a busy beehive most of the time."

Rebecca sat up tall on the carriage seat, waiting.

"The next few months—years, actually—will be extremely busy for me. I have reason to believe that the good people of Nauvoo will, in their wisdom, ask me to be their mayor. This will involve incredible responsibilities. There is the Nauvoo Legion to organize; I must do it. President Smith will hold a commander's rank in it, but he knows nothing of military matters and he expects me to advise him as his major general. I already hold the rank of brigadier general in the Illinois Dragoons, as you know."

"Oh, yes, I know."

"Well; I am drafting plans for a Nauvoo University. This involves selecting regents, professors, designing a curriculum . . . the work of a university chancellor, in fact. And all these things must of necessity come into play all at once, so to speak. Brother Joseph is anxious for Nauvoo to grow as fast as it can, and as well as it can. And I have given him my pledge to do all in my power to see this city into greatness."

Rebecca, spellbound, merely nodded and watched his darting eyes as he spoke.

"But there is another part to a man's life," he said, his voice softer now, a throaty huskiness in it. "Apart from all his, and my medical practice, of course, there must be some time left for the Inner Man. Do you know what I mean?"

He had turned to look intimately at her, the meaning inescapable in his voice and eyes. Rebecca nodded hesitantly.

"I must declare myself," he said. "I am thirty-six. I am in excellent health, in the very prime of my vigor, you might say; I have property and considerable influence here and elsewhere, and a classical education. I know the law and I know medicine. But there is one thing, one part of my life, which my responsibilities in serving others have denied me." He now took both her hands in his. "And I think you know what that is."

He was so close to her, he spoke only in a deep whisper, and Rebecca was almost hysterically impatient to hear him continue.

"I have no one close to me," he said. "No wife waiting for me in the evening. No children playing at my feet. No one to carry on my name." He seemed suddenly overcome, and turned his head away.

Rebecca's mind whirled. Was this a proposal she was hearing? Why else would he be telling her these intimate, personal thoughts? The carriage jolted slightly as its wheels passed over a rut in the street, jouncing her shoulder into his bicep. He turned back to her, an earnest expression in his eyes. "Rebecca," he said, "I require a giving, loving woman. A woman willing to bear my children, a woman capable in all ways of returning the affection I so earnestly desire—**need**—to express. A woman patient enough to endure long absences at times when my presence is required in other quarters. **And**," he said with emphasis, "a woman mature and faithful enough to the Restored Gospel to welcome the revelation, when it is announced, of the principles of Celestial Marriage."

It **was** a proposal! He was asking her to become Mrs. John C. Bennett! The natural rhythm of her heart seemed to palpitate, her eyes fixed his in a glassy stare. Marriage! It was the only word she heard, the only word she responded to.

"May I ask your father for your hand?" he said, tenderly.

Rebecca felt she was in a dream. In her wildest fancies she had conjured up intimacies with Bennett which were never so bold, never so fulfilling, as this moment of reality was now! "Yes," she breathed, "Yes, ask him! Oh, Doctor Bennett!" Impulsively she threw her arms around him and kissed him so energetically that he was nearly thrown off balance. He dropped the reins and held her as tightly as she held him, and when their lips separated at last and she pressed her cheek against his, he opened his eyes and looked out at the night, smiling knowingly to himself.

Chapter 16

Orrin Porter Rockwell had scavenged enough food from the tables at the grove to satisfy even his prodigious appetite. He had never let Joseph out of his sight for longer than a few seconds, yet had managed to complete the emptying of a complete pint bottle of corn whiskey and had cleaned the two pans of food he had provided himself by purloining plates left on benches while their owners danced.

In one of his circuits of the bower he had seen the couple stroll away from the rest of the celebrants, out toward the line of carriages and wagons, and to his surprise and anger they had mounted Joseph's own black carriage as if it were some public taxi! He had crept up behind it and sat directly under the body of the buggy, where he could hear every word they said. And what sparking was going on! He had grinned and lifted his head so that his good left ear was pressed against the floorboard. Love-sick calf that he was, the man was being a perfect gentleman, he had to give him that.

He had awaited the inevitable first kiss, and decided that at that moment he would break upon the couple, providing them the maximum embarrassment and confusion. But he hadn't counted on his victim's reaction. This young Sharp fellow had struck out at him and caused him to lose his balance on the step of the buggy, and he had fallen, hurting his back on something on the ground. He had longed to use the Pepperbox on him, but Joseph had repeatedly warned him about that. So when the girl seemed to swoon and the Sharp fellow had whirled, defiant, it had seemed to Orrin best to depart, which he did, on silent moccasined feet.

He chuckled to himself now as he left the hut down near Joseph's house, to go out and use the privy. He enjoyed the astonished look on Andrew's face, the shock in the girl's eyes. Pretty girl, a ripe looking girl. Too bad for her to get tangled up with a number like Sharp.

This new reporter asked too many questions about things that shouldn't concern him—plural wives and the Danites. For another, he was smooth. He didn't have the rough edges that Mormons developed from undergoing years of privation and persecution. He had learned to read sign from the Indians and faces from his own father, and the face and hands of Andrew Sharp bore no signs whatsoever of sacrifice, hard work and privation. To Rockwell, that augured no good for Sharp. And so he collected a mental dossier of information about him, as he had done for so many years on others who might prove to be enemies of his beloved friend, Joseph Smith. One day he would assemble what he had learned, and use it in the protection of his dearest friend, one of the only ones he had ever had.

He sat with the door to the small outhouse propped open, looking across the river. When he rose, he felt clearer-headed, and thought about going upriver a ways to select something for his breakfast in the morning. There was a cache of negligently guarded hens in a coop on Cutler Street, which had provided him with eggs for months. Living hand-to-mouth as he was obliged to at present, it seemed only fair to Orrin that Nauvoo's henhouses be available to his appetite in return for keeping the city safe from marauders. He decided to stalk silently up and purloin a few eggs.

He didn't like roads, so he kept to back fences and alley ways, walking in the soft grass that didn't make sounds beneath his moccasins. He proceeded on up the road, noting that a buggy was standing still in the middle of empty Hotchkiss Street. Curious, he circled and came up behind it, noting it was a hired rig from the livery stable. The voice from within instantly identified one occupant as Dr. Bennett. Grinning, Rockwell padded up silently and crept beneath it.

Fancy words, fancy words, thought Rockwell. The man could charm the skin off a snake. Well, tonight he would have his way with another girl and under other circumstances it would have been a pleasure to have listened to the proceedings, but Rockwell was single-purposed and, having decided on eggs, eggs it would be. He backed out from under the buggy and circled far to the east, remaining low, until he was out of sight.

When the targeted henhouse appeared, it was wreathed in the fog coming off the river, which was all to the benefit of the poacher who now approached it downwind, careful not to arouse the troop of neighborhood dogs. They might sniff out a 'coon or a fox, Orrin thought, but never would they catch old O.P.

Skillfully he navigated until he was within an arm's reach of the desired aperture in the henhouse. He knew exactly where the setting hens nested, and he snaked his arm in just above the straw.

Suddenly in the night, there was a scream, far off, piercing the silence. Rockwell froze. Then, another scream, and even with but one good ear he had managed already to locate the source. It was north and west, toward the river, two to three thousand feet away, and it was a woman in trouble—probably hurt. And, although he had promised himself eggs, some other impulse within him overruled, and he started off at a dead run. Someone hurt? Someone dead? He belonged there and it was more important than his breakfast. The dogs awoke, grumbling, breaking into howls and alarmed barks as he leapt almost unseen barriers as he dashed through the fog. He would steal some eggs later; now, he had to steal a lantern.

Andrew hadn't known where to turn for help. There was no police force in Nauvoo to initiate a search, only the volunteers—most of whom had tired themselves out at the Christmas party and no doubt were snug in their beds. But he was desperate, and so he went to the only source of help he knew, Jock McCann. He ran the entire distance back to the McCann house, hoping to find Jock had not yet retired for the night, for they had left the party some time before Andrew had discovered Louisa missing.

Dashing to the door, he flung it open and ran panting into the house and up the stairs, hoping to see a glimmer of lamp light under one of the bedroom doors—but there was none. He tapped on Angus' door and stood, chest heaving, waiting for a response. He knocked again, and called Angus' name.

"Yes, what is it?" Angus said, drugged with sleep.

Quickly, Andrew opened the door and poured out the problem. In a moment, Angus came awake and sprang out of bed. "Good heavens, man," he said, pulling on his trousers, "how long has she been gone?"

Andrew wore no watch but he estimated it had been two hours since she had drifted away from him at the party; a good two hours, maybe more.

"And there's something else that worries me," Andrew added. "There's someone out there with a pistol; we were sitting in the prophet's buggy having supper and he leaped up on the step and pointed it at us!"

Angus paused long enough to ask if Andrew had gotten a look at him.

"No, but I've heard the voice somewhere, I'm sure of it," Andrew said.

"Do ye still have that pistol your brother gave you?"

"Yes."

"Ye best bring it," Angus said grimly. "Now, go wake up William and I'll get Jock and some lanterns."

In five more minutes, the McCann men were in the hired wagon and racing for the grove. It was arranged that each man would go a separate way from the bower where Louisa had last been seen, and would give a shout if he saw anything or needed help. Pulling up to the glen where the party had been held, Jock assigned William to go north, Angus south, himself east, and Andrew west. They split up and hurried off into the night, lanterns bobbing.

It was close to two a.m. Andrew plodded along, heading toward the river. In the distance he heard dogs barking.

Louisa had lost all sense of direction, and her panic was such that she was no longer directing her actions, but mechanically plowing through the menacing brush until stopped by a thorn bush or tree, then abandoning that direction to set off randomly in another. Her dress was torn, she had lost her bonnet, her gloves and arms were raked with hundreds of scratches, her cheeks were flecked with insect bites and dirt, and she continued the choking sobs which had begun when she had fallen backwards and seen the snake. Her slippers, hose and leggings were soaked with moisture from the marshy ground, and the temperature continued to fall, so that she was growing almost numb with cold. She had experienced the same detachment from reality that she had felt at Haun's Mill, where the enormity of the calamity she found herself in seemed beyond belief. She hadn't thought of calling for help because part of her brain refused to believe that all this was really happening.

Her wandering and thrashing were gradually growing faint, and more indefinite. She vaguely knew that she was weakening, succumbing to the damp cold, and now, almost unbelievingly, came to the realization that she might die. She remembered bitterly that night, just that week, when she had said she wanted to die. How ironic, she thought, that this wish of all wishes was now to be granted her! On the night she found the love she had dreamed of, she dies! Alone, lost within only a few miles, surely, of Andrew! She found herself sitting in the heavy underbrush, exhausted, cold, numb. She curled up and almost consciously resigned herself to the brambles, insects, and mist, waiting for death to come. As she lay, her breath growing shallower, she heard a strangely comforting sound of dogs barking in the distance.

Running low and stopping to listen, Orrin Porter Rockwell followed rabbit trails, dog trails and shortcuts known only to the wild inhabitants of the old city of Commerce to reach the area where he knew the screams had come from. His instincts soon proved him right. He loped along, scanning the ground a few feet before each footfall, pausing, searching, sniffing, and continuing.

He was looking for anything foreign to the wild growth of the neighborhood, anything a person might leave behind, and presently his eye caught sight of a patch of foreign color, something gay and artificial in a morass of mossy browns and ochre. The lantern sputtered. He held it closer. It was something pink. He picked up Louisa's bonnet.

He rose, cupped his hands around his mouth, and called, "Haloo, haloo," to the four points of the compass, and then waited, breathlessly, for a response.

In Louisa's weakened condition, the spark of life burnt lower. She lay gasping, trying to raise her head, trying to take in enough wind to call back, but she couldn't do it.

Andrew heard the call, far to his right. He thought it might be William, and he called back, "Haloo! Did you find her?"

Orrin Rockwell swore and muttered out loud, "Shut your face, whoever you are, and let the woman answer!" He called again now, and held his lantern high.

Andrew's heart lept. He saw a lantern swinging in the distance and he felt sure Louisa had been found. He plunged into underbrush and became enmeshed in thorn bushes, but ripped free and plowed on toward the light.

Louisa could hear the sound of brush breaking and she forced herself into a sitting position again. From a great distance she heard a man calling her name.

Andrew paused every few feet and called, "Louisa" at the top of his voice. The other voice was still now and the lantern was no longer visible.

Rockwell knew who else was searching for the woman and he decided to try to signal him to come and join him, else he would continue making so much noise, thrashing around in the underbrush, that nobody would ever hear the weak voice of a woman if she did try to call out. He raised his lantern again and swung it.

Andrew made for the light, and got to within ten yards of it before he saw the same man he had seen earlier that evening with a gun in his hands. "Rockwell!" he gasped.

The short man stood in a dim circle of light from his lantern. Andrew made his way to him. "Have you found her?" he asked.

"No, and not much chance of it with you crashing around out here," Rockwell said in disgust. "Now, walk beside me with your lantern high and keep **quiet!**"

No mention of their confrontation earlier in the evening, no explanation of why he was here now; well, Andrew felt grateful that the strange little bodyguard was willing to help. They started forward, looking in every direction.

Seated now, Louisa found she was having less difficulty in breathing, and she began to try to call for help. Her first attempts were nothing but vapor exhaled from her tired lungs into a cloud of condensation in the cold air; she kept trying until she began to feel in danger of fainting with the expulsion of so much oxygen, but she still hadn't made any real sound.

"What was she doing out this far in the first place?" Orrin Rockwell asked.

"I don't know," Andrew replied. "She was so upset by your coming at us with a gun . . ."

"I'm here to protect the prophet and keep order," Rockwell snapped. "You or nobody else has the right to use the prophet's carriage. Now shut up!"

The two men plodded carefully onward.

From where she sat, Louisa could watch the two lanterns move across her field of vision, and she knew she would have to stand up, somehow, to attract their attention. Painfully, every muscle shaking, she got to her feet, and with every ounce of effort she could muster, she called, "Here I am!"

The lanterns stopped. Both men shielded their eyes and stared into the darkness. It was Rockwell who spotted her. "I have her," he cried, and plunged off to his right, Andrew following immediately behind. In a few seconds, Louisa was in his arms.

"Anybody else hunting for her?" Rockwell asked.

"Jock McCann and his brothers. We have a wagon."

"We'd best signal them we've found her."

"I'll do that," Andrew said, bringing out his gun and firing it into the air. As the report echoed across the landscape, Rockwell stared at him with interest. "So you have a gun, do you!" he said. "What would a newspaper man need with a gun like that?"

"It was given to me by . . ." Andrew suddenly couldn't remember whether he had told Louisa he had a brother or not. ". . . a friend," he concluded, lamely.

Within minutes, the rescuers were reunited, Louisa was taken quickly to the Bennett household, and she was turned over to the care of Maude Gaines.

The McCanns put their wagon and horse away once more, Orrin Porter Rockwell slipped away in search of breakfast, and Andrew remained downstairs in the Bennett house. Maude busied herself upstairs with Louisa, but she came to the head of the stairs and loudly whispered Andrew's name.

"Louisa said for me to tell you thank you and good night. She apologizes for all the trouble she's been, and she hopes you'll call on her in the morning."

Andrew was delighted. "Tell her I'll be here before she's awake," he said with a smile. Maude paused in the upstairs hall.

"Brother Sharp, it's well past two-thirty, and Dr. Bennett and Rebecca aren't home yet. You didn't happen to see any sign of his carriage, did you?"

Andrew told her he hadn't. She thanked him and disappeared into Louisa's room.

As Andrew prepared to let himself out the front door, he heard a horse in the street and looked out to see the carriage stop in front of the Bennett house. He stepped back into the parlor and waited until he heard the front door unlatch and open. John C. Bennett was first into the hallway, and then he assisted Rebecca in. He turned, pushed the door gently shut, and enveloped Rebecca in his arms. Andrew was astonished, and stood rooted to the rug in the center of the parlor. When at last the embrace was through, the couple walked silently into the entry hall. Andrew dared not make a move. Dr. Bennett had nearly walked beyond the hallway door to the parlor, when he happened to turn and look into the room, and there he saw Andrew. He recoiled as if he had been whipped. With one arm he thrust Rebecca away from him, and then he whirled and stormed into the parlor. "What, may I ask, are you doing, skulking in my house?" he demanded.

"I---I was just seeing Louisa home. She's been missing for half the night and . . ."

"It looks to me as if you were spying! Is that your reason for being here, sir? To spy on citizens?"

Andrew spread his hands in dismay. "I was just leaving when you drove up. I thought I'd wait and speak with you, sir, but when you stepped inside the door I . . . I didn't want to disturb you!"

The doctor seemed to gain control of his temper and he grudgingly accepted the explanation. "I see, I see," he said. "Well, it is very late indeed and I won't keep you longer."

Andrew hurried to the door and let himself out. As he tried to close the door he felt something tugging on it from the other side. Into the darkness beside him stepped Dr. Bennett. He then eased the door shut behind them. "Look here, Brother Sharp," he said in a low voice, "I'm quite sure you misunderstood what you saw just now. That's why I was so short with you."

"Misunderstood, sir?"

"Well—you see, I feel very warmly toward Rebecca; like the daughter I never had, you might say. And she is an impulsive girl. Her . . . her kiss was merely out of gratitude. I'm sure you understand, don't you?"

"Why, of course, doctor."

"Excellent. Well, good night again." He let himself back into his house and left Andrew to muse over the strange climax to a tumultuous evening as he walked slowly back to the McCann's.

Excitement ran high in Nauvoo during the ensuing week, as the city prepared for its first election of civic officers. When the polls opened at the Law brothers' store, a long line of residents had already queued up to cast their ballots. There were many positions to fill on the city council and four aldermen to select, and competition among some of the candidates had been lively. But nobody had filed against John C. Bennett for the top office—mayor of the city.

Andrew, as a reporter for the *Times & Seasons*, was watching the election closely. The prophet and Emma had appeared early to cast their ballot, and were immediately surrounded by a throng of admirers, each wanting to shake hands and have a word with him. Equally as popular with the women, but considerably more reserved, was Emma, attired that morning in a plain but attractive mauve outfit, prim black leather shoes peeking from beneath the hems of her long skirts, a starched neckpiece of glistening white setting off her smooth olive complexion. Joseph wore the frock coat he usually wore when speaking at Sabbath meetings.

It had been determined that most of the votes were in long before noon, and the stewards began their count in the back room of the store. John C. Bennett had modestly stayed away from the polling place, other than to cast his ballot at about ten a.m.

By nightfall, Bennett had been elected mayor, and as he had suspected, the vote was nearly unanimous; he had had no write-in opposition and nearly everyone who voted at all had signified that they wanted him for their first mayor.

It would take several days for the entire state to collect its ballots and count them, but in Illinois there were few surprises; Thomas Carlin was returned to office. Across the Mississippi in Missouri, however, the fates had again turned against Lilburn W. Boggs, who was defeated by Thomas Reynolds after he had served four years as governor. Boggs considered himself largely a victim of the bad publicity poured out on Missouri in Washington D.C. by the Mormons, and his desire for vengeance burned brighter than ever as he and his family packed their belongings for the move back to Independence, where he would resume his occupation as a merchant while planning his next entrance into state politics.

Andrew studied the complexion of the Nauvoo election returns carefully. At home in his room, he thoughtfully composed the next dispatch for the *Argus*. It was evident that the population of Nauvoo sought Joseph Smith's opinion before forming their own. At supper that evening, he had spoken of that with the McCanns.

"Would you have preferred the prophet to be the mayor?" he had asked Jock.

"No, I wouldn't," Jock had replied. Seeing Andrew's surprise, he continued, "President Smith made it plain that he felt Doctor Bennett was the better man for the job, and that's good enough for me."

"Well," Anne put in, "the prophet is busy enough as it is, heaven knows, without having to be mayor as well."

William said, "He'll be the general of the Nauvoo Legion and he does have to have some time to himself. No wonder he doesn't want the job of mayor."

But Jock overruled the family. "That all may be true," he said, "but the prophet is a prophet of God, and if he supports a man in an office, then that's who I shall support."

Andrew had to add his question: "Then the prophet cannot be mistaken—ever?"

Jock glowered at him. "Read that book I gave ye," he said in a menacing voice. "And then see if ye can ask that question!"

A DISPATCH FROM A TRAVELER IN NAUVOO
January 4, 1841

A New City Rises On The Mississippi; Nauvoo Buries Her Past

Those journeying north from the Principal Cities along the River will recognize a great change in the community named "Nauvoo" by Jos. Smith, Jr., the prophet, seer and revelator of the Mormon Church., as this settlement has now received a most beneficient Charter from the Illinois Legislature, which was signed into law on December 16th last.

On Saturday, January 2nd, 1841, a majority of the eligible citizens of Nauvoo selected a Mayor, nine City Councilmen, and four Aldermen. The populace selected the well-known physician and educator, Dr. John Cook Bennett as their mayor, and the following day the popular Dr. Bennett delivered a brief inaugural address, in which he made sweeping proposals for Civic improvement.

Among these propositions was the abolition of tippling houses within the city limits, the establishment of a municipal force of men-at-arms known as the Nauvoo Legion, and that a University be organized.

It is estimated that some two-thousand citizens witnessed the swearing-in ceremony, which was also attended by the prophet Jos. Smith and his Council of Twelve Apostles.

Not mentioned in the speechifying were the grevious hardships suffered by numerous Mormons on their way to this new haven, nor the charges still at large against Jos. Smith and some of his confederates; nor was there mention of the fact that nearly one-half of the original settlers of Nauvoo have perished from the ague, despite Mr. Smith's valiant attempts to save them through the laying-on of hands.

Despite the setbacks and the overfilled graveyard, the new City of Nauvoo bids fair to become a power to be reckoned with amongst the communities along the Mississippi, and indeed, throughout this region of the Nation.

Chapter 17

Snow blanketed Nauvoo through the first ten days of 1841, and more was falling. The white blanket covered the rich black farmlands, clung to the trees, covered the raw diggings and half-finished houses and absolved the eyesores of dirt-floor cabins down by the river as it graced the finer homes completed uptown on the slopes.

In the home of John C. Bennett, Louisa had lain sick since Christmas, suffering from the chills and fever of the ague. Around the corner in the Mc-Cann household, Andrew had suffered with her, discouraged from visiting her as often as he had wanted to by Doctor Bennett, who had said he believed in isolating swamp fever patients and accordingly had ordered Rebecca to move her bedclothes downstairs to his study, where, he said, she would be less likely to become infected with the fever. It also made her considerably more accessible to his own ministrations, a fact which Rebecca appreciated as much as he. Rebecca's parents, unaware of the new relationship, saw nothing unusual about the arrangement. Nor did Rebecca, who had abided by Bennett's insistance that they keep their engagement strictly secret for the time being, in order, as Bennett had explained it, to permit him to direct all his energies toward setting up the new city affairs and those of the Nauvoo Legion and the University.

Of one thing, Andrew was immensely relieved. On Christmas day, when he would have certainly been forgiven for remaining with his own family, President Joseph Smith and his brother Don Carlos called on Louisa. Andrew had poured out his concern to Don, who was fast becoming a surrogate older brother to Andrew, and that evening the prophet and Don Carlos surprised the Bennett household by appearing there, asking not for a conference with the doctor, but a private audience with his sick boarder upstairs. Bennett had hoped to remain in the bedroom with them, but the prophet had asked for privacy. Bennett felt a tremor of fear. What could the girl report to Joseph? Nothing, probably, he told himself, and went back downstairs.

Joseph and Don Carlos had spent fully an hour with her, Louisa told Andrew some time later when she was much improved, and in that time she had grown to know that her actions at Haun's Mill were not only not a sin, but in Mormon understanding were honorable. Joseph patiently explained to her that she had had every reason to expect that she would be raped, very possibly killed—as had been a number of innocent women and children, that dark day—and that under those circumstances she was certainly justified in trying to free herself from a similar fate. "I can assure you, Sister," he had said, "you are not under condemnation by man or God. You must go on and make a good life for youself, free from the slightest fear of that judgment which the Savior will pronounce upon us all. The Church is proud to have you," he had said, "and Jesus Christ is still your kind and loving Elder Brother."

Before they left, Joseph and Don Carlos had placed their hands on her head and pronounced that she was healed from that moment and would regain all her natural strength and health. They had left her weeping with relief and gratitude, and the next thing she asked for was Andrew.

On their way out of the house, the two brothers seemed to have their customary calm confidence about them. John C. Bennett saw no indication that Louisa might have reported to them anything detrimental about affairs she had heard of in the Bennett household—for he was now living in agitation that his impulsive new lover, Rebecca, might have already confided in Louisa, and that Louisa might have relayed such news to the prophet. But all seemed normal, and Joseph and Don Carlos stepped into the parlor where the rest of the household was grouped around the Christmas tree, to wish them the greetings of the season.

Louisa later testified before a Sabbath meeting in the grove that she felt a drenching warmth pass through her body from the hands laid on her head and knew that she was being healed. Later that night she had risen from her bed and, while still weak, knew the exulting feeling of being cleansed of all possible evil.

What she did not share with the Nauvoo stake at that Sabbath meeting was the fact that, ten minutes after the prophet left her bedroom, Andrew Sharp was there, kneeling by her bed, kissing her brow which was still warm. He sought to kiss her lips, but she forbade him, worried that he might come down with the ague himself. He protested mildly, pointing out that he and Don Carlos worked side by side in the damp basement of the *Times & Seasons* and were still healthy, but so as not to exercise her, he agreed. They talked quietly of the miraculous way in which Joseph had healed her spirit as well as her body, and then their conversation turned to the future. Haltingly, Andrew repeated his confession of love for her and said he hoped she would feel the same for him. And Louisa, freed now from the weight of guilt that had prevented her from accepting his love, wept with joy as she gripped his hands and told him that she was deeply, everlastingly in love with him.

They talked until late, each rehearsing their movements of the night of the party after they had been separated. Louisa wanted to know everything Andrew had done since she had seen him last, and what he planned to do until she could be with him again, and he itemized his activities in great detail, excepting one thing: still that night, Christmas night, he would have to write notes for an *Argus* dispatch. As he realized how forthright Louisa had been with him in disclosing her life and sharing her experiences, he felt again the shame of having to hide from her the other half of his work—and the fact that he was posing as a Mormon. He could see now how much a part of her life the Church was, and how she relied upon it for support and guidance. He felt cheap and ashamed that he wasn't able to be as frank with her as she had been with him. He had walked home that night, overjoyed at the seemingly miraculous recovery in Louisa—but dismayed that she could believe it had been brought about by a man who called himself a prophet. He was interested in Joseph Smith, fascinated by the man's magnetism, his seemingly boundless confidence, and warmed by his apparent friendship . . . but in his heart lay insurmountable doubts that Joseph was anything more than just another religious entrepreneur.

The packet boat had made its way through the swirling snow to dock at Nauvoo. The countryside now lay under more than a foot of snow, and the pilot had not expected to find anyone waiting at the Nauvoo dock, in the wind-whipped somber afternoon, but there stood a man, waving an envelope. Groaning, he steered to the left and stood up in the stern of the boat. "Stand by for a line," he yelled, and heaved the ice-stiff line out as the boat grazed the dock. The man was a landlubber for sure, the pilot saw, in the awkward way he grabbed for the line, and the unsure way he had of twisting it around a bollard sticking up out of the frozen bank. The boat snubbed against the line, creaking and complaining, and then halted. "I got no freight for Nauvoo," the bearded pilot said.

"Will you take this to Quincy?" Andrew Sharp asked him.

As he accepted the envelope and the coins, the pilot now saw that this was the same man who had appeared periodically since the end of the previous summer, always handing him an envelope addressed to someone at general delivery in Quincy. "Always do," the pilot said.

"It has to be in his hands no later than Wednesday the sixth," Andrew said.

"What's today, January fourth, ain't it?" the pilot asked. Andrew nodded. "It'll be there waitin'," the pilot assured him. Why did this young fellow always seem to be so tom-fool anxious about his letter? Why didn't he use the U.S. Mails like everyone else? He flipped the letter over and glanced at the address. Yes, as before, to just one name: **Ketchum**. It sure beat all, he thought, why a man would spend a quarter of a dollar just to mail someone his diary, or whatever you call it, for that was all he could make out of the other little letters the man had sent. He wondered if there was something more interesting in this one. Well, he'd open it up and find out before he got down to Quincy.

Andrew unlooped the line and tossed it back to the pilot and the boat cut out into the sluggish river, resuming its' two-mile-per-hour course southward. The pilot bundled up again back at the tiller, then removed the letter from his jacket and, taking a knife, slit it where it had been sealed, unfolded the two pages inside, and began to read.

"Oh, this makes my blood boil," Louisa said as she put down a copy of the *Argus*.

Maude looked up from her potato peeling. She had taken to bringing a basket of work upstairs to Louisa's room while she visited, since the doctor had suggested Louisa keep herself isolated from the rest of the family until all traces of weakness had left her, and so Louisa, on this Tuesday afternoon, January 11th, 1841, had her company for an hour. The youngsters were in the tiny one-room school down the street, and Samuel, of course, was at work. Rebecca was feeling out of sorts and was keeping to the former study of Dr. Bennett, covered with a quilt, reading. "What have you found in there that makes you say that?" Maude asked.

"Oh, there's a regular article in every issue that's written by someone they call 'A Traveler In Nauvoo,' and he doesn't sign his name. And no wonder. Listen to how he talks about the prophet: 'Not mentioned in the speechifying were the grevious hardships suffered by numerous Mormons on their way to this new haven, nor the charges still at large against Joseph Smith and some of his confederates . . .'!"

Maude looked vexed. "Who would write that sort of thing?" she asked.

Louisa read further, and then cried, "Ooh! Listen to this: 'nor was there mention of the fact that nearly one-half of the original settlers of Nauvoo have perished from the ague, despite **Mister** Smith's valiant attempts to save them through the laying-on of hands.' Well," Louisa said, "I'd like to tell whoever wrote that about my recovery and see what he has to say about that!"

At that moment, a tap was heard on the half-open bedroom door, and Andrew stood there, hat in hand. "Rebecca said it was all right if I came up."

Maude picked up her potatoes. "I'll just see how supper's coming," she smiled at Andrew as she left the room.

Louisa held out her arms and Andrew sat on her bed and kissed her. "I love you," he said softly.

"And I love you," Louisa replied.

Andrew looked down at the bed, where the latest *Argus* reposed. "Oh, you've been reading the *Argus*," he said.

"Yes, but I'm going to give it up!"

"Why?"

"Because they print trash like this column by 'A Traveler In Nauvoo'! Rebecca thinks it's someone who lives here and is spying on us!"

Andrew saw the paper open to the article he had most recently sent in. His own copy of the newspaper was under his bed, at home. "What's wrong with the article?" he asked.

"Well, he insulted the prophet," she said indignantly, and read him the reference to the charges still outstanding against Joseph Smith.

"But it's true, there still are charges against him in Missouri, aren't there?" Andrew asked.

"They're all lies, darling," Louisa said. "Everybody knows that."

"Maybe every Mormon does, but that will have to be proven in a court of law. Until that happens, the fact that there are charges is . . . a fact.''

Louisa put the paper down and looked at Andrew with exasperation. "You sound as if you're siding with the Gentiles!"

"I'm not siding with anybody, Louisa," Andrew said. "A good reporter doesn't take sides, he reports facts—as he sees them."

"Well, whoever's writing this in the *Argus* is certainly no friend of ours," she said.

Andrew was silent for a moment. "That's not necessarily true, Louisa," he said softly. "Don't you remember how you used to feel about the Mormons before you joined the Church?"

"No, because I never even heard of the Mormons before Ma and Pa started talking about them, and then I was baptized."

"You mean, you never thought about them before you became one?"

She hesitated, thinking. "No, I guess I never did." She pulled the blankets up to her chin and drew up her knees beneath them. "What about you? You joined the Church a full grown man, so you must have had lots of time to think about it."

"Well, it was pretty fast, I'll tell you. I still don't know that I understand much about the Church."

"But Brother McCann gave you a *Book of Mormon* for Christmas. Are you reading it?"

Andrew couldn't lie to her any further. "I haven't had time to begin yet," he said. "But I will, I promise. Anyway," he said, changing the subject, "I've been reading some of those *Argus* articles and I think the reporter is pretty truthful. At least, he tries to be accurate."

"You sound as if you admire him."

"No, no, I don't admire him. Let's just say I . . . I can understand him. Being a reporter myself, that is."

Louisa, still in a half pout, snuggled down in the bed. "I think tomorrow Dr. Bennett will tell me I can get up and stay up. Will you come and see me?"

"Always."

"I love you, Andrew. Even if you are a reporter."

Andrew had a stricken look on his face for an instant, causing Louisa to smile at him and say, "I would love you no matter who or what you were."

He looked at her soberly. "I hope that's true," he said.

Despite the cold winter weather and the large number of sufferers still plagued with swamp fever, the early months of 1841 in Nauvoo were remarkable for their progress. Preparations were made for a survey of a canal through the city to a point two miles east of the river, where a huge reservoir would be built. All remaining hardwood within the city boundaries was to be cut and the final undrained part of the city trenched to allow spring water to run down to the river, instead of filtering through the upland causing marshes and swamp fever.

Industry began to thrive; more streets were paved, and the *Times &*

Seasons was able to report that the prophet had received a revelation pertaining to the building of a hotel to house commercial travelers, who were expected in great numbers as soon as the weather warmed.

But of greatest interest to Andrew was the organization of the Nauvoo Legion. Long before the ground thawed, men of almost all ages could be found outside in the streets and on vacant land, drilling in military close-order marching. Some had uniforms of a sort, but practically all of them had arms—not muskets, the common type of weapon throughout most of the United States—but rifles, the most coveted firearm of that generation. These had been shipped in and stored against the hour when the Legion had its charter and could train in the open. But recruiting had started long before, and hundreds of Mormon men eagerly spent hours after supper and before bedtime, learning to become soldiers, to defend their families and homes against marauders.

Don Carlos was so enthusiastic about the formation of the Legion that he could speak of little else as he, Robert Thompson and Andrew chatted during their workdays. Don Carlos had been a commissioned officer in the Hancock County Militia and the precision of the military drills, the horsemanship and the finery of the officers' parade uniforms appealed to him. He found Andrew less enthusiastic. "Where's your patriotism, Brother?" he had asked him on the day that the printing order for a bulletin arrived from the First Presidency.

Andrew studied the language of the bulletin. "Every able bodied man in Nauvoo must join the Legion?"

"Of course! It's an honor, and the training will be good for them!"

Andrew kept his thoughts to himself. He was getting deeper and deeper in the affairs of Mormonism, and felt he was in danger of losing his perspective. Still, from what better vantage point could he view the activities of the Church and its leader than from deep within one of Joseph Smith's favorite organizations?

"We shall train until we are the finest crack troops in all America," Joseph Smith said, "and then we shall perform demonstrations for our Gentile neighbors and show them what the Saints can do!"

Sitting on a stool, John C. Bennett agreed. The fitting for their uniforms in the tailor shop of William Onyx was taking much longer than Bennett had hoped but the prophet seemed to be enjoying himself in the tall mirror. It reflected a striking picture: a contemporary U.S. Army uniform of high black boots, striped parade trousers, a vivid blue coat heavy with golden epaulets, and piping and braid, worn with an air of nobility by this man, better than six feet tall, whose costume was topped off by a plumed hat and an ornate sword.

Bennett, however, had designed a slight variation on the General's uniform for himself. It was so heavily decorated with gold piping and braid and devices made of gold embroidery that he glittered as he moved. "What an inspiration for the men," Bennett said. Onyx, the tailor, busied himself around the prophet until he was certain his uniform fitted him perfectly. At last he stepped back and clasped his hands together under his chin, almost as if in prayer. "I think it's perfect, President," he said.

"I do too," Joseph replied. "Brother Bennett, you're next."

Onyx began fussing with the ornamentation on Bennett's breast, requiring the tailor to bend over continuously, due to Bennett's small stature. Observing this, Joseph handed Onyx the low stool on which Bennett had been sitting, and said, "Brother Bennett, why don't you stand up on this so Brother Onyx won't have to bend over?" Miffed, Bennett did so and the tailor continued his work.

"The tailor reached for the insignia of rank which would be sewn to the epaulets. "Now, which is the correct number of stars for you, Doctor?" he asked.

"General," Bennett corrected him. "Two stars for a Major General; General Smith has three."

"Yes, Will," Joseph told the tailor, "this humble New England farmer has become the highest-ranking military officer in the United States!"

It was true; not since George Washington had there been a man holding the rank of Lieutenant General, and although the rank placed him in charge of the Nauvoo Legion only, it had been authorized, as had Bennett's, by the governor of Illinois, which was sufficient to enable Smith and Bennett to call themselves "General."

In the door stepped Porter Rockwell. Immediately, Joseph saw that his friend required a private word with him, so the two stepped into the small field behind the tailor shop. Bennett could see them through the back window, but he couldn't hear what they were saying. It was obvious, however, that Rockwell was giving Joseph some information which shocked the prophet. He had stepped back in astonishment when Rockwell had said something, and then put his hand on the small man's shoulder, as was his custom when wanting a sincere answer, and Rockwell was wagging his head in affirmation. The prophet ran his hand over the back of his neck and walked around in a circle, obviously agitated.

"Stand still, please, for just a moment, General," Onyx said with a mouthful of pins. Reluctantly, Bennett turned away from the window, a deep fear beginning in his bowels. What had Rockwell found out about him? What was he telling Joseph?

When he next was able to steal a glance through the window, he saw that the two men were now walking toward the fence at the rear of the lot, and were standing by the privy. The faithful little bodyguard was listening intently as Joseph stood over him and spoke rapidly, punctuating his speech with short, choppy gestures. Bennett, in his short acquaintance with Joseph Smith, had learned to recognize those mannerisms—they meant he was holding in a ferocious anger. At last, Joseph dismissed Rockwell and the small man hurdled the back fence and made his way off behind lots, as

Joseph, hands behind his back and head down, stalked slowly back into the tailor shop. He closed the door quietly and sat in a chair, chin on clasped hands, a morose and detached expression on his face.

"Is there anything wrong, President?" Bennett asked.

Joseph looked up with an intent expression. "Yes," he said, but returned to his thoughts and said no more. Bennett trembled in rising panic. There's no question about it, he thought, he's been told something about **me**! Everyone knew Porter Rockwell was Joseph's spy, and that Joseph trusted him above anyone else in the Church. For a moment Bennett considered dismissing the tailor and begging Joseph to tell him what he had heard, then and there, but he realized that to do that might be to invite a disaster which could yet be forestalled. He decided to wait and watch and listen.

Finally, Onyx, the tailor, said he was finished, and held up the long mirror so that Bennett could admire himself, but by now Bennett was thoroughly out of the mood. He feared that Joseph had lost confidence in him, and if he ever fell out of favor with such a powerful man, he knew his position and reputation—possibly his very safety and freedom—would be in jeopardy. He couldn't wait to get out on the street with the prophet and try to find out what was troubling him.

When the two men had changed to their civilian clothes and had left the shop with their uniforms boxed under their arms, John C. Bennett spoke to the brooding prophet, whose long strides down Main Street forced Bennett to skip four or five steps to keep up with him.

"President, if you consider me the friend I believe myself to be, will you tell me what's concerning you? I have never seen you so troubled!"

Joseph waited for so long to answer him, that Bennett feared his silence was an accusation in itself, but finally he said, "I have had some bad news, and I fear it will bring trouble."

Fearfully, Bennett asked, "What news?"

Continuing to look straight ahead, Joseph said grimly, "Someone I trusted appears to be unworthy of that trust."

He knows, Rockwell found out, Bennett thought. "Can you be sure your information is correct?" he asked at last.

"My information from this source is never wrong," Joseph said.

Bennett's mind, long accustomed to framing precise phrases in difficult situations, now presented him with a direction to follow which might probe to the source of the matter without admitting his complicity in any immoral activity. "Is this something I should be concerned about as mayor?" he asked.

"Very possibly," Joseph said.

What kind of an answer was that? Bennett frantically tried to recall what Rockwell might have seen or heard. The other night in the carriage with Rebecca? Or had Rebecca herself been talking? Or might it go back much farther than that? To Ohio? *Oh, please, God, don't let him find out about Ohio!*

161

"Jospeh, I am terribly distressed to see you concerned like this," Bennett said, putting his hand on Joseph's arm. "Can you not confide in me so that I can be of help?"

"No," he said, shaking his head sadly. "Others are involved, and I shall say no more."

Others? What others? His heart sank. *It must be Rebecca. If not, it must be . . . who? There have been so many!*

"I will leave you here," the prophet said, and turned abruptly down Sydney Street, leaving the newly-elected mayor standing at the corner, wishing he were dead.

Andrew retired to his bedroom to add a few lines to the dispatch he was preparing to send to Quincy. He lighted the lamp and placed it on the desk, then pulled open the drawer to reach for the paper, and froze with shock. His pistol, which he had kept at the front of the drawer, was nowhere in sight. He pulled the drawer all the way out and saw that it was gone. He frantically got down on his knees under the desk and felt everywhere, but there was no pistol.

His notebook was gone too, and with it, the notes for the *Argus*!

He stood in the middle of the small room, holding his hands to his head, wondering what to do next. Someone had robbed him. Well, in Nauvoo that was ridiculously easy to do, since—as Jock had discovered on the day they arrived—nobody kept locks on their doors. He tried to enumerate the obvious suspects. One of the McCanns? They were the most obvious. Anne cleaned his room and would have had plenty of opportunity to open the desk and find the gun and the notebook. If she had, she would have gone straight to Jock. But if not Jock or Anne, would it be Angus or William McCann? He trusted them implicitly and couldn't imagine either of them rummaging through somebody else's belongings.

Well then, if nobody in this house, who? There was plenty of whispering going on about Mormon thievery, but most of it from dissidents who were falling away from the Church, or from outsiders who were sworn enemies of it. Could it have been a passing burglar? And then he thought of Orrin Porter Rockwell. Rockwell was the only other person in Nauvoo who knew he had the pistol. He had even questioned him about it.

Nevertheless, he brought the subject up with the family at breakfast the following morning, but made no progress. Anne hadn't seen the gun, and Jock, William, and Angus hadn't seen it since the night of the search for Louisa, and none of them fancied firearms anyway. As for the notebook, they looked annoyed that he would suggest any of them would care to handle anyone else's property.

Well, that left Orrin Porter Rockwell. Angered, Andrew decided to confront the little man and tell him he wanted his property back.

On his way down to the *Times & Seasons*, Andrew scoured his memory for anything he had written in his cryptic code to himself that might be con-

sidered damning, and couldn't think of anything in the notes that a *Times &
Seasons* reporter might not have written.

When he reached the basement press, he saw Don Carlos already there,
stripped to the waist despite the damp cold, turning out a printing job.

"You're at it awfully early, aren't you?" he asked. "You warm
enough?"

Don Carlos looked up as Andrew came down the ladder. His face was
gray and his eyes wore a haggard redness Andrew had seen all too often in
Nauvoo. "Don!" he cried. "What's wrong with you?"

"The fever," he said. "I'm burning up, but we have to get these hand-
bills out. I thought I'd work as long as I could and then go home."

There was a printing order locked into the press, and after long practice,
Andrew could glance at the tray and read the type even though it was revers-
ed. It was about the recent Missouri elections, and it seemed to be a violent
message denouncing Lilburn W. Boggs. Andrew picked up one of the wet
copies. "Who wrote this?" he asked.

"Mayor Bennett," Don Carlos replied, as he pulled down the handle to
make another copy. Scanning it to the bottom, Andrew saw that the tirade
was signed, "Joab, General in Israel."

"Joab?" Andrew remarked.

"It's Bennett, believe me," Don Carlos said wearily, pulling the handle
again.

"Here, let me take over," Andrew said, and for once Don Carlos relin-
quished the labor without protest. "How many more to make?"

"Five-hundred and thirty," he said, picking up his shirt. He coughed a
wracking dry series of coughs that all but doubled him up with pain. Andrew
was concerned for the man. He had grown to have a strong affection for him
and he had grown to count on his unfailing humor—it was one of the things
that helped Andrew through laborious days such as the one he now had
ahead of him. He hated to work the press alone in the "Pit" as they called it.
Don Carlos put on his coat and reached for his muffler, when Andrew
blurted out what he had discovered in his room the night before.

"Robbed?" Don Carlos said in surprise. "Are you sure?"

"Yes, and I think I know who did it. Orrin Porter Rockwell."

Instead of registering more surprise, Don Carlos looked away, eyes
hooded. "What are you going to do about it?"

"I wanted to ask your advice."

Don Carlos coughed again, wrapped his muffler around his throat and
shook his head as if to clear it. "I wouldn't advise your facing him with your
suspicions," he said. "Port is a violent man."

"There were notes stolen, too," Andrew said. "Even if he kept the
pistol, the notes couldn't possibly be of any use to him. They were in a sort of
code I use. You know, my short-hand."

"Just use discretion. In fact, suppose I speak to him about it?"

That was what Andrew wanted to hear. "But you're too sick," he said.

"I'll stop by and see if he's at home on my way," he said, and climbed the old ladder and was gone. Andrew heard him in another coughing spasm as he stepped out into the swirling frozen air above.

It was long past dark, and several hours after his normal quitting-time, that Andrew Sharp pulled the door closed on the print shop and walked, drugged with fatigue, up the Water Street hill toward home. Robert Thompson had come to work at the shop, but he, too, had evidently contracted the chills and fever, so it fell to Andrew either to labor alone or shut up shop, and he felt he had no right to close the office. As a result, between laboring down in the pit on the handbill order, and taking new business upstairs at the counter, he reckoned it must have been at least half-past eight in the evening before he was able to start for home.

As he turned north on Granger to walk up to Sydney Street, he saw the carriage of Dr. J. F. Weld clattering up the hill, fast. He knew the doctor's old horse was on its last legs and that the doctor was sparing her all he could, so he assumed this was an emergency. He quickened his pace to see if he could see where the carriage was going, and to his surprise and mounting fear, he saw it stopped in front of the Bennett house. Andrew broke into a run and dashed the remaining two blocks. Before he reached the front door, he could hear Rebecca wailing in anguish inside. Forgetting himself, he hammered on the front door and then let himself in, fearing the worst for Louisa. Samuel, a nightshirt tucked into his trousers, met him in the hallway.

"Is it Louisa?" Andrew gasped.

"No, it's Doctor Bennett!"

Then his eyes shifted to the open door to the doctor's study. Andrew looked in. In the dim lamplight he could see Dr. Weld bending over someone on the couch. The smell of vomit was souring the air, and at that moment Maude Gaines hurried down the hall from the well, with a bucket of water in her hand. "Go fetch another," she whispered to Samuel, and then, recognizing Andrew in the house, she shook her head. "It's terrible," she said, and hurried into the study.

Andrew looked in. He wanted desperately to be with Louisa, but he knew as a reporter he should follow this story. He slipped into the room and stood inconspicuously in a corner where he could see John C. Bennett.

He was lying on the couch, bedclothes draped over him, a chamber pot on the floor near his head. He was alive, moaning in utter agony, his face a twisted mask of pain.

"Doctor, you must tell me how much you took," Dr. Weld was saying, insistently.

Bennett stopped his moaning long enough to gasp, "I want to die, leave me alone!"

"Do you know how to give an enema?" Dr. Weld asked Maude.

"Of course I do."

"Well, I'm going to try that. Help me haul his trousers off."

She went for his trouser buttons, and Bennett howled in protest, but shortly the trousers were around his knees and the sturdy Dr. Weld had turned the writhing man over onto his stomach. His cries were now muffled in the upholstering, as the doctor and Mrs. Gaines prepared the enema from powders Dr. Weld had brought in his bag. Andrew slipped back out into the hallway. He could still hear Rebecca sobbing, and he realized she was upstairs. He took the stairs two at a time, and found her in the bedroom she had shared with Louisa, curled on her bed, her head in Louisa's arms.

In a few moments, the story came out. Rebecca had been helping wash dishes after supper and had heard the front door close. Expecting Dr. Bennett, she excused herself to go to him—(Andrew had raised his eyebrows at this but a look from Louisa stilled him)—and she found he had gone into his study and had closed the door. Unlike the McCann house, which had no locks on its inside doors, the study did have a lock and he had locked it. Rebecca tried to speak with him but all she heard inside was a whimpering noise. Alarmed, she ran for her father, who got a key and pushed the other one out of the keyhole, unlocked the door, and saw Dr. Bennett gasping for breath in a chair, a small vial of liquid marked "poison" clutched in his hand.

"You mean, the man tried to kill himself?" Andrew asked, incredulously.

"It seems that way," Louisa said, answering for Rebecca, who was still completely engulfed in tears.

"But why?"

Louisa shook her head sadly. Andrew stood there, trying to make sense of it. The most popular man in Nauvoo, just elected mayor, respected and depended upon . . . a suicide? And why, apart from her emotionalism, did this affect Rebecca so profoundly? As Louisa followed his silent train of thought with her eyes, she waited until the truth suggested itself to him and he looked at her questioningly. "Are they . . . ?"

Louisa put a finger to her lips and nodded sympathetically. Then she lifted the sobbing girl off her breast. "Rebecca," she said, "you really must stop this, now. If he pulls through, he will need your strength—all our strength," she corrected herself. "And if he shouldn't . . . crying won't help. It only weakens you."

Rebecca sniffed and tried to stop the sobbing. She seemed unaware that Andrew was in the room. She said, "I want to be with him," and climbed off the bed.

"Do you think that's such a good idea?" Louisa asked.

"I don't care," Rebecca replied vaguely, and she walked out to the stairs and hurried down them.

"Where were you when this happened?" Andrew asked Louisa.

"Up here, still following doctor's orders! What a terrible thing for anyone to do, especially him!"

"He must have been terribly distraught to try to kill himself."

"Oh, I don't mean just that," Louisa said. "I mean, for him to do what he's done to Rebecca! She just told me everything, in the last ten minutes!"

"Can you tell me?"

"If I do, you must honor this as a confidence and never repeat it," Louisa said.

"I promise." He sat on the edge of her bed. Louisa's long lashes hooded her eyes. "It isn't very pleasant," she began.

Andrew watched her forming in her mind a delicate way to tell him what he had begun to suspect already. "The night of the Christmas party," she said, "when Dr. Bennett took Rebecca home in his buggy, he proposed to her and made love to her."

"No!"

"He's told her that they can't tell her parents yet, because he's going to be so busy with everything he's doing that he won't have time for a wife for a while . . ."

". . . But he would have time for a mistress?"

Louisa looked up, shame in her glance, and down again. "Yes, that's what it amounts to."

"That poor girl!"

"Andrew, what kind of a man is Dr. Bennett? Why, he must be twice her age, and he's so suave and sophisticated and she's such a child . . ."

"Do you think what he tried to do tonight has anything to do with Rebecca?"

"She thinks so. She thinks he loves her so much that he can't live without her. And she thinks she's responsible for his trying to kill himself because earlier she wouldn't let him . . . have his way with her."

"The man's insane."

"I'm beginning to think so."

Andrew rose and walked agitatedly around the room. "I don't like the idea of your living under the same roof with a man like that, you or Bobby—or any of the family, for that matter."

"Shhh!" Louisa cautioned. "We'd better not talk any more now."

Andrew was content to spend several more minutes alone with Louisa. They were in no mood for the intimate conversation they usually had each evening after Legion drill, when they would spend a few minutes in the parlor before Andrew hurried back home to bed. Now they said little, shocked by what they had learned that night.

Downstairs, they heard the resonant voice and the whistling sibilance of Joseph Smith. Andrew kissed Louisa and hurried downstairs in time to see Maude step out of the study with Dr. Weld, and the prophet step in and close the door. Andrew asked the doctor, "Will he live?"

Dr. Weld shrugged. "If I could be sure how much he took, I could tell you," he said. "But I think we've flushed his system well enough that he'll pull through. He's in much less pain now, and I've given him a sedative." Then, to Maude, he said, "I want you to look in on him throughout the night and have someone stand by to run and get me if he gets worse.''

Andrew would have given a month's pay from both newspapers to be on the other side of Dr. Bennett's study door at that moment. As it was, all he could do was ask Dr. Weld one more question. "Do you know what he swallowed?"

"Arsenic," he said.

Joseph pulled a chair beside the sofa. The waxen face of John C. Bennett, taut with the recent agony, showed no sign of recognition. "Brother Bennett," Joseph said softly. "It is Joseph."

Quietly, without opening his eyes, Bennett said, "I know."

"Why did you do this?"

"Because I wanted to die."

"Taking one's own life is a mortal sin."

"But I have committed worse, far worse."

Joseph was silent for a full thirty seconds. Then he took one of Bennett's hands in his own. "I know," he said.

Bennett began to weep, hot tears squeezed from under his clenched eyelids.

"But your sins are forgiven you."

It took several moments for the words to reach him, but when they did, Bennett chanced opening one eye, then both. "Oh, Brother Joseph," he whispered, grimacing through his tears, "when I knew that my sinful past had been disclosed to you, this afternoon, I . . ."

"This afternoon?"

"When that Rockwell man talked to you . . ."

"That was on another matter entirely. No, Doctor," Joseph smiled, "I've known your past for several months. But I also know that you have been cleansed through baptism in the Church of Jesus Christ, and that a repentant soul can be made whole again."

Bennett looked at Joseph now for the first time, and through his flowing eyes, a look of pure adoration grew. "Do you mean to say that you accepted me, supported me, honored me as you did . . . knowing about my . . . past life?"

Joseph nodded, still smiling. "We don't require perfect people in our Church. Who among us is perfect? I am not, although many of my people impute such qualities to me. We are all subject to temptations, Brother, and when we finally cast aside our weaknesses, take upon us the name of the Savior, and are baptized of the water and the fire . . . we are as newborn babes; pure as the driven snow!"

Bennett lifted his head off the pillow as if straining to hear every word. Then, slowly, he let his head fall back, exhausted, but a look of peace on his face. "Then I have done this awful thing for nothing."

"And if I were you, I would forget it and get to sleep. I bless you that you will be well in the morning, and full of your old strength." At that, he placed a warm hand on the perspiring man's head, then turned and left the room.

"God bless you, President," Bennett called after him.

Joseph left the house and walked back to the carriage. As Orrin Porter Rockwell nipped the reins over the horse's back and they jerked into motion, he turned to his passenger and asked, "Well, how is he?"

"Better," Joseph replied.

"He really tried to do himself in?"

"He certainly made it look that way, Port."

"My, my," Rockwell said, turning back to his driving. He was thinking about all the affection the amorous doctor would be missing had he succeeded in his attempt.

"Port," the prophet said, "Giver Brother Sharp his notebook."

Rockwell shrugged. "Whatever you say, Joseph." The carriage rocked along the dark street. "What about the gun?" he asked. "It's a dandy!"

"The gun, too. You've no right to it."

Port had his weaknesses, Joseph realized. But he was so loyal that he would lay down his life for him if the need arose, and Joseph knew that greater love hath no man. For this reason he tolerated the lively underground dram shop which Port operated. He knew that his friend brought in barrels of rum and sold it by the drink to thirsty patrons, but he liked to think that the only ones quaffing ardent spirits in Nauvoo were nonmembers of the Church. Besides, if Nauvoo were to take its place as a center of commerce, it would have to cater to some of the requirements of the commercial traveler, including the availability of alcohol.

Joseph consoled himself with the thought that Gentiles, attracted by the booming city and its familiar comforts, might see the light of the Gospel here, and forsake their bottled spirit for the holy variety. It had happened before.

And so Orrin Porter Rockwell was permitted to scrape along, supporting himself and Luana, his wife, on what he was paid as Joseph's bodyguard, and what he could make retailing rum.

Rockwell was at heart an entrepreneur, marching to his own drum and following his own conscience. He was ever alert to a new possibility for profit, and the same single-mindedness that made him an unshakable friend to those he favored, also made him an implacable enemy to those he didn't. He was thought of as an eccentric by all. He was the most laughed at—and the most feared—Mormon of all.

His devotion to the prophet was so absolute that it blinded him to all else, and his hatred of those who opposed the prophet was maniacal.

It was this fanatacism burning within him like an underground peat fire, which would soon place a price on his own head, and plunge his adored friend Joseph Smith into mortal danger.

Chapter 18

Spring, 1841, crept up the Mississippi from the Gulf, repainting the wildflowers at Natchez and Memphis, warming St. Louis and Hannibal, Quincy and Keokuk, passing its benediction over the rich black soil of Nauvoo, bringing plentiful game in the hardwood forests and fish to the river, and grain to the till plain. The City of Joseph wore an air of optimism.

And so did Joseph. He had published a revelation he had received in January, on the 19th—the day after John C. Bennett's apparent suicide attempt—in which he said the Lord had called on him to proclaim to the world, to "bring your gold and your silver to the help of my people, to the house of the daughters of Zion."

The Saints heard, and obeyed. Three, four boats a day now called at Nauvoo and hundreds of recent converts disembarked each week, swelling the town's population, driving prices for land and houses up, and multiplying the ranks of the Nauvoo Legion, which was fast becoming the largest, best-equipped and best-trained military organization on the continent, exclusive of the United States Army itself.

Joseph was working harder than ever, and so was John C. Bennett, who did indeed rise from his couch the morning after his ingestion of the poison, conducted all of his business as mayor and topped off the day with a smart military retreat ceremony, astride the spirited stallion he rode expertly, and not a word was said outside of those four households which knew of it, about the despondency of Major General John C. Bennett, for all signs of it had evaporated with the swamp fog and he seemed as commanding and sure-footed as ever.

Joseph had announced that work on two important projects should begin immediately. The first, the temple, to be built on the block bounded by Wells and Woodruff on the east and west, and by Knight and Mulholland on the north and south. These and other street names were to be changed from time to time before they became officially accepted, but the prophet had chosen them to do honor to his most trusted inner circle of elders, who comprised foreign missionaries, members of the Twelve, and benefactors of the Church.

The other project was a hotel suitable to attend the needs of the increasing numbers of tourists and official visitors who were now calling on Nauvoo. The power exuded by the prophet and his faithful was sought by politicians in search of votes, businessmen and drummers in search of dollars, and the simply idly curious, to whom the sight of a prophet would be an interesting subject for conversation at parties and clubs. Joseph had a hand in almost all building designs, and he sketched a plan for "Nauvoo House" which would be erected near his home, near the river. Still cash poor, the hotel would be financed by stock Joseph required to be purchased by himself, Sidney Rigdon and Hyrum Smith, who were his counselors in the First Presidency, and others. The temple would be built through the diligent labors and sacrifice of every man, woman and child who would give a tenth of their increase, plus a tenth of their time, for the project.

The spring was especially memorable for Andrew. One moonless night in March he awoke, sensing someone in his room. Upon investigating, he discovered the drawer to his desk open, and that the gun and notes stolen two months earlier had been returned.

He had little time to wonder about this, though, because he and Louisa were enjoying each other's company so thoroughly, and Andrew was considering his future. Clouding his personal skies, though, was the nagging realization that he could not found a marriage on dishonesty, and somehow he would either have to divest himself of his dual role as an employee of both the *Times & Seasons* and the *Argus*, or find some way to tell her about it. He had searched for the right words but never found themn.

There was also the matter of the Church. Everybody in Nauvoo assumed he was a member. He was becoming more knowledgable about the Church, but he wasn't baptized and had no desire to be. Yet, Louisa . . . what about her? She loved him. Did she love him as a Mormon, or as a man?

A Mormon . . . a man. In another sense, this dilemma also faced Emma Smith. She had married Joseph fourteen years earlier, believing in him completely. She had believed him when he told her of his first vision, back in Palmyra, New York, in which he had been visited by God the Father and Jesus Christ, who told him that no church then on earth held the authority of the Gospel Jesus taught. She had believed him when he told her how, three years later, in 1823, he had been visited by the Angel Moroni, who disclosed the hiding place of the gold plates on which the history of the lost tribes of the Americas had been written, and she knew for a fact that he had translated from these plates the most controversial book of the Nineteenth Century — the *Book of Mormon*. She believed he had been visited by Peter, James and John, and had been given the keys of this dispensation with which to restore the Church of Jesus Christ. Yes, in every way that a wife could know her husband, Emma Hale Smith knew that Joseph was a prophet of God.

And yet, he was also a man. He never had pretended to be anything more than mortal. But was there—in the **man**—something more or less than a faithful husband? She had heard rumors for years, seen the pious and sympathetic looks on purse-lipped faces among a few women of the Church, and knew what they were saying among themselves. But when she had taken her concerns to Joseph, he had told her that he continued to live God's commandments as he understood them, and for her to pay no attention to what she heard. But what she had heard was that her husband might be a bigamist!

Months passed. Rumors became more specific, and there was always a well-meaning "sister" to pass them along to her. Now the rumors had coalesced: Joseph had been urging the Brethren to take other wives. Emma was too intelligent and refined, too much aware of the delicacy of her position as the prophet's wife, ever to approach any of the other people whom, rumor said, were informed about this. She loved and trusted her husband as a man and respected him as a prophet, and would be content with whatever he, as a prophet, was commanded by the Lord to do.

But other wives? In secret? It was abominable—**unthinkable!**

It was a fine spring night. The Nauvoo Legion had practiced for the cornerstone-laying ceremony at the temple site which would take place in two more days, and Joseph, his brother Hyrum, and younger brother Don Carlos, sick though he was, had participated in the maneuvers. All had gone off exceptionally well, and Major General John C. Bennett, who had commanded the two cohorts in the drill, seemed to have turned a ragged group of volunteers into a crack unit. Joseph should have been his usual glowing self, but he was not; he had asked Hyrum to meet him on the levee just off Water Street, southeast of his house, for an urgent conversation. He seemed worried.

Hyrum walked with his brother now along the path which paralleled the Mississippi. "Something's on your mind, Joe?"

"Yes. I need counsel from you, Patriarch," Joseph replied. And Hyrum knew when his brother used the title of the office to which he had been ordained following the death of Joseph Smith Sr., that their talk was to be on matters pertaining to the Gospel.

"Then go ahead, President," Hyrum said.

"How many revelations have come through me to date?"

Hyrum paused to think. "Counting your last one in March—the one for the Saints in the Iowa Territory, there have been one-hundred and twenty-five."

"No."

"Then I've miscounted?"

"No. No, you haven't miscounted, Patriarch. I have received two revelations which I have never spoken of, never repeated, never taught."

Hyrum stopped. "When?"

The first one was ten years ago. The Church was a year old."

"But, why do we have no record of it? Wasn't it clear?"

"Oh, very clear."

"Then I don't understand."

Joseph turned and faced his brother. The rising moon shone on his chiseled face, the river rolled placidly in the background. "I had been pondering the Old Testament, and I had asked the Lord to help me understand whether I was as the prophets of old—Abraham, Isaac, Jacob—in His eyes. I wish to God I had never asked."

"Why?"

"Because I received a revelation—a commandment—that . . . that I should be ready to receive additional wives, just as Abraham received Hagar and Keturah, and Jacob received Rachel, Bilhaha and Zilpah."

"Be married to more than one wife?"

"Yes. Well, here was I, married then only four years to Emma, whom I love with all my heart . . ."

"Then . . . the rumors have been true!"

The prophet's shoulders sank. He looked up into the shadowed face of his brother. "Hear me out, Hyrum, as the **Patriarch**, please! I know there have been rumors, and I mean to set them to rest, but first you must hear me out! The revelation warned me to speak to nobody about this, but to find for myself a second bride, to raise righteous seed. I know what it must have looked like. I was sick, I was physically ill at the thought of violating my sacred vows to Emma, but what was I to do? Like Father Adam, I was given two conflicting commandments: which do I break and which do I obey?"

Hyrum watched his brother in silence.

"So, I did nothing. I prayed to have this burden lifted from me, but nothing happened. I knew it was true, but I purposely ignored it! Ignored a revelation, a commandment of God! I, the chosen prophet of this dispensation! Can you imagine the torment of my heart?"

"Joseph, you preached against it, denied it, time and again . . ."

"Do you have any idea of what would happen to this church if I had preached plural marriage?"

"I don't know what to think," Hyrum said, shaking his head in dismay.

"There's more," Joseph said. "The commandment went beyond what I've told you. I was commanded also to teach the principle to the Brethren. They must also take spiritual wives."

Hyrum realized what he was hearing. "The Brethren? You mean . . . Sidney Rigdon . . . William Law . . . **me**?"

"And, when the time is right, the entire church."

It was almost too much for Hyrum. He looked at his brother as he would look at a madman. "Joe," he said, carefully, "if you were given these commandments and you have disobeyed them, then aren't you under condemnation right now?"

"No."

"Why not?"

"Because I have taken a spiritual wife—back in Ohio. And tomorrow I shall take another."

Hyrum stared in disbelief at Joseph. "Wife? Or concubine?"

"We shall be legally married in the eyes of God. Bishop Noble is performing the ceremony."

"And who is the bride-to-be?"

"The bishop's sister-in-law, Louisa Beman."

"And does Emma know all about this?"

"No. But she suspects. There have been rumors, as you said . . ."

"And I have denied them, time and again! Joseph, this makes me sick! This is hideous! Why would the Lord impose this upon a people who are already outcasts from the rest of the world?"

"To produce a righteous seed, and to weed out the weak among us who cannot stand the pure light of revelation."

Hyrum sank to his haunches in the trail and idly pulled at a weed. "You said there is another revelation you haven't taught."

"There is. I call it 'The Drawn Sword' Revelation. After I had been rebellious, had refused to take part in this commandment, an angel appeared before me as bright as the sun, with a drawn sword in his hand, and he said to me, 'Joseph, if you will not live this commandment, you will be replaced by someone who will!'"

There was bitter silence. The two brothers stood inches apart, but a gulf seemed to have opened between them. Finally, Hyrum said, in a choked voice, "It could destroy us. It would be used by all our enemies to blow the Church apart!"

"I know. I expect mass apostasy."

"And do you expect me to find another wife and live with her?"

"The Lord expects it," Joseph said softly, wearily.

A DISPATCH FROM A TRAVELER IN NAUVOO
April 6, 1841

Temple Begun; Mormon Military Prowess Demonstated

On this day in the Holy City of Nauvoo, a cornerstone was laid whereon will be constructed a temple to the "Most High God" in whom the communicants of Joseph Smith's religion profess their belief.

The site is a fair one, commanding a view of the entire city and the banks of the Mississippi on the far off Iowa shore. From the river and from Iowa, the temple, if it is completed along the lines which Jos. Smith designed, will become a landmark for miles around.

Prior to the placement of the cornerstone, an audience of several thousand was treated to a demonstration of close-order drill in which most of the ablebodied male population of Nauvoo participated. Rumors of the high quality of the Nauvoo Legion have scarcely done justice to the precision of this body.

The commander in chief of the Legion is Lieutenant General Joseph Smith, the same individual who is also the spiritual head of the city. Acting as his second in command is the noted political and medical figure, Major General John C. Bennett. Major General Bennett seems fully recovered from a recent mysterious illness which attacked him.

Meanwhile, an alarming number of Nauvoo residents are still ill

173

with ague, and a number are dying of it.

Drums awoke Nauvoo on the morning of Tuesday, April 6th, 1841, the drums of the Nauvoo Legion, over a thousand men, anxious to put their newly learned military skills to the test.

The rattle of parade drums was heard on the upper plains east of the city, where an encampment of over two thousand visitors had spent the night in tents.

It poured into the streets and echoed among the buildings in the commercial district, where merchants were hastily throwing open their doors to serve the largest crowd in the city's history. American flags were everywhere, and everyone abroad on the streets that morning seemed to be in a hurry.

The black buggy of the prophet skimmed along Munson, skirting the center of town on Main, and turned instead to go down Bain Street, Port Rockwell driving, and Joseph riding concealed beneath the top in back.

He kissed Emma and held her tightly when he stepped inside his house, and said into her hair, "I love you." Then he took his wash basin and hurried out to the pump to dash cold water on his hands and face. Emma had spent the night alone, but then, Joseph had told her he would be away all night. She presumed it was on Church business.

In her sister and brother-in-law's house, Louisa Beman Smith sat in her bed, cherishing every moment of the night, her first with any man, spent with her new husband. He had been as honorable and tender as she had dreamed he would be, and her joy had been complete with this fascinating man who was still such a mystery to her. He had carefully explained why she must not reveal their relationship, and this was her only frustration. But she and her sister and her brother-in-law, the Bishop Noble, had all fasted and prayed until they knew that the revelation on Celestial Marriage was true. If she could but prove worthy, she would be exalted, and she wanted that more than anything in this world or the next. Bishop Noble had married them using words suggested by the prophet himself; her sister and Orrin Porter Rockwell had been witnesses, and then after a wedding feast, the newlyweds retired. Joseph had said it had been a perfect ceremony, except for one thing: he wished Emma had been there.

The military review began. Sixteen companies of men in all kinds of partial uniforms marched and wheeled so splendidly that when Major General Bennett barked an order, and the cry was repeated by captains of the companies and lieutenants of platoons, the throng of some twelve thousand onlookers applauded and cheered. Few had ever seen anything so grand, nor on such a large scale, as the Nauvoo Legion.

Marching among them, Andrew had surrendered to the cadence and precision of the disciplined cohort, concentrating on exact movements—keeping his rifle angled precisely at the right degree on his shoulder, snapping it off his right shoulder and into the palm of his left hand,

174

slapping right hand to rifle butt, snapping the piece onto his left shoulder, all in strict marching cadence at the command. Executing square-cornered **columns-right** and **columns-left**, keeping his equilibrium on the command, **to-the-rear-march**, and then, standing at rigid attention, feeling pride in executing a perfect **present arms** when Lieutenant General Joseph Smith rode by on his shimmering black stallion, Charlie.

The audience was impressed by the precision, and there was pride in the face of Major General Bennett when, at the end of the review, he executed a perfect **about face** and barked "dismissed" to the Legion.

The cornerstone had been laid and the ceremonies were over. Andrew began searching the nearby crowd for Louisa, when a man in a beaver hat and swallowtail coat walked toward him. He wore a dark muttonchop beard and walked with a slight limp. "Andy," he called.

"Tom!"

"It's been a long time."

Andrew embraced his brother and exclaimed, "When did you get here? I didn't know you were coming!"

"Got here this morning on the ferry. I'm just up for the day. Where are you staying?"

Andrew realized that the two brothers hadn't exchanged letters in the eight months he had been in Nauvoo. "I board with a family here, the Mc-Canns. You may remember them; I met them on the boat, and we saw them waiting on the Warsaw dock."

"Ah, the Mormons. Well, isn't everybody in Nauvoo?"

"Practically."

"Are you one yet?"

Andrew looked around nervously. They were still surrounded by a swirling mob of Legionnaires and spectators, and he realized the danger of being overheard. "Tell you what; let's go somewhere and talk."

Tom pulled out his watch. "It's dinnertime," he said. "Has this prosperous city got a restaurant that serves food to Gentiles?"

Andrew grinned and took his arm. "Not so loud, Tom," he said, looking straight ahead.

Thomas cupped his ear. "You'll have to talk louder, Andy," he said. Andrew realized his brother's hearing was worse than it had been when they had last talked. "Come this way," Andy said, guiding him toward a coffee house which served fresh-baked bread.

"A **coffee**-house in Nauvoo?" Thomas said as they sat down. He made a mock look of disapproval. "Next you'll be telling me there's a dram house here too!"

"There is," Andrew said. "But the city council will be closing them down. Oh, yes, there's more than one place serving liquor."

They ordered coffee and a loaf of bread. The proprietor brought a fresh-baked loaf still warm from the oven, a sharp bread knife and a plate of butter, and a pot of preserves. Tom dug in with a vengeance. "They do know how to bake,'' he said, his mouth full.

"Well, tell me all about Warsaw and your law practice."

"I've given it up."

Andrew was astonished. "Given it up? Not enough clients?"

"I don't need it any more," Thomas said. "I've taken over the Warsaw *Signal,* just as I said I would, and it's doing very well."

"I'm glad to hear that."

"Now, tell me what's happened to you, Andy."

"Well, I'm working at the Nauvoo print shop on our newspaper, the *Times & Seasons,* and . . ." he turned to see if the proprietor was in earshot, "you know what else I do."

"Yes," Thomas replied. "That's why I asked you what's happened to you. Where was that objective young reporter I put on the boat last year? What became of him?"

"What do you mean?"

"I've been reading your stuff in the *Argus,*" Thomas said. "Have you capitulated to Holy Joe and his bunch?"

"I don't know what you're talking about."

"Like hell you don't," Thomas snarled. "You came up here and sold out to them. And you've got an angry editor in Quincy."

Andrew was alarmed. "Who says so?"

"He says so. I've talked with old man Ketchum. He's about to cut you off. You're only writing what the Mormons want to let out."

"That's not true!"

"I've read your articles," Thomas repeated. "Not a word about the fortress they're building up there that they call a temple. Not a word about the outlaws who call themselves Mormons so they can steal people blind and run hide under Joe Smith's skirts. Not a word about the whoring going on. . ."

"Now, wait a minute, Tom," Andrew interrupted. "I've been reporting what I've seen!"

"Then you've had your eyes closed for eight long months," he said. "What happened? You fall for one of the 'Sisters of Zion'?"

"No!"

Thomas studied his brother's face. "You've had a perfect opportunity to get on the inside, working for their newspaper. You're a member of the militia. Good; you should be able to get closer to Bennett, who as you ought to know is one of the most dastardly characters ever expelled from the territory of Ohio . . ."

"Where do you get your information on these things?"

Thomas spread his hands. "It's common knowledge everywhere else but here," he said. "I'm sure Joe Smith knows the kind of man he's hired to run his town."

Andrew's thoughts were confused. Had he been filing stories that were that naive? "What did Mr. Ketchum tell you?" he asked.

"I went down to Quincy to do some business and I called on him, introducing myself as your brother, and he told me he was disappointed in the stories you've sent him. I read them and agreed with him. They're watered milk, Andy.''

Andrew's heart sank. "I've tried to be honest," he said.

The proprietor appeared again with a steaming pitcher of coffee and refilled their cups. When he left, Andrew leaned closer to his brother's ear again. "He wanted me to find out about Joseph having more than one wife. Well, there are rumors but I can't print them."

"And why not?"

"Because they're leads, not stories," Andrew protested.

"You're wrong," Thomas said. "People love to read juicy gossip. If people in his own town are saying Joe is bedding other women, that's news!"

"Would you print such a thing in your paper?"

Thomas laughed. "Would I? That's what I have been printing, and the public is eating it up! You can't keep a copy on the street every time we publish! I tell you, little brother, you could learn a few things from me and the *Signal*. And I can still use a good hand down in Warsaw. Why not jump out of the *Argus* before old man Ketchum sacks you, and come to work with me? You'll catch on to the style soon enough."

"I can't."

"You'd damn well better. Your days are numbered, Andrew."

Andrew sat in a daze. His brother had changed so much in these few short months. He had never heard him use such coarse language so often before, nor had he seen him so opinionated. And the thought of working on the *Signal*, writing stories designed to inflame public sentiment against the Mormons made him feel sick in the pit of his stomach.

"I think I know the Mormons better than someone living in another county," he said. "I live with them on a day-to-day basis. I know them. I know some of them very well."

"What do they pay you on the *Times & Seasons*? Could you live on it?"

"If I had to."

"Well, if you don't start sending some meatier articles down south, you may have to, little friend."

Andrew felt a sudden flash of anger at being patronized so. "If it happens, let it." He rose from the table and threw a few coins down. "Nice seeing you again," he said, and stalked out of the coffee shop.

Thomas watched his brother disappear in the busy street, smiled, and took another large mouthful of bread and butter.

A DISPATCH FROM A TRAVELER IN NAUVOO
Mormon Prophet Arrested on Missouri
Charges; To Stand Trial In Monmouth

June 8, 1841: Jos. Smith Jun., the Mormon prophet, made a bold move to call in person upon Governor Thomas Carlin of Illinois, while Gov. Carlin was visiting Quincy on the 4th inst.

Following his interview, upon Smith's departure, Gov. Carlin dispatched a posse consisting of a Constable and a Sheriff from Illinois and a Peace Officer from Missouri, to apprehend said prophet who was at that time still a fugitive from justice, wanted in Missouri under a writ signed by the former Governor Boggs.

On June 9th, Smith goes before Judge Stephen A. Douglas to receive Justice on charges of treason, murder, arson and larceny.

Mormon residents in the prophet's home town of Nauvoo are said to be rallying support behind their leader, and it is being bruted about that Gov. Carlin may look no longer for the slightest support in any future political enterprises from the disillusioned citizens of Nauvoo.

Chapter 19

Governor Thomas Carlin was flabbergasted. He had carefully planned his Friday to permit him to enjoy most of the afternoon off, so he could use some of this rare time away from gubernatorial duties to travel the countryside around Quincy. It was a prettier town than Springfield, nestling as it did on the Mississippi, and he was ready to tell his aide to turn away the Illinois citizen who had applied for a meeting with him, when the aide whispered in his ear, "He says he is Joseph Smith of Nauvoo."

Outside of the suite of rooms in the tiny Quincy hotel which served the governor and his party as a traveling headquarters, waited the man wanted in two states, who had eluded justice for more then two years. Now he was calling on the very man who had most recently ordered his arrest! With him were two other men the governor didn't recognize. "Send them in," he said, and stood up to greet his visitors.

Joseph Smith stood half a head higher than Thomas Carlin, and his commanding presence dominated the small room. Behind him was a ferret-like individual with uncommonly long hair, introduced as the prophet's traveling companion, Mr. Rockwell, and a journalist from Nauvoo, Andrew Sharp. The three visitors were seated in the governor's room and a chair was quickly brought in for Carlin.

"To what do I owe this surprising pleasure?" the governor asked, using a formality he had reserved heretofore for persons of equal or superior rank.

To his surprise, the long-haired Rockwell replied. "General Smith wishes to confer with you on the development of Nauvoo, Sir."

"Very well," Carlin said with a smile. "They tell me your city is becoming almost as large as Springfield."

"Yes," the prophet said, the sibilant whistle more pronounced now, as it always was when he was orating. "We have the finest and most advanced city in the state, and I have come to thank you for making that possible, your excellency, by signing our city charter."

"I am delighted to hear of it."

"And to issue you my personal invitation to visit Nauvoo as our guest," Joseph said. "Every modern convenience is provided for a comfortable visit. We have wide streets and plentiful shops, and I am particularly proud of the industriousness of the Latter-day Saints; we have craftsmen doing the best work in the world, for they have come to Nauvoo from all over the world!"

Carlin nodded agreeably while thinking the man was certainly not lacking in self-assurance. But then his visitor's expression changed to one of concern. "It is of utmost importance, your excellency, that you see with your own eyes the nature and quality of the people whom Missouri has oppressed; that you appreciate the high moral standards and the peaceful industry which is threatened by ill-considered and illegal acts."

Carlin noticed that the journalist Smith had brought with him was taking down every word being spoken. The interview was becoming too one-sided, and Carlin knew that he himself was far from being a commanding speaker; he wanted to exert his presence now before this became a case of the governor being the audience to a harangue.

"The charges Governor Boggs brought against you, sir, are very serious; I cannot dismiss them lightly."

"Indeed, you are right," Joseph replied, leaning forward in his chair. "They are serious and should be understood for their insidiousness. If your deputies had happened to find me in this spring when you sent them after me, a great injustice would have been done . . ."

"You would have been brought to trial where the charges could be explored," Carlin interrupted.

The prophet leaned back and smiled. "Governor Carlin," he said, "do you honestly believe that Joseph Smith, the president of The Church of Jesus Christ of Latter-day Saints, could find justice in Missouri? Have you read my charges against Missouri?"

"Oh, yes," Carlin said, "I am quite familiar with them. They cost Lilburn Boggs the state. You have turned a nation against him."

"And he has turned a nation against me," Joseph said, his voice ringing in the small room. Andrew looked up in surprise.

"We have been denied our Constitutional rights, and there was no one in Missouri, save a very few, who would stand up for us. We were to be destroyed by executive order of their infamous governor, not merely dispossessed of all our belongings, but exterminated!"

And then his voice softened. "We sought refuge in this state, in this very city, and found that in the state of Illinois, law and order still prevailed. We were taken in, clothed and cared for, and given your esteemed friendship. And so I thank you, governor, and invite you to partake of our hospitality in return. When can you come to Nauvoo?"

"I should very much like to visit Nauvoo, General, but I will have to consult my calendar—which, unfortunately, is back in Springfield."

"You shall always be made welcome," Joseph said, smiling.

"Uh, getting back to those charges Governor Boggs lodged," Carlin said, "there is much talk of lawlessness among your people, you are surely aware of that. Four of your men were caught with quantities of stolen goods, and it is said that you yourself authorized the taking of property from non-Mormons, to compensate for the property taken from you."

"There is not a word of truth in either of those rumors."

"I'm glad to hear that."

Joseph changed position in his chair, assuming a more relaxed pose. "I have been told that some—a few—of our newer converts may have accepted membership under false pretenses, in order to shield their criminal activities from discovery. We are a large and fast-growing Church, your excellency, and it is impossible for me to keep a record on every new member. Why," and he turned toward Andrew, "this brother has been with us for three-quarters of a year now and I still haven't seen his baptismal records."

Andrew fastened his eyes on his notepad, not daring to look up.

"But whenever a Latter-day Saint is found in violation of the law—God's or man's—he is caused either to confess and repent, or he is cut away from the Church."

"A very wise course."

"Governor," Joseph said, rising and walking around the room, "as membership in all other sects and denominations in Christendom is falling, why is it that our converts number in the hundreds every month? Why, do you suppose, over two thousand people have accepted baptism in this church in England in less than two years' time? And what kinds of people are joining us?" He turned and placed both hands on the back of his empty chair. "Excepting those few rabble who sought to use us for protection while they continued their sinning, we are an incredible body of people! Skilled, educated, hardworking and honest, faithful to God and ready at a moment's notice to make any sacrifice in His name! We represent the very cream of society for Illinois—or for the world!" He leaned up, arms folded, as if waiting for applause. Andrew scribbled furiously to catch up.

Carlin was becoming anxious. How much longer would this man go on sermonizing? "Would you gentlemen care for refreshments?" he asked.

"No, thank you," Joseph replied. "We shall take no more of your valuable time. I thank you for this opportunity to introduce myself to you, sir, and I hope you will visit me again in Nauvoo. We are building a large new hotel and I shall personally arrange a Governor's suite for you and your party."

Carlin stood up and shook hands all around, promising to make a visit as soon as possible. Andrew completed his shorthand notes, and Porter Rockwell went to the door of the room, opened and stepped into the hall, returned and nodding at Joseph. The way was safe for the prophet.

Governor Carlin and his staff were amused by the pomp attending the Mormon leader, but after they were sure the trio from Nauvoo was out of sight and hearing, Carlin motioned for a meeting behind the closed door of his hotel room.

To have found himself back in Quincy on almost no notice was a surprise to Andrew, but he was finding that being around Joseph Smith provided him with many surprises. Joseph, four days before, had stated that he had business with the Saints in Quincy, and that he wished Andrew to travel with him as scribe. Porter Rockwell would go along, as usual, as bodyguard and major-domo to all the prophet's needs.

Now as the three men walked into the street, Joseph asked Andrew if he had gotten all of the conversation.

"Every word, I think, President," Andrew replied. It struck him that Joseph had two imposing titles—President and General—and that he was forever in a quandary, wondering which one to use. Since the rise in prestige of the Nauvoo Legion, however, Joseph tended to use the military rank most often. Well, Andrew mused, he is entitled to it. "Would you like me to read back some of it to you?" Andrew asked.

"Not just now," Joseph replied. They were free now until Saturday morning, when they were to take the boat north to Nauvoo. "I have some friends here in Quincy," Andrew said. "If it's all right with you, I'd like to call on them."

Joseph readily agreed, and Andrew said farewell to him and Rockwell in downtown Quincy, only about three blocks from the office of the *Argus*. Andrew set off in an oblique direction so that nobody would later think that he might have intended to visit the newspaper, and after ten minutes' walk through town, during which time he stopped to inspect goods in shop windows, he deemed it safe to return to the main downtown section where the *Argus* was printed.

He slipped in through the back door to the printing office and surprised a pressman, asleep in a chair by the idle press. "Where's Mr. Ketchum?" he asked the embarrassed man.

"Upstairs, I guess," he said. Andrew hurried up to the office.

Elias P. Ketchum was collarless, a towel around his neck, sleeves rolled to his elbows, a thatch of yellow-white hair that looked uncombable sprouting from his head, matching great bushy eyebrows beneath which were the eyes of a professional skeptic. But he was kinder than he looked, patient and encouraging, and in Ketchum Andrew felt he had a friend. He stepped into the large loft-like open room that served as the general office for the small newspaper's staff, and greeted the editor.

At first, Ketchum didn't recognize Andrew, but then he threw up a hand and walked over. "Well," he said, "what are you doing here? Give it up in Nauvoo, did you?"

"No, sir! Joseph Smith is right here in Quincy. I came down with him!"

"You don't say," the editor replied, pulling a chair out. "What's he doing here?"

"He just saw the governor and I took down every word!" Andrew displayed the notebook.

"Anything interesting happen?"

"He thanked him for signing the Nauvoo charter and bragged about the Mormons. Oh, and invited Carlin to come to visit."

"Did Carlin's men ever serve that arrest warrant on Smith?"

"No. He must have found out about it and cleared out by the time the deputies got there."

"Hmm," Ketchum said. "Seems to me they could still serve it on him if they were a mind to."

Andrew put a finger to his lower lip and considered that. "Where is he staying?" Ketchum asked. Andrew leaped from his chair. Suddenly he realized that Joseph was in imminent danger of being arrested, now that he was here in Quincy, away from friends who might hide him. He dashed to the door.

"Hey, where're you going?" Ketchum asked in surprise. "I thought you had a story for me!"

"I may have a better one," Andrew yelled, already half way down the stairs. Ketchum hurried over to his window and looked down on the street. Andrew was dashing north, as fast as he could run.

Of course, Andrew thought as he darted among the pedestrians; Joseph had walked right into the lion's den, a typically bold move for this bold and dramatic man. But he was on the Governor's home ground, away from Mormons who would hide him on a moment's notice. If the governor wanted to serve papers on him, he would be a sitting duck! Then, it occurred to Andrew that he was running to warn Joseph Smith of his danger, and not to merely be on hand to report what happened. He slowed to a walk, analyzing his own thoughts.

What had become of the objective reporter? Had he sold out, capitulated to Joseph Smith as Tom had charged? Had he succumbed to the prophet's charm as so many were accused of doing? Just what was he going to do when he got up to his hotel room? Would he try to warn Joseph to leave before a posse arrived to arrest him and drag him to jail? Or would he stoically wait for fate to deal its next hand, then report what happened?

I have no right to interfere, he told himself. *I'm a reporter, not a member of the Twelve.* But, climbing the hotel stairs, he had another thought:

He has befriended me and he trusts me. And another: *If I sell out Joseph Smith to get a good story for the Argus, how am I different from Judas?*

He walked down the narrow hallway to the door of Joseph's room. There was no sound. He was about to knock, when suddenly from behind him came the thin, nasal voice of Orrin Porter Rockwell.

"Have a nice visit with your **friends**, Andrew?" His tone was thick with insinuation.

Andrew whirled, startled and angry. "Where did you come from?"

The small man deliberately shifted a cud of chewing tobacco from one cheek to another, smirking. "Oh, I get around some," he said. "You got a message for the President?"

Andrew studied his insolent face—a defiant school bully in men's clothes. What kind of man could call this specimen his closest friend, Andrew wondered. How this little toad swaggered, displaying his gun in his belt, defying any controls of society. Well, he concluded, at least Orrin Porter Rockwell had helped him make up his mind about warning Joseph Smith. "No," he said, his tone indifferent; "I have no message for the President."

The three departed for Nauvoo the following day, as planned. Andrew had returned to the office of the *Argus* and written a full account of the meeting with Governor Carlin, but he was never sure that he had not somehow been followed—either by Rockwell himself or by some footpad in Rockwell's employ. **Nerves**, he decided, when he had returned to Joseph's side for the carriage ride to the dock and saw no sign of suspicion on the face of either man.

Now, the steamer *Celeste* was pulling into Warsaw. Andrew had no plans to disembark, because he didn't want to encounter Thomas, after their stormy leave-taking at Nauvoo two months earlier. They hadn't corresponded, but Andrew still was furious over the remarks his brother had made. He was all too worried that they might have been true.

As the ramp from the boat was lowered to the dock, Andrew saw a group of men, standing all together, move quickly, in a body up the gangway onto the ship. Too quickly! Suddenly he knew who they were and what was about to happen. The men fanned out, each going to a different part of the vessel. One of them approached Joseph Smith, who was comfortably seated, talking animatedly with another passenger.

"Are you Joseph Smith of Nauvoo?" the man asked.

Joseph looked up at him questioningly. The man opened his hand. The five-pointed star of a sheriff's badge lay in his palm. In the other hand was a long-nosed revolver. "I'm Marshall Tolbert from Quincy. I'm placing you under arrest, sir, and taking you off this vessel."

"Under whose orders?" Joseph asked, imperiously.

"Orders of Governor Carlin," the man said, pocketing the badge and reaching for the prophet's arm. Joseph wrenched free of the man's touch and rose slowly, without aid. "May I send a message on ahead to Nauvoo?" he asked.

"You can give it to me and I'll carry it to a mail rider."

Joseph sized up the man. "Just tell the rider to tell anyone in Nauvoo that I have been illegally taken back to Quincy."

A cry and a scuffle went up from somewhere astern. Passengers made way as four men dragged Orrin Porter Rockwell along the deck, his moccasins lifted completely off the planking, legs flailing as he tried to kick his captors. "You infernal pukes!" screamed the little man, but the quartet of lawmen only laughed and two of them seized the determined quarry and immobilized his legs. "I'm going with the prophet!" he screamed, when they began taking him down the gangway to the dock. "You shore are," one of the deputies chuckled.

Through it all, Andrew had kept silent. Now he stepped forward as Joseph was being led ashore. "Do you want me to go on to Nauvoo, President?" he asked.

"No! I want you with me, taking down everything that is said and done!"

The marshall scrutinized Andrew. "And who are you, sir?" he asked.

"He is my personal scribe," Joseph said, before Andrew could answer. "His name is Andrew Sharp and he has no part in this affair. But I insist that he accompany me."

The marshall shrugged. "Come along then, but the state of Illinois won't pay for your keep."

"I shall pay, sir, have no fear," Joseph said, and then to the marshall who still gripped his arm, he demanded, "turn loose of that arm so I can give my scribe some cash!" When he was freed, Joseph dug into a pocket and handed a roll of bills to Andrew. "See that Port is taken care of." The phalanx of lawmen, surrounding Joseph and Rockwell, walked onto the dock and into a waiting two-horse wagon. Accompanied by two lawmen in the wagon and the others on horseback, the procession started south. Andrew found himself sitting between Joseph and Rockwell, facing the deputies.

They had searched Joseph and found nothing worth taking, but from Rockwell they had removed his Pepperbox six-shooting pistol, a knife and a small flask of rum. When Rockwell complained about the rum, they gave it back.

It became apparent that Joseph was almost more angry over being deceived by Governor Carlin than he was by the danger of facing the hearing. He seemed to have no doubt about his innocence or concern about proving it.

Andrew was prepared to spend several more days in Quincy, but as soon as an appointment for a hearing date was set in the Monmouth courthouse, Joseph was released and Porter Rockwell got his gun back. Andrew managed to slip away to the *Argus* and file a story which delighted Elias P. Ketchum. "Go to it, by Ned," he shouted at Andrew, as he darted off to rejoin the prophet. At least, Andrew thought as he hurried back to the others, I've got my job nailed down again.

It was by now too late to take another boat north, and since Joseph had had to post bail which took almost all the available cash among the three of them, they were obliged to take lodging in the Quincy home of Matthew Rainey, a stalwart defender of the Mormons who, although not a member himself, had lodged several refugees from Far West when the Saints first began arriving in Quincy. He not only gave the three men beds and fed them royally, but he insisted on giving a purse to Joseph containing a hundred dollars, to be spent on decent transport to Nauvoo and the remainder on his defense. Touched by this generous gesture, Joseph embraced the elderly man the next morning before taking the stage north. "God bless you and keep you, my friend," Joseph said. "Kindness such as yours will be rewarded a thousandfold in heaven."

Most of the daylight was consumed on the drive north with frequent stops and a change of horses. When they finally arrived in Nauvoo it was sundown and Joseph discovered that the word of his arrest and arraignment hadn't been heard there yet. He went directly to see Mayor Bennett, to arrange for a legal defense against the several charges in the warrant. But before he retired for the night, he stopped off at the home of Don Carlos

Smith, Andrew still with him.

Don Carlos' wife, Agnes, and their two children, were overjoyed to see the prophet, and embraced him lovingly. Don Carlos, lying on a bed improvised from a couch in the small living room, was too weak to stand up.

Joseph was alarmed at his brother's condition, for he had worsened in the few days Joseph had been gone. "But you will be well," the prophet told him, "I know it."

"Are you speaking as a prophet . . . or as a brother?" Don Carlos asked.

"I am both," Joseph said, placing his hand over those of Don Carlos', folded on his blanket-wrapped chest.

The two men spoke quietly together for a few minutes, while Andrew waited in the balmy evening outside. He desperately wanted to see Louisa again, but Joseph had requested him to stay at his side. When the front door opened and Joseph appeared again, Andrew saw that his eyes were wet.

On the morning of June 9th, Andrew was discovering what it was like to be considered a Mormon outside of Nauvoo. Here, as the entourage approached the town of Monmouth, the county seat of Warren County, angry crowds began to form. Joseph had engaged six lawyers to defend him, and they—together with Joseph, Andrew and the ubiquitous Porter Rockwell—had to force their way from their wagons up the steps of the County Courthouse, assisted by a handful of deputies from the Sheriff's office. Jeering shouts of "Holy Joe" and "Here comes the Mormon Jesus" were heard, and of particular offense to Joseph, a disreputable old crone—toothless and half in her cups, sidled up next to the prophet and cackled, "Why'n't you marry me, reverend? Can't you use another wife?"

Porter Rockwell was so agitated by the menacing throng that he seemed ready to explode. Prudently, Joseph had ordered him to accompany him unarmed this time, for the little bodyguard's temper was reaching the boiling point and there was murder in his eyes as he pushed along beside the prophet, shoving people out of their way.

Inside the courtroom reserved for the hearing was another group of spectators who had gathered early for the spectacle, and in the open windows leaned everyone who could pry his way for a glimpse of the Mormon. Small boys hung from the branches of trees outside the windows.

The magistrate presiding in the court was Stephen A. Douglas. He had a reputation as a just man, and Joseph knew that he had supported the signing of the Nauvoo city charter into law. After the warrant from Missouri was read, the judge called on the defense to speak. Taking the floor was O. H. Browning, a respected lawyer chosen as spokesman for the team of attorneys representing Joseph.

"Your honor and ladies and gentlemen," he began. "Remove from your minds for the moment, any consideration of religion here. We are not concerned now with what a man's religious beliefs may be, for our Constitution assures that each citizen of this great nation should be free to think and worship as he sees fit. It is not the question, whether Mormonism is right or is wrong, whether it is popular or unpopular. The issue is one of human values. Should a man upon whom the wrath of an entire state has been poured out, be handed back into that pack of ravening wolves who have sworn to tear him apart? If you return Joseph Smith to Missouri, that is exactly what will happen!''

Browning began to pace around the front of the room as he continued. "Now, let us look into our hearts. Suppose that there is someone here today who would say, 'Why, the world would be better off with Joe Smith dead.' Think a little farther, friend! When we have killed Joe Smith because of his unpopular beliefs, what is there to prevent the next person with unpopular beliefs from being killed? And the next? What is there to prevent **you** from the same fate? Now, I present to you in evidence, this exhibit,'' and he picked off the table a document and handed it to the judge.

"This is an accurate, notarized copy of an order signed by Lilburn Boggs, governor of Missouri, which instructed his forces to exterminate the Mormons if they had to, to get them out of his state! It is only because of the humanity of some of the officers charged with the duty of carrying out this unspeakable killing, that Mr. Smith and his party were allowed to escape! And when those officers turned on their superiors and refused to comply with this illegal order, those who issued the orders slunk away like whipped dogs, knowing full well that what they had ordered was totally reprehensible and illegal!''

Then Browning shifted his position, halfway turning toward the spectators. "But that didn't stop them," he said, dropping his voice so low that everyone in the room had to strain to hear. "Oh, no indeed! For they still lusted after Mormon blood, and Mormon property. In Far West, Missouri, where the Latter-day Saints numbered in the thousands and had built up a civilized city, the citizens defended themselves. They had no help from the state militia which should have been defending the rights of citizens; they had to do it themselves. It was all right for marauders to steal and plunder from Mormons, but let one Mormon turn around and fight back, and it was considered treason!''

"And then," he said, his voice dropping further, "there was Haun's Mill. Two-hundred and forty maniacs on horseback rode into this tiny Mormon settlement, comprised of a mill and a dozen or so poor log cabins, and opened fire. They killed nearly every man, many women, even a few of their children. They shot them, they stabbed them, they quartered them alive with their swords, they raped mothers in front of their children . . .'' his voice quavered and broke. He took out a pocket handkerchief and wiped his eyes. "And these," he said, turning now to face the hushed audience, "are the people to whom you would send this man?'' He held his stance for a few seconds, then dropped his head and walked to the table, where he sat down beside Joseph Smith.

187

The courtroom was still silent except for a few coughs and a sniff from several of the women present. Browning noted, as he took his seat, that several handkerchiefs were out.

Judge Douglas, who had appeared unmoved during the lawyer's speech, now studied the writ in front of him for several seconds. He fiddled with it, picked up the papers and stacked them on end, then flattened them on the bench again. At last he spoke.

"Apart from the possible danger to the welfare of the defendant if he were to be returned to Missouri," he began, "it is the judgment of this court that this writ, having been returned to the governor by the sheriff of Hancock County, back in April—without it having ever been served—and the governor accepting it again—is dead."

A murmur began to rise from the crowd.

"This court will not rule on whether the evidence in the case is admissible," he said, "since there is no known precedent for such a decision, and it is the opinion of the court that there yet may be future considerations between the states which will have a bearing on extradition proceedings. Consequently," he said, "this court rules that the writ requiring the extradition of Joseph Smith Junior to Missouri is null and void," and he rapped his gavel on the bench. "Case dismissed!"

The spectators broke into an uproar of applause and rising voices. The attorneys gathered around Joseph to shake his hand; the courtroom was finally cleared of spectators and Joseph, Porter Rockwell and Andrew stepped out into the sunshine.

"It's just noon, Port," Joseph said, clapping an arm around his friend. "Let's see if we can get back home to Nauvoo before dark."

A DISPATCH FROM A TRAVELER IN NAUVOO

City Rejoices! Population Soars! Missionaries Bring New Converts from England Amid Land Speculation Scandal!

July 1, 1841: A celebration was staged at the Nauvoo dock today to welcome returning members of the Council of the Twelve Apostles who had spent the past two years in England where they were busily converting thousands of New Believers. Among those returning to the City of Joseph were Orson Pratt, Wilford Woodruff, John Taylor, George Albert Smith, Willard Richards and Brigham Young.

Due to the exceptional labors of the proselyters, Nauvoo has in the past months seen a most dramatic increase in population, with an estimated 2,000 more souls settling here from England alone. While an accurate census will not be made for yet another nine years, city officials are claiming that Nauvoo now boasts a population of over eight thousand, thereby making it perhaps the second largest city in Illinois.

All is not tranquil amid the spectacular growth of the city, however, as the prophet Joseph Smith himself has been accused by some of profiteering on the sale of lots to some of the arriving newcomers. There are those even among the Faithful who resent their "Prophet, Seer And Revelator" speculating on the land he sells.

In particular question is land located near the center of the city which has remained undeveloped until the present need to expand. This land, sold by Dr. Isaac Galland, a land agent, on behalf of Horace R. Hotchkiss and partners from New Haven, Connecticut, represents a parcel of five hundred acres and is reportedly worth well over $50,000. This, the Mormon church purchased under agreement signed by Joseph Smith as Trustee-In-Trust. Smith, it was said, intended to repay the Hotchkiss interests with deeds on property handed over by Converts from the East who were willing to trade their property for land in Nauvoo. Some of these recent Eastern arrivals, however, are complaining that the price of Nauvoo property is too dear, and have petitioned the prophet to reduce the prices to a more equitable level. The controversy continues, amid rising tempers in the Mormon's "Holy City."

Chapter 20

"Lies!" shouted Brigham Young, throwing the folded copy of the Quincy *Argus* on the table in the prophet's office, where Joseph had just shown some of the Brethren what the outside world was saying about Nauvoo.

"No, Brigham," Joseph replied. "Not outright lies, merely not enough truth. You have been away, but as President of the Quorum of the Twelve Apostles, you must be informed of all these developments." Joseph stood before the small group. "As you know, Isaac Galland sold us the Half Breed lands, on behalf of the Hotchkiss interests in Connecticut. It has been my intent to pay for these lands by tendering the deeds from property that had been owned by some of the new converts from the east. They who wished, would be able to trade their old land in their former home state for new property here in Nauvoo. It was operating just as I had envisioned, when I received this letter," and he produced a few pages of stationery.

"This is a dunning letter from Hotchkiss, saying he had received the principal but none of the interest from Isaac Galland, and he accused me of holding out on him."

"But had you paid him the full amount?" Young inquired.

"I sent it to Galland, his agent . . . and my friend," the prophet said. "I cannot understand why Isaac hasn't forwarded the full payment to Hotchkiss, but Hotchkiss says he has left New York without making full payment."

"But meantime, the press is insinuating you're profiteering on the resale of the Half Breed lands," Brigham Young said.

"It is true I have charged slightly higher prices than we had to pay," Joseph said, "but this was to enable me to provide free land to widows and orphans of the Haun's Mill massacre, and that is all."

"Then tell the writer of this article!"

Mild-mannered and handsome John Taylor spoke up. "Who is this 'traveler in Nauvoo,' President? Does he live among us?"

Joseph shook his head. "I don't know. Port has told me he is suspicious of someone, but it's still inconclusive. Ah, well," he said, and his tone brightened, "what does it matter if our hearts are free of offense, correct?" The men in the room nodded agreement.

"Now, about the Fourth of July, Brethren," Joseph continued. "I wish you all to be special guests of honor on the reviewing stand. Brother Brigham, we should like to hear a report from you on your experiences in England. I have also asked Mayor Bennett to speak to a patriotic theme. The Legion will pass in review, the arrangements have been made for a fine dinner to be served in early afternoon, and I have invited a special guest to join Emma and me at our table.''

The Brethren raised their eyes in interest. "Most of you don't know of him, since you have been away these two years,'' the prophet said, "but if we can win him to our point of view, many of our troubles will be over. For if you think our 'Traveler In Nauvoo' is a nuisance in the Quincy paper, he is as nothing compared to the editor of the Warsaw *Signal*!''

"And you've invited him here, Joseph?'' asked the prophet's cousin, George Albert Smith. "Was that wise?''

"He will see with his own eyes the falsity of his position,'' Joseph replied. "If there is a drop of honesty in him, he will moderate his attacks on us. I wish you all to treat him with every courtesy.''

"Well, what's his name?'' asked corpulent Willard Richards, his three-hundred pound bulk propped against the wall since no chair could support him.

"Thomas Sharp,'' Joseph answered.

In 1841, the Fourth of July fell on a Sunday, making the Nauvoo celebration a combination of patriotism and religion, and providing reason enough for every inhabitant of the city who was old enough or well enough to gather for festivities which had been touted as being the grandest spectacle yet staged by a prophet who had already shown his delight in recreation, drama and major gatherings.

A delegation awaited the arrival of Thomas Sharp on the dock at Water Street, including Emma Smith, who was there to represent her husband while he tended to other matters. In due course, the *Cicero* pulled into the dock and from it stepped a hundred tourists. The welcoming delegation was swamped and had to step back from the gangway to let them all get off. They were attired for a holiday, whole families of them, with picnic baskets, parasols and top hats much in evidence. Many children ran toward the new adventure.

But how to recognize Thomas Sharp, the anti-Mormon newspaperman? Eliza Snow, the slender young poetess and close friend of Emma's, clung to her arm as they scanned the sea of new faces. "There,'' she suddenly said, tugging on Emma's arm. "That will be our man.''

By some instinct her sharp eyes had perceived one man of the entire throng who appeared to be traveling alone, and who was less enthusiastic about running down the ramp onto Mormon soil. He hung back, observing the crowd with a trace of a smile on his face. He wore thick mutton-chops and a black beaver hat despite the rising temperature of the morning, and he walked with a slight limp. His clothes were poorly pressed, and not as light as the summertime wear of a man who could afford a good tailor.

"I do wish Joseph hadn't asked me to do this,'' whispered Emma. "It's not proper, a woman approaching a perfect stranger!''

"But my dear,'' Eliza said sweetly, "I'm sure that's why he asked me to go with you. Surely two women together wouldn't arouse even a blackguard's suspicion," and she laughed, looking up at her taller friend. Emma patted her hand and said, "He does seem to be looking for someone to meet him. Well, let's go." And they both walked over to the stranger, their arms still locked together.

"I beg your pardon sir," Emma said in her most correct manner, "but we have been asked to look for a gentleman by the name of Thomas Sharp, of Warsaw."

He removed his hat and smiled. "You have found him," he said. "Thomas Sharp, at your service."

Emma offered him her gloved hand. "I am so pleased to make your acquaintance," she said. "I am Emma Hale Smith and this is my dear friend, Eliza Snow."

He shook both hands. "I'm delighted," he said, "to have such a pleasant and charming reception committee."

"Mrs. Smith is the wife of the prophet Joseph Smith," Eliza chimed in, "and I am her best friend."

"We have a carriage waiting," Emma said.

"Ah, what a shame you went to that trouble, Mrs. Smith," Sharp said with a deep breath. "Your air here is so delightful, I was hoping to stroll up to the city. However, if it is too strenuous a climb for you . . ."

"Oh, no," Eliza interjected. "We'd love the walk, wouldn't we, Emma?"

"Of course," Emma replied. "I'll send the driver back, if you'll excuse me." She picked up her skirts and hurried up to where Orrin Porter Rockwell waited on the seat of the carriage, the folding top down. "You may return the carriage, Port," she said, forcing herself to use the familiar nickname her husband had always used. She had tried to be tolerant of Joseph's oldest friend, but she detested his crude arrogance and uncouth manners. "We're walking," she said.

Rockwell shrugged. "President ain't gonna like it," he said, and clicked the reins. The horse trotted away with the carriage.

Andrew stood in the parlor of the Bennett house, where he now spent more time than in the McCann house which was still his home, while Louisa fussed with the neatly pressed new tunic he had just put on. She admired the chevrons on his sleeve, a sergeant's grade accorded him only the week before by Major General Bennett himself.

"I'm so proud of you," Louisa said. She was wearing a white organdy dress with cascades of ruffles edged in red piping, over a series of crinoline petticoats. "We'll make a handsome couple."

Andrew was less impressed with his advancement in rank than was Louisa, because he knew that the Nauvoo Legion contained far more officers than the size of the organization warranted, and a correspondingly top-heavy contingent of non-commissioned officers, such as himself. He suspected that the advancements, which were announced at special ceremonies, were part of the inducement to keep the Legionnaires active and interested, for there was no pay to consider and, in Andrew's case, no significant change in his responsibilities.

But it was an altogether beautiful day he looked forward to. The Legion would put on their performance for Joseph and Bennett to review, then he would be free to sit with Louisa for the rest of the program. They would hold hands tightly beneath the concealing edges of the ruffles she was wearing, and from the varying pressure of their handclasps an astonishing variety of emotions could spring. In the past, even at church meetings, when they could hold hands in secret, they each developed such voluptuous feelings for one another that their cheeks would become flushed, and they could scarcely look at each other for fear of releasing all the pent up passion they had generated. Andrew was looking forward to this Sunday, completely unaware that before the day was done, his world and most of what he held dear would be in ashes around him.

Thomas Sharp was seldom in the company of ladies. Women, yes; he had paid for the attentions of women a few times, since he felt he was unable to attract females in any natural way. But these two were ladies, indeed; the taller, older one, Emma Smith, still had a classic beauty about her despite the fact that she was angular to the point of seeming almost bony. Her eyes were sunken deep in her head, always in shadow, giving Thomas the impression that she had perhaps recently recovered from an illness which might have taken the flesh off her. He was unaware that Emma had had seven pregnancies, most of them very difficult, and that she had seen hundreds of people die as she had fought to nurse them back to health.

And as for Eliza, whom he presumed to be several years younger, but who was in fact a few weeks older than Emma, he put her down in his mind as an attractive little woman in her mid-thirties, still a spinster, apparently—or maybe one of the hundreds of widows he had heard lived in Nauvoo. Widow or spinster, she still had her figure and she seemed to have a cheery disposition as well. He was rather taken with her, in fact.

Now he was preparing to probe these two, to get beneath their composure so that they might inadvertantly reveal information he could turn against the Mormons. "By the way," he said in a conversational tone, "have the Danites been active since moving here to Nauvoo?"

Eliza glanced at Emma. Emma responded to the question with a raised eyebrow. "The Danites, Mr. Sharp?"

"Yes; the group of men who enforce the church laws."

Emma looked at him innocently. "Enforce church laws? Why should God's laws require enforcement from men?"

"You mean," he countered, "that anything the prophet says is regarded as 'God's law'?"

Emma smiled disarmingly. "Well, hardly; being granted the gift of prophecy doesn't remove a man's nature from him, so far as I have been able to see.''

"What I mean is, there was a great threat to the Gentiles by a group within the church calling itself the Danites three years ago. Isn't it true that some of the best of your own men swore they feared for their lives if it were known what the Danites were ordered to do? Is that group still organized?''

"Why, Mr. Sharp, a man of your sophistication—asking a mere woman such a question,'' Emma said. "I am truly honored that you think I could have such information, when in fact I haven't.''

He looked at Eliza, who nodded her head in agreement. "We're only women,'' she said meekly.

The conversation, he could see, would need to take a different turn if he were to glean anything useful from it. He decided to change the subject. "Ah, I see your progress on the temple is moving along,'' he said.

They looked up to the top of Nauvoo hill, where the foundation of the temple was just visible over the rooftops below.

"Has your husband decided just how to convert it to a fortress?'' he asked Emma.

"A **fortress**?'' she asked, looking incredulous. Eliza laughed. "All it lacks is a moat,'' she said.

"Well, it's common knowledge in many parts of the state that what you're calling your temple will in fact be a fortified strongpoint from which to defend Nauvoo.''

Unruffled, Eliza said, "You know, Emma, he's right; that would make a wonderful place for a cannon. Why, you should be able to see all around the horizon from up there, especially from the tower. We must mention it to the prophet.''

"Yes, I'm sure he will be amused,'' Emma said, pleasantly.

"Ladies, I did not mean to be amusing.''

"Well, you are, sir, nevertheless,'' said Emma. "Now, instead of plying us with provocative questions, why not relax and enjoy your stay here? You will see a spectacular performance by the Legion and I think you'll find our food second to none in Illinois. And when you have sensible questions on subjects in which we are acquainted, we shall be delighted to try to be of service.''

Sharp felt thoroughly squelched. He had learned nothing and only managed to put them firmly on their guard. He walked the rest of the way glumly silent except for occasional replies to comments the women made.

The hour of the Independence Day ceremony struck, marked by the report of a cannon, and before the thundering echoes returned, the skurl of snaredrums announced the arrival of the Nauvoo Legion. A pair of grandstands erected for spectators overflowed, and the streets of the city along the route of the march were five and six deep with excited visitors and townspeople.

Joseph and Emma rode in a carriage which pulled up in front of the reviewing stand. A landau had been obtained and riding with the General and his lady were John C. Bennett and the guest from Warsaw, Thomas Sharp. Uniformed officers of the Legion were on hand to assist the quartet down from the landau, and while Generals Smith and Bennett mounted their respective horses for the review of the troops, the others joined guests on the podium.

When the Legion was at last marched to a halt in front of the platform and Andrew, standing in a file of men just opposite the reviewing stand, looked up at the dignitaries, he saw Thomas for the first time. He felt a shock of—*what was it*? Fear? Anger? Yes, both. His own brother, causing him to feel as if he were an enemy who had infiltrated a friendly camp! Then his eyes traveled to the left, to the bleachers where Louisa waited for him. She was sitting not fifty feet away from the man who could destroy them if he chose to.

When the Legionnaires were dismissed to take their seats with the guests, Andrew circled the back of the file and approached the bleachers from the rear so that he would not be seen by Thomas, if in fact he had not already been seen. For a wild moment Andrew thought of taking Louisa from the stands and hurrying away with her, leaving it all behind—Nauvoo, the *Times & Seasons*, the *Argus* and his dual role—and starting all over somewhere else. So pronounced was his presentiment of doom that he scarcely listened to the speakers at all, but kept his eyes fastened on the face of his brother, who sat smiling in the stands as if he were a friend and supporter of all that went on here. As Andrew's fear and anger mounted, he also realized that **he** was here under pretenses just as false . . . and the desirable young woman whose hand he held trusted and believed in him. He was as shocked at his own duplicity as he was at Thomases', and then he realized that at least Thomas had never pretended to be a friend to the Mormons, let alone a member of their church! Of the two Sharp brothers, Andrew thought, **I** am the hypocrite!

When the last speech was over and the music ended the proceedings, Louisa took Andrew by the hand to lead him to the shady spot beneath the reviewing stand where she had left the hamper with their picnic lunch in it. The route there took them close—too close—to the stand. Just as they passed the side of it, Joseph Smith conducted Thomas Sharp down the steps. They passed within inches of each other but Thomas was looking the other way and didn't see his brother. Whispering a prayer of thanks, Andrew gratefully hurried to the spot where he, the McCanns and the Gaines family were to merge their picnic foods. It was back of the grandstand, half a block from the reviewing stand and behind it. Andrew was sure now that Thomas' time would be occupied by Joseph, and that he himself was free to enjoy the afternoon.

The four McCanns—five, counting the baby James—and Samuel and Maude Gaines, Elizabeth and Louisa's brother Bobby, Louisa, Andrew and, arriving late, Rebecca Gaines, crowded around the huge gingham tablecloth spread on the ground. The hampers were unloaded and soon dishes of food were circulating. The talk was light and pleasant, and happiness returned to Andrew.

The Fourth of July orating was discussed. Most agreed that Apostle Young was the best speaker; he had a robust and forthright way of talking and was easy to hear from any quarter. General Bennett seemed to be better educated, but his voice didn't carry as far when compared to the thunderous baritone of Brigham Young. As Jock said, "Between those two men lies a great cultural gulf, but Brigham Young speaks with awful, awful power!" The others nodded in agreement.

"But General Bennett has such a great mind," Rebbeca put in, and then flushed with embarrassment when all eyes turned to her. "Aye," Jock said, "It's as we say. The better speaker, though, is Brigham Young." And then he went on to discuss the thrill it was for him to greet again the first Mormon he had ever heard, Willard Richards, who had just returned that past week from the English mission where the McCanns had been converted.

Andrew wasn't listening. Where he sat, the sun was in his eyes. But coming toward them through the haze of afternoon, stepping among the other picnickers who rose and shook his hands, was a figure who could only be Joseph Smith. The tall, broadshouldered man, the feathered headpiece denoting his rank, the large light-haired head. And, just behind him, Emma and another man, a man who walked with a slight limp and wore a beaver hat.

He started to get up, started to pull Louisa up with him in a spasm of terror, in a last-second attempt to avoid the inevitable, but it was too late. Joseph strode up to the gathering with a wave of his hand, and said loudly, "Ah, there's the man I want to see!"

He was looking down at Andrew, still crouching from his attempt to flee. Louisa was looking at him curiously. All the rest at the table had turned to look at him too. "I have the honor to introduce the brother of our friend, Brother Andrew Sharp. Here is another newspaperman, from Warsaw—Thomas Sharp!"

Introductions were made all around. Andrew stood lamely beside Louisa, knowing that Thomas would see in her the explanation for what he had accused Andrew of: "falling for a Daughter of Zion."

"Please join us, won't you?" Jock said. "We've more than enough food."

Emma spoke up. "We've sampled food at a hundred picnics already, it seems to me, and we've still half the city to visit with."

"But Thomas may want to stay here with his brother for a while," Joseph said heartily. "We'll be sure to come back for you."

"No, no," Thomas said, "I don't want to intrude on your lovely picnic, and I have a boat to catch before long. And besides, Andy and I write to each other all the time, don't we Andy?"

Andrew was speechless, trapped, waiting like a cornered animal.

"By the way," his brother went on, "Mother and Dad send their love."

Andrew felt Jock McCann's stare. "Andrew, didn't ye tell us that your parents were dead?" he asked in surprise.

196

All eyes turned back to Andrew. He could say nothing, explain nothing. He knew now that the final blow was coming and he could do nothing but stand there and hear it rain down upon him.

"Oh, you must be mistaken, Mr. McCann," Tom said. "Why, just the other day they wrote to say how proud they are that Andrew is the Nauvoo correspondent for a fine paper like the Quincy *Argus*!"

Eyes went blank, mouths stopped chewing.

Joseph Smith looked from one Sharp brother to the other.

Rebecca gasped, delightedly, "There! Didn't I tell you?"

Thomas feigned embarrassment and uttered a groan, putting his hands to his mouth. "Oh, no, Andrew-- you didn't tell them that you are the 'Traveler In Nauvoo' that everybody's talking about?"

Suddenly Angus McCann detached himself from the circle and stalked up to Andrew, his face contorted into an ugly snarl. He stood face to face with Andrew, his arms stiff at his sides and his fists doubled. "Is this true?" he demanded.

Andrew hadn't dared to turn and look at Louisa until then. She was standing with her head bowed, her eyes staring at the ground, waiting for the worst.

Angus moved in. He shouted, "I want to hear it, Andrew! I want you to tell us you're not the one who's been writing that trash about the prophet, and the Church, and Nauvoo!"

Andrew tried to look him in the eye but he couldn't. Instead, he turned again to Louisa, who had not moved. "I tried to write both sides," he said. "I didn't mean to hurt anyone. I wrote what I thought was the truth---"

"So you're not an orphan, you're a Gentile spy! Now, tell us this," Angus raged, "are you a Latter-day Saint or was that a lie, too?"

Andrew hadn't taken his eyes off Louisa. She hadn't moved, but stood perfectly still, lips slightly parted, waiting.

Softly, Andrew whispered, "No."

Louisa seemed to sink slightly. He started to reach out to her, when a crashing blow under his eye sent him off his feet and he felt himself being propelled backward until his head smashed into something so solid that a sharp **crack** was the last thing he heard before he went tumbling into oblivion.

"The Blacksmith Shop"
Painting by Al Rounds

Part 4:

The Outcast

Chapter 21

The *Cicero* glided down the Mississippi into the gathering dusk, its smoke plume drifting off into the trees along the Illinois shore. Tired and cranky children with spoiled holiday clothes were arm-yanked by mothers, out of patience from the fatigue and heat of the day. Fathers with their collars off fanned themselves with their hats to keep away the insects and stir a little breeze.

The interior cabin was alive with card players brandishing cigars and drinking rum. A bench ran along both sides of the cabin for those waiting their turn at a hand, and those dealt out of a game. From time to time these spectators looked at the two young men who had come aboard at the last minute at Nauvoo, one of them limping slightly and the other obviously injured in the face. The light-haired man held a rag over his eye and appeared to have trouble walking. The curious pair sat together on the portside bench, the dark one talking to the light one, who kept his head in his hands.

"A damned unfriendly people," Thomas commented as he pulled the cork on his whiskey flask and sampled its contents, then he passed it to his brother. Andrew did not look up. Thomas tried another swallow before pushing the cork back in with the heel of his fist.

"I should've taken that blow instead of you," he said, in a fair imitation of remorse. "It was my idea in the first place for you to pretend to be a Mormon." Andrew remained silent.

"Why, your articles in the *Argus* were just beginning to get good, really good!" Even this compliment did not encourage his brother to lift his head. "You want me to wet down that rag?" Tom asked. Still no reply. He put his arm around Andrew's shoulders. "Well, now that you've seen with your own eyes how they treat Gentiles, I expect you'll be able to turn out some mighty interesting articles for the *Signal*."

This remark brought Andrew's head out of his hands for the first time since his brother had led him to his seat aboard the *Cicero*. He turned and regarded Thomas with his still tearful, inflamed left eye. His right eye was swollen completely closed and a huge purple bruise was beginning to turn jaundice yellow beneath it on his cheek. Dried blood still caked the inside of his lips and stained his teeth, and his look bore utter contempt.

"I'm not going to work for you," he said. Loathing was in his voice.

"Oh, pshaw, Andy; you'll get over this. There'll be other stories, other girls. . ."

Andrew stood up and turned around to his brother. "Just don't say anything else to me," he said, and made his way through the smoke to the cabin door. Several men who had been amusing themselves by watching the pair craned their necks to see what the blond-headed man would do, but to their disappointment he just went outside and leaned against the portside railing.

Illinois was slipping past. Nauvoo was long out of sight in the gathering gloom. Still, he tried to make his vision from his one good eye penetrate the thick tangle of growth along the riverbank, and catch one last corner of a home, or the splash of color from the flag that flew at the temple site. But in his imagination, he saw himself back on the wide street that leads uphill to the house where Louisa lived, saw her face and heard her voice.

"**Oh, God!**" he cried into the hazy dusk, his hands gripping the rail until his knuckles almost splintered, his anguish pouring from him, unashamed.

A somber supper was served in the McCann house. The McCann men were usually sparing in their conversation, but there was now even less said than usual, as Anne quietly laid the bowls of soup before her family, trying to make no noise to break the melancholy silence. Only the baby, pounding chubby fists on the tray of his tiny feeding chair, made a sound in the stillness of the room.

Jock took a spoonful of soup, swallowed it and wiped his beard with a napkin. "After supper," he said, his rumble shattering the vacuum, "I want ye to go over to Sister Stephens and apologize to her."

William and Angus looked at each other and then down into their bowls.

"I know how ye felt," Jock went on, "but ye should'na have hit him. Angus, ye'll do that. Tonight."

"All **right**, Jock."

The family ate again in silence. Anne, ever sensitive to the moods of her men, had no appetite. She picked up the wooden bread dish and offered it to her husband. Silently, he took the loaf in his huge hands and tore off a chunk, which he pushed into his mouth as he passed the dish to Angus. Angus shook his head.

"I'll have some," William said. Angus passed it to his brother.

The baby began to fuss, and Anne lifted him into her arms, unbuttoning her dress. The infant, sensing satisfaction was near, broke into an anxious panting cry which was stilled as Anne turned him to her breast. "What do you want done with the room?" Anne asked.

"Scrub it down," Angus said.

"Angus!" Jock glared a warning to him, and the three men finished their meals without another word.

The door to the Bennett parlor was closed. Inside sat Maude Gaines on the maple deacons' bench with Louisa Stephens at her side. Maude had asked Louisa to come and talk, but now that they were alone, she didn't know exactly how to begin.

Louisa had not uttered a word for some six hours, since she had screamed for Angus to stop his wild fists. Angus hadn't been satisfied with knocking Andrew to the ground, for then, although Andrew had been unconscious, Angus had leaped on him with the evident intent of destroying his face. Louisa had screamed and tried to pry him away until someone lifted her aside, and Joseph Smith, himself had wrestled Angus away from Andrew's senseless body.

Then Louisa had picked up her skirts and started to run. When the Gaines family came home, they had found her sitting in her room, and not a word had come from her since. She sat next to Maude with her dry eyes staring and her lips slightly apart, giving her an expression of uncomprehending detachment.

Maude reached over and took one of her hands in hers. "You must remember one thing," she said. "Just because Andrew wasn't completely honest about part of his life doesn't mean that he isn't truly in love with you. After you ran away, you know, I sat with his head in my lap while they bathed his face and brought him 'round, and the first thing he said when he came to himself was, 'Louisa!' The very first thing!"

She wasn't sure Louisa had even heard what she had said, for her eyes didn't change, and her hand lay in Maude's like the hand of a corpse.

"And when he got to his feet and they were stripping his uniform off him, all he could do was call for you and look around for you. You were all he could think of!"

Now, a tear appeared in the corner of each of Louisa's eyes and rolled down her cheeks.

Someone knocked at the parlor door. "We're busy," Maude shouted, but the door opened, and Rebecca stepped in.

"Not now, Rebecca," Maude said impatiently. "Louisa and I are having a private talk!"

In a small voice, Rebecca said, "I just wanted to say how sorry I am. . ."

"You can tell her later," her mother said, nodding at the door. "Please leave us alone now."

"Mother . . ."

"Do as I say!"

Piqued, Rebecca stepped out, slamming the door.

Maude offered Louisa her handkerchief. Dabbing at her eyes, Louisa tried to smile. "I want to thank you for everything that you and Brother Gaines and Rebecca have done for Bobby and me," she said with great composure. "I shall never be able to repay you."

"Nonsense, dear, we don't want to be repaid."

"And I have been doing a great deal of thinking," Louisa went on, "and I have decided to leave."

"Leave? Leave the family? Where would you go?"

"I don't know yet," she said, "but that is what I have decided to do." She sniffed and dried her tears. "I have to make plans for the rest of my life, you see."

Maude understood. Until this afternoon, Louisa had her future wrapped around Andrew, and suddenly he was gone. "But things may not be as you think," Maude put in hopefully; "Andrew certainly still loves you. Do you still love him?"

Calmly, Louisa turned away. "I don't intend ever to see him again as long as I live."

"Oh, now I . . ." Maude began, but was interrupted by the sound of a firm knock on the front door. "Rebecca will get that, whoever it is," she said, and Rebecca's step could be heard hurrying to the door. Her muffled voice and that of a man's conversed briefly, and then came another knock on the parlor door.

"Well, we'll talk some more later, dear," Maude said, and got up to go to the door.

Filling the hallway were Jock and Angus McCann. Their expressions told her that Jock was here as an enforcer, determined that Angus do his courtesy.

"Angus has come to speak a word with Sister Stephens," Jock said somberly.

Defensively, Maude said, "Well, Louisa may not be up to much company just at the moment, Brother McCann. Wait here, and I'll see," and she vanished inside the parlor again and shut the door.

Rebecca stood with the McCanns, admiring these two sturdy men. "Quite an exciting time of it this afternoon, wasn't it?" she asked.

"Quite," Jock said, glancing her way and then back again to the door.

The parlor door opened again, and Maude stepped out. "She asked you to come in," she said, holding the door. When they had gone in and closed the door, Maude steered Rebecca down the hall by the elbow.

Louisa was standing at the end of the room, in front of the hearth, wearing the same dress she had worn at the picnic. Now, Jock prodded Angus forward. Angus turned to his brother and said, "Do ye mind, Jock? I'd like to do this on my own!" There was a fierceness beneath his hushed tone. Jock stepped back, nodded at Louisa, and left the room.

"Hello, Louisa," Angus said.

"Hello, Angus."

"Mind if I sit down?"

"Not at all." He sat on the deacons' bench, but seeing that Louisa wasn't sitting, got up again. "I'll stand, then," he said.

He took a look around the room. "I've come to ask for your forgiveness for what I done this afternoon."

They were eight feet apart, neither looking at the other.

"I've an awful temper, sometimes," Angus said.

Louisa found it hard to think what to say to this man. She knew how uncomfortable he was, especially with his older brother pushing him into the room to say his piece. But, since she saw he might say nothing else until she replied, she found words.

"You needn't apologize to me, Angus."

"Oh, yes I must. I know how you feel about Andrew."

She opened her mouth, but the words wouldn't come.

"I hope he's not badly hurt," Angus added. "It's not Christian of me to do what I done."

"I forgive you."

He rotated his cap in his hands, looking down at it, then he looked at her. "If ye ever write to him . . ."

Louisa looked levelly at Angus. "I don't expect to ever hear from him or see him again," she said.

Angus paused, then took a step toward her. "Ah, Louisa, what I hit him for was for the hurt he done to you, the way he betrayed you! I could'na stand for that." He dropped his eyes. "Well, I'd best be goin'."

He turned to the door, then he turned around again. "Can we be friends?"

Louisa nodded. "Of course, Angus."

He clapped his cap on his head and opened the door. "Good night, then, and thanks."

Jock stood alone in the hallway with his arms folded. "Well?" he said expectantly.

"I apologized, and she accepted," Angus said.

"All right; tomorrow's Monday," Jock said, ushering his brother out of the Bennett house, "and we've work to do at the river."

The *Cicero's* steam whistle shrilled into the night, announcing to Warsaw that there was a load of passengers back from the Mormon holiday doings upriver.

Lanterns hung on the dock and back through the vegetation twinkled oil lamps in a few windows. Andrew had spent the entire journey at the ship's port rail, lost in his thoughts. Now he was made more conscious of the miles between his heart and his battered body by the slowing of the ship's motion and the hiss of escaping steam, as the paddle wheel stopped. It meant he was fifteen miles away from Louisa. Not such a great distance by water or road, but the gulf might as well be from here to the stars, for them. He could not go back, could not erase the shame of the afternoon; that would always characterize him to her, he knew. And he had his brother Tom to thank for it all.

At least he had had the decency to leave him alone. But now, with passengers lining up to leave the ship, Tom appeared beside him and dumped his traveling bag at his side. "Want me to carry this?" he said, attempting to sound as if nothing had happened between them.

"No, give it here," Andrew said, picking up the bag.

"There's a good bed waiting for you at the newspaper," Thomas said. "I moved out of Mrs. Wilson's — remember her? — because the newspaper office has rooms right above it. Very cozy, and the rent is free!"

"I'm not spending the night with you, Tom. And I'm not working for you tomorrow, or any time!"

"And what do you think you'll do now?"

Andrew turned to his brother, a murderous look on his battered face. "Whatever I may do, I'll do it without your interference. You're right, Tom; you should have gotten this," he said, pointing to his own swollen cheek, "but from **me**. I deserved this, but so do you. For creating a little world of lies, and then destroying it. Well, be proud of yourself, Tom: you destroyed me right along with it! And whatever else I have coming in this life, I'll take it — but without your string-pulling, do you understand? Now, thanks for the boat ride."

Andrew hefted the bag and edged around his stunned brother, joined the debarking throng, and set off into the dim, narrow lanes of Warsaw without looking back.

He was grateful for the darkness which concealed his injuries, but he knew he couldn't get a ride to Quincy until morning. He had no plans now, for suddenly he felt like a man without a future. Like Louisa, he had set a course to be traveled in tandem. What he should do with the rest of his life, he couldn't imagine.

The Warsaw streets looked familiar. Had it been only eleven months since he had stopped here on his way to Nauvoo? Into less than a year, he felt he had packed the best part of his life. As he walked, faces appeared to him: proud, devious John C. Bennett; tough and unswerving Jock McCann, his quiet wife and — painfully recalled — pugnacious brother, Angus; jovial Don Carlos, motherly Maude Gaines, her flirtatious daughter Rebecca — but beyond them all, the face of Louisa loomed in his imagination. He could still feel the touch of her lips, still hear the sound of her voice, still see the love in her eyes. Could it all be gone? Could he really be away, and alone? His one serviceable eye filled now with tears, and he had to lean into a darkened doorway until he could seize control and go on.

He discovered that his feet had carried him to the veranda of Mrs. Wilson's roominghouse, and the aroma of fried chicken told him that the establishment was under the same management. On the porch sat three men, quietly taking the evening with their pipe and cigars. He decided to walk around back, for he supposed that the pleasant proprietress would be found in her kitchen, and he was correct.

The back door was propped open for ventilation and under lamplight from a four-lamp chandelier, the black-haired landlady labored. Just as the last time he had seen her, he was too late to eat one of her meals, but the scent lingered tantalizingly in the air. He knocked on the open door.

She looked up from the sink, took a swipe at a lock of jet hair that hung on her forehead, and squinted into the black night. She had to step away from the sink, dish in hand, to see who had knocked, and when she caught sight of Andrew's mangled face, her mouth dropped open, and the dish fell from her soapy fingers to shatter on the floor.

"Oh my land!" she cried.

Andrew dropped his traveling bag and hurried in to help her collect the pieces. "That's two I owe you."

She turned, on her haunches, and examined him closely. "It's you! The lawyer's brother! Only he's not a lawyer anymore!"

"And I'm not his brother anymore," said Andrew grimly. "Here, let me pick these pieces up."

She got her breath back and blew a sigh of air at the lock of hair still exploring her forehead. "What on earth happened to you?" she asked.

"Everything," Andrew said. "Can you rent me a room for tonight?"

"Of course. But you don't make any sense. Weren't you the newspaper writer?"

"That's right, I **was**."

"And you're not Mr. Sharp's brother any more?"

"Biologically, yes. Mrs. Wilson, I'm in terrible shape," and as he said it, he had to stop to wipe his watering good eye. "Could you tell me which room?"

"The same one, would you believe? You remember which?"

"I think so. Top of the stairs and to the left?"

"What happened to your face? Were you in a fight?"

"Uh, yes." He picked up his bag and headed for the hall.

"Where? Where?"

"In Nauvoo."

"Ugh! Mormon town? Is that where you've been?"

He loved her direct curiosity. "That's where I've been. Do you have anything to make my face any better?"

"Listen here, what was your name again, Mr. Sharp?"

"Andrew."

"All right. Mr. Andrew Sharp, I will fix your face and feed you if you will tell me about the Mormons and Nauvoo. All I know about them is what I read in your brother's paper, and it's not good."

He laughed. "I know. It's a deal, Mrs. Wilson. You fix my face and feed me, and I'll tell you about Nauvoo!"

He found that in the telling, the story lived again. As he introduced her to each of the people he had met, she stopped him to ask details — what did he look like, where did she come from, how big was the house — and as he fleshed in the descriptions, he realized that he should write this way, too, if he could talk this way; people seemed interested in details, descriptions.

He told her how he had first seen Louisa on the *George Washington*, and about the storm and his broken rib, about the McCanns and the Gaines family and meeting Don Carlos.

"Ah, you liked him, I can tell," she had said.

He went on, telling of the little gunsel, Orrin Porter Rockwell; of the big Smith men, Joseph and Hyrum, and the love and respect they engendered throughout Nauvoo; he talked of the Nauvoo Legion and the curious little man who seemed to have every talent an intellect could produce — doctor, educator, politician, military leader — but who was possessed of one major weakness.

"Yes, and what was that?" Mrs. Wilson asked, eagerly.

At this, Andrew stopped. Here he had been gossiping about a man with a major weakness, when he had been guilty of living a lie every bit as much as he suspected John C. Bennett of doing. Mrs. Wilson saw the pensive look in his eye and asked him, "So, you care for Louisa, I can tell." It was half statement, half question.

"Yes, very much."

"Is that what the fight was all about?"

He took a deep breath. "Yes, and no."

He then admitted that he had been living in Nauvoo under false pretenses, and that as he found he had fallen in love with Louisa, he hadn't dared confess his dual role to her for fear that she would drop him. Then he told how his brother had intentionally disclosed his secret, and how Angus — whom he had felt all along had strong feelings for Louisa — had hit him, knocking him out.

Mrs. Wilson put another cold compress on his face. "Then what happened?" she asked.

"When I came to, all I could think of was what Louisa would think. But it's obvious what she thought; she was gone."

"And you didn't go looking for her?"

"No. They brought me my things jammed into my bag and made me take off my Legion uniform right there under the grandstand," he said, "and by then it was time to go down and get on the boat. And so here I am."

"So you don't really know how she felt about you? Why didn't you just stay in Nauvoo and explain things to her, the same way you've explained them to me?"

"Stay in Nauvoo?" He laughed bitterly, "I was given to understand that the sooner they saw the south end of me, the better for my health. Mormons don't take kindly to Gentile spies."

"Gentiles?" Mrs. Wilson asked. "They don't like Gentiles? That sounds like my people. I'm Jewish, Andrew, and I married a Gentile, and my father disowned me. I'm dead, to him! Is that how Mormons feel about Gentiles?"

He considered his answer carefully. "No, not all Mormons hate all Gentiles. But the Mormons went through living hell for their beliefs, at the hands of Gentiles."

"Now, why don't I read some of this in the papers?" she asked.

"Maybe you would have . . . if I'd been able to remain with the *Argus*."

"You've lost your job?"

"I suppose I have. I was hired as their Nauvoo correspondent, and I'm not in Nauvoo any longer."

"So, what are you going to do?"

"Tomorrow, I'm going down to Quincy and talk to the editor. From there — I don't know."

She got up, patting his hand. "It's late, get some sleep. Tomorrow I pack you a good lunch. Oh, did you like the last one I packed?"

His memory shot back to the trip upstream, the beginnings of his life in Nauvoo and the start of his cherished association with Louisa. "Oh, yes," he said, a distant look in his eye, "I liked it."

The Hancock County Stage Lines served Warrsaw at about ten A.M. Andrew was aboard it as it rattled south through Tioga, Lima, Marceline and Ursa, down just west of Fowler, and finally, Quincy. He sat with five others in the dusty coach, enjoying a finer repast from his lunch sack than any road-house could offer, and he blessed raven-haired Mrs. Wilson with each mouthful. She had not only sent him off with a substantial lunch in his sack, but had fed him a good breakfast at her table after all the other boarders had left for work, and her ministrations with the compresses had reduced the swollen eye enough that he could now see through it to some extent, but the bruise was still ugly enough to cause heads to turn at the wagon stops.

The verdant town of Quincy loomed ahead, and Andrew's pulse quickened. Soon he would know whether he still had a job or not. He got his bag off the rack and hurried to the office of the *Argus*.

Today, late in the afternoon though it was, the press was running. It was a modern steam-driven model, much like those in use in larger cities, and the engineer and pressman were vigilant, lest one of the wildly oscillating levers, whirling cams, or other machinery jam, loosen or attempt to destroy the efforts of the small newspaper staff to publish a competent newspaper. The hot moisture emanating from the engine softened newsprint into soggy rags, so a steady shuttle of blank paper had to be provided by hand from a storage room, and the finished pages had to be taken out to a drying shed before they became waterlogged. Andrew stood and watched the fascinating process for a minute or two before he hurried up the stairs to Mr. Ketchum's office.

Ketchum, having worked the clock around to meet the printing deadline, lay asleep in his chair, apparently lulled by the rhythmic thumping and hissing of the printing plant just below him. Andrew was disappointed, but was reluctant to interrupt his sleep. His very presence in the cluttered loft somehow alerted some still-wakeful sense in the old editor, however, and as Andrew tiptoed back to the door, he swung his bulk upright in his chair and called, "Huh? Who's that?"

Andrew stepped back into Ketchum's sight. "Andrew Sharp," he said.

The editor found his eyeglasses and hooked them over his ears. "What happened to you?" he asked. "Did you write a story somebody didn't like?"

Andrew smiled wryly; everyone who spoke to him asked something different about his injuries. "No, sir, not exactly, but in another way — yes."

"Which requires some clarification," Ketchum said.

And so, once again, Andrew related the story of his expulsion from Nauvoo, omitting the personal details which preyed so much on his mind.

Mr. Ketchum listened attentively until he was done. "You mean to tell me," he said, "they won't tolerate anyone among them who's not a member of their church?"

"No, there are several other Gentiles living there; it's that they thought I was spying on them, and writing things that weren't true."

"And were you?"

"Spying? No; observing. I never pried into anything that I wouldn't have been told about as a reporter for their own newspaper. And as for what I wrote, I stand by it."

"Good!" ejaculated the editor. "It didn't seem to me that your articles were defamatory in the slightest. Certainly, they don't resemble your brother's work. Maybe they got suspicious of you just because of Thomas Sharp's attacks on them in **his** newspaper."

Guiltily, Andrew shook his head. "No, I might have been allowed to stay in Nauvoo if it hadn't been for something else. You see, I let them think I was a Mormon, too!"

"Oh."

"And, like a fool, I even invented a story the first time I talked with a Mormon, that I was orphaned. Just to make them think I'd suffered some hardship, too, I suppose. Anyway, they lost all confidence in me when that came out, too."

"I suppose they take that kind of thing pretty seriously — pretending membership in their faith."

"They do."

The old man leaned back in his creaking office chair and put his hands behind his head. "Well, Andrew," he said, "I'm sorry to lose my Nauvoo correspondent, and I'll be dogged if I know what I can put you to doing now."

Andrew's heart lurched. Mr. Ketchum looked genuinely sympathetic. He bit his lower lip and tilted his head back in thought. "No sir," he said after some thought, "I can't afford to pay a salary to a reporter unless he's reporting, and it doesn't take any more than a man up at the court house and one man here in Quincy to do the job. And we've got those jobs filled."

Andrew managed a rueful smile and stood up, feeling that the interview was at an end.

"Unless, by Ned," the editor said, leaning forward again, "you want to handle our advertising?"

"What kind of a job is that?"

"Going out and selling ads in the paper," Mr. Ketchum explained. "Some papers carry a whole page of advertisements. Those are paid notices. Brings in revenue. I never had many of 'em, but we sure could use the money. 'Course, I couldn't pay you a salary, but I'd give you a commission on every dime you bring in."

Andrew thought it sounded a far cry from reporting. "Would there be any writing to it?" he asked.

"Oh, sure," Mr. Ketchum replied. "You'd be helping customers write up their ads."

It sounded simple enough, and he had to have some kind of income. Besides, it meant he could still remain employed by a newspaper and not have to take work out of his field. "I'll try it," Andrew said.

The old man stood up, chuckling. "Well, now, if you're going to just 'try it,' I don't know as I want you for the job. But if you were to say, 'I'll **do** it,' I'd say you and I were going to be pretty successful. How about it?"

Andrew nodded. "All right, sir; I'll do it. Thank you."

"That's the boy," Mr. Ketchum said.

The days dragged by for Andrew. He found a room to rent in the home of an elderly couple who would accept him and his battered face only after a recommendation by Elias P. Ketchum himself. There was a period of enforced idleness suggested by Mr. Ketchum, to allow the wounds to become less noticeable. It was true that Andrew's injured face looked grotesque, but each day brought an improvement.

But no such improvement took place within. He mourned for Louisa, wrote her a long and impassioned letter explaining how he had permitted himself to be led into his impersonation by Thomas; he declared his desire to report only the truth; he said how he regretted deceiving anybody; he recalled the friendships he had made in Nauvoo; and he closed with the most carefully-constructed part of the long epistle:

> Now I realize more poignantly than ever, that I may have forfeited not only the respect of many who trusted me, but most especially your own respect and love, for I do truly believe that you were as honest with me in declaring your love, as I was in telling you of mine. I swear to you that, of all my many deceits, I never lied to you on that tender subject. I loved you then, Louisa, and I love you even more at this moment. May I dare to hope that you might forgive me and send me my heart's fondest desire — your assurance that your feelings for me still exist?
>
> Your contrite and dearest friend,
> Andrew

Chapter 22

Being the county seat of Adams County, Illinois, Quincy enjoyed the annual Adams County Fair, which was held early in September, to coincide with harvest time. Prosperous farmers and their wives spent hours inspecting new machinery from Moline, the best livestock from the county, homespun and honey from the settlers in the lonely Quincy Hills, and new patents to make healthier and happier the sturdy lives of the local fairgoers.

It was a time of gently warm days and chilly nights, of turning leaves which made a blizzard of color when the wind tore them from their branches and sent them flying across fields and lanes. Catfish fries were again in fashion, and smoke of a thousand perfumes drifted through the land.

Through this seasonal bazaar, Andrew walked with order pad and pencil, disconsolately transformed from a journalist to a drummer. He had found that those persons willing to advertise in the *Argus* claimed to be a doctor and who marketed a salve which, it was claimed, would remove all wrinkles if applied frequently enough to the female epidermis; a jocose gentleman with a still in his back yard, whose "tonic" would knock over a horse, but who claimed it would restore youth to the aged and health to the sickly; and a poultryman who wanted to tell all the county about his special feed mash which would double egg production, if it didn't kill the hens.

Andrew, of course, had been told to help these customers draft their advertisements, but being trained to report facts and not hearsay, he found it galling to be part of the process that would place into public print such outrageous claims as his clientele were making. Invariably, when he would write up an ad and show it to a prospect, the advertiser would reject it on the grounds that it wasn't compelling enough. Claims were made which were purest invention, and the eager seller seemed to care not at all that his first sale might be his last.

Andrew felt his credibility as a journalist slipping from him, and he longed to be able to report news again. But the correspondent at the Court House, while easily as old as the venerable Elias P. Ketchum, showed no signs of weakening, and the other reporter held tenaciously to his beat and spoke as little as possible with Andrew, proving that he wouldn't give an inch of his constituency to any johnny-come-lately ad drummer who wanted to report the news.

And so Andrew prowled the fairground for prospects, and found a handful who would risk a one-time-only insertion in the newspaper. Taking money — as little as it was — from this kind of enterprise seemed more dishonest to him than any of his covert reporting had in Nauvoo. He thought often of the orderly, spotless city and the pride its residents took in it. But he thought most about Louisa. It was a hopeless effort, though, he knew; she had had his letter for over two months and had not written him an answer.

At the end of a dismal day drumming business for the *Argus,* he walked back into town, calculating his commission for the day's efforts at about fifty cents. He couldn't afford a decent meal (how he dreamed of the food at the McCann's, or at Mrs. Wilson's!) so he went up to his room hungry and took out the purse in which he kept his money. He was wearing out his only pair of boots and was saving for the price of a re-sole. His only serviceable suit of clothes was already so patched that he knew he looked more like an itinerant beggar than a sales representative of a newspaper, and unless his fortunes changed drastically within a few more days, he knew he was going to run out of money just trying to keep body and soul together.

The fireplace in his room held a few sticks of unburned but slightly charred wood, and he made a low fire and sat by it as the night came on. There was, of course, one alternative he could fall back on; he could return to Warsaw, beg Thomas to forgive him for the tongue-lashing he had given him when they had last met, and ask for the job he had offered him. But to work for the Warsaw *Signal* would be to sell his soul for an even lower price than drumming for advertising. Thomas would expect him to write violently Anti-Mormon articles. That, Andrew knew he would not, could not do. But what **could** he do, to survive?

It was in this desperate frame of mind that he now drew up his knees and cradled his tired head on folded arms before the wan little fire. He was so tired, so discouraged, so lonesome.

How long he had sat there in the darkness he didn't know. But suddenly he heard a knock on the door to his room. He had not lit the lamp, and the fire had gone out; it was almost totally dark, and as he got to his feet, he wondered who this could be. He hadn't had a single visitor in the two months he had been staying there. He went to the door and saw the old landlord holding a candle. "Visitor for you, Mr. Sharp."

"Just a second, let me get some light," he said, reaching for a match on the table by the door. The match flared, and he touched it to the wick of the lamp, replaced the chimney, and then looked up — into the face of Samuel Gaines!

"Brother Gaines!" Andrew cried, pulling his door wide open. "Come in! I'm so glad to see you!"

Samuel walked into the tiny room, in which there was a narrow cot and one chair, the table by the door and a low stand which held the chamber pot and a pitcher. "Please, sit down," Andrew said, pulling out the chair for him. Andrew would have been delighted to see any face from Nauvoo, but to have someone from the very household in which Louisa lived was like an answer to a prayer.

"Well, Andrew, and how have you been?" Samuel asked.

"Oh, well enough," he replied. "How are you? And Sister Gaines and

213

Rebecca?"

The Englishman's smile faltered. "Quite well."

"And . . . Louisa? Is she well?"

"Well, so far as we know."

Andrew was alarmed. "What do you mean?"

"Louisa moved out of Dr. Bennett's house nearly two months ago, into the home of Brother and Sister Richards."

"Richards?"

"Willard Richards. He's an apostle of the Church. He's just back from England as a missionary. Now he's one of the Twelve."

"Why did she move out?"

"Well, after you left, she didn't quite know what to do with herself, and . . ." He shrugged. "Shall we say, a very mixed-up young lady."

"It's all my doing," Andrew said, looking away. Samuel didn't reply.

"Well," Andrew said, looking back at him again, "what brought you to Quincy?"

"I came to see you," he said.

"Me? After everything . . . why?"

Samuel shifted in the chair, looking uncomfortable. "There have been a great many changes in Nauvoo since you left," he said. "I suppose you know about Don Carlos and Robert Thompson?"

"No."

"Both dead, Andrew. Don Carlos, then only a few days later, Brother Thompson."

Andrew was stunned. "No!" he said, shaking his head, "I can't believe it! Not Don Carlos!"

"Yes, I'm afraid so," Samuel said. "The ague. You know how damp it was in that cellar where they kept the press."

"What about the *Times & Seasons*?"

"Ebenezer Robinson has taken over as editor, and I've taken your old job, but I'm not good at it."

"What about your book-binding?"

"I'm going to go back to it, it's all I know. Ah, Andrew, so much has happened, both good and bad."

"Tell me, I've been perishing for news from Nauvoo!"

"Well, just after Brother Smith and Brother Robinson passed away, the Prophet and Emma lost their little one, too."

"Little Don Carlos?" Andrew's eyes filled.

"Yes. It's been terrible, Andrew, the way that fever takes them."

"Can't anything be done? What is Dr. Bennett doing?"

"Organizing a university," Samuel said, bitterly. "There's naught to be done for the sick, it seems, except to pray for them, and some recover, some don't. President Rigdon is still down with it — it's been three years, they say!"

"It seems all the news from Nauvoo is bad!"

"Oh, no, not all. There's been some good in it, too. You wouldn't recognize the temple, it's grown so much. President Smith has everyone working on the temple every tenth day, and it's going up quickly. And he's building a general store, he calls it a 'country store,' made all of red brick and two stories high. It's a fine piece of work. And the city's growing. They say it's up to ten thousand now."

"How are the McCann's?"

"Their shipyard is coming along. They hired a steam dragline, you know; I'd never seen such a monstrous thing before, and they work it all day and half the night, digging muddy dirt for their inlet from the river. A hard-working bunch, that."

"But now," Andrew said impatiently, "tell me why you came all this way to see me. What can I do for you?"

"You can come back to the *Times & Seasons*."

Andrew was dumbfounded. "Come back to Nauvoo?"

"Yes. We need you."

"Why, they wouldn't let me off a boat or a stage!"

"Oh, nonsense, of course they would. You don't know this, of course, but right after your sudden departure on the Fourth of July, the Prophet asked to see samples of those articles you'd written in the *Argus* as the 'Traveler In Nauvoo,' and after he'd studied them, he stood right up in a meeting with the Brethren, so I'm told, and said he couldn't find fault with them, that they were true! And after that, you were absolved of any blame!"

"But there's the little matter of my pretending to be a member of the Church . . ."

"What harm did you do? Did you try to perform any priesthood functions, baptize anybody, that kind of thing?"

"Well, of course not."

"Well, we know that. As a matter of fact, some of us think it would be a fine thing to have a perfectly impartial observer in our midst, writing objectively about everything that transpires. Might even make us behave more like Saints!"

Andrew laughed delightedly. "Brother Samuel — if I may still call you that, knowing that it's done out of friendship rather than Church member-ship — I should love to be that 'impartial observer'!"

"Well, what about your position with the *Argus*?"

"My position today is barely keeping me or the *Argus* alive. I'm sure Mr. Ketchum would be delighted to have me back as the 'Traveler In Nauvoo' — if Nauvoo would have me!"

"Well, Nauvoo will have you. Gladly. Oh, and I almost forgot! Soon, the *Times & Seasons* will be moving into a grand new brick building up on the corner of Main and Kimball! Out of the swamp!"

"Well, that clinches it!" Andrew laughed. "I'll speak to Mr. Ketchum the first thing in the morning!"

Two trails of dust rose from the tracks of the iron tires as the coach bearing Andrew, his worldly goods and his hopeful heart, clattered west on the road out of the Hancock County seat, Carthage, toward Nauvoo, on the last lap of Andrew's pilgrimage.

It had been a tiring day-long journey, and the three other passengers to Nauvoo were showing signs of fatigue, but Andrew — who had slept almost not at all the night before — was straining through the dusk for his first sight of the city.

Where the Carthage road became Parley Street, the city spread out before them like an opened book, and Andrew clung to the sill of his open window to take it all in. In only two months, he was sure there were fifty new buildings, and when they got to where he could look north to the temple site, he was amazed at the progress on the building.

He knew nothing of where Apostle Richards lived, but he asked for directions from the first man he saw when he got off the stage, and was directed to a tidy new brick house only a few blocks away. On his way he had encountered a dozen or so people in the street, but it was by now so dark that none recognized him. Besides, as Samuel Gaines had said, there were so many new arrivals, he might not meet anyone he had ever known before. It didn't matter to him; he would do whatever he had to to reconstruct a reputation in Nauvoo, once he had established himself again with Louisa.

The Willard Richards home was serene, just completed, by the looks of its bare surroundings. Andrew bounded up to the front door, heart racing, and knocked.

The man who opened the door looked like a giant. His bulk filled the doorway from side to side and top to bottom. Standing on a lower step and looking up at him, Andrew thought the man was almost too big for the modest dwelling. He looked down at Andrew and said, in the pleasantest of voices, "Good evening, brother."

"Good evening, sir. Would you be Willard Richards?"

"I am."

"I'm looking for Louisa Stephens; I'm told she lives here."

Richards stepped outside and closed the front door behind him. "It's Brother Sharp, isn't it?" he asked.

"Yes! How did you know?"

"You were somewhat — notorious around here a short time ago, you know, and we were told that you were to be invited to return, to help with our newspaper. So you were expected."

Andrew couldn't understand why the interrogation in front of the house; why didn't he just let him see Louisa? "Does Louisa expect me?" he asked.

"I don't believe so. Louisa and my wife, Jenetta, are away at the home of another sister, on Church matters. Would you like to come inside?"

Andrew accepted, and found the remains of supper on the table. "Jenetta prepared only enough for me," Richards said apologetically, "and I've just finished eating, or I'd be glad to share with you."

As hungry as he was, Andrew had no thought for food — not until he had seen Louisa. The thought of seeing her walk through the door thrilled him. He seated himself at Richards' invitation, in a chair that gave him a view of the front door.

"I have been wanting to talk to you," Richards said. "Joseph has often mentioned that you have a means of taking down conversation as rapidly as it is spoken."

"Well, if the speaker doesn't talk too fast, yes."

"I am the Church historian, and also Joseph's personal secretary. Such a talent as you have — do you think you could teach it to me?"

"I'm certain I could."

"Would you be willing to do so?"

"Of course. However, there is the problem of where to teach you. I haven't any idea of where I'll be living."

"Ah, then it takes a long time to learn the technique?"

"I don't know, I've never tried to teach it. But it might take quite a bit of time."

"Well then," Richards said, looking about him, "would this room be acceptable?"

With a smile, Andrew said, "It would be ideal." He realized that this assignment would place him in close proximity to Louisa, and on official business, at that! "When would you like me to begin?" he asked.

"Oh, gracious, you have so much to do to get settled; let's talk about that later."

They sat mute for a moment. "You just got in on the stage?" Richards asked.

"Just a few minutes ago." The loud ticking of a clock marked the dragging seconds.

"And how is Quincy these days?" the apostle asked, big hands tapping on the arms of his chair.

"Busy. They're having the Adams County Fair just now." They were rapidly running out of sensible conversation, and Andrew couldn't take his eyes off the door. "When do you expect Sister Richards and Louisa to be home?" he asked.

"Why, any time, any time. They haven't gone far."

Andrew saw in the man's face a look of friendliness, so he risked a personal question. "Brother Richards — what does the town think of me?"

The tapping hands paused. "Well," he replied carefully, "the town, of course, is made up of thousands of people. Your, ah — sudden departure on the Fourth of July was mentioned — ah, somewhat."

"Did they think I was an enemy of the Church?"

Richard ran a hand over his mouth. "I never heard that word used," he said. Then, with a frank smile, he said, "You were much more unpopular with those who never read anything you wrote in the *Argus,* than you were with those who took the time to read your articles. That's why the Prophet wanted you to come back, Andrew. You wrote the truth, so far as you were able to determine it. And that is much better than vicious lies, such as — forgive me, I know he's your brother — such as Tom Sharp's Warsaw *Signal* is doing."

"I want to write the facts," Andrew said. "Not Mormon facts or Gentile facts — just facts."

Gently, Richards said, "'Ye shall know the truth; and the truth shall make you free.'!"

At that moment, voices were heard at the door, and Andrew shot to his feet. The door opened, and an attractive dark-haired woman stepped into the room. Seeing Andrew, she smiled in surprise and stepped away from the door. Behind her stood Louisa.

Her mouth was open, her eyes grew large, and they darted first to Willard Richards and then to Andrew.

Richards had struggled out of his chair and was making introductions. "Jenetta, this is Andrew Sharp, who just got in from Quincy. Mr. Sharp, my wife, Jenetta . . ."

Andrew heard himself acknowledge the introduction, but his eyes and mind were on Louisa. She was wearing a dark blue skirt with matching vest and jacket, and a small hat. Around her neck was a white knit shawl. She was more beautiful than he had remembered.

"And you both know each other, of course," Richards said.

"I'll fetch some chairs," Jenetta said.

"Oh, let me help you," Louisa said, fleeing from the room. Andrew was stunned. She hadn't said anything to him! "Why don't I go help the ladies with those chairs?" he said, and strode after them into the next room, where the apostle had recently eaten.

He couldn't identify the look he saw on Louisa's face. Did it say, "You shouldn't be here, now go away"? Or did it say, "You shouldn't be here, but I'm so glad you are"?

He covered his confusion with a smile and hefted two chairs, managing to knock one of the legs sharply against the doorjamb as he brought it into the parlor.

The chairs in place, Andrew turned to greet Louisa, but the two women had remained in the dining room, and he could hear the sounds of hasty whispers.

The men remained standing, and at length, Jenetta came into the parlor. "How nice to meet you, Mr. Sharp," she said, in a formally pleasant way. "I've heard so much about you."

She sat down as if Louisa had never existed. Andrew remained standing by a chair. "Isn't Louisa coming?" he asked.

"Louisa said she has a headache, and has gone up to her room. She asked to be excused."

Oh no! So close, now to be denied even a word with her! Andrew sank ruluctantly into the chair he had been holding for Louisa.

The minutes of irrelevant conversation dragged by, with Andrew becoming more frantic by the second. If she wouldn't even talk to him, how would he ever explain? What good would he be, to the *Times & Seasons*, the *Argus*, to himself?

The conversation was delicate, impersonal, formal to the point of being ridiculous, Andrew thought. Why couldn't he break through to these people and tell them he hadn't come here to discuss weather and crops; he had come here to see the woman he loved, and whom he thought might still love him!

Seizing an opening, Andrew said, "I wonder if I could ask you to — to take a note up to Louisa before she retires, Sister Richards?"

Jenetta looked doubtful, as if this would implicate her in some impropriety of the Gentile world. She turned to her husband.

"Oh, I think that would be all right," he said, smiling.

"Yes, all right," Jenetta said, not convinced. "Do you have the note?"

"I'll have to write it," Andrew said. "Oh, I have pencil and paper."

He had to improvise. What could he write, a love note under the noses of an apostle and his wife? Impossible. Besides, what if Mrs. Richards read it on her way up the stairs?

They were standing by, waiting for his creation to take form. At last, with grim dedication, he wrote a note far removed from the urging of his heart, folded it tightly, and handed it to the primly waiting woman. "This is awfully nice of you, to be a message-bearer," Andrew said with as much graciousness as he could muster.

"I'll take it up to her," she said, holding the tiny missive between her thumb and forefinger. He heard her mount the stairs, heard the discreet rap on an upstairs door, heard the door open, listened intently for words but heard none, and then — to his dismay, heard the same footsteps coming down the stairs again.

"I was hoping she might reply," Andrew said lamely.

"I didn't know if you expected her to reply immediately," Jenetta sniffed. "Shall I go up and see?"

Suddenly, the huge bear of a man who had kept silent exploded, half in jest, half seriously. "Oh, for heaven's sake, Jenetta," he admonished, "Tell Louisa it won't kill her to talk to Andrew for a few minutes! The poor man is dying!"

His wife flushed deeply, said nothing, opened her mouth but thought better of it, and stalked out of the room and up the stairs.

Richards sat down now, folding his hands over his belly like a happy buddah, and nodded for Andrew to relax. The seconds ticked by, marked by the brass and mahogany voice of the ticking clock. Now, Richards and Andrew were conspirators in a farce, it seemed to Andrew. He would glance at Willard Richards, and Richards would raise his eyebrows until they almost met his hairline. Then he would look away in the direction of the stairs, and look back, head bowed so that a collar of fat that hung below his jowls completely masked the top of his shirt, and smile a knowing, benign smile. It was his way of signaling pleasant encouragement and patience.

At last, the sound of a door closing. The sound of footsteps. Slow footsteps, moving in an upstairs hall to the stairs. Then, slowly, a step at a time, reluctant steps coming down the stairs. One set only! Not the rapid stacatto of the upset Mrs. Richards. No! A different tread, a precious one! Andrew found himself on his feet.

Louisa stepped around the corner into the room. She stood motionless at the doorway.

Providence, move that enormous man out of here! Andrew thought, and almost as if he had heard it, Willard Richards heaved himself out of his chair and said, "Well, here she is. You see, all things come to he who waits," and he walked into the dining room, where he could be heard picking up dishes — a signal that he wasn't listening.

Louisa had moved into the parlor to allow Willard Richards to pass. Now she stood, the unfolded note in her hands, her head slightly lowered, her eyes demurely downcast.

"Louisa, I . . ." Words failed him. He wanted to stand and look at her, slenderer than he remembered, more beautiful than he had dreamed.

"Louisa, I meant it. What I wrote in the note. Believe me!"

She looked up at him only momentarily, slowly nodded, and looked down again.

"My letter, did you get my letter?"

The same response, a slow nod.

She didn't move toward him, so he had to move to her. He edged across the room. Now he wouldn't have to whisper so loudly. "There's so much I have to say to you . . . I couldn't put it all in a letter . . . Louisa, you must believe me, I love you! Maybe — maybe you thought I had deceived you, that I wasn't the man you thought I was . . . but I came back to prove to you . . . and to Nauvoo and the whole Church . . . that I **am** an honorable man, and I did write only the truth . . . why, Brother Gaines says even Joseph himself admitted that! If you loved me once, Louisa, I'm the same man you believed I was . . . only better, more repentant . . ." He ran out of words. She hadn't moved or looked at him. "It was all in the letter," he finished, weakly.

She wet her lips with the tip of her tongue as if she was preparing to speak. But she merely stood waiting, just as she had done on that terrible Fourth of July, as she had listened to Andrew confess. She had stood silently, accepting each revelation like a rifle ball, and when she had heard it all, she had run from him.

She stood waiting now, to be sure she had heard all there was to hear, letting him wring from himself the last drop of desperation.

"All right," he said, in a voice just above a whisper, "if you want me to prove myself to you, I can do it. I'll win you back all over again, only you've got to give me the chance!"

And then she looked up, dry-eyed. *It hasn't moved her at all,* he thought. She looked at him compassionately. But the look didn't contain love, it contained sympathy. **Sympathy!**

At last, a tear detached itself from one of her lashes and rolled down her cheek. "Oh, Andrew," she said, "it's too late now!"

"Too late? I don't understand."

She sat down, wiping her eyes. "That afternoon, when you admitted you weren't a Mormon and you were writing those nasty articles . . ."

"Louisa, they weren't nasty! They were nothing but truth!"

"Well, you see," she went on, "I saw that what your idea of truth was — was different from mine. I went home and began to think that maybe you saw everything different, altogether. And I began to think that — what I thought of as love, was different from what you thought of. And so I . . ."

"You what?"

"I decided not to be in love with you any more."

"You **decided**? Can a person just **decide** to be in love or not in love?"

"Yes. I can."

"Well, I can't!" Andrew said. "I spent two months of misery away from you, not hearing a word from you, not knowing if I'd ever even see you again, and I assure you that if there'd been any way I could have just decided not to be in love with you, I would have done it. But I can't just snuff my love, as you snuff a flame. Love becomes a part of you, and you are a part of me now, forever, and I'm still a part of you!"

She shook her head. "No," she said, weakly.

"Yes, I am, Louisa! You may deny it, but it's there, I know it's there! Louisa, is your religion so blind that it shuts out everyone who ever made a mistake?"

"No!" she said, eyes blazing. "I once thought it was, but I found out you can be forgiven."

"Exactly!" Andrew cried. "And I made a mistake, a terrible one, I grant you. Am I not to be forgiven?"

"I forgive you," Louisa cried, "I forgive you with all my heart, Andrew. But I can't love you any more!"

And with that, tears coming again, she jumped up and ran up the stairs. He heard the door open and shut.

Chapter 23

Andrew had never been in Joseph Smith's private office before. It looked a great deal more like the quarters of a busy merchant than like the head-quarters of a religion which its founder had prophecied would sweep all over the world. There were, in fact, no chapels, meeting-houses, or any other 'church' buildings in Nauvoo, so that all the Sunday services were held outdoors in one of two "bowers," or in private homes when it was too cold or wet to go outside.

Here, in the upstairs of a store, the twelve apostles met with the President and conducted the ecclesiastical business of the Church, as well as the financial and political. Grouped around the center table were the President of the Quorum of the Twelve, Brigham Young — a stern-faced middle-aged man with a thrust chin; balding Heber C. Kimball, seated next to him; then there was handsome Orson Pratt, at thirty, one of the most popular of Joseph's inner circle; the Prophet's younger brother, William Smith, tall and imposing like his siblings; 42-year-old John Edward Page, ordained by Brigham Young at Far West before the fall; sensitive, handsome John Taylor, an Englishman; the intense Wilford Woodruff; Joseph Smith's cousin George Albert Smith; mountainous Willard Richards, besting three hundred pounds but known as a gentle spirit; and newly-called Lyman Wight. Orson Hyde and Parley P. Pratt, Joseph explained, were still overseas preaching the gospel in Jerusalem.

"I have asked you to appear before the Brethren," Joseph said, "so that your new residence here will be approved and understood by all." And then, turning to Brigham, he said, "President Young has had misgivings about taking you back with us — something about 'a viper in our breast.'"

Brigham's defiant chin lifted a fraction as he glanced at the Prophet, and then at Andrew. Then Joseph continued.

"I have read your writings in the *Argus* and have asked the Twelve to do so as well. We have found them to be frank and truthful, as far as they go. Unlike your brother Thomas, who has taken it upon himself to villify us in every possible way, you seem devoted to the truth."

There was a pause. Andrew was about to say, "Thank you," when Brigham Young turned to his chair and looked up at the Prophet who stood beside him. "President," he said, "I'd like to ask Mr. Sharp something about the honesty we can expect from him."

Joseph nodded agreement, and Brigham stood up. He was square framed, with a bulging chest and broad shoulders. "Why," he asked, narrowing his eyes into a squint as he looked at Andrew, "did you find it necessary to pose as a member of the Church when you first came here?"

"I never told anyone I was a member," Andrew said. "But it's true that I let people assume it. I thought if you knew I was a Gentile, you would never let me see you the way you really are. You would show me only your best side. I just wanted to live among you, take part in your lives, and write what truly happens here, that's all."

Willard Richards leaned forward, a finger raised. "Now, Brother Sharp, there was one other minor indiscretion, I believe. Did you not represent yourself as being orphaned?"

"To my shame, I admit that I did."

"And what was that all about? Did you know there are dozens of young people in Nauvoo right now who indeed were made orphans by the massacres in Missouri?"

"I know about Far West and Haun's Mill, yes sir," Andrew replied, "and I certainly never would cheapen the memory of those who died there by claiming that I fought there, or that I was one of the sufferers! I suppose that I just wanted sympathy."

That reply seemed to satisfy Richards. "It couldn't have been done to help along your relationship with a certain young lady?" he asked, with a benign twinkle in his eye.

"It certainly wasn't," Andrew said. "I hadn't even met Louisa then!" As he realized what he had said, the Quorum broke into laughter. He realized she was dominating every thought he had.

"Well, gentlemen," Joseph said, "we have much else to discuss tonight, so let us come to a point. As you know, now that Don Carlos and Robert are both gone, Eb Robinson and Samuel Gaines have their hands full, and we need to get that paper out. Does anyone here have an objection to our sustaining Andrew Sharp as an employee of the *Times & Seasons,* and welcoming him in full fellowship back into the community?"

There was no response.

"All those in favor?"

"Aye." It was as if one voice had spoken.

"Those opposed?"

Andrew looked at Brigham Young, whose lip twitched at that moment, but said nothing.

"Then you have it from the highest authority on earth, Andrew, that we welcome you to Nauvoo and expect fine things from you."

"Thank you, President."

The men at the table got to their feet to shake his hand. He went around the circle, saving Brigham Young and Joseph until last. When Brigham took his hand, he said, "If you keep your eyes open, keep your heart open also, brother, and soon you won't have to pose as a Saint; you'll want to become one!"

Joseph smiled and took Andrew's hand in his. "You have stood by me in difficult times, and I'll not forget that. We're glad to have you back."

The fall of 1841 turned cold, presaging an even colder winter. The burying ground was filling with victims of swamp fever, and now the small body of Hyrum Junior, son of Hyrum Smith, was tenderly placed near one-year old Don Carlos, namesake of his uncle, who lay there as well. Funerals were so frequent that a common funeral service was read each week.

Migration from Europe hardly slowed for the season, however. Housing became an acute problem, and land prices rose. Andrew had been fortunate to find a reasonably-priced room to rent in a house at the corner of Ripley and Granger, but many who had families were obliged to spend the winter under tents or share crowded houses, until a way could be opened for them to acquire separate houses for themselves.

Still, Joseph Smith's undimmed vision pushed him to create new projects. As the temple was being built of stone quarried nearby, Joseph designed a hotel to be called "Nauvoo House," on a tract of land directly across the street from the Homestead where Joseph and Emma lived.

Since visitors were often crowding into the President's private residence, Joseph undertook to have built, less than a block away, the Mansion House, where Emma would know the luxury of six rooms to live in, for the first time in her life.

And then there was the country store, which townspeople came to know as the "Red Brick Store." Joseph delighted in playing the merchant when time permitted, and just before Christmas of 1841, after helping his clerks lay in supplies just off the boat from St. Louis, he donned an apron and doled out merchandise at the grand opening celebration. In the space above the store there was room for Church offices and a meeting space.

Christmas of 1841 passed sadly for Andrew, because it marked the one year anniversary of his and Louisa's love pledges. Gradually, he began to feel that his efforts were futile, and he tried to concentrate his life on the newspapers he worked for.

Ebenezer Robinson was a man cut from the same cloth as Andrew Sharp. As Andrew threw himself into the work of the *Times & Seasons,* he soon realized that it was Eb Robinson who must have petitioned for Andrew to be invited back to Nauvoo, because they thought so much alike.

They both held a high regard for accuracy. Robinson kept a personal journal and wrote in it several times a day. "Someday, folks will argue about who said what," he explained to Andrew, "and if they find my old journal lying around, they can read it and see what really happened."

As editor of the newspaper, he applied that same philosophy. The three of them, Ebenezer, Andrew, and Samuel Gaines, worked in virtual harmony. Nothing was said to Andrew about his previous misrepresentations, and through the efforts of Eb and Samuel, he began to learn a little more about the Church. He became familiar with the structure of its framework, its priesthoods and its leaders. He learned of Joseph Smith's historic first vision in Palmyra, his unearthing of the gold plates from the Hill Cumorah in New York, and the later visitations which guided him to found the Mormon

Church.

And in the printshop, no topic was taboo. If Andrew asked a tough or embarrassing question, it was answered forthrightly, and Andrew would unfailingly tell Eb ahead of time if it was information he needed for an *Argus* article. "D'ruther have 'em print the truth than lies," Eb would say, cheerfully. "If we can't stand up to the truth, then we're not the true Church."

Down in Warsaw, Thomas Sharp evidently had abandoned any pretense of fair journalism, and had turned the *Signal* into the official voice of the Anti-Mormon Party. As its editor, he also became the leader of this hate-filled group who clutched at any crumb of scandal that could blacken Joseph Smith's name and sew more antagonism against the Mormons. The break between the Sharp brothers was irrevocable now, and Andrew had to admonish himself not to strike back against the *Signal's* lies through his own *Argus* articles, because that would identify him as a Mormon apologist — which he did not want to be. Respect was growing in Nauvoo for Andrew. In fact, he remarked to Eb one day, "The whole city has accepted me back, but I'm still an outcast to Louisa." He threw himself into his work to try to forget.

But the busiest man in Nauvoo — save for the Prophet, himself — was John C. Bennett. With the perfecting of the Nauvoo Legion and its frequent drills and parades, Bennett as General was increasingly popular and visible. He was mayor, bringing him temporal powers second to no one in Nauvoo, not even the Prophet. And he was deep in the throes of assembling Nauvoo University, of which he, naturally, would be chancellor.

With all of these activities, his private medical practice had been all but abandoned, except in special cases in which the patient interested him. One of these cases was Rebecca Gaines.

As spring approached, and he continued making surreptitious visits to his vivacious boarder when her parents were fast asleep upstairs, he had to repeatedly reinforce his intent to marry her "as soon as the pressures of responsibility lessen." This fabric, however, would stretch only so far, and on one stormy April night in which Rebecca had refused his attentions, matters came to a boil.

He had let himself into his study, which continued to serve as his den of assignation, and was met there, as usual, by Rebecca. But instead of romance, she requested medical attention.

By lamplight with all shades drawn, he gently prodded and poked her abdomen. "How long has this been?" he asked her.

"Last month, and again this time."

"Hmm," he said. "I'm afraid I must make a complete pelvic examination."

When he explained to her what would be entailed, she rebelled completely. He tried to explain that he was, after all, a gynecologist and knew precisely what he was doing. As usual, he prevailed at last; hushed preparations were made in his study, and the doctor performed, not a routine investigation, but an abortion, stifling Rebecca's cries with a bed pillow as he removed the fetus he had been certain he would find. He did not tell her what he had done. After all, it would be inconvenient for him to marry her, now or later, and the arrival of a baby in the Gaines household would inevitably indict him. It was an old story to him; abort and forget.

There was only one annoyance this time. Rebecca turned out to be a bleeder, and his primitive cauterizing methods didn't stop the flow of blood completely. As dawn approached, he still labored with her, and his study went cold from the untended hearth. Rebecca went into shock, and the doctor's usual composure began to crack. A baby would have been bad enough, but if the girl died. . .

At last, the hemorrhaging ceased, and he carried her upstairs to her own bedroom. When Samuel and Maude Gaines awoke to discover the haggard physician coming out of their daughter's bedroom, he quickly explained that he was treating her for a serious urinary tract infection which had flared up overnight, and admonished them to keep her very quiet for several days.

Rebecca's own constitution began slowly to rebuild her ravaged body, and in her enforced isolation from the rest of the household, she had much time to ponder her position with respect to John C. Bennett. She came to the conclusion that he had used her, that he had no intention of marrying her, and that she had been a fool. Now, she firmly decided, he must pay. As soon as she was able, she would speak to one of the Church authorities and confess everything. If Bennett had done this to her, might he not have done it to women before her? After all, he was thirty-seven and worldly. If she didn't take whatever steps a woman could to put an end to his debauchery, how far would it go? She lay in her bed, weeping for her lost maidenhood, and plotted her course of action.

As many as four and five steamships a day were now calling at Nauvoo's dock, and the commercial trade helped the city to flourish. The flood of new residents continued and increased. With astonishing vigor, Mayor John C. Bennett administered the civic affairs of Nauvoo with a firm, if flamboyant, hand, while Joseph Smith continued to publish new scripture, including his translation of The Book Of Abraham, which he had printed in two successive issues of the *Times & Seasons*. Joseph continued to manage his new Red Brick Store. He conducted all Church business on weekdays, preached sermons on Sundays, in March had taken part in the installation of a lodge of Free Masons, and had helped the sisters of the Church organize the Female Relief Society, a charitable organization founded along the lines of the male priesthood. He supervised the temple building and the work on Mansion House. He sold real estate, entertained dozens of visitors each week in his home, found time to play with his children and visit with his extended family. In his enthusiasm for communication he found himself at the *Times & Seasons* so often that he decided to take over as editor, himself, to shorten the route between his dictated articles and publication. Willard Richards was at his side almost constantly, using the shorthand system he was learning from Andrew Sharp.

But beneath the dynamic progress of Nauvoo, forces were forming which even Orrin Porter Rockwell, Joseph's self-ordained intelligence agent, was not yet aware of.

Polygamy was now an open secret and several outraged members of the Church determined that Joseph was a fallen prophet and had to be removed. At first their ranks were small, and they could meet to discuss plans in any secure house, or in an open field. Among them was Alanson Brown, who had earlier been found guilty of theft and bore a deep grudge against Joseph — and William Law, Joseph's own second counselor in the First Presidency. Law not only felt that Joseph was a land profiteer, but suspected him of making advances toward his wife, as well. The antagonist forces started to grow and attract more disenchanted people, both in and out of the Church, who resented Joseph's enormous power, and they swore to bring him down.

They would have help from an unexpected source: Orrin Porter Rockwell, himself. Rockwell was given to taking unannounced and erratic leaves of absence from his assignments for the Prophet, and in early May, he and his wife, Luana, simply disappeared. This didn't provoke much interest; everyone knew Port's bizarre behavior. And what was about to happen, when Porter surfaced in the city of Independence, Missouri, also didn't surprise those who knew him well.

It had come on to rain heavily on the night of May 6th, 1842, and Independence was mostly indoors. The rain whispered through the thick leaves of the trees and shrubbery surrounding an imposing house on Pleasant Street, and wind gusts dashed droplets against the pane of a downstairs window. Just inside the window with his back to it sat Lilburn W. Boggs, former governor of Missouri, reading the evening paper. At his feet was a six year old daughter rocking a cradle containing the Boggs family's newest baby.

A figure materialized in the shrubbery and crept along the side of the house until he was just under the sill of Boggs' window. The sill was too high and the intruder too short to see down to the floor of the room in which Boggs sat. It appeared he was all alone. The figure took from beneath his poncho a gun with a large barrel, aimed it squarely at the back of Boggs' head, and fired. The report sounded like a small cannon.

The window glass disintegrated as a thick charge of buckshot crashed into the graying head, which pitched forward as the body crashed down on the terrified children.

The gun's barrels had been crammed with buckshot and black powder and when all fired at once, created such a recoil that the small hand that had held it lost its grip, and the weapon flew into the darkness. The shooter didn't waste time looking for it, he had to get out of there! Besides, the important thing had been done. Boggs — the worst enemy the Mormons ever had —

was dead!

Only he **wasn't** dead! He was carrying two balls in his brain, one in his neck, another which had passed through to the roof of his mouth, but was clinging to life when Sheriff J. H. Reynolds dashed in. Doctors were summoned, a minister, friends. Governor Boggs couldn't last more than a few more minutes, at most.

Outside, a deputy gave a whoop. "Stand back, boys, here's the weapon!" Out of a mud puddle he fished a Pepperbox pistol.

The rains that soaked Independence that night also fell across a broad striper of Iowa and northern Illinois, and blessed the black soil on Nauvoo's bottomland.

In her room, still giddy from the unexpected exertion, Rebecca Gaines now wrapped her woolen scarf around her neck, put a warm shawl over her head, and made her way to the door. She had planned what she must do and now she was just strong enough to do it. She went downstairs as quietly as her shaky legs would permit, and slipped the front door open. Suddenly, the door to John C. Bennett's study was flung open, and there stood the man in his shirtsleeves. "Where do you think you're going?" he asked her.

"Out."

"You're not strong enough yet, Rebecca. Let me help you back to bed."

"I don't want to go back to bed, John, I'm going out."

Bennett came up beside her and in a low voice, said, "You are taking a terrible chance. Now get up to bed. It's cold and raining outside!" He took her arm, but she pulled away from him.

"I am well enough to do what I am going to do."

"And what is that?"

"That's my business," she said, and in her determined tone, Bennett heard something he had never heard before from this girl, and he was suddenly wary.

"Well, if you must go out in this weather, at least let me get a carriage, and I'll drive you where you're going."

"No. I must do this alone." And she pulled the front door open again. She walked down the steps and into the rain, careful to keep her equilibrium.

"Rebecca!" he called to her. "Come back, don't go! Please!"

She reached the street and turned to the left. Bennett dashed out into the street after her, caught up with her, took her by the arm. She yanked free and continued to walk unsteadily toward her goal, the house of Hyrum Smith.

Bennett looked down at his feet. He had no shoes on, and he was standing stocking-footed in the water. He ran back into the house, hoping no one had seen him. Drying off in his bedroom, he consoled himself. Whom would the Brethren believe, if it came down to that? A little coquette, or the most admired man in Nauvoo, save for the Prophet himself?

Hyrum took the shivering Rebecca into his small parlor and drew up a chair by the fire. His wife gave her tea with honey in it to warm her, and then she left the girl with the Patriarch, and closed the door.

"Brother Smith," Rebecca began, in a soft and steady voice, "I have come to confess my sins."

Hyrum Smith had listened carefully as Rebecca Gaines had unburdened herself about the long relationship she had had with John C. Bennett. None of it surprised him in the least. Port Rockwell had brought him mounting evidence that Joseph had placed his trust in a brilliant but utterly corrupt man. Hyrum was saddened that honest Saints had been exposed to Bennett's chicanery. He had pleaded with Joseph to renounce him and have him removed, but for some reason the Prophet wanted to give Bennett the benefit of the doubt.

It wasn't a surprise, either, for Hyrum to learn the next morning that Bennett was part of a plot on Joseph's life. Rockwell had predicted that, too, but Joseph had scoffed at it. Now, Hyrum was hurrying to the Homestead to warn Joseph before it was too late.

Both families had been laid low by sorrow. The ague which had taken Hyrum and Joseph's beloved brother Don Carlos had snatched baby Don Carlos, barely one year old, from Emma and Joseph's midst, and it took Hyrum's seven-year-old son. Now, Hyrum thought, here am I, coming to their door with more bad news.

Emma greeted Hyrum warmly, and he kissed her on the cheek. Joseph was finishing dressing in his General's uniform. The plumed hat hung on a peg by the door. "Jo, I've got to talk to you," Hyrum said.

Joseph told him to go ahead, but he would have to continue putting on his elaborate uniform.

"Last night and this morning, I've received news about John Bennett. Jo, the man has no morals whatsoever!"

Joseph stopped what he was doing to listen.

"I know now that what Port has been telling us is true," Hyrum continued. "Last night, a sister confessed she has been his mistress for over a year, with him promising to marry her. She says she became pregnant by him, and he performed an abortion on her!"

Joseph's shoulders sank. "Go on."

"Now, this morning, a man I trust implicitly but who is in fear of his life has warned me that Bennett has it fixed with some others to kill you in the sham battle this afternoon."

Emma, overhearing, ran into the room. "How do they plan to do it?" Joseph asked.

"With you commanding the cohort of cavalry, someone will simply shoot you — by accident, of course," Hyrum said.

"Joseph, you're not to go out of this house!" Emma exclaimed. "Hyrum, make him stay!"

"No, no, I have to be there," Joseph said, rejecting the thought. "But I don't have to play target to Bennett's men." A plan formed in his mind.

"We'll go through everything as planned, until the sham battle. I'll alert Captain Rockwood, and he'll tell the other guards."

"Shall we have Bennett arrested? Why take a chance? Let me have him locked up!"

Joseph shook his head sadly. "It wouldn't do any good to lock up just one man. There are others." He turned back to his dressing.

Hyrum smiled at his sister-in-law as he left. "Joseph will be all right. I'll see you at the parade ground." But he wasn't as confident as he sounded.

The next morning was a long-awaited demonstration of skill by the Nauvoo Legion, to be climaxed by a sham battle, in which one cohort would be commanded by Major General John C. Bennett and the other by Lieutenant General Joseph Smith.

John C. Bennett was humiliated and terrified. Humiliated because his usually well-oiled precision on the parade ground had been thrown off completely by Joseph's refusal to lead the second cohort. And terrified because he now knew that his hours were numbered in Nauvoo. Gone would be the impressive house which he had only begun to pay for. Gone would be his prestige and influence. And all because of one man: Joseph Smith. He detested him for having life-and-death control over him, for his arrogant use of his power. But he hated him mostly because he feared him, and what he would do when all the truth came to light.

And that stupid girl, Rebecca! Who would have thought that the dazzle would wear off and that she would have the temerity to accuse him, which she surely had done when she left the house the previous night. It was written all over her.

He sat gloomily in his study, surrounded by the trappings of honor, and wondered what to do next. He decided finally to play the cards to the very last hand, and see if he might yet salvage his repute in Nauvoo.

He was removing his heavy parade uniform when there was a firm knock at his door. He opened it and found Samuel Gaines standing before him. The mild Englishman had an unholy look in his eyes as he backed John C. Bennett into the study and slammed the door behind him.

"You scoundrel!" Samuel said. "I should thrash you within an inch of your life!"

"In heaven's name, man, for what?"

"For what you've done to my daughter," he said. "Under our very noses, for a year and a half, you've had your way with her, you miserable scum!" And he let fly a straight-armed blow with his open hand that staggered Bennett and sent him against his desk.

Bennett edged his way around the desk, putting it between him and Samuel Gaines. "Is that what she told you?" he asked, feeling the blood on his numb lip. "Your precious little innocent isn't nearly as innocent as you thought she was," he snarled.

The enraged man started toward the desk as Bennett hauled open the drawer where he kept a spare surgical kit. Flipping the case open, he drew out a long scalpel. He held it out in front of him and brandished it like a miniature sword. "You're really too upset,   Brother Gaines," he said. "I can give you something for it. This!" and he lunged across the desk at Samuel's face, connecting with his chin. A bright red line of blood spurted from the slicing wound.

Leaping back, Samuel tripped and fell over a chair. Bennett saw his chance to escape. He ran out the door of the study and into the street. He knew of only one sanctuary, one person who would protect him now, and, officer's jacket flapping wildly, he ran as fast as he could down the street, toward the Homestead.

Joseph and Emma had enjoyed a bite of food together following the sham battle, and then he had changed into his workday clothes, and had just left his back door to go to his store when he heard running footsteps on the road. John C. Bennett approached, coat flapping, a wild look on his face, and he dove through the gate and fell to his knees at the feet of the Prophet. Grasping Joseph by the legs, he burst into tears. "Joseph, oh Joseph, forgive me!" he cried.

"What have you done?"

"I have conspired against you! And I have been immoral, I confess it!"

"Since your baptism?"

"God forgive me," he choked. "Yes! Many times!"

Joseph took the sobbing man by the arms and pulled him to his feet. He looked him in the eye, but Bennett turned his head away. "And have you taught this immorality in my name?"

"Oh, no! I swear before God, I never taught wickedness in your name!"

"Did you learn this life you have been living from me?"

"No, Joseph! I will take an oath and sign it!"

Joseph released the man's arms. "I shall require you to do exactly that," he said.

"What will you do with me?"

"You will be tried for your Church membership. I shall have you relieved of command of the Legion, and the City Council will remove you as mayor. You will be cut off from everything you have in this city, sir!"

Bennett now looked into the eyes of Joseph Smith, searching for some sign of sympathy, but there was none to be seen. He slowly slipped to his knees again and threw his arms around Joseph's legs, pressing his face to his boot tops. "Please say you understand and will forgive me again!"

"That is for the Brethren to decide, at your excommunication."

On May 19th, 1842, a special session of the City Council met. The small loft was jammed with spectators. John C. Bennett presented his resignation as mayor, and it was accepted. Joseph Smith was acclaimed mayor pro tem, with his brother Hyrum as assistant.

On May 26th, Bennett appeared at the Masonic Hall, which convened at that time in the room above the Red Brick Store, and confessed his immoral behavior, begging to be spared from dismissal. Joseph was so touched by his tears of remorse that he prevailed upon the brotherhood to give him one more chance, but soon they found that Bennett had been expelled from an Ohio lodge for "rascally conduct." That finished him in Nauvoo. He left, not in the least abashed or contrite, but shaking his fist and warning that he would publish an expose which would tell the true story of his mistreatment at the hands of a fallen prophet and his henchmen, and that Joseph would rue the day he had sent him away.

A DISPATCH FROM A TRAVELER IN NAUVOO
By Andrew J. Sharp

JOS. SMITH NAMED INSTIGATOR IN BOGGS SHOOTING! PROPHET DENIES HE WAS IN MISSOURI WHEN DEED WAS DONE! NAUVOOITES DEFEND HIM!

July 22, 1842: As has been widely reported in other papers, former Governor Lilburn W. Boggs has sworn an affadavit which charges the Mormon prophet Joseph Smith, Jr. with being an accessory to the attempt on the life of the Missouri politician.

This is denied by Mr. Smith on two grounds: Firstly, that he has not been out of the State of Illinois for two years, and secondly, that it is not logical to seek a Mormon assailant, since the unfortunate Mr. Boggs was one of the least popular politicians in recent Missouri history, and had many enemies in his own state.

In Nauvoo, feelings are running high that their prophet is once again being made the scapegoat in a matter in which he was never involved.

O. P. ROCKWELL ACCUSED AS GUNMAN PROPHET'S BODYGUARD DENIES ALL!

In a related development, the man accused of actually pulling the trigger in the shooting of Gov. Boggs, Orrin Porter Rockwell, a Mormon from Nauvoo, has informed the former mayor of Nauvoo, Dr. John C. Bennett, that his articles in a Warsaw (Ill.) newspaper naming him as the would-be assassin are false. The deposed mayor has been active of late in writing colorful exposes of Jos. Smith and the Mormon activities in and around Nauvoo.

Chapter 24

Lilburn W. Boggs never expected to die, even as he had fallen to the floor of his study and, in his waning moments of consciousness, seen and felt his precious blood gushing from his wounds. He had wavered between life and death for weeks, gaining a little strength, much of the time unable to talk.

But his mind — despite the presence of two balls of buckshot which were still in his brain — was clear on one subject. He had been shot by a Mormon, there was no doubt of it whatsoever, and he would live to see Joseph Smith hang for it. The dedication helped keep him alive.

Missouri papers were filled with accusations. They quoted a story saying that Joseph had prophecied that Boggs would be dead within a year after he had tried to have him extradited. To Boggs, his shooting was obviously Joseph Smith's way of insuring that his prophecy would come true. But, by God, he'd show him. He would live to dance on his grave!

Sitting by the huge brass bedstead in the flowery master bedroom in which Boggs was recuperating, was his old friend and Judge of the Superior Court, A. B. Perkins.

"Governor," Perkins said to the bandaged head of his friend, "I'll do anything I can for you; you know that."

Boggs' salivary canal had been injured by one of the pistol balls and scar tissue prevented him from speaking in his usual deep voice. He spoke slowly and intensely, spitting out each word so that the judge would understand. "I want to swear out an affa-da-vit."

"Affadavit, yes, I have it."

"I want Jo-seph Smith and Or-rin Por-ter Rock-well ex-tra-di-ted to Missouri!"

"Extradite Joseph Smith and Orrin Porter Rockwell, yes, sir."

"And this time I don't want any mis-takes!"

"No mistakes, Governor, I understand. They're fugitives now, and we can bring them in without any mistakes, I guarantee it."

"Good." His energy spent, the heavily-swathed head fell back against the pillows.

The judge stood up. "If that's everything, Governor, I'll get to work on this right now. And you just take care of yourself so you'll be well enough to watch those devils stand trial."

"I'll be well enough," the head said. "You just get me those men!"

A DISPATCH FROM A TRAVELER IN NAUVOO
BY Andrew J. Sharp

PROPHET ARRESTED! ILLINOIS SHERIFFS CANNOT REMOVE HIM, SAYS NAUVOO JUDGE. THEY LEAVE EMPTY-HANDED!

August 8, 1842: The Mormon prophet Joseph Smith again escaped extradition to stand charges of attempted murder in Missouri today, as the Nauvoo Municipal Court ordered him released on a writ of habeas corpus.

This marked the third time that Mr. Smith has eluded the long arm of Missouri law. In an earlier attempt to extradite him on charges of murder, treason and arson, a judge in Monmouth, Illinois ruled the writ dead, as it had been returned to Governor Carlin once before without it being served.

Following the departure of the officers from Missouri, the Nauvoo City Council enacted an ordinance empowering the Municipal Courts of Nauvoo to rule on the validity of any writ served upon a citizen of this city.

"Mr. Rockwell!"

It was the first time he had seen Port wearing civilized, city-cut clothes, and Andrew almost didn't recognize him as he and his wife and baby drove east on Parley Street. The buggy slowed to a halt. In the back were suitcases.

"Are you leaving Nauvoo?" Andrew asked.

"Just for a spell," Rockwell answered. "Thought we'd visit some relatives."

"Where are you headed?"

"Oh, just Carthage." The volume of luggage indicated otherwise, but Andrew said nothing about it.

"Off the record, Orrin," Andrew said, "did you shoot Boggs?"

"Never in my life have I ever done anything I was ashamed of. I can go back anyplace I've ever been, and have nothing to fear!"

"But did you shoot Boggs?"

Rockwell laughed. "Well, I'll say this," he said, picking up the reins again. "He sure had it coming!" He clucked to the horse and started on, then hollered, "Whoa."

Andrew walked back up to him. "Forget something?"

"You said you came from some town in Pennsylvania, didn't you?" he asked.

"That's right. Meadville."

"Where's that? Near Philadelphia?"

"Middle part of the state."

"Oh," he said, flipping the reins once again. "Be seein' you." Andrew stood in the road, watching the buggy disappear. It was the day after Rockwell and Joseph had eluded arrest, and it was certain the sheriffs would be back again — soon. "He's almost told me where he's going," Andrew said aloud to himself. "Or, has he?"

He put his hands in his trouser pockets and continued his walk toward Willard Richards' house. Nearly a year had elapsed since he had come back to Nauvoo, a lovesick boy chasing a dream. Eleven months of hard work and the mounting drama of the Prophet and his troubles, his more frequent deadlines, now that both the *Times & Seasons* and the *Argus* were published bimonthly — these had drained most of his time and energy.

So, it was no longer the gnawing hunger for an old romance which led Andrew's steps toward Louisa's home; he felt a vague emptiness where her friendship had been. He was no longer worthy of her love. Was he worthy of her friendship?

Apostle Richards was pleasantly surprised to see Andrew at his door, and he invited him in to share a bowl of nuts Jenetta was passing around. Jenetta, too, was most hospitable now, since Andrew had stopped his almost nightly pilgrimages to her door in hope of seeing Louisa.

And Louisa? She was out for the evening with Angus McCann, Richards said. "But you're a welcome sight, Andrew. Come on in."

They spoke of the weather — very cool for August; the growth of Nauvoo — past eleven thousand now; the promise of a good crop in Nauvoo's farmlands, and, at last, their beautiful boarder.

"I'm a plain sort of man," Willard Richards said. "It drives poor Jenetta to distraction, sometimes, but I like to say what I'm thinking."

Jenetta smiled in agreement. "I'm that way, too," Andrew said.

"Then I'll say it," Richards said. "Why don't you join the Church?"

Andrew stopped to think of an answer. "You think Louisa'd have me then, is that it?"

"Oh, no, I don't know about that. But I mean, living here among thousands of Saints, you apparently feel comfortable with us."

"It's an exciting city, for a small-town boy like me."

"Now, now, let's talk plainly. Are we a bunch of fools, or do we have something?"

"Oh, you have something."

"What? What is it we have?"

"Loyalty, for one thing." He was thinking of the devotion Joseph Smith generated wherever he went in Nauvoo.

"Anything else?"

"You're hard workers. You like business."

"True. Anything else about us you've noticed?"

Andrew thought it over for a moment. "You believe in the future. Yes, that's it. No matter how many times you're knocked down, you seem to get back up again."

The huge man was silent for a minute. "Why do you suppose that is?"

"I don't know. Sometimes, when I see the troubles President Smith has on his mind — he's wanted for this, he's wanted for that, his Church doctrine is under fire from Gentiles everywhere — I wonder why he doesn't just give it up, and tend his store, or something."

"Might be a lot easier, mightn't it?"

Jenetta looked on, interested in the exchange. "I'm sure he knows why he can't give it up," she said.

"You ever asked him that?" Richards asked.

"No."

"Do it, some time," he said. "See what he tells you."

"All right, maybe I will."

"And whatever he tells you will be my reason for sticking. The reason Brigham Young and Heber Kimball and the rest of us set out to go preach the gospel in England when we didn't have money or a purse to put it in! 'Without purse or scrip,' as the saying goes! And Brigham and Heber were so sick they could hardly stand up. And Vilate Kimball and the children were half dead, too. What would make a man leave at a time like that, with nothing in his pockets? No way of knowing where he'll lay his head that night? Or how he'll eat?"

Andrew shook his head, fascinated at the apostle's account.

"We did it," he continued, "not because we're any brighter or duller or more righteous than the next fellow. Why, we in the Quorum of the Twelve are exactly like you, like everyone you know — except for one thing." He paused. "Do you know what that is?"

Andrew shook his head.

"We have what is called a 'testimony' of the truth of this work. And if a man gets a testimony of something, it becomes a part of him. It motivates him, drives him on, makes him impervious to fortune. He can't stop. He can't give up. He just goes on."

Jenetta spoke up. "Some people think we're daft."

"I don't think you're daft," Andrew said.

The big clock took a mechanical breath and struck the hour. Nine o'clock. It seemed a good time to divert his host to something closer to his heart at the moment. "Does Louisa see a lot of Angus McCann these days?"

Richards looked at his wife. "I don't know, you'd have to answer that, Jenetta."

"Oh, she's good friends with him, but I think that's all," Jenetta said.

"Are they serious about each other?"

"That, I couldn't tell you."

Andrew stood up to go. "Well, I want her to be happy. She's had enough misery in her life, God knows."

"Yes, He does," Richards answered gravely. "That's a nice thing for you to wish for her. You ought to tell her that next time you see her."

Whenever that will be, Andrew thought, wistfully. "Thanks for giving me something to think about," he said, shaking hands with the Richards. He left, tasting the chilling air, and walked home.

MORMON PROPHET DISAPPEARS!
Smith and Rockwell escape arrest again! A Bounty On Their

236

Heads; Springfield Sheriffs In Nauvoo!
By Andrew J. Sharp
Special Nauvoo Correspondent to the *Argus*

For the fourth time, Joseph Smith, Jr., prophet of the Church of Jesus Christ of Latter-day Saints, has slipped through the grasp of law officers who were dispatched from Springfield to arrest him in connection with the shooting of Lilburn W. Boggs, former governor of Missouri.

Despite elaborate precautions by the officers, T. O. Brown, Isaac Borden and William I. Prince, no sign was found of Smith or his confederate and bodyguard, Orrin Porter Rockwell.

This correspondent has been told that Rockwell has gone east, but nobody in Nauvoo is speculating as to the whereabouts of the prophet. The law officers are remaining in close proximity to Nauvoo, in hope of capturing Smith and Rockwell. They refused comment on the tactics they will employ to snare the fugitives.

Meanwhile, Governor Thomas Carlin of Illinois has posted a reward of $200 for the arrest of either of the missing men.

SEARCH FOR JOS. SMITH CONTINUES:
Rumored To Be In Canada; Officers Still Suspect He Is In Nauvoo District; Government Is Baffled!
by Andrew J. Sharp
Special Nauvoo Correspondent to the *Argus*

September 27, 1842, Nauvoo, Ill.: From first light until sundown each day, teams of lawmen are roaming the city of Nauvoo, largest city in Illinois, searching for any sign of the vanished prophet of the Mormons, Joseph Smith, Jr. To date, no sign of him has been reported.

Rumors persist that the prophet was seen aboard a steamboat heading for Canada, but this information has not discouraged searchers who have made a permanent encampment in empty fields around Nauvoo, where they can hope to apprehend the leader of the Mormon church for the stipend of $200 which lies on the head of Smith and his accused associate, in the shooting of Lilburn W. Boggs, former governor of Missouri. Smith is wanted for extradition to Missouri on charges of accessory before the fact. His associate, O. P. Rockwell, has also disappeared.

Correspondence between the wife of the prophet, Mrs. Emma Hale Smith, and Governor Thomas Carlin of Illinois, has not pursuaded Carlin to change his mind. Meanwhile, in the closing days of his term of office in Springfield, Carlin is the butt of almost daily comment in many newspapers for having never been able to apprehend Joseph Smith.

EXCLUSIVE REPORT FROM SECRET

HIDING PLACE FOR JOS. SMITH!
Prophet To Submit To Arrest! Agrees To Come To Capitol;
"Argus" Correspondent In Exclusive Interview With Prophet!
by Andrew J. Sharp, Associate Editor,
The Quincy *Argus*

December 27, 1842: Determined to start the new year 1843 as a free man, Joseph Smith told this correspondent today that he has been assured by God that he will be protected from all harm until "his work on earth is done."

The controversial Mormon prophet has been hiding in homes provided by friends for four months, while forces from Springfield and many volunteer posses have combed a three-state area.

The crime Smith was accused of was aiding and abetting the planning of the attempted murder of Lilburn W. Boggs, former governor of Missouri and a long-time foe of Smith and his church. Boggs is recovering from injuries received when he was shot while at his home in Independence, Missouri.

This correspondent was able to travel several miles in the party accompanying Smith out of hiding. He is in custody of Wilson Law, a fellow Mormon and Major General of the Nauvoo Legion, replacing the deposed John C. Bennett in that position. Also traveling with the party are numerous Mormon church leaders, including the prophet's older brother, Hyrum Smith.

In an exclusive interview, the prophet prophecied to this reporter that "no power can stay the hand of God, and His work with roll forward; I fear no one and no thing, for no harm will come to me until my work on earth is finished."

The months of exile for Joseph Smith have not been without their exertions, but he has also communicated with his church several epistles on doctrine, which he said came to him as he meditated. He told this reporter that he is "looking forward to 1843, exonerated by the courts of Man," as he obviously believes he has been exonerated by the Court on High.

MORMON PROPHET'S PROPHECY FULFILLED!
JOS. SMITH RELEASED! RETURNING FREE TO
HIS CHEERING FOLLOWERS IN NAUVOO
by Andrew J. Sharp
Associate Editor, Quincy *Argus*

The Mormon prophet Joseph Smith will arrive in Nauvoo, Illinois to a flag-waving multitude of thousands of his faithful on January 10, restored to freedom once again because of a flaw in Missouri's writ-writing process.

Judge Pope in Springfield ruled that since the offense of which Smith was accused, (accessory before the fact in the shooting of Lilburn W. Boggs) did not take place in the state of Missouri "if, in fact, it took place at all," that the writ was void and Smith should be released.

All along the snow-covered route the prophet's party is taking, well-wishers have bestowed gifts upon Smith and many have taken up in the procession, to accompany the prophet back to Nauvoo in triumph.

Orrin Porter Rockwell, close friend and bodyguard of Mr. Smith, has remained unseen since the same day the prophet went into hiding. A $200 reward remains for the arrest of Rockwell, who is accused in an affadavit by Boggs, of his attempted murder.

Chapter 25

The singing could be heard all across the covered plain. It was a new song, sung by men's voices, punctuated by laughter. As the horses plowed their way through the muddy track across Illinois, inside the two lurching wagons sat the vindicated prophet and his party. Riding with Joseph were Wilson Law and Willard Richards, who had composed this "Jubilee Song" for a celebration the night before at the farmhouse of a Mormon family who lodged the returning party on their way back from Springfield.

They sang it again, and then again. In the second wagon, Andrew Sharp smiled to himself. If he didn't know that those men in the front wagon were the leaders of the Mormon Church, he would have thought they were drunk.

And drunk they were — with relief and gratitude. Now, for the first time in three years, no charges remained hanging over the head of the prophet. They could tolerate the infamous lies being printed by John C. Bennett; they were so extreme, so outrageous, that Joseph felt few reasonable people would believe them.

And Nauvoo continued its growth. Imagine! The outcast Mormons now had the showplace of the plains, the largest city in the state, and a thriving economy which resulted from the blend of skilled European craftsmen and venturesome Yankee merchants.

So peace and prosperity lay ahead, at the end of the wintery trek — so far as they knew.

But Bennett, the deposed Nauvoo mayor and former Major General of the Legion, had his followers. He united with Thomas Sharp and the Anti-Mormon Party; he charged stiff admission to his lectures, in which he revealed the lurid details of "spiritual wifery" as taught and practiced by the heathen prophet. He explained his own difficulties with the Church by revealing he had come to Nauvoo on a secret investigative mission, in order to amass the facts which he now was making public. And all of this, in order to spread the warning throughout the country that the Mormons had plans for national domination; they would spread their tentacles, would entrap more thousands of innocent dupes as contributing members, build up their treasury, multiply the Nauvoo Legion into hundreds of thousands of battle-ready soldiers — and then, with the means to control the ballot-boxes in twenty-five states — they would seize the nation. From there, they would launch a spiritual, then a financial, and finally, a military attack on the rest of the world. Such were the infernal plans of Joseph Smith, Bennett had claimed. And he drew large crowds who believed him. He wrote articles which were printed and reprinted across the east and middle west in papers large and small, and he was preparing a book which would go into greater detail to expose Smith and the Mormons. Bennett had climbed out of the muck of his own exposure in Nauvoo, to new heights of notoriety and fame, as the eloquent declaimer of the Mormon Threat.

It was the last night's encampment for the prophet and his party before his triumphal entry into Nauvoo. Word had been sent ahead from the County seat of Carthage, that Joseph was back in Hancock County and would arrive in Nauvoo on the Carthage Road by noon the following day, January 10th. He would spend the evening in the cottage of Heber and Mary Blake, preparing a talk to give to the welcoming crowd expected at Nauvoo.

After their supper, Joseph, Willard Richards and Andrew sat in the small front room, discussing the talk. Should it be a recital of all that the prophet had done while in hiding, where he had been staying, and with whom?

"No," Andrew said, "you may need those friends again sometime, President, and if you disclose who hid you, you place them and yourself in jeopardy."

Joseph turned in admiration to Andrew. "Now, that is good thinking. You are absolutely right; I must protect my friends, just as they protected me. I'll speak on what transpired at the hearing, what Judge Pope had to say — that sort of thing."

Andrew was warmed by his acceptance. From time to time he had suggested a few tactics and phrases which his journalism experience had given him, and Joseph had appreciated the help. Not an accomplished writer, he composed most of his talks in his head and delivered them beautifully from his well-organized thoughts. But so complex were the proceedings of the legal matters he had just experienced, he thought it best to confer with the two scribes — Richards and Sharp — who were available.

The talk droned on, the hour grew late. Willard Richards at last excused himself and went outside, preparing to retire. Suddenly, Andrew remembered the conversation he had had with the apostle months earlier. Joseph seemed in a reflective mood, not yet ready to go to sleep, so Andrew said, "President, Apostle Richards once said I might ask you something that has been a puzzle to me."

Leaning back before the fire in the hearth, Joseph turned his mild blue eyes on Andrew with a smile. "By all means."

"Well — it's this: you seem to enjoy your life as an editor, the mayor, the commander of the Legion, as a merchant and a land dealer; you could have a rich and peaceful life in Nauvoo, with all your talents, without being the prophet."

Joseph leaned forward with interest. "What are you asking?"

"I'm asking, why do you continue to undergo all the torment and criticism heaped on you over your religion?"

"Ah, you wonder why I don't just give in to my enemies and tell them it was all a great joke? A misunderstanding between me and the Lord?"

"Well . . ."

"And what of the thousands of faithful who have given up all they had to follow me? Should I disinvest them of the root of their faith?"

"They have prosperous lives now in Nauvoo. You've succeeded, Joseph! You've built a marvelous, thriving city! There's plenty for everyone now."

"So what need do they have for religion, is that it?"

"No. I'm asking, what need do **you** have for persecution? Do you believe all your troubles are over now?"

He sighed. "No, there will be more trouble ahead. But you overlook one fact, my friend, a fact which burns in my breast night and day and is relentless in the hold it has on me. It's something I can't expect you to understand, or possibly even to believe. But it is a fact to me, and has caused me as much agony as it has joy."

"What is it?"

"I am a prophet of God." His eyes fastened on Andrew's in a kindly gaze. Andrew said nothing.

"And I cannot retire from that fact," Joseph continued. "If you only knew the times when I cried to the Lord to remove this burden from me. There have been commandments, Andrew, that I wish to God He had never given me! But it has never been in my nature to shirk a job, and this is the greatest job a man can be given — to act in the name of the Lord. Now, do you see?"

"I see."

"But, do **you** believe I am a prophet of God?"

It was the one question Andrew did not want to be asked, especially by Joseph. He had grown close to this remarkable man, and had felt the glow of his friendship. He didn't want to offend him or risk losing his friendship, but he could not give him the answer he wanted to hear. He could only answer as truthfully as he knew how.

"I don't know."

"Andrew, would you like to know?"

"Yes . . ."

"Even if the knowing were to change your life forever?"

"I think . . . yes."

"Then I will tell you how you may find out. Do you pray?"

"Not much . . . no."

"Neither did I. Andrew, when I was a young boy I faced a similar dilemma. I wanted to know which of the many churches was true, which one I ought to join. I had never prayed before in my life, but I knew what the Bible taught, in the Epistle of James . . . do you know it?"

"I'm afraid not."

"In the first chapter, fifth verse: *'If any of you lack wisdom, let him ask of God; that giveth to all men liberally, and upbraideth not; and it shall be given him.'* Well, I went out into a grove of trees near my father's farm, and knelt down, and asked."

"And got an answer. President, I have been told about your first vision. Do you think, if I prayed about **you,** that I would get such a vision as you did?"

"Such a vision would not be necessary. I shall not suggest to you what will happen if you ask, with an open mind and a contrite heart. You must do that on your own. But if you do," he warned, "you must be content to act upon what you learn!"

Willard Richards banged back into the room. He stopped, sensing he had interrupted something. "Shall I leave you for a while?" he asked.

Andrew stood up. "No, no, apostle. President Smith has just helped me with a question I had. I'm quite ready for bed, and I'm sure you are, too." He looked at Joseph, who was still sitting. "Thank you, President," he said.

"You are very welcome. Good night, Andrew."

Andrew put on his coat and stepped outside. He looked up at the stars for a long time, and began to recognize a curious thought which had formed in his mind. It hadn't been there before; he hadn't even toyed with the idea, but now it presented itself and would not leave. It disturbed him, but at the same time, it intrigued him: *What if Joseph Smith really is a prophet of God?*

The Nauvoo Legion stood at attention. As the wagons rattled down Parley Street toward the center of town, the captains of all of the assembled companies called for "present arms," and hundreds of rifles flashed in the sun, and the precision of the ranks of men was something to behold.

The Nauvoo Band crashed into action, and the cannon mounted near the temple boomed and boomed again, sending echoes cracking across the valley. The big bell which had been mounted in the workings of the temple dinned, and a crowd Andrew estimated at procession was accompanied by scores of men on horseback who trotted alongside the wagons.

Despite the cold temperatures, mothers held babies so that they could see their prophet returning victorious, and have a memory of the moment to treasure for the rest of their lives.

The parade ended in front of the brand-new Mansion House, where Emma and the children, Hyrum and his family, and scores of well-wishers surrounded the prophet, bestowing handshakes and kisses on him. At last he mounted the back of the wagon he had ridden in and motioned for quiet.

"One week from this day," he announced, "Sister Smith and I will lead you in a day of celebration and thanksgiving. It will be a civic holiday. After so long a period of tribulation, Nauvoo needs a celebration!" The crowd cheered. "Thank you, my brothers and sisters, for your prayers. And now, I should like to spend a little time with my family. God bless you!"

He stepped down from the wagon, put his arm around Emma, and walked into his spacious new home.

Andrew concluded his notes and put away his notebook. When he looked up, he looked directly into the eyes of Louisa Stephens.

The crowd was walking away now, moving past them on all sides. Shoulders brushed against her but she stood in her place, looking at Andrew.

"Welcome home," she said.

"Thank you."

"I heard you have been with the Prophet."

"That's right."

"I've been reading your reports in the *Argus*. Congratulations, I see you've been promoted."

That came as a surprise to Andrew, who hadn't seen a newspaper for weeks, nor had any mail been forwarded since he had been with Joseph and his party. "Promoted?" he asked.

"According to your dispatch of December 27th, when you wrote about your personal interview with him. The article said it was by Andrew J. Sharp, **Associate Editor!**"

"I didn't know. I haven't had time to pick up my mail. Must be Mr. Ketchum has written to me about it."

"Yes, you should get your mail."

"Well, I have a lot of things to do. How have you been?"

"Oh, fine. And you look fine."

"Oh, yes. The trip was exciting. I got to spend quite a lot of time with President Smith."

Her eyes glowed. "He must like you. I mean, to grant you an interview. Did he know you would send it to the *Argus*?"

"Of course. I inform anyone when I'm writing for the *Argus*. I wouldn't want any more misunderstandings."

"No," she said, glancing down again, "they can cause so much . . . sadness." And she looked up at him with a look he hadn't seen since that long-ago summer.

"Well," he said, "how's Angus McCann?"

"He seems to be well, too."

"Good," Andrew said, "give him my regards, won't you?" And he touched the brim of his hat, smiled at her, turned, and walked away.

Louisa stood, lips apart, hurt welling up in her eyes, as she watched him disappear amid the crowd.

Sidney Rigdon had resumed the duties of postmaster, and the Nauvoo Post Office had been moved back from Jensen's store to Rigdon's generous-sized front room. The fifty-year-old first counselor to Joseph Smith was emaciated from his long bout with the ague. Andrew found him sorting the mail when he called to see what had arrived for him. The dour Rigdon had a small packet of mail tied together with a string, efficiently separated from the sacks and bundles which now came in with every boat. "Here's yours, Mister Sharp." Rigdon had never gone out of his way to be friendly toward Andrew, having not gotten over Andrew's deceptions of the past.

Walking slowly toward his rented room, Andrew leafed through the letter. He was looking in particular for something from the *Argus*, and when he spotted the envelope he wanted, he tore it open and read it as he walked. It was from Elias P. Ketchum, and under the date of December 25, Christmas

Day, it read:

Dear Andrew:

You are entitled to know the effect of your efforts upon our readers. The notices you sold have turned out to be hard to collect on, but I forgive you in view of the great popularity of your authoritative reports at the side of the Mormon prophet. Much excitement greets each issue of the *Argus*, and needless to say, our circulation has grown. Much of this, and our attendant prosperity, I attribute to your dispatches.

I think it is time we stopped referring to you as "A Traveler In Nauvoo." In the interest of truthfulness, you are living there, not traveling, and for your own sake it is no longer needful for you to write under that imprimatur. Therefore, commencing with the next issue, I am dropping that byline, and adding one which I hope meets with your approval.

I am promoting you to Associate Editor, and increasing your salary to $14 per week.

Merry Christmas,

E.P.K.

Associate Editor! Andrew could hardly believe it! He wanted to shout it out, to at least tell somebody about it, but who was there to share it with? His brother Thomas? They hadn't spoken in months and were philosophically poles apart. His parents? He would write to them and hope that this increase in his stature and income would make them less disappointed that he hadn't become the engineer his father had wanted him to be, or the doctor of his mother's dreams. There was Louisa; but she already knew.

He leafed through the rest of the mail, finding an advertising letter from a Nauvoo store where he had purchased some few necessaries for his wardrobe a few months ago, advising him that a new shipment of goods was unloaded and being offered at good prices.

And then he saw an envelope addressed to him in feminine handwriting which he could not identify, but it was postmarked in Nauvoo also, with no return address. He tore it open and read:

My Dearest Andrew:

The events of the last several weeks have proven me wrong. I had harbored thoughts of you which were unkind and groundless, and I find that I cannot find peace of mind without confessing them to you and begging your forgiveness.

Will you call on me, Andrew, so that I may tell you what is in my heart?

Love,
Louisa

His hands shook slightly. He read the letter again. What was this? What about Angus McCann? Just when he thought he had found a distant corner in his heart to tuck his memories of Louisa and the love they had known, and had managed to reconstruct his life without her, twice in one day she had come to haunt him! He could do nothing more with his day until he saw her and let her, as she requested, tell him what was in her heart.

He hurried through the slush, barely feeling the sting of the cold January afternoon. In his imagination he fashioned a scene of tearful reconciliation, with those sweetest of all words, "I do love you," pouring from her contrite lips. He would be stern at first, not letting her forget the misery she had caused him, but then he would take her in his arms and lovingly forgive her. With new-found purpose, he plowed even faster through the crusty frozen snow.

It was Louisa herself who answered the door. She let him into the Richards house with a curious half smile. Andrew looked around for the apostle or his wife. "They are out for a while," Louisa said in answer to his unspoken question.

"Well," Andrew said, as they stood facing each other in the quiet room, "I got your letter. And here I am."

"Thank you for coming. Let's sit down." She indicated a love seat, the only piece of furniture in the room in which two could sit together. It usually was the seat Willard Richards occupied, since no ordinary chair scaled for normal-sized people would hold him without sticking to his rump as he tried to rise. Andrew noticed a pair of smoking pipes and the reading glasses the apostle used. "He's seeing someone who's sick," Louisa said, detecting Andrew's gaze at the articles on the table.

It was lovely being this close to her again. Andrew couldn't recall a time, since the night they pledged their love to one another, that he had felt as happy as he did at this moment. A substantial advancement and a raise from the *Argus*, and Louisa about to ask him to resume their courtship! What could be more fulfilling? And in return for her confessions, he would tell her that now he was in a position, at last, to take a wife, and would ask her to set the wedding date. Yes, he couldn't be happier.

He turned to her and said, "I believe there was something you wanted to tell me?"

"Yes, Andrew." She placed her hands flat on the top of her skirted lap. "Before anyone ever takes an important step in their lives, one should make amends for any wrong that was done, don't you agree?"

"I certainly do. That's what I was trying to do in this very room last September, if you remember."

"Oh, I do remember," she said, turning toward him. "That's what I wanted to talk to you about. That evening, I told you that I was afraid that you understood things quite a bit differently than I did, and I was afraid that . . . that things wouldn't work out between us."

"And I remember **that.** Vividly."

"At that time I believed that you cared very little for the truth, and that you were an enemy to the Church. But since then, I have seen how you have been accepted by the Twelve, Apostle Richards speaks so highly of you, and now you even travel with the Prophet. I can see that whom I thought was an enemy to the Church is really a very truthful writer about the Church."

"Well, thank you for that. As I tried to tell you in my letter to you last July, I only pretended to be a Mormon so that I would be exposed to Mormon life the way it really is."

"Yes. I understand that now."

Andrew was anxious to get past the question of his professional objectivity and her loyalty to the Church, and come to the real reason she had asked to see him. "And so," he prompted her.

"And so, I want to confess my mistake, and ask for your forgiveness."

"Of course," he said, placing his hand over hers and curling her fingers into his palm. "You are completely forgiven."

She looked up at him. "Thank you, Andrew, for understanding." They were close now. And she glanced down at his waiting lips, and he kissed her. It was tender, not passionate, strangely unrewarding to him. He looked at her as their lips separated, and saw that her eyes were closed.

"And now, about that important step," he said, about to tell her he wanted to set a wedding date, but she interrupted him.

"Yes," she said. "Before I could feel right about it, I had to know that everything was all right between us."

He cupped her face in his hands. "Everything is all right," he murmured. "Now, what is that important step?"

"Well," she said, her voice softening. "Angus McCann has asked me to marry him."

Andrew's hands dropped from her face. "Angus? I thought you wanted to talk about **us!**"

"I had to know that we were friends, before I could give him my answer," she said, falteringly.

He stood up, scratching his sideburn, uncertain of what to say or do. "Then you love him?" he asked, at last.

She didn't answer. He turned to look at her there on the love seat. "You do love him?" he repeated.

Without looking up at him, she nodded her head.

"And you don't love me? Oh, that's right! You **decided** not to love me, I think you said."

"Don't be angry."

"Angry? Of course not. You've decided not to love me, you've decided to love somebody else instead. That's fine."

"No!" she said, and stood up suddenly. "I was wrong about that, too! I found out that I couldn't tell my heart what to do . . . it kept telling me what to do! I never stopped loving you completely, Andrew! But when you stopped coming around and we didn't see each other for so long . . . what was

I to think?"

"What was I to think?" Andrew fairly shouted. "And so far as I knew, you'd snuffed me out of your life. What was I supposed to do, sit around and mourn? Pray for a miracle?"

"Don't shout at me!"

"Would it make a difference if I happened to be a Mormon, too?" he asked bitterly. "A rich Mormon from a rich family?"

She sank to the love seat again. "That sounds terrible," she said weakly.

"And it is terrible," Andrew replied, "when a church stands in the way of two people's happiness."

"But you don't understand," she said pleadingly. "The Church was put on earth to **help** people live happily!"

He laughed bitterly. "Is that so? Did it help Joseph Smith live happily? Or Emma? Or any of the people like your own mother and father, who died because of the Church?"

"At least they died for what they believed in," she said, quietly. "They had a faith that was stronger than death. That's what I want to share with my husband!"

"Well, Louisa," Andrew said, knowing all was lost now in their relationship, "better tell the bishop to get ready for a wedding."

She stood up slowly, expectantly.

Andrew jerked open the front door. "But I won't be there," he said, and slammed the door.

The January day turned bleak. The sun was behind clouds, and a frigid wind clawed the bare trees as Andrew stalked back through the snowy streets to his room.

Once inside, he found wood for a fire and pulled the woolen blankets down from the closet, spread them over the tick on the bedframe, and unloaded his traveling bag. As the room warmed enough that the rime of ice on the inside of his window began to drip, he shrugged into his heavy coat again and went out for a solitary supper.

On the way, he saw smoke coming from the chimney of the new *Times & Seasons* building and diverted his steps there. Inside was Samuel Gaines, working by himself at the desk.

The two men exchanged greetings. "I'm trying to write down an account of the Prophet's return," Gaines said.

"Let me help you with it," Andrew said. Gratefully, Samuel handed him what he had written. In a few short slashes here and a little re-arranging there, Andrew managed to edit the story into printable form. He handed it back to Samuel, and walked stiff-legged around the small room, hands on his back pockets and back arched.

"You've had a long time of it," Samuel said. "Why not go home and get some sleep?"

"My room is as cold as it is outside. And I'm afraid I'm too upset to do much sleeping at the moment."

248

Samuel watched his friend pace. "We have the extra room now," he said. "It's just Maude and the girls. You could have Bennett's old room. It's huge and comfortable, and we could use the rent."

Andrew knew that the City Council had taken over the Bennett house and mortgage and was renting it now to the Gaines family. Samuel added another thought:

"Unless, of course, it might contain too many unpleasant memories."

"Of Bennett?"

Samuel smiled. "No; I was thinking of Louisa."

Andrew turned a chair around and straddled it, leaning his chin on his folded arms atop the chair back. "I just came from Louisa's. She tells me she's going to marry Angus."

"And you'll let her?"

"Let her? Her mind's made up."

"Is it, now? And you didn't try to change it?"

"Change her mind? I'm afraid not. I'd have to get baptized to do that."

"Did she say that?"

"Just about." Restlessly, Andrew swung off the chair and began to pace the small office again. "Ah, it would never have worked. She wants a good Mormon man, strong in the faith. And that's Angus."

"And you, Andrew: what do you have faith in?"

He looked up at the ceiling, remembering the stars over Carthage the night before, remembering the challenge Joseph had given him. "I don't know. I just don't know."

The act of moving his residence had become simple for Andrew. It consisted of folding his clothes and blankets into two good-sized trunks, putting one across his shoulder and hefting the other one by its handle. But this time he loaded his goods into a small handcart, which he rented from the Nauvoo Wagon and Carriage Shop, and pushed it through the slush and mud to the familiar door of the old Bennett house — the house in which he had spent such magical hours with Louisa — the house which sent memories racing back.

What Andrew didn't realize was that the invitation to him from Samuel to take a room there hadn't been a spur-of-the-moment thought. Samuel and Maude had talked about it at length in private conversation. Having Andrew there would place him in daily contact with their daughter Rebecca, who had been excommunicated from the Church and immediately rebaptized, Hyrum himself officiating, in view of her obvious repentant attitude. She was as contrite as she could be over the affair with Bennett, to the extent that she avoided all contact with eligible young men, and kept away from social gatherings entirely. What she needed, her parents decided, was a male friend with whom she could feel safe — and someone who, unlike many of the young men of the town, would not treat her as a fallen woman. After all, the Gospel said that when one is totally repentant, baptism washes away all sins.

Andrew would benefit from this association, too, in the minds of the Gaines. They had been watching the courtship of Louisa by their neighbor, Angus, and although he was probably far less exciting a person than Andrew, he was part of an extremely prosperous family and, of course, he was a Mormon. All of which was evidence that Andrew would find pursuit of his former love quite hopeless, and it was felt that the daily exposure to Rebecca might take his mind off Louisa. All in all, it seemed to Samuel and Maude to be an ideal situation.

Andrew installed himself in the big corner bedroom and made his bed. He hung his clothes in a large closet and placed his boots and shoes on racks thoughtfully provided at the back of the closet. He pulled down the ceiling chandelier and saw that scented coal oil was in all four reservoirs. A commode stood against one wall beside the bed in the corner, while a night table with a small candle lantern flanked the bed on the side next to the door. There was wallpaper on the walls and a braided rug on the floor; a rocking chair in one corner and a small wooden chair in the other. In all his twenty-three years it was by far the finest room he had slept in.

Sister Gaines cooked and baked heavy foods; mutton pies, fruit pies, cakes and fried dishes. There was little variety, and she urged Andrew to take second helpings on everything, appearing hurt if he didn't. He wondered how Samuel remained so slender. Elizabeth, their ten-year-old, was becoming chubby. Rebecca was becoming buxom.

It seemed to Andrew that Rebecca had changed much for the better. Where before she was forward and inclined to be sassy, she now was refined and reflective, much more mature than she had been before her relationship with Bennett ended. She was courteous to Andrew, but her flirtatious ways had flown. Andrew found that he could relax around her in the few hours he was able to spend in the house each week. She made no demand upon him, but behaved like a friend. He never used the name of Bennett, and she never mentioned Louisa. He tried not to think of her in the arms of a lover, and she avoided the memory of Andrew kissing Louisa, which she had secretly witnessed through the keyhole on several occasions.

Around the corner, at the McCann's, a new carriage stood outside a new stable in which two fine horses lived. Dray wagons drawn by oxen from time to time brought new crates of furniture to the house from the Nauvoo dock. South of the dock, not far from the Law's new mill, McCann Shipbuilding Company had gone into business. There were dories and catboats, hulls made for breasting open ocean, and those ideal for cruising the rivers. They sold every boat they could build, and had orders waiting to be filled. The canny Scotsman had chosen his site well. No visitor coming to Nauvoo by water could possibly overlook the shipyard and boatworks, and the undelivered products were in plain view, as was the company sign. Anyone with the time to spare could stand and watch Jock and William and the handful of other employees carefully fabricating the boats, bending the steamed lumber, filing, matching, lovingly crafting a product superior to most of those for sale anywhere in the area.

Andrew spent more time at the *Times & Seasons,* drudging at his work as much as Angus had at his own. The two men never met each other, although Andrew had seen Angus departing or arriving on occasion, and had side-stepped the opportunity to be seen by him.

And so, spring came, and another summer. Early in June, 1843, Joseph decided that Emma needed a change of scene, so he took her and the children northeast across Illinois to visit her sister, Mrs. Wasson, who lived near Dixon, the County Seat of Lee County on the Rock River. With the prophet gone from Nauvoo, Andrew relaxed, knowing that the city always quieted down when Joseph was away. He seemed to be the vortex of all activity wherever he was, and it had been a long time since Andrew had had a vacation.

Besides, he didn't want to be in town for the wedding of Angus and Louisa, which was announced for the twenty-fifth of June. If he were out of Nauvoo, his absence wouldn't cause any hard feelings. He mailed a letter to Elias P. Ketchum, asking for some time off, and received a letter by return mail granting it.

His plans were changed abruptly, though, by — of all people — the absent prophet. Five days after Joseph and Emma had left for Dixon, Hyrum received a message by an express rider. Judge James Adams had written from Springfield that he was required to issue a writ against Joseph. The governor of Missouri had demanded that Thomas Ford, who by now had succeeded Thomas Carlin as the governor of Illinois, turn Joseph over to him to stand trial on the old Boggs charges in Missouri. Ford had ordered Judge Adams to sign the writ, and there were two riders on their way at that moment to arrest Joseph, and they knew he was in Dixon; they'd read the paper.

Hyrum wasted no time assigning William Clayton and Stephen Markham to ride to Dixon to warn the prophet. They nearly killed their horses and exhausted themselves to reach the Wasson place in Lee County in sixty-six hours — a trip of 212 miles. But Joseph wasn't at the Wassons that day, June 21st; he had just left for Dixon, where he had agreed to speak that Friday night. Clayton and Markham leaped back on their staggering horses and rode after him, found him, and convinced him to turn back.

Joseph seemed only mildly disturbed at the news. He was in one of his supremely confident phases, and assured them, "I'll find friends, and I tell you in the name of Israel's God, Missouri cannot hurt me!" Well, be that as it may, Joseph sent Clayton on into Dixon to cancel the speaking engagement for him, and to scout for any news.

Two pious-looking Mormon elders arrived in Dixon that hot Wednesday afternoon, garbed in black coats, straight-brimmed black hats and beards. One of them wore thick, gold-rimmed spectacles. They were aware that the prophet Joseph Smith was staying with his wife's relatives, they said to a storekeeper, and asked directions to their farm. He was expecting them, they said. The storekeeper gave them the directions to the Wasson place, and they thanked him kindly, calling him "Brother."

The two men hired a team and wagon and set off down the road. On the way, they passed William Clayton heading in the other direction, and remarked to each other after he had passed, that a man ought not to ride a beat-up nag like that on such a warm day. And Clayton never paid any attention to the wagon and its passengers.

The elders drew up in the brush outside the front fence of the Wasson spread and looked it over. Smoke curled out of the stone chimney, and there was the smell of supper in the air. Pots and pans banged from inside the house; children could be heard playing, and women's voices drifted on the early evening breeze from the Wasson home.

The two men eased themselves down from the wagon seat, stepping down onto the hubs and then the ground, and began to stroll toward the house, their long black coats sweeping through the weed tops.

Then they saw a tall, light-haired man emerge from the back part of the house and begin to walk in the direction of the barn, which stood with its open door in the blue shade of the setting sun. The men quickened their pace. Constable Harmon T. Wilson of Carthage, Illinois reached him first. "Joseph Smith?" he asked. The man whirled, taken by surprise. Wilson whipped his pistol out from under his coat and cocked it as he pressed it against Joseph's chest. Missouri Sheriff Joseph H. Reynolds of Jackson County jammed his pistol against Joseph's temple, pulling back the hammer.

"What is the meaning of this?" Joseph demanded.

Reynolds said, "I'll show you the meaning of this, by God, and if you move one more inch, I'll shoot you!"

Joseph was stunned. They had him again, here in this peaceful valley, two hundred miles from his friends and protectors. "Oh, go ahead and shoot," Joseph cried. "I've been through enough that I am getting tired of living!"

"Take him to the wagon," Reynolds said, and walked behind Joseph with a drawn gun as Wilson pushed him forward by the arm, his own gun still buried in Joseph's back.

Suddenly a door in the Wasson house banged open and Stephen Markham dashed toward them.

"Stop right there or you're a dead man!" Wilson yelled. Markham skidded to a halt in the dust. Emma ran out to see what was the matter, and put her hands to her mouth. Her husband was being marched away to a wagon, and she didn't know where they were taking him or whether she would ever see him again.

Markham ran toward the wagon, and grabbed the bits in the horses' mouths and hung on grimly.

"Get your damned hands away from those horses, or I'll shoot you, by God I will!" Wilson shouted.

"No law on earth says a sheriff can take a prisoner without his clothes," Markham said. Sister Emma, seeing it was futile to try to help rescue her husband, ran in the house to get his warm coat and hat, and ran up to the wagon to hand them to her husband.

The Missouri sheriff took the reins while Wilson sat in the back with the Prophet, and the team started up. "God bless you, Emma," Joseph called. "Stephen," he shouted to Markham, "ride to Dixon and tell the sheriff I've been kidnapped!"

Markham rode into Dixon to see the justice of the peace, while William Clayton took a steamer down to Nauvoo to ask Hyrum to send help. One of the people who heard of the Prophet's latest peril was Andrew Sharp. He packed his traveling bag and set out upriver for Lee County, and another story for the *Argus,* as well as the *Times & Seasons.*

JOS. SMITH KIDNAPPED BY MISSOURI SHERIFF! NAUVOO POSSE RIDES TO THE RESCUE! THE CAPTORS BECOME CAPTIVE! LAWYER CYRUS WALKER INVOLVED!

by Andrew J. Sharp,
Associate Editor

June 26, 1843: Dixon, Lee County, Ill.: Mormon prophet Joseph Smith has again been apprehended on charges dating to the shooting last year of former Missouri governor Lilburn W. Boggs. In the latest incident, Smith was taken captive by Sheriff Joseph H. Reynolds of Independence, Jackson County, Missouri, and was assisted by Constable Harmon T. Wilson of Carthage, Illinois. These lawmen asserted that they were going to transport Smith to stand trial in Missouri. When word of the abduction reached Nauvoo, a detachment numbering some three hundred volunteers departed to search for their prophet.

Meanwhile, however, a justice of the peace in Dixon ordered the arrest of Reynolds and Wilson, for conspiring to illegally remove an Illinois resident to Missouri. Hence, while the two officers still held Jos. Smith as their prisoner, the officers were themselves made the prisoner of the constable of Lee County!

This correspondent has just learned, in addition, that Mr. Cyrus H. Walker, prominent lawyer and candidate for Congress, was campaigning in the Dixon area and has been interviewed by Jos. Smith, with reference to becoming Smith's attorney in the Missouri matter.

Chapter 26

"Andrew is here? Bless him! Send him to me!"

Seeing another face from home seemed to enormously cheer Joseph. He embraced Andrew and told him all that had happened since his abduction.

"They put me in this hotel room," he said, "but made the mistake of not barring my window. Since it appeared that I was to be denied legal counsel, I simply opened the window and used my best preacher's voice to summon some help!"

"You mean you hollered out the window and asked for a lawyer?" Andrew asked, unable to avoid laughing at the picture that painted in his imagination.

"I did, and it brought results. Two Quincy lawyers were in town and tried to see me and our friends, Wilson and Reynolds, forbade it — until the generous owner of this establishment demanded they be let in. And do you know what they've done?"

"No."

"They have sent for the master in chancery and the honorable Cyrus H. Walker, who should be here any moment!"

Andrew said, "Walker — who's running for Congress?"

"The same!"

Andrew whistled. "If he comes up here to see you, you'll be as good as free."

And at that moment, with a brief rap at the door, Mr. Walker himself arrived.

"May I remain?" Andrew asked.

With a gesture, Joseph indicated that he should sit on the bed. With another, he invited Walker into the small room and offered him the only chair. After introductions were made, Joseph swiftly outlined his plight. "They never contended with the plan of the Lord, to place you here at hand just when I needed you," he concluded.

Walker, who was somewhat overdressed for a hot day in a small town, pulled off his gloves and fanned his face. "I am in the middle of a very tense campaign, Reverend Smith. I can't afford to take time off for your defense — although your case seems straightforward enough — unless I can be assured of one thing."

"And what is that?" Joseph asked, chancing a sly look in Andrew's direction. He saw that Andrew had his notepad out and was keeping busy with a pencil.

"If I could be assured of your support in my campaign for the Congress, it would be worth my time to be your counsel."

Unruffled, Joseph replied, "And since you have the reputation as the best criminal lawyer the state of Illinois has yet produced, I would be a fool not to vote for you."

It was not until then, when the deal was made, that Walker took notice of what Andrew was doing. "Here," he asked, "what are you doing there?"

"Mr. Sharp is my personal scribe," Joseph explained. "He takes down everything I say."

"And everything that is said to you?"

"Why, Mr. Walker? Have you said anything you are ashamed of?"

Walker recognized he was obtaining a shrewd man as a client, and with the expectation of Joseph's influence on ten thousand or more Mormon votes, he walked out of the room feeling assured of a seat in the United States Congress.

By the time the men from Nauvoo had been organized and sent on their way to search for Joseph. Reynolds and Wilson were served a writ from the master in chancery to appear before the judge at Ottawa, Illinois. Since Joseph was their prisoner, they had to take him with them. Along the way they stopped for the night in the town of Pawpaw Grove, and again, Joseph was incarcerated in a hotel room. It was late in the day, but word spread fast through the little town that the Prophet Joseph Smith was there, under arrest. A crowd numbering in the hundreds demanded he be allowed to preach to them.

Wilson and Reynolds had had enough of this, and tried to disperse the throng, but an old man, grizzled white hair and beard flying and grasping a huge staff, banged it like a gavel for silence, and when the astonished lawmen let him speak, he shouted at the sheriff, "Stand off, you puke! Let the man speak! And if you don't, Pawpaw Grove has a committee you see here before you who will handle your case, and there'll be no appeal!"

The audience whooped into laughter and applause, and Reynolds and Wilson had no choice but to back down. Joseph addressed the throng on the subject of God's law on marriage, and was still going strong an hour after he had begun.

The subdued Wilson found a seat beside Andrew, and became immediately suspicious at the strange markings — not quite English — which he saw as he looked over his shoulder at the notepad he was filling. In a whisper, Andrew explained what he was doing.

"Looks like Hebrew," the man said.

"I've never seen Hebrew, so I wouldn't know."

"Well, I saw enough of it when I was married to a Heeb," the constable said with distaste.

Andrew continued his jottings, listening with one ear to Joseph, the other ear tuned to what Wilson was saying. "A Heeb? You mean a Jew?"

"Jew bitch. Didn't last too long. I took up with someone of my own race, which I should've done in the first place and high-tailed it one day. But I saw some of her Jew books with that kind of writing in it."

Rapidly filling the page, Andrew listened to another few words from the Prophet and continued his cryptic note-taking, flipping to the next page and continuing on.

"Yeah, the only thing I miss about her is her cooking," the constable said. Part of Andrew's brain received that and suddenly, an odd thought struck him.

"Your name's Wilson?"

"Yeah."

"You ever work on the Illinois levee?"

"Yeah. How'd you know?"

"Near Warsaw?"

"In Warsaw. That's where we lived!"

"Whatever happened to your wife?"

"Which? The Jewish one? She's still there, running a boarding house."

Andrew almost said, *And whether you know it or not, you're dead to her!* But he didn't. He just thought about all the good meals the man had missed.

COURT FINDS MISSOURI WRIT INVALID; SMITH FREED BY NAUVOO CITY CHARTER!

by Andrew J. Sharp
Associate Editor

After a surprise reunion with nearly a hundred volunteers from Nauvoo, Joseph Smith and his captors have returned to Nauvoo, where the City Council insists the Municipal Court has the right to rule on the Missouri extradition writ. Upon examination of the Nauvoo City Charter, this power was granted to the Nauvoo court and Joseph Smith was ordered turned free.

CRIMINAL ATTORNEY VERIFIES IT

Still traveling as counsel to the prophet, Cyrus Walker, noted criminal attorney, said it was his opinion that the Nauvoo City Charter possessed the power to try writs of habeas corpus.

REYNOLDS, WILSON FEAST AT SMITH TABLE BEFORE HEARING DECISION

In the unprecedented case, prisoner Joseph Smith invited defendants/captors Joseph H. Reynolds of Missouri and Harmon T. Wilson of Carthage to dine with him the night before the case went to the Municipal Court. When the court found Joseph innocent the next day, it closed yet another chapter in Missouri's untiring — but so far, unsuccessful — efforts to bring Smith to Missouri for a hearing on charges that he was an accessory before the fact in the attempted murder of Lilburn W. Boggs.

Back home again in the beautiful home most people still called "the Bennett house," Andrew caught up on the small amount of mail and the large amount of gossip he had missed. His informant was Rebecca, who sat comfortably on a large pillow at his feet. Maude and Samuel were also present in the spacious parlor.

"The wedding was beautiful," was all she would say when he asked her about it. Whether to spare his feelings or to divert his thoughts away from his former love, Rebecca hurried on to other things.

"Joseph is adding on to their house and is going to make it into a hotel," she said. Samuel nodded confirmation.

"And there's more and more talk about polygamy."

"'Becca!" Her mother, who had been knitting, dropped the yarn in her lap.

"Well, it's true; everybody but the Twelve is talking about it."

"What are they saying?" Andrew asked.

"We don't discuss such things in this house," Maude said.

"Well," sniffed Rebecca. "Anyway, it's your turn to tell us all the news," she said, looking up at Andrew.

"The Springfield papers say Governor Ford may send the militia to bring Joseph back to the Missouri border, where the Missouri militia can take him!"

Maude asked him if he thought he really would. Andrew said he doubted it. "But Illinois is getting pretty tired of hearing how the Mormons wriggle away from everyone who is sent in to get them," he said. "And they're especially angry at the Nauvoo City Council, claiming to have the power to reject any writ that's served on Joseph."

"What do you think of that?" Samuel asked.

"I think it's dangerous. I think the Council is acting as if it were the supreme power in the state, and the state isn't going to tolerate that much longer."

At this, Maude put her knitting down and stood up. "Oh, how depressing to hear all this. Come on, Rebecca; I know how to sweeten their dispositions. Let's go make fudge!"

Louisa stood in the dark bedroom, the southwest corner bedroom in the McCann household that she shared with Angus, and carefully parted the white curtains. She was staring into the black October night, not really looking for anything or anyone. It was too early to expect Angus to come home, even though it was half past nine. But she looked anyway — not at the street, but at the dim lamplight in the windows of the Bennett house, around the corner.

He had really acted like a beast, she told herself for the hundredth time. She had given him every opening, every opportunity to meet the challenge she had thrown down at him; she hadn't said she was going to marry Angus; she had carefully rehearsed how she would say it, and she had said it just that way. **Angus has asked me to marry him.** Why, she'd even told him that money and family position meant nothing to her, that she would have been very happy to marry a reporter, but he had to be willing to join the Church. Was that so much to ask? Then he would be hers, safely hers. Nobody could take him away from her. No differences, no arguments. *But I've adapted to the circumstances quite well, really.*

She thought she saw Andrew in the old bedroom she used to share with Rebecca. But no, that was Rebecca herself, drawing the curtains.

She had adapted to Angus working all day and half the night at the boat works, to his coming home most nights long after she had gone to bed, him smelling like a catfish, never washing unless she demanded it, then climbing into the bed along side of her and putting his filthy hands on her . . . her flesh crawled.

She had even adapted to her brother-in-law, Jock's, regulations. No lamps lit unless you were doing something in a room; ask Jock or one of the "boys" (and that included her own husband, Angus!) to adjust the damper on the fireplaces so no heat would be lost; and bathing! She used to love to take long and beautiful baths as often as three times a week when she was living over there at the Bennett house. Here, the men bathed weekly, the women every ten days! She knew Anne cheated on that rule because she was always sweet-smelling.

And the working hours. As soon as the boat yard opened, it had become successful. To handle the orders and draw the plans took all the daylight hours; that's why the three McCann men went back to work in the evening — to build what they had sold! Rather than hire outside help, they kept all the profits in the family that way. No wonder Jock had seemed so reluctant for Angus to marry — it might distract him from making more money!

She kicked at the long white curtain with one bare toe. Well, Jock had spared no expense for Anne and their son, James; he did love them and provided everything a wife could reasonably ask for.

She thought she saw a light in Andrew's bedroom. She did! There was someone moving around. Was there more than one there? She looked over quickly at Rebecca's room. No, there was Rebecca, combing her long hair. All was still well.

Jock expertly drew the adze down a timber which would become the keel of a dory. Beside him, William and Angus whittled strakes for the same boat, using drawknives. They had to work with their eyes close to their work in order to see in the dim light from the oil lamps. Yet, so precise was their craftsmanship, when the boat was assembled, it was a matter of family pride that less stuffing and chinking and caulk was used on a McCann boat than on any being made.

"Jock, it's ten o'clock," William said.

With a sigh, Jock looped the leather apron off over his head, rubbed oil on his adze and locked it away in the toolbox he carried with him. He saw that Angus was already standing, ready to turn down the lamps.

"All right, home we go," Jock said, and the other brothers fell into line behind Jock, who carried a lantern, across the plank which spanned the boggy area between dry land and the dredged inlet in which rested their new boats.

They walked up past the sign Joseph had just set out in front of their grand new house. "Nauvoo Mansion," it read. Jock had never approved of it, grunting every time they passed it on their twice-daily round trip between home and the boat yard. Tonight they had to walk the center of the street; there were six carriages parked in front of the place. From the windows could be heard conversation, and through them the McCanns saw several men earnestly discussing something. The three men walked past in the night, wondering what Joseph was up to now.

MORMON PROPHET RUNS FOR PRESIDENT OF UNITED STATES! WOULD FREE SLAVES, FORGIVE DEBTS, MAKE SCHOOLS OUT OF PRISONS! DECLARES ALL OTHER CANDIDATES UNWORTHY!

by Andrew J. Sharp
Associate Editor
The *Argus*

Nauvoo, Ill., January 4, 1844: It is no longer being denied by Joseph Smith, the Mormon prophet, that he is a serious candidate for the office of President of the United States.

Encouraged by his popularity in Mormon circles, and having determined to his satisfaction that no other Presidential candidates have the qualifications which he feels he, himself has, Smith has published a platform outlining his creeds.

Long opposed to slavery, he proposes the sale of public lands to raise the funds to buy the slaves from their masters, and then offer the freed slaves free passage to Africa, or an equivalent amount of land on which to live and farm.

On the subject of debt, he would close debtors prisons and would turn prisons into palaces of education, except for those convicted of murder and other base crime.

Smith and his counselors have recently petitioned all other candidates for statements in reply to questions sent them on issues of concern to Mormons, and according to the prophet, only a handful of replies were received, and these, not satisfactory to the Mormons.

Large campaign gatherings, complete with the Nauvoo Brass Band and marching by the Nauvoo Legion, have so far marked the opening of the Smith campaign.

"Seventies Hall"
Painting by Al Rounds
Courtesy of Nancy Rounds

Part Five:

The Downfall

Chapter 27

The temple was rising, tier upon tier, until it became the focal point to which the eye was drawn as Nauvoo came into view, from whatever direction the traveler approached. Some thought it was a church in which ordinary worship services were held. Some had heard whispered rumors of bizarre rites that would be performed there—something about the baptizing of dead bodies! (Joseph had laughed when he first heard this; it was understandable that his revelation on baptism **for** the dead might be misconstrued to mean baptism **of** the dead. After all, the doctrine was mentioned only once in the Bible, and most people hadn't heard of it.)

There were other rumors. Polygamy was now an open secret among the members, and the farther one went into Gentile land from Nauvoo, the more lurid the tales became.

A growing body of formerly loyal friends and followers of Joseph Smith were becoming his enemies, and by April of 1844, cells of conspirators had sprung up.

The prosperous Law brothers, William and Wilson, were now estranged from Joseph and the Church over the subject of "spiritual wifery," as well as their disapproval of Joseph's mixing of political and religious authority. They were not alone.

Joseph had ordered them excommunicated, along with a group of other men who had raised their voices in protest. But unlike the dishonored John C. Bennett, who departed from Nauvoo immediately upon his severance with the Church, the Law brothers had scores of friends and good customers and a thriving business in the city, which they had no intention of giving up. Besides, they had plans of their own to strike back at the man they believed was now a fallen prophet.

Andrew Sharp was walking along the road in front of the temple one May morning when he saw a team of oxen plodding toward a new building which had excited some interest because nobody seemed to know what it was to be used for. But Andrew understood immediately. The machine in the back of the wagon was a printing press. He ambled into the still damp brick building as workmen wrestled the iron monster down out of the wagon and onto a skid, to drag it inside. He asked Wilson Law about it.

"In three more days, Andy," he said, "the *Times & Seasons* is going to have some competition."

"Competition is healthy, I've heard."

"Well, this competition isn't going to be very healthy for Joe Smith!"

Andrew strolled out of the building and started down Mulholland Street, picking up speed as he approached the heart of town. This break in Joseph's authoritarian grip on Nauvoo was inevitable, he knew, but this was the first overt act of opposition. Once again he found himself in the position of a reporter who could alter the outcome of the event by reporting it. Should he hurry and tell Joseph Smith that a dissident press was about to start up in his city? Knowing Joseph, Andrew was certain that he would take some means of preventing it. But if he did that, he would be acting against the Constitution of the United States, and even Joseph Smith wouldn't dare do that---would he? He decided to wait, and watch.

On May 10th, the first sheets from the new press were handed out around Nauvoo. The prospectus announced the establishment of a new newspaper to be called *The Nauvoo Expositor*, and it heralded its editorial policy: UNMITIGATED DISOBEDIENCE TO POLITICAL REVELA-TIONS! And on the polygamy issue: WE SHALL CENSURE AND DECRY GROSS MORAL IMPERFECTIONS WHEREVER FOUND, EITHER IN PLEBEIAN, PATRICIAN, OR SELF-CONSTITUTED MONARCH!

Joseph struck back immediately by suspending Wilson Law as Major General of the Nauvoo Legion.

Wilson Law rode to the county seat and obtained an indictment from the Carthage Grand Jury against Joseph Smith on charges of adultery and polygamy. Another dissident Mormon, Robert Foster, who believed Joseph had tried to seduce his wife, accompanied Law and got an indictment against Joseph for "false swearing."

Now that the charges were out in the open, Andrew could write about them for both newspapers. Wording his *Argus* article slightly differently, because its readers would not necessarily know the personalities involved as intimately as would Nauvoo readers of the *Times & Seasons*, he sent off a dispatch to Quincy by express, and did so with a heavy heart. The signs of disintegration were all around him. They were more evident to him, as one of the few non-Mormons who had the confidence of both Joseph Smith, as well as his disillusioned former friends.

He rode with the prophet to Carthage on May 26th to cover the trial, but he was back home again that night; the case was put over until the circuit court met for the next term.

Late that evening, just before Andrew started to undress for bed, Samuel came to his door and said he had a visitor. "Jock McCann," he said, sounding mystified.

Andrew hurried down and saw the burly Scot standing in the entry hall with his cap in hand, his work clothes dusted with fine wood chips and sawdust. He shook hands gravely, and Andrew showed him into the parlor.

"I come to ye," he said, "seeking information on a delicate matter."

Andrew thought of Louisa, shut up in McCann's house. "On what matter?" he asked.

"Ye seem to know the prophet quite well."

"I have been with him a great deal, recently."

"And since ye're not a Church member, ye owe him no special loyalty?"

"Only as a friend; that is, I think of him as my friend and I believe he thinks of me that way."

"Then what I have to ask of ye, ye'll tell me as honestly as ye can?"

"Of course."

"Have ye seen the man change?" Andrew was puzzled. "Is he any different now, than when ye first met him?"

"I don't think so."

Jock compressed his lips into a straight line and seemed lost in thought.

"What sort of a change do you mean?" Andrew asked him.

"Anything—nothing. I don't know. I don't know why I came here to ask it. I'm not sure of a lot of things, any more."

Coming from Jock McCann, Andrew thought, that is a remarkable statement. If there had ever been a man who seemed as resolute as Jock, Andrew hadn't known him. Now, however, he was troubled and uncertain. He pulled at his black beard and stared at the ceiling. "Well," he said suddenly, moving to the door and putting on his cap, "I'll take nae more of yer time."

"It's the polygamy, isn't it?" Andrew asked him.

Jock stopped and turned back to him. "Well, that—and his making law and politics a part of the religion. I thought I had escaped from a country that had a state religion!"

He walked back toward Andrew. "Y'see," he said, "I know he's in trouble and I want to help him if I can. I have a few dollars put by." Andrew saw in his mind's eye the two-foot-long box of gold coins. "And I'd be able to pay for the best lawyers to defend him . . . if I could just be sure the man wasn't . . ."

"A fallen prophet?"

"Yes." It was painful for the man, Andrew could see, even to openly discuss such a thing. "I've read that apostate newspaper, the *Expositor*, and I started to tear it up—but then I thought, are they attacking an innocent man? Or is he guilty, as they say?"

"He's never discussed any of it with me."

"Nae, of course not," Jock said, making again to leave. "And I shouldn't trouble ye with my worries. After all, it's of no concern to you."

No, that's not quite true, Andrew thought, as he saw Jock out the door. *I am as troubled as any Mormon about the source of Joseph's ideas.* It would be good to know if the man was a prophet, ever had been a prophet, or if he was innocently deluded into believing he had been chosen, or—most chilling thought of all—was he a conspiring, knowing liar? Could he be any of these, one of them, none of them? He climbed the stairs again, slowly, trying to make sense out of it.

Joseph was enraged at what he read in the first issue of the *Expositor.* His friends had tried to keep him from seeing a copy, fearful of what he would do. He sent word to the members of the City Council that he was convening an emergency meeting the next day, June 8th. Andrew, of course, was in attendance.

"This infernal tripe," Joseph thundered, holding up a copy of the *Expositor*," is filled with the most pernicious lies any demon from Hell could conjure!" Then, for the benefit of any who had not read them, Joseph recited aloud the charges made against him.

"Yes, it's all over the city," one of the councilmen said. "There's talk of nothing else."

Joseph looked as haggard as if he had spent months in prison. "Then what are they saying of me? What do they think of me? Can one abominable edition of an apostate paper destroy all that has been built up?"

One of the members rose and said, "The Law brothers have been guilty of the very things they say the prophet has done! They're trying to cover their own guilt by accusing him!"

Another man shot to his feet. "Everyone knows they're just trying to get back against President Smith because he beat them in a real estate deal!"

Other voices added more accusations: theft, pandering, seduction—even counterfeiting.

At last, it was the Patriarch of the Church, Hyrum Smith, who galvanized the council into a united action. "The *Expositor* should be condemned as a public nuisance," he said.

One of the councilmen reached for a copy of *Blackstone* which was kept handy for legal reference, and as the other men discussed the correct definition of a public nuisance and what should be done about it, he found and quoted a passage to Joseph that seemed to satisfy him that the *Expositor* indeed qualified as a public nuisance. Andrew's pencil flew over the notepaper as he tried to keep up with the heated exchange.

"I say those devils should be run out of town," one of the men cried. "That paper is a disgrace to the whole city! We can't let them run another issue off their press."

And again, Hyrum spoke. "The thing we should do, is to fix that press so it can never print another lie!"

Andrew was alarmed. Didn't these men realize they were talking about violating the United States Constitution if they suppressed a newspaper? "Under the first amendment to the Constitution," he said, "all Americans are guaranteed freedom of speech and freedom of the press!"

"That doesn't mean we have to stand for libel!" Joseph shot back, and the councilmen voiced their agreement. Andrew sat back, aghast at what was taking place.

"Gentlemen," Joseph said, "Let us bring it to a vote. All those in favor of abating the *Expositor* press as a public nuisance, say aye."

A chorus of agreement.

"Opposed?" There was no reply. Suddenly, Andrew could bear it no longer. He stood up again.

266

"Gentlemen, I realize I have no official status here, that I am merely an observer; but I must remind you that the very Amendment you are about to violate is the same one that protects your church, that has permitted you to even have a church!"

Joseph and the rest of them ignored him. "The ayes have it," he said.

William Law hadn't returned from Carthage, where he had gone to press charges against Joseph Smith. The *Expositor* building was dark on the night of June 10th, when the Nauvoo Marshall, backed up by troops from the Nauvoo Legion under the command of acting Major General Jonathan Durham, smashed in the door, hauled the type out of its boxes and threw it into the street, took heavy mauls and smashed the press into junk.

A crowd of several hundred people poured into the street to watch the destruction of the *Expositor*. There were many cheers as the remaining copies of the paper, and even the blank newsprint stacked and waiting for the second edition, were set on fire and burned. Andrew watched from concealment, making notes, and feeling a wave of sadness and foreboding that made him almost ill.

Dr. Robert Foster chose to ride a fast horse down to Warsaw to inform Thomas Sharp of the occurrence. Together they composed the first printed notice of the attack, and Thomas added a flourish of his own:

CITIZENS ARISE, ONE AND ALL!

TOO OUR FRIENDS AT A DISTANCE, WE SAY, COME! WE ARE TOO WEAK, IN THIS COUNTRY, WITHOUT AID, TO EFFECT OUR OBJECT. COME! YOU WILL BE DOING YOUR GOD AND YOUR COUNTRY SERVICE, IN AIDING US TO RID THE EARTH OF A MOST HEAVEN-DARING WRETCH.

The countryside from St. Louis to Springfield and up through the top of Illinois was aflame with indignation. To try to explain his actions to the Governor, Joseph wrote that the *Expositor* was removed to keep peace in the city, and that Nauvoo would welcome the Governor's presence to investigate the entire affair, with the Nauvoo Legion at his disposal to put down any disturbance.

Nevertheless, once again a warrant was issued out of Carthage for the arrest of Joseph Smith and more than a dozen others—and once again Joseph invoked the Nauvoo court's authority to hear the charges, and he, his brother Hyrum, John Taylor and others were acquitted by Judge Daniel H. Wells. The sheriff returned to Carthage empty-handed again, touching off a riot among the population.

MORMON WAR THREATENS! PROPHET CALLS OUT NAUVOO LEGION, ASKS FOR VOLUNTEERS! CITY BEING FORTIFIED AGAINST EXPECTED ATTACK!
By Andrew J. Sharp

Associated Editor
The *ARGUS*

June 20, 1844: The largest city in Illinois is now being fortified with trenches dug at the outskirts, as the prophet Joseph Smith is arming Nauvoo against any attack from forces of the state or the general population.

The Nauvoo Legion, largest militia in the state, is under alert. Some five thousand armed men, except for a handful who are serving as missionaries, are prepared to defend the city in the event that a move is made to seize Joseph Smith by force, to stand trial on charges in Carthage which include willful destruction of property, arson, and moral misconduct.

In a speech in this city, Smith called for volunteers to assist this military defense. It is not known whether any Mormons living outside Nauvoo have made themselves available for this purpose.

Andrew sensed that his next trip out of the city was in the offing, and packed his traveling bag again, this time to go to Carthage to cover a hearing at which Governor Thomas Ford himself would be present. Ford had written to Joseph, asking that he send a delegation which could present the Mormon side of the fray. Joseph appointed John Taylor and John M. Bernhisel. The meeting did not go well.

GOVERNOR, MORMONS CONFER IN CARTHAGE: FORD REBUKES SMITH AND COUNCIL FOR "GROSS OUTRAGE," CONSTITUTIONAL CRIMES!

By Andrew J. Sharp
Associate Editor
The *ARGUS*

June 22, 1844: Governor Thomas Ford late tonight handed a stern message for Joseph Smith to Smith's representatives at a meeting in Carthage, in which Smith and the Nauvoo City Council were accused of "a very gross outrage upon the laws and liberties of the people" in the destruction of the *Expositor* press twelve days ago.

The Governor pointed out that the Mormons had violated at least four principles of the Constitution: freedom of the press, the right to give evidence in one's defense, no search and seizure without due process, and no union of legislative and judicial powers in the same body.

GOVERNOR FEARS DESTRUCTION OF NAUVOO! DEMANDS SURRENDER OF SMITH!

Governor Ford concluded in his statement to Joseph Smith that he feared that uncontrollable mobs would take matters into their own hands and destroy Nauvoo if Smith and the others charged with him did not surrender.

As a reply, the Mormon prophet wrote that he and his men were afraid for their lives to submit to the writs, especially since the Governor admitted that mobs might be uncontrollable by governmental force.

By the time Andrew had ridden back into Nauvoo, the city had taken on the look of a town under seige. Trenches were in place along the Carthage road and Legion members and volunteers challenged him with swords and muskets, until they recognized who he was and let him pass. Many wagons were leaving town.

What had become of the orderly, civilized City of Joseph? Townspeople were running here and there, wagons were driven at breakneck speed through the streets, the mills and factories seemed to be at a standstill, and men everywhere carried weapons. He hurried down to the *Times & Seasons* office and saw Samuel Gaines laboring with the press, trying to get out an extra edition. His first words to Andrew told the story.

"Joseph has gone into hiding again, sent his family away!"

"Oh, so that's it," Andrew said. "The town looks as if it's lost its head."

"I'm running off a special edition," Samuel said, "but I wonder whether there'll be anyone left in the city to read it!"

"Do you want any help?"

"Not yet. You're the reporter, Andrew; go get the news!"

He did just that. Starting out on horseback, Andrew moved through the city. He saw men and women frantically hauling carts of staples from the stores, carts piled high with more food than they could consume in a month. As he made his way down to a variety store which also sold medicinal drugs and herbs, he saw the carriages of two doctors tethered outside, and a swarm of people clamoring to buy the remedies their families might need if there was to be a long seige.

He rode down to Water Street and saw the Nauvoo Mansion, closed and deserted, and a little farther down, the three McCann men laboring frantically to remove as much of their portable goods as they could. He rode up beside Angus, who was helping William load a workbench into a waiting wagon. "Moving out, Angus?" he asked.

"Aye!" We're taking everything we can, before the mobs get here!"

"What mobs?"

"What mobs? The Gentiles, mon! They've got an army marching in here, ready to kill every one of us and torch the town!"

"Where did you hear that?"

"Everybody knows it, except for you, I guess."

Andrew turned his horse around and started up Sidney Street. Hand carts, ox carts, teams hauling wagons—the streets were filled with vehicles and shouting men. As he rode through the chaos he saw a trunk lowered out of a second-story window on a rope into a waiting wagon, and then two men holding a bedspread below the window started catching bedding being thrown.

So, Joseph had flown. And when the word spread, this is how the faithful react. He wondered whether Jock had made up his mind about Joseph Smith. He turned the horse around again and trotted back to the boat works. Jock was just getting onto the wagon seat now, the back piled high with lumber, tools and workbenches.

"Jock!" Andrew called, "Where are you bound?"

"East," he said, "Carthage by tomorrow morning if we ride all night."

"Where are the women?"

"They've gone on ahead," he said.

"You're leaving your home?"

"Aye." Andrew looked for any sign of the two-foot box, but decided the women must have been entrusted with it.

"I was wondering," Andrew said, "if you ever made your mind up about the prophet."

Jock looked at him with scorn. "He's run out on us. The mon's a coward, leaving us to face the mobs. No prophet would do that!" And with that, he cracked the whip over the team and the wagon jolted into motion.

"Good luck," Andrew shouted.

They made no reply.

Andrew turned around again and rode past the Mansion House when he saw Orrin Porter Rockwell suddenly slip out of the side door and run to a horse tied nearby. Rockwell! What was he doing in the Smith's house? Looting? Vandalizing? No, Andrew realized, whatever the man's morals, he was too devoted to the prophet to victimize him. He spurred his horse and dashed up to the small man as he was about to swing into the saddle.

"Hello, Port, where're you going?"

Rockwell hauled out a pistol and aimed it directly at Andrew's face. "None of your damned business, Sharp, and if you know what's good for you, you won't even watch where I'm going!" And with that, he stuffed his feet into the stirrups, reared his horse, and galloped off to the south, beyond the boat yard and the mill. Andrew considered following him; he was undoubtedly going looting. He tied his own horse to the hitch rail and tried the door Porter had come out of, and found it open. He walked into the house and stopped to listen. "Anybody home?" No answer. He walked slowly through the big kitchen, remembering the last time he had been there—the Christmas party when Porter Rockwell had stumbled in covered with filth from his weeks-long journey up from St. Louis where he had been in jail. The women had screamed at the sight of this apparition with a matted beard and long filthy hair, and Joseph had come running, pulled the man to his feet, for he had fallen onto the floor, and cried out "Port!" It seemed only days ago. Now the house was still, deserted, and not a pot or pan seemed to be missing.

"Stand where you are!"

Andrew jumped in surprise. There in the gloom stood a woman, both hands clutching a pistol which was wavering but aimed generally at his head.

He was too astonished to talk, and he raised his hands slowly into the air. As he did so, the muzzle of the gun dropped. "Mister Sharp!" It was Emma!

"Sister Smith, what are you doing in Nauvoo?" Andrew gasped.

"And what are you doing in my kitchen?" she replied.

"I saw Porter Rockwell run out of here. The place looked deserted and I was afraid he might have been looting."

"A natural mistake," she said with a wry smile. "Thank you for being concerned. I'm sorry I can't offer you much hospitality just now---"

"I understand. I hear that the prophet has gone somewhere?"

"Yes. I just sent Port off with a message to him."

"Oh! That explains why he greeted me the same way you did!"

"Are you planning on staying in Nauvoo, Mr. Sharp?"

"I don't know. Are you?"

Emma looked around her to the door from the kitchen to the hallway. He could see several small trunks and bags piled there.

"You'll be joining Joseph, then?"

"Perhaps not," she said. Andrew studied her face. As sick as she had been, as many years of fighting and weeping and burying her dead children as she had been through, she had a rare kind of beauty. Maybe the strength he admired in her made her glow a little brighter. "Could you tell me where he is?" he asked.

"That I cannot tell you," she said. "I'm sure you understand."

"Can you tell me what was in your message?"

She smiled. "You are a very persistant man, Mr. Sharp; that must be what Joseph so admires about you. And he does admire you, you know; he has spoken to me many times about what an honorable man you are, how he trusts you."

"Will you trust me now?"

"In what way?"

"Tell me how to get to him. Sister Smith, this city is going crazy. People are running all over, hoarding, fortifying, leaving their homes and businesses . . ."

"And if you could find him, what would you say to him?"

"I'd say, 'Come back and be with your people. Don't run out on them at a time like this!'"

She looked at him sadly. "That is exactly what is in the note that Porter Rockwell is taking to him, right now."

Chapter 28

A hoot-owl called from the thick underbrush just east of the tiny house on the Missouri shore. Dawn was just breaking, but the three men inside were instantly awake. Willard Richards poked his head outside and cocked a ready ear. The bird call came again, and he whispered, "Be alert!"

Joseph and Hyrum, both fully dressed, rolled out of their blankets and stood beside the single door to the shack. Each man carried a pistol.

Suddenly the thin voice of Porter Rockwell came from just outside the door. "Joseph, it's Port!"

Hyrum let him in. He was drenched from the crossing of the turbulent Mississippi in the skiff that had brought them there only 24 hours before.

"Well, how is Nauvoo?" Joseph asked.

Rockwell pulled off his hat and shook his long hair like a dog. "Half the town's moving out," he said, "and the other half is digging in for a fight."

"What are they saying about me?"

"There's a lot who wish you well, Joseph. There's some who think you should've stayed with them. Oh, here," he said, fishing the note from a small purse tied around his neck.

Joseph unfolded it. "It's from Emma," he said, as he began to read it to himself. His eyes tracked back and forth, and the smile of anticipation that had come over him when he saw the note, now faded. He looked up. "She wants me to surrender and let them try me. She says Nauvoo will be sacked unless I come back."

The others were silent. "They think I'm a coward." Joseph turned and looked out the window toward the pink dawn in the sky above Nauvoo, across the river. "If my life is of no value to my friends it is of no value to me." He turned back to Rockwell. "What should I do?"

"You're older than I am; you ought to know best, Joseph. As you make your bed, I'll lie with you."

Headstrong, self-confident Joseph now turned to his quieter, older brother, Hyrum. Of the two, Joseph had been the natural leader, almost from the beginning of his life. But now he said to his brother, "Hyrum, you are the oldest. What shall I do?"

For Hyrum, the answer was simple. A plain and law-abiding man, he was ready on the moment for his reply. "Go back and give up."

"We'll be butchered!"

But Hyrum was calm. "The Lord is in it. If we live or die, we shall be reconciled to our fate."

Andrew decided to take advantage of the mild June weather to camp across the street from the Mansion House, in the yard of the prophet's former dwelling, the Homestead. At 4:00 am Monday, June 24th, his vigil was rewarded. Up from the river crept four men, and let themselves into the Mansion by the side door.

With the dawn, around 5:30, came other men, singly and in groups. Most entered the house while others cared for the horses tied to the hitch rail outside.

The eastern sky was just beginning to grow light when Joseph and the others came back out of the house. By now other men had arrived, and Andrew obtained a horse so that he could ride with them. At the door of the Mansion House, Emma and the children gave long and heartfelt embraces to the prophet, who went from one to the other and held them so long and firmly that it was obvious he feared he might not see them again.

They set off just as the sun rose above temple hill. Andrew saw the poetess, Eliza R. Snow standing with Emma and the family, and came over to them just as Joseph and the party rode away.

"Can you tell me what he said?" Andrew asked Sister Snow.

"He said—to all of us—that he was going like a lamb to the slaughter, but that he was as calm as a summer's morning. He said, 'I have a conscience void of offense toward God and towards all men . . .'" then she suddenly sobbed and tears sprang from her eyes—"I shall die innocent, and it shall yet be said of me, **'He was murdered in cold blood!'**"

Andrew paused to write the words in his notebook before he rode off to join the others.

Andrew wanted to spend as much time with the prophet as he could, for indeed, as Eliza had indicated, these might be the last hours he would spend on earth—riding toward a district in which ferocious anti-Mormon demonstrations had burst out spontaneously on countless days, whenever news of new Mormon "Outrages" reached them. But he couldn't get more than two horse lengths from Joseph.

As he rode behind him on the eighteen-mile journey to Carthage, Andrew wondered over and over, what makes the man persist? Why not merely say what they want him to say, take a little prison time, and free himself from the entanglements of legal penalties? If he renounced polygamy, it might not be too late. If he ordered the Nauvoo Legion disbanded, people would relax. **Why not, Joseph?**

He recalled asking him that, on that winter night in Carthage, and remembered his strange reply. **"I am a prophet."** Well, Andrew mused, he certainly must believe it, or he wouldn't be going back to Carthage now.

But he didn't make it to Carthage. Three miles west of the town at about 10:00 am, a troop of mounted soldiers appeared in the road. The Mormon procession stopped, and an officer rode up to Joseph.

"General Joseph Smith?"

"I am he," Joseph replied.

Saluting, the officer said, "I am Captain Dunn of the Union Dragoons. Governor Ford is in Carthage, and has ordered me to intercept you and give you this order," and with that he handed over a rolled paper affixed with a red wax seal.

Joseph broke it open and examined it. Andrew tried to move closer to the prophet, but there were too many men between his horse and Charlie, the big black mount on which Joseph rode.

Joseph looked up and turned to the others. "I'll have to go back to Nauvoo."

"Go back?" several riders said in unison.

"Governor Ford has ordered the Legion to turn in the state's arms. I'll have to ride back and see that they do it."

A groan of dismay went up from the party. Andrew could hear someone comment, "They're taking no chances with us, are they?"

Captain Dunn asked Joseph if he would countersign the Governor's order, and Joseph did so immediately. Then he called Willard Richards to ride over beside him, and looked around for Andrew for the first time. The others made way for Andrew's horse to come up beside the prophet.

"Brother Andrew," Joseph said, "ride with me back to Nauvoo, and I'll dictate some to you." And then to Brother Richards he said, "Willard, please take a note to Governor Ford. Tell him I've had to go back to Nauvoo to disarm the Legion," and his voice cracked and he hesitated, finally continuing, "And tell him I shall return as ordered as soon as I have seen that all is well." Then he asked Marshall Greene to ride ahead to Nauvoo to open the armory.

The Nauvoo group turned their horses around and started west again, while Willard Richards rode with the Dragoons into Carthage.

Joseph was flanked on the left by Andrew and on the right by Porter Rockwell, who looked glum because much of the time Joseph spent talking to Andrew.

"May I stay with you and the others?" Andrew asked him.

"Yes, for as long as matters are under my control," Joseph said. "When we return to Carthage, though, I shall submit to arrest and they will do with me as they please."

"You have dictation to give me?"

"Yes. Some personal letters I shan't have time to deliver myself. I want to get back on the road to Carthage as soon as possible, to show my good faith to the Governor. And there is no need for another leave-taking at home."

"You won't be seeing Emma, then?"

"No." They slowed their pace so that Andrew could make notes as he rode. Shortly past two in the afternoon, they breasted the crown of the rise just east of Nauvoo and rode down into the city again.

"There never was such a beautiful place, in Greece or ancient Rome," Joseph said reflectively.

It took little time for word to spread through the city that Joseph had returned, and hopeful citizens poured toward the parade ground for a chance to hear good news, but Joseph made no public speech, only busying himself seeing that the two hundred firearms and three small cannons were collected and placed on wagons. Many members of the Legion stood around the armory building, looking on with apprehension, remembering that the last time the Mormons had laid down their arms in the face of a military order a massacre had followed. Without the weapons the state had issued them, the Legion would have only personal arms to fall back on if they needed to defend the city.

Six p.m., June 24th. The prophet, Hyrum, and his party started back toward Carthage. Everyone was growing weary by now, and a long ride faced them. In the woods just east of Nauvoo, a man named Abraham Hodge came riding back from Carthage and stopped the prophet's group.

"What is the news in Carthage, Abraham?" Hyrum asked him.

"If it was my duty to counsel you," he said, "I would say, don't go another foot, for they say they will kill you in Carthage!"

Hyrum and Joseph looked at one another, but neither one seemed to hesitate. They thanked him for the information and rode on into the gathering night.

Just outside of Carthage at eleven-thirty, Captain Dunn and the sixty cavalrymen from the Union Dragoons intercepted the party. Andrew rode up through the ranks of the fifteen Nauvoo City Councilmen and others who had made the trip with the prophet.

"Well, Captain," Joseph said wearily, "in these wagons are all the arms the Governor asked for."

The young Captain looked back and saw two wagons covered with canvas, and could make out cannon muzzles beneath them. "Sir, I'm relieved that you complied with the orders, and I thank you. Now, I want you to know—and to pass on to your men, here—that I shall be responsible for your protection in Carthage, and I mean to see to your personal safety, sir, if it costs me my own life!"

With that, he wheeled his horse around and ordered the Dragoons to form two files, one on each shoulder of the road, and to flank the Mormon party as they rode into Carthage.

Joseph looked at Andrew and the others who had ridden with him from Nauvoo. "There is no call for you men to go with me," he said. Nobody said anything in reply. "God bless you," Joseph said, and rode Charlie into the hollow square of Dragoons which waited to accompany him and the others.

Ahead and around a bend in the road, a glow lit the sky. The rhythm of a bass drum resounded, setting the tempo for a mass of hundreds of voices shouting in a chant. Torches shooting flaming pitch illuminated the town square, where well over a thousand men had gathered. The torches were brandished up and down as the frenzied mob shouted in rhythm, "Kill Joe Smith! Kill Joe Smith." It reminded Andrew of a scene out of Dante's vision of purgatory. There was no mistaking the purpose of the enormous mob, for there were many times more people standing in Carthage square than lived in the town under normal conditions. They had come here to get rid of Joseph Smith, once and for all.

As the Dragoons drew closer to the edge of the town, a boy who had been stationed along the road as a lookout sprang from the trees and ran ahead of the party, shouting "Here they come! Here come the Mormons!" As he reached the fringes of the crowd in the square, the mob turned and began milling toward them, and in moments, a thousand rioters, some on horses, descended on the Mormons and their escorts.

One of the Councilmen said, "Oh my God!"

Andrew saw hundreds of uniformed men in the milling throng, just as unruly as the rest. He saw a battalion from neighboring Schuyler County and a regiment from McDonough, and thirty or so gray-jacketed militiamen who seemed louder and more depraved than any of the rest—the infamous Carthage Greys.

Captain Dunn of the Union Dragoons unsheathed his sword and held it over his head, its blade glinting in the torchlight, and he drove his horse through the frenzied mob with his men closing ranks behind him to protect Joseph and Hyrum. The others in the party rode as close together as they could. Andrew had never seen such concentrated hatred in his life. Men and even boys, screaming so shrilly that he thought his ears would burst.

As the Dragoons escorted their prisoners slowly through the ravening mob, a voice screamed beside him, "Stand away, Dragoons, so we can shoot the damned Mormons! Stand away and we'll kill 'em!" It was a Carthage Grey, not over eighteen, Andrew guessed, and he had a musket to his shoulder and his finger on the trigger. The gun was aimed at the back of Joseph's head.

Captain Dunn led the beleagured party to the door of Hamilton's hotel and tavern, and formed a tight cordon around the entrance as Hyrum, Joseph and the others climbed down from their horses and hurried inside. Joseph turned at the last moment and took a fleeting glance at his prized black stallion, Charlie, but was pushed inside by others.

At last, everyone was safe inside and Captain Dunn posted a detachment of men with them, not only to guard the Mormons, but to protect them. The planked oak door was shut and barred, but a hundred fists pounded on the door and smashed through the glass panes in the windows. Bayonetted rifles poked through the openings, and the Dragoons smashed at them with their own guns. The mayhem from outside made conversation in the tavern impossible. Joseph and Hyrum were led upstairs to a small room overlooking the square.

In the room stood the Governor of Illinois, Thomas Ford. "I am Joseph Smith and this is my brother, Hyrum," the prophet said, "reporting as you have ordered, Sir."

"A terrible night, a terrible night. I must try to quiet the men, the

Governor replied, and went to a window and opened it. He stuck his head and torso out and held up his arms. When someone noticed him, a call went out to hush the noise, and in a few moments, the more than thousand men fell silent.

"Now I know your great anxiety to see Mr. Smith, which is natural enough," he shouted, "but it is too late tonight . . . but I assure you, gentlemen, you shall have that privilege tomorrow morning, as I will cause him to pass before the troops upon the square! And now, I wish you to return to your quarters."

Some of the crowd cheered. Others groaned and cursed. Someone sang out, "Hurrah for Tom Ford." Gradually the crowd dispersed, the Governor retired to his own room in the hotel, and Joseph, Hyrum, John Taylor, Willard Richards and Joseph's old friend William W. Phelps fell into a fitful, exhausted sleep in one room.

Andrew found a room across the square, only after assuring the landlord that he was not a Mormon, but a journalist from Quincy—and paying in advance at double the usual rate.

It seemed to Andrew that his head had barely touched the rough pillow before he was awakened by the shouts of a crowd again, and this time it was broad daylight—8:30 in the morning—and the square had filled again with a mob bent upon getting a look at the Mormon prophet. He was separated from the prophet now by the bodies of over a thousand hostile people; no way to get across to be with Joseph and his party. He had to content himself to witnessing the events at a distance. He found a way to climb to the low roof of the building where he could observe all that went on.

The Carthage Greys reassembled. Despite their reputation as a crack and orderly outfit, their commander, General Deming, seemed to have no control over them today. He pushed and hauled at them until they formed a box of sorts around the door to the hotel where Joseph, Hyrum, the Governor and the other Nauvoo men had stayed. Andrew saw the door open and before anyone could see who was coming through it, a screeching roar went up and a musket, pointed in the air, discharged with a puff of smoke. But the man who emerged was Governor Ford. A table was provided and he was helped up on it, where he held up his arms for quiet.

Andrew recorded in his notebook that the Governor said little that could be considered encouraging for Joseph. He declared that the prisoners were dangerous men, guilty no doubt of all charges that might be brought against them, but in some deference to justice, he admonished the crowd that they must not interfere with the due process of the law. "This was not what they wanted to hear," Andrew wrote. "The people were enraged that there would be any hinderance to their assault upon the prisoners."

And then the Governor went inside and reappeared moments later with Joseph and Hyrum, then Richards, Taylor and Phelps. The sheer volume of noise put up by the mob amazed Andrew for its palpable force; he felt it literally shake the roof.

"The Greys surround them now," Andrew scribbled, "and they march the prisoners through the crowd to the troops of the 57th Regiment, who were promised an introduction to Joseph and Hyrum."

Down in the square, General Minor Deming fell in behind the Governor, and Joseph and Hyrum walked behind the General, as they made their way before the troops. Over and over, Governor Ford introduced the prisoners as "Generals," as they passed along the line of men. The title of General did not set well with the officers of the 57th Regiment nor the men of the Carthage Greys. As the prisoners were caused to walk slowly past the files of men, the last semblance of military courtesy and discipline disintegrated, and the men cursed at the Smiths while still standing at Order Arms. Ramrod straight, the two ranks of men through which the prophet passed hurled insults and threats, and several soldiers spat at Joseph and Hyrum at point-blank range. The prophet recoiled but had no choice but to walk silently on, spittle dripping from his face and hair. On his rooftop vantage point, Andrew searched for a simile to use in describing the incredible scene unfolding before him, and surprised himself by scribbling, "Joseph is walking with his own crown of thorns."

Governor Ford finally saw his mistake. The crowd outside the ranks of militiamen had picked up the new mood of rebellion and the Governor feared that open warfare might break out at any second. Calling for the small table he had used as a platform before, he scrambled up on it.

"No! No! You must not think I meant any military honor to these prisoners! They are not Army Generals, they merely wear that title in their own militia! You need not fear!"

The temper of the mob gradually subsided and Ford gratefully hurried back into the security of the Hamilton hotel, believing that he had prevented mass bloodshed.

The mob seemed to be without direction. The objects of their anger had once more been taken out of their sight, back into the hotel, and they didn't know where to turn next with their hate, so they began to rush the hotel again, slamming their hands on the doors and even the walls, demanding the blood of the Prophet and his brother.

At last, the greatest part of the throng grew tired of waiting and drifted back to other pursuits. Andrew climbed down from his rooftop perch and made his way across the square to the hotel but a guard barred the door and refused to let him in, credentials or no. Andrew felt foiled now that he had come so far at the side of Joseph Smith, not to be with him to record his words at this perilous period in his life. He decided to stay down in the square, close to the door to the tavern, in hopes that he might find some other way of gaining entrance.

Inside in his room, Joseph Smith dictated several notes to Willard Richards, who was able to move throughout the hotel and tavern with less restriction, possibly because of his 300-pound bulk, which tended to dominate any room he was in, or possibly because he had let it be known that he was a doctor—and therefore considered above suspicion, even if he was a Mormon.

About 4:00, Joseph was alerted by the approach of a Carthage Justice of the Peace, who was also Captain of the Carthage Greys. Robert F. Smith walked up to the door and the sentry recognized him immediately and opened it for him.

"Captain, I'm a reporter for the Quincy *Argus* and I must see Joseph Smith," Andrew said.

"Not on your life," the Captain replied, and the sentry stepped in front of Andrew as the officer slipped in the door.

Discouraged, Andrew resumed his vigil and waited for another chance. Shortly after five, lawyers H. T. Reid and James W. Woods arrived and after considerable negotiation with the sentry and the captain of the guard, they were admitted. Again Andrew applied to enter with them and again was barred. He had almost given up, when a constable worked his way through the crowd. He was a man Andrew had talked with in Carthage before, and he hurried to his side as he came to the door. "Constable, do you remember me? I'm a reporter from the Quincy *Argus*, and I've been covering Joseph Smith now for a long time. Will you tell this guard to let me in to see him?"

"He'll be coming right out," the constable said gruffly, as he motioned for the guard to open the door for him. "I've got a mittimus here that says he has to go to jail."

"Jail? Where?"

"Right here in Carthage," the constable said, hurrying in the door.

A crowd, mostly drunk, began to gather to wait for the appearance of the prisoners, and Andrew found himself pushed up against the wall of the tavern. Then the crowd began yelling, each man with his favorite epithet or curse, making threats, obscene remarks—anything that might get a reaction from the prisoners.

As Andrew waited among them, the mob roared with dismay as a detachment of the Greys arrived with fixed bayonets to force the crowd away from the door. It was obvious to Andrew that he would get no closer to Joseph than any member of the mob, so he decided to worm his way through the gathering crowd toward the jail, a low stone building not far from the square, and try to find his way in there.

He cajoled, he threatened, he tried bribery, but to no avil. The jailer, George W. Stigall, who lived in the small stone building with his wife, refused to admit anyone unless they were approved by the proper authority. The best Andrew could do was stand near the door and watch as Joseph and Hyrum were led through the crowd.

Stigall welcomed them as if they were customers, rather than prisoners, (for in fact, they did represent cash to the proprietors of the jail; it was operated for the profit of the owner), and Joseph and Hyrum were assigned to a minimum-security cell, the debtors room, and John Taylor, Willard Richards and William W. Phelps were permitted to spend the night in the same room.

279

Chapter 29

Joseph stood at the single east window of the debtors' room and watched the sun rise on Thursday morning. It was June 27th, without a cloud in the sky. It would be another warm day. He felt considerably better about their chances for a safe stay and a fair and impartial hearing after his long talk with Governor Ford the day before. Joseph had been alarmed when word reached him that the Governor was going to leave Carthage and go to Nauvoo.

"We owe our safety to you, sir," Joseph had said. "If you leave us here, our lives will be in grave danger!"

"Oh, I think you are unduly alarmed about that," Ford had said, but then he assured Joseph, "If I go to Nauvoo, I'll take you and your brother with me." Relieved, Joseph had gone on to talk of the charges against them, his feeling of justification for destroying the *Expositor* press, and the sincerity of the councilmen who only meant to do their duty in the name of public order and decency.

Before he had left their cell, Ford mentioned their safety again. "I've never been in such a dilemma in my life, but your friends shall be protected. I have the pledge of the whole army to sustain me." And with that assurance, he had departed and Joseph and his party settled down for a peaceful night. It had been disturbed only once, by a gunshot which sounded right outside the jail, and someone drunkenly making a noise like a turkey. He had sent Dan Jones out a few minutes ago to inquire what that had been all about.

Dan had gone directly to the officer on duty, Frank Worrell of the Carthage Greys, and demanded to know what had caused a man to fire off a gun outside the jail. Had there been any danger to the prisoners inside?

"Listen," the man said, "we had too much trouble to bring Old Joe here, to let him escape alive, and unless you want to die with him, you'd better leave before sundown! You'll see that I can prophesy better than Old Joe!"

Jones ran back to the jail to tell Joseph, but now was told that he couldn't go back inside. The Welchman was frantic now. Whom could he turn to for help? Here was the first overt threat from an officer of the military that Joseph would be killed! Then he remembered that the Governor was staying at the Hamilton Hotel, and he ran there and asked to see him.

"Hell, Ford's went down to Nauvoo," the clerk at the hotel said. "Took some troops with him."

Jones was beside himself. With nobody left to appeal to but the Carthage authorities—who seemed to be part of the conspiracy to kill the prophet—his last source of help was gone! He left the Hamilton Hotel and in the square he saw a Warsaw soldier shouting to a group of eager townspeople. "We're going to be discharged this morning, but now that the Governor and those troops from McDonough are on their way to Nauvoo, we'll be back here and take care of those men, never you fear—even if we have to tear the jail down!"

That was enough for Dan Jones. He ran over to the jail and when the jailor opened the door, Jones told him that there was every likelihood that the Carthage Greys or some soldiers from Warsaw would storm the jail and murder the prisoners if something couldn't be done to protect them. He demanded to be let in and allowed to report this to Joseph and Hyrum. The jailor refused, but he was worried enough by the earnestness of the little Welshman that he promised to deliver the message to Joseph, himself, and try to find more secure quarters for him and his party.

There were no locks on the room the men were in. Debtors weren't as likely to escape as felons, and locks cost good money. Jailor Stigall reported what Jones had told him, and Joseph was appalled. Ford had betrayed him! Instead of taking him with him to Nauvoo, he had fled and left them to the mob! Stigall wanted to do whatever he could to keep his prisoners safe, so he offered the lockable cell, and apologized, saying there wouldn't be room for more than four. Joseph and Hyrum and two friends. John Taylor and Willard Richards, loyal as always, stayed on with the prophet.

Andrew felt absolutely useless now. He had amassed many notes illustrating the temper of the crowd and the ineffectiveness of the forces on the side of the law in Carthage, but what was he to do with them? They were incomplete. Something was imminent—a breakout? A release through more tricky legal maneuvering? That seemed most unlikely now. Ransacking his knowledge of the law, which was only what he as a reporter had gleaned in covering the courtroom adventures of Joseph Smith, Andrew thought there might be reason for a change of venue, should he have to stand trial; there could not be a disinterested party in any western Illinois county, when it came to the Mormons in general or Joseph Smith in particular.

And then, there was the other possibility. Joseph might never leave Carthage alive. He had never faced such uniform hostility and such unbridled violence as he did on the night he arrived. And the very troops assigned to protect him were the most vicious of the mob!

He had seen the Governor and the McDonough militia ride out of Carthage early this morning and in short order discovered that this left "the fox in charge of the henhouse." Who was there now to bar the door if a mob wanted to assault the jail and kill the prisoners? Andrew wandered around the streets of Carthage, picking up stray bits of gossip, listening, putting pieces together in his mind.

The weather, which had dawned promisingly, turned cloudy and a chill rain suddenly swept in across the plains. Unprepared for the changed weather, Andrew huddled under a narrow eave on a building which permitted him to watch the company of Carthage Greys which was encamped on the public square. The second company of Greys had been disbanded, and these were here only to stand guard shifts at the jail, half a mile away. Eight members of the company, Andrew had noted, were walking guard duty at the jail at any given time.

Inside the jail, Stigall came upstairs and saw that Joseph and Hyrum and their two friends were still not making any move to come downstairs to the cell. John Taylor lay on the straw tick in the corner. The rain hadn't cooled the room and it was hot and sticky. From time to time, Joseph asked Taylor for a song, and the handsome Englishman complied. The sound of his true baritone made the Greys on guard duty jeer. No man they knew of would be caught dead singing **hymns**.

The rain squall passed and the sun came out again, causing wisps of steam to rise from the roofs of Carthage. Joseph barely heard the song his friend was singing; his mind was on Cyrus Wheelock, his friend who had managed to visit him in jail during the morning rainstorm, attired in a long coat, in order to exchange mail and take to Nauvoo some letters the Brethren had written. He had also produced two pistols, a six-shooter and a single-shot gun, and silently handed them to Joseph and Hyrum. Then, without a word, he had taken the letters for Nauvoo. "Ride like the wind," Joseph had told him, "because everything may depend upon this one," and he had tapped a letter on which was the name of Jonathan Dunham.

Joseph and Hyrum had the secret guns; in a few hours, General Dunham would have his secret orders. Mobilize the Nauvoo Legion with whatever arms remained in the city and ride for Carthage prepared to storm the jail and rescue the prisoners! It was his last and most desperate plan to save their lives. John Taylor was singing, "A Poor Wayfaring Man Of Grief."

By five o'clock, Andrew was finding it hard to concentrate on what he had come to this town to do. He had been so thirsty recently! Yet he dared not leave the post he had assigned himself to stand, an excellent vantage point where he could watch the Greys and also see the jail. The Greys were obviously waiting for something to happen; from time to time one of them would look down the road toward the jail, then another one would do the same thing, and then there would be a huddle of grey uniforms and snickers and guffaws, not quite under their breaths. He decided to walk toward the jail again. If only this buzzing in his head would leave him, this insufferable thirst! And why was he feeling cold one minute and boiling the next? He put it down to nerves, ragged nerves. If he was this close to cracking, how must Joseph feel?

He walked along the road, smelling the dust and the vapor from the rain. When had it rained last? This morning? He looked at his watch. Just past five, and he had forgotten to eat lunch again. He was definitely off his feed, he decided, and wished he were back in the big, neat bedroom at the Bennett house.

Why was everyone walking as if they were in some kind of stage play? Was it his queer condition—maybe it was indigestion—or were the people on the road all walking as if they thought someone was looking at them? As if they had been told to walk just thus-and-so, just this way and that way? To provide stage dressing, to make things look **normal**? And didn't he hear somebody **singing**?

He approached the jail. The Carthage Greys were on guard duty. Suddenly, something caught his eye, something to the west. It was something moving fast and then halting. He squinted into the sun, and then he saw it again. Two this time! They were boys playing in the fields. No! They were full grown men! He stood immobile on the Carthage street, watching a group of men—were there four or five?—running as if they were playing tag. Only these men carried guns, and there was something on their faces. They were painted, like Indians! Black smears on cheeks and noses and foreheads. And then they were at the jail and the Greys were firing, firing point blank at them, but the men didn't halt or even hesitate. One of the Greys seemed to be running after one of the black-faced men, and the man stopped and shouted something and pushed him back, and the Grey picked up his gun and fired!

Andrew ran across the street. The jail was northwest of him now, only a hundred yards away, but he ran as if in a dream . . . his legs pumping too slowly, as if he were running in thick molasses. He couldn't reach the jail, it kept staying too far from him, and then there were more shots and still more! He ran toward the south corner of the jail, approaching the well, when suddenly a flash of something white caught his eye in the upstairs window. A man had just smashed out the window pane! But below were more men with guns, just in front of him! As Andrew watched, the man in the window turned, as if to leap, and suddenly crimson blotched his white shirt—once, twice—and he lost his balance and fell to the ground by the well, hitting on his left shoulder, and he rolled onto his back and lay still. The attackers ran up to him, saw him, turned and saw Andrew coming, and then ran. Andrew ran too—slower and slower, dreading the knowledge he was about to have, dreading the story he was going to write, dreading the face he was about to see, lying by the well.

It was Joseph Smith. Dead.

In the jail, pandemonium had broken out. Down the stairs came four men, some wounded, holding their arms, limping, dragging themselves into hiding.

Out of the door sprang the jailor, waving a pistol, not knowing who to shoot at.

Andrew tore his eyes away from the face of Joseph Smith in the grass, and looked up at the broken window. He looked at the street, where the people who were posing and play-acting as walkers and strollers were just now beginning to come back to their natural lives. One of them yelled, "Get out of town! They've killed Joe Smith and the Mormons are coming!"

There were more shouts, more people pouring out of the jail now, and running. Running from what? They had killed him. The act they had all lusted to do was done. Andrew was having trouble understanding anything now, except that Joseph Smith was dead at his feet.

The whole town was back in the streets again, but this time instead of running toward the Prophet, they were running away from him as fast as they could go. They hated him alive, they feared him dead, Andrew thought. Doors were left gaping open, food was left on the tables, shops were left unlocked, Carthage was evacuated. "The Nauvoo Legion is coming," some woman screeched. "Get out of town! Take to the woods!"

Suddenly it was quiet. The afternoon breeze sprang up and rustled the leaves in the tree over the well. A shiny shred of glass still lodged in the window casement fell with a sparkle to the ground beside Joseph's outstretched hand.

A shadow by the corner of the building. A young man, Andrew's age, with a shock of corn-tassel hair, wearing a grey uniform, came edging around the corner of the jail with a long musket in his arms. He halted at the sight of Andrew. He looked confused, dazed by it all. The young soldier cautiously approached Andrew and the man on the ground. The soldier looked down at the face of the dead man. "That him? That Old Joe Smith?"

Andrew didn't answer. The soldier didn't care. "Hmmm," he said, shrugging as he turned away. "Never did get to see him before."

ASSASSINATION IN CARTHAGE! JOSEPH AND HYRUM
SMITH MURDERED IN JAIL BY MOBS! CARTHAGE
EVACUATED IN FEAR OF REPRISAL! CHURCH
IS LEADERLESS!
By Andrew J. Sharp
Associate Editor
The *ARGUS*

Carthage, Ill. June 27th, 1844: Joseph Smith, Jr., founder and President of The Church of Jesus Christ of Latter-day Saints, and his brother Hyrum Smith, the Patriarch to the church, were both slain at 5:16 p.m. this date, as they were held prisoners in the Carthage Jail. John Taylor, an apostle of the church, was critically wounded. A fourth church official, Dr. Willard Richards, escaped with only a nicked ear.

This correspondent saw a group of four or five men with blackened faces approach the jail from a woods nearby. The Carthage Greys, assigned to guard the jail, fired directly at the oncoming men but failed to stop them. The black-faced men then were seen running up the stairs to the living quarters of the jailor and his family, in which Smith and the others were staying. Shots were heard inside the building, and Joseph Smith leaped to a window, crashing through it. He was shot several times in the chest, and was dead upon striking the ground outside the window.

Hyrum Smith was the first to be hit by a ball, according to Richards, as he, Richards and Taylor sought to hold the door to their room.

Taylor was struck in the back of the knee, in the hip and suffered other wounds not yet determined at this time.

Upon learning of the attack upon the Smith party, most citizens of Carthage fled the city, in fear that the Nauvoo Legion would strike in retaliation, but no reprisals took place.

The bodies of the Smith brothers were taken to the Hamilton Hotel, and will be carried back to Nauvoo tomorrow.

(EDITOR'S NOTE: This dispatch was found on the person of Associate Editor Sharp, who collapsed behind the Carthage Jail, and was taken to Nauvoo for treatment of an undiagnosed illness. His reports will resume upon his recovery.)

"Heber C. Kimball Home"
Painting by Al Rounds
Courtesy of Wally Rose

Part Six:

Farewell, Nauvoo

Chapter 30

There was something familiar about the room he was in. If only he could keep his eyes open long enough, keep his mind focused on it, he knew he could bring it into his head — where he was. But then, he would drift away. Sometimes at night, he was sure he was wide awake and rational. He would lie and listen to the incredibly true sounds from somewhere outside. Voices outside himself, that he knew as well as he knew his own voice. Or was it his own voice? That made it harder to tell where he was, if every voice was his own.

He was sure that sometimes he wasn't alone. He felt hands ministering to him, felt coolness on his face, and felt moisture on his swollen tongue. Was he drinking, or had he forgotten how to swallow?

It was important for him to remember what he was supposed to do. There was something important about his life, he knew that. He had learned something that he had to teach. That was it. He was a teacher. He was satisfied with that for quite some time, until he began to think, one day — one week, maybe one month — later. . . If he was a teacher, where were his pupils? He couldn't seem to remember having pupils. But why, then, did he teach? And what was his subject?

The truth, that's all. All sides.

That was satisfying for another month. Or was it a year? He really ought to get up. He was sure he was lying down, and he couldn't remember when he had walked last, really walked. He knew he could dream about walking, and it was a good feeling, walking — even running. He could do it again, if he could just remember how it was done. He would work on that, too. Another time.

Suddenly it was he, himself, he saw in the classroom. He must have walked to get there. And so now he knew who the pupil was. **He** was the pupil. He was here to learn the truth. All sides. But how could that be? How could he be the pupil if he was also the teacher? There was a teacher in the classroom, but he couldn't see who it was. He should sit closer. Why couldn't he get closer to the teacher? If he could, he could listen so much more! He tried to get closer, but his legs were thick with molasses, and he couldn't get through the crowd of people and horses, to be close to the teacher. But he could see him better now. And he wore a white shirt with crimson on it!

I have to learn all sides, he explained to the people with their molasses horses in his way. *So I can know the truth, and the truth will make me free.*

But how do you know the truth? he asked. The teacher smiled, even though the crimson was spreading. "Epistle of James, Epistle of James." **My** middle name is James. Is that a sign, President?

I am a prophet of God. The crimson was spreading, spreading.

Don't you wish you weren't? Just sometimes?

There were daylight hands and night hands, he had come to know that. The daylight hands were soft and smooth, and there was a different kind of voice with them and a different kind of smell.

The night hands were rougher but gentler, and the smell was familiar. There was a different night-time voice, too. And sometimes tears, he was sure. Were the tears for him?

If he awoke from this dream in the daytime, would he find that the night-time hands and voice and tears were a dream, and would go away? He decided he wouldn't want that to happen, so if he had anything to say in it, he would awaken in the night-time and make the daytime hands into a dream. Strange how he could decide this, and still not have decided where he was, or what it was he was supposed to be doing.

And then, one day he was better. Just as the sun comes up after a long, dark night he was better, and he knew it. He could feel the soft edges of his mind beginning to firm themselves up.

He was perfectly able to remember all the dreams he had dreamed, and he knew that he had been sick. The only thing was, he didn't know how long it had been or precisely where he was, but wherever it was, he was where he should be, he felt that comfortably. Because he had been right here before.

All this took perhaps thirty seconds. He didn't want to go too fast into this new consciousness because he didn't want to open his eyes and find himself somewhere he hadn't planned on being, and he definitely knew by now that he wanted to be with the night-time hands and voice — and tears. He had fallen in love with those hands and that voice, and he wanted it to be the right person when he opened his eyes.

He opened his eyes. He felt cool. There was a pale gray space over his head and a very, very bright light by his left side. He looked for where the space ended, and found what he took to be a wall. He followed the wall down until he came to a window, which had drapery on it, and he followed the drapery down until he could only see the end of his bed. And then he turned his eyes to the left and saw the chair and the chest of drawers, and then he saw the hand. It was the good, rough hand. It was holding another hand, if he could feel the rough hand, maybe it was his own hand it was holding! He would test it. He would squeeze that hand. He did it.

"Andrew?"

The light moved and a shadow came over his face, the smell of freshly-washed hair with familiar body oils came to him. He turned his eyes far, far, to the left, to see.

"Andrew? Can you see me?"

Like a newly-discovered comet, yes, I can see you. Like a great natural law just unearthed, a Newtonian, Olympian truth, I can see you. Like a rejuvenation, a rebirth, a reincarnation, I can see you! Like a fulfilled promise, I can see you! *I can see you, Louisa! I am back, Louisa!*

"Oh, Andrew, you're smiling! That's the first time you've smiled in months, do you know that? Andrew, can you heart me?"

Like a baby's first cry, I can hear you. Like a volcano's eruption, I can hear you. Like a blossom bursting into bloom, I can hear you! *I can hear you, Louisa!*

"Then say something, darling!"

This first word should be everything that has been inside me for as long as I have been unable to express things the way I want to. This is a very important word, not to be uttered with casual abandon. This word is an immortal word, a word the world is waiting to hear.

He pondered. He said it.

"I love you."

He had a fascinating time catching up on his lost life. He had been found wandering with a high fever in Carthage the night of the martyrdom, June 27, 1844, shaking and burning up at the same time, and so incoherent that it was morning before he could be positively identified. Carthage was still largely deserted for fear of a Mormon assault. A kindly hotel keeper, Mr. Hamilton, had dispatched his son to fetch a doctor and the doctor had him carried back to Nauvoo, where most of the medical talent and medicine in Hancock County could be found.

He was diagnosed as suffering from a very serious case of the ague, and was put to bed in the room he had been renting from the Gaines family. He had been completely out of his head for many weeks, with only brief spells of rationality. Dr. Wells, one of the three physicians remaining to treat the sorrowing population of Nauvoo, spent as much time with Andrew as he could spare, but he had confided to Samuel and Maude that this case was too severe to expect a recovery and that it would be only a matter of time before he succumbed.

Maude, however, would have none of it. She organized ladies from the Female Relief Society to come in on shifts to bathe his face and try to keep his parched tongue moist, and to change his bed linen and wash it as often as it was soiled. Maude and Rebecca spent hours feeding and comforting him every day, but the weeks became months, and the doctor was suggesting the intensity of the fever had damaged his brain and that if he did wake up, he would be so impaired that it would be a blessing if he passed away.

Into this somber household one day, returned one of its first tenants, Louisa. Louisa and Angus had returned from Carthage to try to salvage the family business. Jock had been so disillusioned by the scandals of Nauvoo that he had sternly ordered the family to join him in returning to Scotland, but Louisa had refused to go. Her home, she had said, was America, and she had deep feelings about Nauvoo. Angus had been torn by indecision, but when he saw that his wife would not be dissuaded, he agreed to return to Nauvoo and take her back to the McCann house and try to get the McCann Boat Works going again and send money to Jock and Anne every month.

Louisa had been dismayed to find Andrew so sick, and so while she worked beside Angus down at the boat yard by day, she spent hours nursing him at his bedside at night, until Angus came and called for her on his way back home from his labors.

And what of Nauvoo in the meantime? Andrew's first view from the bedroom window seemed familiar. But then he saw the temple, its tower gleaming against the sky. And the clusters of new brick homes. New businesses dotted the streets. Factory smoke drifted.

And what of the Church? Had it collapsed with the loss of its leader and the Patriarch? There had been a struggle for control. Sidney Rigdon, long estranged from Joseph, said he had been told in a vision that he was to be the caretaker of the Church until the proper prophet could be found; but somehow the speech he made at the grove had failed to rouse the throng, and Brigham Young, president of the Quorum of the Twelve, called for an afternoon session. When he spoke that afternoon, hundreds believed they saw him transformed into the image and likeness of the Prophet Joseph Smith, and that was enough for them; the Lord had spoken, and Brigham was to be their leader.

But the acceptance of Brigham Young had been far from unanimous. Many had dropped away from the Church, some to form their own. Many believed Joseph had secretly ordained his oldest son, Joseph III, to take over the mantle of prophecy when he was of age. There was dissent among the Saints.

And now, it was January, 1845. Andrew had been suffering the ague nearly seven months! His recovery was slow, and his strength did not flood back but only trickled back a little at a time. He had not written a line, of course. The mail had brought his regular checks for a while, but then Mr. Ketchum wrote to say, regretfully, that due to reverses he could no longer manage to pay Andrew a salary while he was unable to produce any articles; he hoped Andrew would recover soon and that he would be able to rehire him at that time.

That letter had been written in October, 1844!

Samuel told Andrew not to worry. He wasn't to think of himself as a boarder in their house but a member of their family. They wouldn't dream of taking a cent in rent from him until he got on his feet again. Samuel had taken over the *Times & Seasons* and had hired others to operate the print shop. He had received book-binding orders from as far away as St. Louis and was establishing quite a reputation as a skilled craftsman.

During the day, Rebecca was on hand to help Andrew walk again and to do what he couldn't do for himself. She had become a big, sturdy woman, handsome and desirable, running to flesh like her mother and a far better cook. It was embarrassingly plain to Andrew that, during his months of convalescence, there were now no secrets of his physical self which Rebecca didn't know. Still, like a nurse, she put those thoughts aside and regarded him as if she didn't really know him that well, and he allowed himself to forget that he was an open book to her.

During the night, at least until Angus stopped by and took her home after his evening spent at work, Louisa nursed Andrew more lovingly than anyone except a wife could. In his helpless state, week in and week out, she saw that Andrew was in every way the man she had fallen in love with years before, and as she bathed his fevered brow or took his pulse, or looked hopefully for signs that he might recognize her in the moments when his eyes were open and he was raving, talking nonsense talk about classrooms and molasses horses and epistles, in those moments she thought that she did love him. She decided that she had never stopped loving him. She also decided she would never tell him that. It would just **be**. She had had her chance with him and had lost it. But she could minister to him innocently, hold his hand innocently, late at night, knowing he didn't know, she might cry over him, let her tears spill onto his unknowing cheeks, and in this way share herself with him. It would be the only way she ever could.

Angus had been understanding. In the name of old friendship, and in view of how Andrew had proven himself since he had returned to Nauvoo, it was all right for his wife to spend evenings there. It wasn't as if the man were awake and in his normal state. That, of course, he would never stand for. Why, that would be a scandal! But as it was, Louisa acting as an angel of mercy, it was Angus' way of making it up to Andrew for the beating he had given him. Letting his wife nurse him was a generous thing for a man to do.

Of course, Rebecca was deeply in love with Andrew herself — had been for over a year. But sturdy Rebecca knew she was damaged goods. She would have to settle for somebody equally shopworn.

The meeting was held in Brigham Young's fine new home at Kimball and Granger Streets. Nauvoo had never looked handsomer. It had weathered disease, polygamy, the murder of its prophet, mayor, editor, general, and leading storekeeper. Its people had either deserted the Church or grown rock-hard in their testimony of it. They had been hounded and oppressed, shunted and hated and feared every step of their fifteen year existance. Nauvoo had been a haven, but now it, too, must become part of the Mormon past.

"President Young, I have been unable to reach any conclusion other than the fact that Illinois will never know peace, until the contentions between your people and the rest of the state are stilled."

"Agreed."

"But I know no way to produce that tranquility, other than to insist that the State be vacated by all Mormons."

"Surely you are not serious, Governor Ford?"

"He is quite serious, Mr. Young," put in Stephen A. Douglas. "Wherever Mormons have gone, from Palmyra to Nauvoo, there has been trouble."

"There has been oppression and jealousy!"

"There has been trouble of one kind or another," the Governor continued. "Either Mormons cannot live at peace with their neighbors, or non-Mormons cannot live with Mormons around them. It matters not in the slightest to me which is the true case because my great concern is to end bloodshed on both sides. Your people must leave."

"Leave Nauvoo?"

"Leave the State of Illinois."

Burly-lipped Brigham Young was not to be bullied. "Sir, you are not speaking to serfs, you are speaking to citizens with the exact same rights as citizens of Springfield or Chicago."

"You're referring to the Nauvoo City Charter. I am revoking that charter," said the Governor.

Brigham's jaw fell open. "You cannot!"

"I can, and the legislature will back me. You no longer are the political power you once were, you Mormons. You no longer can terrorize a representative into voting your way by the monolithic size of the Mormon vote. Make no mistake about it, sir, the City of Nauvoo will cease to exist within a few days after my return."

"The other threat to peace and tranquility," put in Douglas, "has been the Nauvoo Legion."

"Also protected by a charter signed into law by Governor Carlin," Brigham said.

"And also about to be abolished by an act of the State Legislature," said the Governor.

Brigham Young was furious, but his rage was impotent against these two men. He no longer had the means to fight back. "Sirs, how shall we defend our city if we have no Legion?" he asked.

"You forget," Stephen A. Douglas said, "in a few weeks, you will have no city."

Elias P. Ketchum looked a decade older than Andrew remembered him. He sat slumped at his desk above the pressroom in Quincy, his hair now somehow whiter than before, his face more deeply lined, and considerably thinner. "Lady luck," he said, "all things change. That's the big joke the Almighty plays upon us poor mortals, and what a chuckle He must get, watching us running around, shoring up first one break in the dike and then a hole in the boat, putting out fires, breathing life into dying things . . ." He paused and gazed at Andrew. "Now, what in the hell was I trying to say?"

"Everything changes."

"Oh, yes! Everything does change. You've changed. You're actually a man, now. What does that make me? An antique, I guess. Well, in this ongoing process of change, cities rise up and disappear like Atlantis; men rise up and are knocked down. And jobs change. My job has changed. I used to be an editor; now I'm a bill-collector. And you used to be the Nauvoo Correspondent; now there is no Nauvoo from which to correspond."

"But there is! There's a tremendous story going on there right now! Brigham Young is trying to sell the city — the whole city — to people in the east. And he's organizing a . . ."

"Did you say sell the city? Who in his right mind would buy it? In a few months all those fine places will just be abandoned. Why would anybody buy something they could just walk in and take?"

"Think of the displacement of thousands of people, leaving prosperous businesses and fine homes! The order states that a thousand families will have to leave Illinois this spring, and all the rest of them will have to be gone as soon as possible afterward — and if they don't leave, they'll be expelled by 'violent means'! The very words of the order!"

"All the same, Andrew, I can't afford a Nauvoo Correspondent. People are dog-tired of Mormons nowadays. It was a fad, like voodoo or something. It passed. It's a new day. The sickness is over."

"Well, I wouldn't call it a sickness."

"Don't argue with an old man! It was a fine madness this Joseph Smith had. Thought himself a prophet and convinced thousands of upright, God-fearing people that he had all the right answers. Andrew, it's happened before, and it'll happen again. You just happened to be around at a time and a place when this sickness broke out on the land. It was a commercial success, Mormonism. I sold a hell of a lot of papers."

"Is that all you got out of my articles?"

"Was there anything else in 'em?"

Andrew put his head in his hands. "Yes, Mr. Ketchum, there was. There was the story of a visionary man who influenced more people in his time than Moses. He moved a whole population across the country, he fought politics, mobs, sickness, death, he even fought conventional morality. And you know why? Because he didn't 'think' he was a prophet. He **knew** it. **He knew it!** He couldn't stop doing what he was doing because he knew that God knew he was a prophet, too! So he couldn't stop it if he'd wanted to. What I tried to write was, underneath his pride, and his ambition, and his love of power and influence, there was a man scared to death **not** to be a prophet! I believe the Lord gave him a choice: be My prophet — or be damned!"

"Well, **I'll** be damned," the old man said. "He's even converted you!"

295

Chapter 31

Angus McCann had brought home the sheaf of boat plans he had always kept down at the yards. The lamp he had rigged over the table in Anne's elaborate dining room burned through the night most nights until dawn, when Louisa came down and shut it off, and put a shawl over the shoulders of her sleeping husband.

He never, positively never, discussed business with Louisa. It was not manly to discuss his utter failure, and besides, he didn't want to cause her distress. But it wasn't working, hadn't worked since he had come back to Nauvoo just to please her, and tried to start up the family business. The truth was, and he had had to face it, the skill and business sense had all gone to Jock. He and William had been good order-takers, and when Jock had shown them how to use the tools properly and had kept his eye on their work, they could get along. But running it single-handedly was impossible. He'd never think of asking for help from the family, not now, not after the horrendous falling-out they'd had in Carthage, Jock determined to go back to Scotland and forget his mistaken religious beliefs, and Angus pulled by his demanding little wife to go back to her "first home." William, of course, went with Jock.

And so he had taken the boat plans home with him to study and see if he couldn't understand what Jock knew, without plans, about building boats. He didn't have the knack, Jock had said. Well, time had proven him right. *As usual.*

He was so tired that the lines scribed so delicately in their father's firm hand had lately blurred and run together. It was just no good.

And now, the town was going to be evacuated. Well, that was all he needed. Like all the other tradespeople and shopkeepers, he was liquidating his assets — only there was nobody to buy them; and so he sat staring at useless boat plans, and boxes of unpaid bills. Only the house was his. And that really belonged to Jock.

He snuffed the light. Pale magenta outside; sunrise coming. Another day of struggle down in the inlet. Nobody buying boats any more, few visitors calling. The ones coming off the steamers nowadays were coming like vultures to carrion — hoping to snatch a juicy bargain off the dying carcass of a city. Well, by God, they wouldn't get a piece of him!

He slipped the door closed, clutching the only comfort he had been able to rely on for many months now, the rum which he kept by the case at the boat yard and which he had only recently brought home. Of all the things in his life, the rum was the only thing that hadn't turned sour. It still fulfilled him, still lit that old flame in his belly. He had nothing else to satisfy him. His work was rejected, his friendships around town rejected, his own wife rejected him in his own bed, night after night . . . Of course, he knew the reason for that.

It had all started, he reckoned, when he had hit Andrew Sharp. Why, he wasn't fit to touch the hem of her skirts in those days, Andrew was everything to her! Then, when Andrew had been exposed as a scoundrel and driven out of town, hadn't she warmed up to Angus! He'd courted her properly, she'd responded. But now he knew why. Andrew had left a gaping hole in her life and Angus had come along to fill it. But it was like stuffing between the strakes in a dory. Oh, it keeps the water out for a time, but eventually it needs to be replaced. Angus had filled her emptiness for a time. He had never expected her to say yes when he proposed, and she had hesitated, put him off, before finally agreeing. Now he knew exactly why. She had seen Andrew one last time before agreeing. But by then Andrew didn't need her! So she chose the last port she'd passed. Just like any good skipper.

He found himself down at the boat yard, the water as still as a millpond, steamy fog rising off it. He looked at the half-finished boats, the stacks of curing lumber that would never be made into boats. He remembered the months of backbreaking labor it had taken to drag the mud out of this huge trench until Jock had finally relented and hired the steam dredge. And all for what? All for **what**? So he could work eighteen hours every day and come dragging home at night without a penny more to his name than he'd started out with in the morning, and find a delicate and sweet-smelling wife who was too sacred to handle!

He climbed down to the narrow planking along which one of the unsold boats was tied, precariously stepped into it, almost throwing himself into the water, and finally sat down in it, reached forward and slipped the rope off the stanchion, and let the almost imperceptible drift take it slowly, slowly out. He lay back, enjoying the sensation of some other force than his own moving him. He had spent all his life moving himself with brute strength and willpower. Now, let some other power take over! The boat glided silently, picking up speed where the eddy from the river current caught it. The boat bobbed and nodded slightly, and a gurgle from beneath the planking delighted him. He celebrated freedom from the land with a deep drink of rum and then threw the empty bottle ahead of him, into the huge river just ahead. Without rudder or oars, Angus' boat slipped into the inexorable moving sea of the Mississippi. It was remarkably warm, he thought, for Christmas morning.

The city that had been the largest and most modern in Illinois was fast becoming a ghost town. Hundreds of homes and stores stood empty, more than nine thousand residents had gone. Some had left with the earliest wagon trains, following Brother Brigham's orders; he had known Joseph had believed in an ultimate Zion, somewhere in the mountains of the West.

Brigham and Heber C. Kimball had pored over the writings of John C. Fremont, who had recently explored the Valley of the Great Salt Lake. The way West was established well enough now that Willard Richards felt good about taking Jenetta and making the move. Brigham himself would be in that company, and George Albert Smith, and their families. The earliest to leave were the most faithful in the Church, the polygamous families.

Not everyone planned to leave Nauvoo for the West. Lucy Mack Smith and Joseph's widow Emma had elected not to follow Brigham, whom they regarded as an usurper of the mantle that Joseph III would one day rightfully wear. Around these two patrician ladies, the roots of the Reorganized Church was plaited.

To Louisa, widowed thirty-six days, the invitation from the gentle-hearted Willard and Jenetta Richards came as a godsend. She had been unable again to cry at the funeral of a loved one, but this time it wasn't because of a deep-seated emotional block too great to express; it had been just the opposite. Poor Angus was gone, and now her life could resume. She felt all the guilt that a proper widow should feel for this reaction; she also felt the hope rekindle in her heart that she might be given a second chance at love. But there was a major obstacle to her new dream of sailing across the prairies with Andrew at her side. He didn't want to go. Since the funeral, he had been in Nauvoo only a few days. He had given her his hand and expressed his deepest sympathy, and had taken a steamer down to Quincy almost immediately.

Observing her torment, Jenetta Richards had suggested that she take this as a sign from heaven that widowed ladies are not to think of new attachments, certainly not this soon. It was God's way of helping her to adjust to the period of mourning she should display.

It was, in fact, quite another thing to Andrew. In the first glimmerings of an awakening faith, it had occurred to him that perhaps the tragic death of Angus McCann was some kind of a signal to him that he might have a second chance with Louisa, but he was so reluctant to permit himself another season of frustration and longing over her that he insulated his feelings a short time after Angus' boat had been found washed ashore near Canton. If God was rewarding him in some way, he wanted to be fully ready to receive this gift in a fiscally sound condition. He had to build a new career, now that Nauvoo was disappearing, and so he had gone to Elias P. Ketchum with an offer. He would take over the rigorous duties of editor from the aging man, pay him whatever he was now taking out of the business, if he would let Andrew run the newspaper for him, living off the accrued profits. A chancey arrangement for them both, but better than seeing the *Argus* expire because its proprietor was no longer able to run it.

Ketchum had been maddeningly indecisive. He had occupied the old creaky chair at the paper-strewn desk for so long that he could not think of a life away from it. There was no doubt he needed a rest, and nobody he would rather see operate the paper than Andrew, but it was such a big change — well, he'd just have to think it over; sleep on it. Besides, what was the infernal hurry, anyway? It could keep another week, another month, if it had to.

Andrew was growing desperate. The evacuation of Nauvoo was something that depended upon the condition of the Mississippi, and now Brigham Young was telling the wagon parties preparing to leave with him that they must be ready to move out when the ice was thick enough. Brigham was told that the Mississippi didn't freeze every year in February, but he was supremely confident — with that same kind of assurance Joseph had had — that his plans were soundly laid, and that the elements would perform as he needed them to, for the righteous purposes of God.

All of which meant, to Andrew, that Louisa must be plucked off the wagon — along with 12-year-old brother Bobby, of course — before it was too late. So it was vital that he be able to promise her that they could live comfortably in Quincy, which was, after all, a comfortable town — a county seat with all of the amenities which would be lacking on the trail to some unknown western destination. He had laid his plans for a sound future, and if Elias P. Ketchum would just make up his mind, he would be off to Nauvoo to intercept the Richards and Louisa, and propose.

On February 13th, the old man wearily gave his approval. Andrew thanked him, told him he would be back within a week, two weeks at the most, to take over his new responsibilities, and with a bride!

STAGE DELAYED DUE TO WEATHER read the sign at the wagon stop where the stage north to Nauvoo loaded. Delayed? For how long? Word had it that there had been a blizzard up in northern Hancock County and it was coming this way; nobody in his right mind would try to drive a stageload of people through that, the agent told him. Well, that same blizzard, Andrew knew, was just the weather Brigham Young had been waiting for, and while Andrew waited down in Quincy, the Mormon wagon trek would begin!

"Then take me, alone," he demanded.

"How's that?"

"Instead of a stageload, just take me! I've got to get to Nauvoo, and the river's frozen, so you'll have to do it!"

"You crazy or something?" the agent asked. "You ever been in an Illinois blizzard?"

Andrew knew there was only one way he could hope to reach Nauvoo without waiting for the storm to abate, and that was by himself, on a good horse. He rented the strongest gelding the livery man had, bought a saddlebag full of food to eat on the way and another bag of oats for the horse, praying he'd find someone on the way with some feed to replenish that — and started out.

The first ten miles of the journey were cold but entirely passable, and he had to resist the temptation to ride faster than an easy, loping gait, so as not to tire the horse. The sky ahead was so heavy with gray clouds that it looked as if it would burst at any moment, and the temperature was dropping. He rode on.

It was impossible to travel by night. With no moon or stars visible, the road was too obscure to risk riding the horse into a hole. If he injured the horse, he could die out there before help arrived. He spent the night with the gelding in a barn and left money stuck in the boards for the grain he took to feed the horse. He was up at first light and back on the road. The blizzard had moved away, leaving it desperately cold, but clearing.

He had made the trip between Quincy and Nauvoo so many times as a stage passenger that he ought to know the landmarks as they passed, he thought, but under the snow and ice, things looked strange. He was sure he was still on the right road, but he couldn't calculate how far along he was, or how much farther he had to go. His mind was filled with Louisa. He understood so much more about her now. He knew now that she had been offering herself to him all through those seven months she had nursed him back to health, saying that the love she had decided not to feel was still there for him, even though she was married to someone else and unable to express it. Then, Fate had stepped in. Or was it fate? Was he trying to avoid thinking of it as an act of God, taking Angus so that he could take his place? He shook off the thought. As little as he knew about God, that idea was blasphemous! All he knew was that he had been given a second chance with Louisa, and this time he meant to have her!

His watch said five-ten, but it was almost as dark as night already, and he was still not in sight of Nauvoo. Should he ride on? It couldn't be much farther. What if Brigham had already gone? He had been in sight of the Mississippi only a few times on this second day of his journey, and he couldn't tell from shore whether the ice was thick enough for heavy wagons or not. Resignedly, he came to Warsaw, slept only briefly, and started north again at dawn.

On Sunday, February 15th, a church bell pealed through the icy air from somewhere ahead of him, and at the same time that he heard this, he began to recognize the thinning brush and forests as the southern outskirts of Nauvoo!

He rode into town down by Water Street, and his heart sank. A train of wagons was lined up on the Nauvoo shore, preparing to make the trip across the river. He had almost missed them! Now he had to find the Richards wagon and Louisa.

She had delayed until the last possible second, hoping that Andrew would return. She and Bobby, a self-reliant young man now, had had a frank discussion about going West, and no matter what happened, he wanted to go. The Richards were delighted to have him and had implored Louisa to realize that leaving Nauvoo and starting all over again was the best thing, the only thing, for a person in her circumstances. She was only widowed less than two months, and although in these difficult times it was important for a woman to have a man at her side, people would surely think the wrong thing if she took up with Andrew again, so soon. There had been enough talk over her nightly nursing of him when he had been sick for so long. The Richards had reasoned with her that, all these things taken into consideration, a separation would be best for both of them. Because, as they finally pointed out, Andrew isn't a Latter-day Saint.

Yes, she thought to herself as she sat in the wagon, there was still that gulf between them. She was even more comfortable in her faith now that the prophet had been martyred, than when he had been alive! He had gone to his death to seal his testimony, Apostle Richards had said. So this was the right way, the true way, and she must teach her heart to forget anyone who cannot share this faith.

Brigham Young walked alongside the wagon train, hands behind his back, his barrel chest thrust out, pacing as he talked with others who walked the crusty snow with him. They were waiting for a report from a scout who had gone out on the river to see how thick the ice was. These wagons looked very heavy, despite Brigham's insistance that the evacuees leave behind everything they possibly could do without.

Suddenly, a horseman drew up beside Brigham, and the rider called down, "President Young!" It was Andrew Sharp, the young Gentile newspaperman. "Have you seen the Richards' wagon?"

Brigham turned and pointed back down the train. "Near the end." Andrew wheeled his horse and dashed off. Brigham resumed his patient pacing.

In the wagon, Louisa and Jenetta sat talking beneath the canvas cover, on two comfortable cushions which would become part of their beds at night. The sound of a horse cantering up and suddenly a voice, just outside the canvas. "Brother Richards? Is Louisa with you?"

Jenetta looked at Louisa with a helpless smile. "Go to him, Louisa," she said.

Willard Richards helped her down onto the frozen ground, as Andrew jumped down from his horse. They came together, and he held her clasped hands in his own, just under her chin.

"Louisa, I've been trying to do something important in Quincy, and now it's done. I have some wonderful news!"

"Just seeing you so well is wonderful news to me."

"Is there any place we can talk?"

She looked around. The closest shelter was the abandoned boat works, only a few yards away. "We can stand over there."

Mindful of what that place had been to her late husband, Andrew said, "Will you mind?"

"Of course not." They walked together to the shed. The inlet was a sheet of ice, locking scraps of lumber which had fallen into the water.

"Louisa . . . I'm going to take over the *Argus*!"

Her eyes danced, and she clapped her gloved hands together. "Oh, Andrew, I knew you would! I knew it that day I saw you had been promoted to Associate Editor! Congratulations!"

". . . And I want you to marry me."

"And I want to marry you, Andrew. I've wanted that for these five years, isn't that sinful? Even when I was married to Angus, you were never far from my thoughts. I prayed to forget you, then I prayed to be forgiven because I couldn't forget you."

"Then we'll unload your things from the Richards' wagon."

"But, darling . . . wait."

"Wait? Why? They may start across any time!"

She took his hands in hers. "I've received a great deal of counsel from Apostle Richards. He is such a wise, good man. He thinks very highly of you, but he sees difficulties for us, if we should marry, because of our differences."

"Because I'm not a Mormon."

"Yes. It causes such strife, he said . . ."

"We're right back where we were before, Louisa," Andrew said, angrily. "If two people love each other, a religion shouldn't stand in the way!"

"But you've seen what it means to be a Mormon in this world of ours; you know it as well as any of us know it because you've reported on it for years."

"Nobody needs to know you're a Mormon where we'll be living."

She looked hurt, disappointed. "You'd expect me to hide my faith, then?"

"No, no, I didn't mean that!"

"Oh, Andrew, I don't know," she said, turning her back to him and looking out at the river. She saw the men who had been testing the ice walking back now toward shore. One of them was waving his arm, pumping it up and down.

"I'm not asking you to give up your beliefs, Louisa. I'm asking you if there isn't enough room in your life for Mormonism and for me."

She turned back to him with tears in her eyes. "Yes, dear, there is," she said. "But I must ask you: isn't there enough room in your life to have me . . . and to investigate the Church? Andrew, you're a reporter, dedicated to the truth. What if . . . just suppose, that this **is** the truth?"

Before he could answer, a shout was heard from the wagons. "Moving out! We're moving out!"

"I have to go," she said.

"No, Louisa, stay here with me."

She started slowly walking back to the wagons. "Promise me that you'll keep on trying to find the truth," she said, her voice choked with emotion, and then she walked on ahead.

"Wait!" he cried.

"I can't," she said. "I've waited too long now; I can't wait any longer!"

Willard Richards helped her up into the back of the wagon. Bobby sat on the driver's seat with the apostle, as the heavily loaded vehicle began to roll, creaking and swaying, down the track and onto the ice. Ahead stretched a line of wagons, slowly making their way toward the center of the frozen

Mississippi. From some of the wagons came the sounds of singing. On the shore stood knots of people, waving, many weeping. In the background stood Nauvoo, now nearly abandoned, the dream of the Prophet returning to dust.

Icy blasts blew down the vast river channel, making the tall canvas wagon covers billow like sails. Andrew rode beside the Richards' wagon. Bobby looked down. "Are you going to come with us, Andrew?" he asked.

"Just a little way," Andrew said. He slowed the walking gait to a halt for the wagon to roll by, and then fell in behind its open tailgate.

Jenetta stuck her head out. "We wish you were coming with us, Andrew," she said.

"Could I talk with Louisa?" he asked.

Jenetta smiled her sad-sweet smile. "I don't think she can talk right now," she said and shook her head slowly.

"Tell her . . ."

". . . Yes, Andrew?"

"Tell her I'll . . . I'll do a lot of thinking."

"I'll tell her."

"And . . . tell her to write to me, in care of the *Argus*."

"Yes, I'll do that."

There seemed to be nothing more for him to say. Except, good bye. He said that now and discovered how close to the surface his emotions lay. He wheeled his horse about and headed back for the shore, the tears freezing on his face.

After all the wagons made it safely across the river, Brigham Young called a halt, and the occupants got down, some to go and relieve themselves in the woods, others to take a last fond look at the city that lay across the Mississippi.

Brigham assembled the wagon company around a bonfire, and conducted a lengthy prayer, thanking God for sparing their lives, for raising up a prophet in these last days, and for showing them their duty and the road ahead. He prayed for divine guidance, and he concluded with a prayer for those loved ones they were leaving behind. Many women and men were moved to tears by the thought.

As the wagons had assembled, the Richards' wagon was the last one in the line. Louisa and Jenetta busied themselves making their first supper on the trail west. Willard was conferring with Brigham and George Albert Smith, while Bobby was, as always, transfixed by the mighty river and had walked several yards down toward the frozen bank. Although night had fallen, the skies had cleared, and the brilliant white of the ice-covered Mississippi seemed to be illuminated from beneath, so brightly did it reflect the light from above. Sadly the boy looked at Nauvoo, his home for longer than any place he had lived. From the vantage point of a twelve-year-old, it was home, and any other place was not. He didn't want to be seen crying, but he felt like crying now, and he decided to do it when he wouldn't be seen. He squatted down and let the tears come.

At last, the feelings were released, and he rubbed his stinging eyes with his mittened hands. At that moment he thought he saw something out on the ice of the river. He blinked and wiped his eyes again, and then he was sure he saw it. It looked like a lone man, but there was something behind him. It looked like a cannon! But then, as the man drew a little closer, he saw that it was a handcart, and it was piled with belongings. The figure was still almost sixty yards away now, and Bobby stood up to get a better look. The man saw him and broke into a run. Bobby felt suddenly frightened. Strangers had always frightened him, ever since Haun's Mill, and he wanted to be back by the fire, with the older people. Looking back at the figure approaching the shore, Bobby hurried to the wagons.

"There's someone coming across the ice," he said. Jenetta and Louisa stopped what they were doing and looked up. "Willard," Jenetta called, "someone's coming."

They paused and walked to the end of the wagon and looked out to the east. Sure enough, whoever it was was struggling in the wagon tracks with a pushcart on which were piled trunks and a barrel and odd assortments of belongings.

Together, Willard, Jenetta, Louisa, and Bobby advanced slowly toward where the stranger was throwing his weight against the handlebar of the cart, trying to get the tall wheels unstuck.

It was Bobby who said it first. "It's Andrew!" he cried, and ran to him.

"Andrew?" Tears sprang to Louisa's eyes, and her mouth was open in disbelief. "Andrew!" she cried, and ran through the muddy slush, and he turned to her, and she flew into his arms. "I can't believe it," she sobbed, shivers in her voice, "I can't believe it!"

He caressed her hair and kissed her cheeks, her eyes, her lips. "I did some thinking, like I said I would," he murmured, "and then I did some praying."

She lifted her head and looked at him wonderingly. **Praying?**

He nodded. **"If any of you lack wisdom, let him ask of God . . ."**

"And you did?"

"I actually did."

"And did you get your answer?"

"Well, I think I did. Anyway, I got enough of an answer that I wrote a note to Ketchum, bought this pushcart and a few things to put in it, and . . . here I am. If you think Brigham Young will have me."

"I'm sure he'll have you," Willard Richards said, putting his huge arm around them both.

"And if you don't mind my tagging along," he said to Richards.

"I've been praying you would," he said.

And then Andrew looked back at Louisa. "And you. Will you let an unemployed reporter walk alongside your wagon while he searches for the truth?"

Her answer was a kiss, a kiss so wholeheartedly given and so lasting, that Willard Richards cleared his throat and turned Bobby around, took Jenetta by the arm, and walked back to the wagon.

Someone had started a song up by the fire. The voices seemed to follow the swirling woodsmoke, up, up into the starry heavens.

Come, come, ye saints, no toil nor labor fear,
But with joy, wend your way;
Though hard to you, this journey may appear,
Grace shall be, as your day.

'Tis better far for us to strive,
Our useless cares from us to drive;
Do this, and joy your hearts will swell —
All is well, all is well!

PS 3557 .R452 N3 1982
French, James R.
Nauvoo